'While Patrick Boyle's first novel *Like Any Other Man* is as Irish as they come, it is hard to imagine it getting past the censors in its country of origin. Though, on second thoughts, a story of sexual indulgence punished by total blindness and final ruin might well be considered worth a dozen hellfire sermons. . . . Half-way through the novel, I thought that Mr Boyle would be unable to maintain the pace he had set himself but the story continues triumphantly to its gory, highly moral climax' – *Robert Baldick* in *The Daily Telegraph*

Also by Patrick Boyle in Panther Books

At Night All Cats Are Grey
The Betrayers
All Looks Yellow to the Jaundiced Eye

Patrick Boyle

Like Any Other Man

Panther

Granada Publishing Limited
Published in 1968 by Panther Books Ltd
Frogmore, St Albans, Herts AL2 2NF
Reprinted 1969, 1974

First published in Great Britain by
MacGibbon & Kee Ltd 1966
Copyright © Patrick Boyle 1966
Made and printed in Great Britain by
Cox & Wyman Ltd, London, Reading and Fakenham
Set in Intertype Times

to Teddy

If I be shaven, then the strength will go from me, and I shall become weak and be like any other man

Samson: *Judges* xvi 17

CHAPTER ONE

TAP-TAP-TAP.

Again the knock at the bedroom door. This time louder. More urgent. The whispered exhortation, too – more imperative.

'Better hurry, sir. The cashier's below in the office. Waiting this twenty minutes.'

It was the third time the housekeeper had called him. 'All right, Annie. All right,' he growled into the mirror. 'I'll be down in a moment.'

Carefully he combed up from the nape of his neck the long dangling lappet of black brilliantined hair, stopping at once where the teeth of the comb became snagged. To free the tangle he gripped the meagre pigtail firmly so that there would be no danger of hairs being plucked out by the roots. Then, cautiously, without tugging, he worked the comb gently against the obstruction until the tangle became unknotted and the teeth of the comb slid freely through. When the queue of hair was combed out he commenced spreading it out over the white shining scalp, spreading it economically so that each hair was plastered into place as equidistant from its neighbour as meridians on a globe, the hair tips forming a decent fringe across his frowning forehead. Before putting away the comb in his breast pocket, he examined it minutely for signs of falling hair. Except for a few flakes of oily dandruff, there was nothing to be seen.

'Good,' he said.

The car engine that had been idling all morning started up again. But now the owner was revving up the engine, which seemed to have developed a distinct knock. Or at least it was pinking badly.

'The silly lug,' he said. 'He'll banjax his engine if he doesn't watch out.'

He crossed to the open window. The morning sun scoured the shabby buildings surrounding the Square, exposing the stained and peeling paintwork, the faded lettering on the dingy signboards, the shop windows cluttered with a jumble of

9

souvenirs as tasteless as the postcards of jaunting cars and fat sweating women that enshrined them. It baked into yellow dust the greasy layer of dung trampled into road and pavement by yesterday's Fair Day rabble of cattle and sheep. It beat down on the shimmering metalwork of the five vehicles parked around the Square – the three private cars outside the hotel, the bread van at the gateway of the Paragon Bakery, the pick-up truck below his window where, for the last six months, on flattened front wheels it had crouched unheeded – no one of which was occupied.

He pulled the window down to the full. Put out his head. Listened. Above the distant mumble of the surf in the estuary and the mingled wailing of gulls and rooks, he heard the steady beat of the engine. A sudden breeze brought the acrid tang of animal dung and rotting seaweed.

Hurriedly he ducked back and slammed shut the window. The sudden movement did it.

'Oh, Christ!' he groaned, clutching at his forehead to still the dull throbbing ache.

The scoundrels. There's not an honest publican in the village. They all tamper with the drink the day of a Fair. If it's not bottling draught porter and selling it across the counter as brown stout in bottle, it's serving out three-year-old rot-gut as guaranteed Jameson Twelve. And, for anyone that complains, it is: 'Drink it up now, you've had enough.' Of course with enough drink put away, a body'll swallow back any class of venom. But who had given him the hammer? What grasping ruffian had dished up this skull-splitting brew last night? It could be any damned one of them, for he could not remember the last pub he was in.

As the ache began to subside he moved back cautiously to the dressing-table where he picked up a bottle of lavender shaving lotion, soaked his handkerchief and laid it across his right temple where the dregs of pain still clung.

'That's better,' he said, smoothed by the prickling chill.

Once more he gazed in the mirror. He stroked the plump palps of his newly-shaven cheeks, plucked a hair from the end of his fleshy nose, champed his dentures more firmly into place. He turned away.

'Now,' he said, making for the door, stooping as he passed under the lintel.

10

At the foot of the stairs he halted, gave a loud sustained belch and called:

'Annie! I'll be back when I open up.'

He heard her flouncing around the kitchen muttering to herself: 'Nice goings on in a Christian country. In under God what will it be next?'

As he opened the office door, the cashier's head bobbed up over the wooden partition like the head of a surfacing seal.

'Good morning, Manager.'

Without replying, he strode the length of the office gangway, twirling his chain of keys nonchalantly, his body swaying at the hips with a boxer's swagger. He turned the key in the upper lock of the strong-room door and marched back up the office to his own box, still twirling the ring of keys. The attendance book lay open on his desk, already signed by the cashier:

F. J. McCann ... 9.20.

In the vacant line directly above this signature he wrote in rapid flowing script:

James Simpson ... 9.00.

Closing the book he hesitated. Checked back rapidly. Changed the last entry to 9.05.

He unlocked his desk, drawers and filing cabinet, watching cynically the frantic efforts of McCann to swing open the strong-room door. Grunting and panting he tugged, lying back on his heels, throwing the whole weight of his sturdy little body into the wrenching open of the massive door.

At length he called breathlessly:

'It won't budge, Manager. It must be jammed.'

Simpson swaggered down the office, rolling his arms to flex his shoulder muscles, spat on his hands and gripped the brass handle of the strong-room door. One tremendous jerk and the door burst open. He hauled it back against the wall, pushed a wooden wedge under the flange to stop it swinging back and straightened up. Only then did he remember the morning's headache. He stood, moodily eyeing the back of the door, waiting for the onset of pain.

The smooth brown-painted surface of the metal was spat-

11

tered with autographs of past members of the staff. Pasted to
the upper right-hand corner was a typed memo:

A typical piece of departmental claptrap. Fat chance there'd
be of freeing this job with a few drops of oil. Hadn't Head
Office sent down a couple of jokers armed with crowbars, cold
chisels and sledges to do a major operation on the bloody door.
The two playboys plowtering around for the whole of a day,
with one idiot jumping on the crowbar while his mate kept
stuffing metal washers into the hinges in an effort to jack up
the door. Then bashing away at the steel door frame with the
sledges and the cold chisels. A proper navvy job. And look at
it now. After six months. Down on its uppers as bad as ever.
Fifteen quid the two hallions charged for their antics.

At his elbow, McCann said:

'It's getting harder to open it every day. We'd want to get the
experts down from Head Office again, Manager.'

Simpson decided the headache had cleared away. He re-read
the notice. Preserving efficiency. Cutting down costs.

'Silly idiot,' he muttered, moving into the strong-room.

He picked his way through the litter of books, parcels and
safe-keeping boxes to the cash safe, where he turned his key
in the upper lock. Through the air vent above the safe came
the faint grumble of Mrs. Mahony's voice and the sizzle and
smell of frying bacon. His stomach turned over gently. He
grimaced as he swallowed back the sour and stinging cud. God
knows, the whiskey could very well have been laced with poteen.
First run poteen, at that. How else account for this imperial
hangover.

Again he belched, sending a flutter through the dusty
webs hanging from the low arch of the ceiling. Really, he must
get Mrs. Mahony to clean out the strong-room. She mustn't
have touched it for months. He looked around. Shelves loaded

with tattered broken-backed ledgers. Shelves piled high with stationery and with cheque books. Shelves of cash books, bill books, draft books, remittance books, blotters of every size and shape: most of them blue moulded and worm eaten. In one corner was a large wooden chest (probably containing family plate) left in for safe keeping. Beside it a battered tin trunk with the sleeve of a shirt hanging out. A case of sporting guns and a long leather container of fishing gear – more items for safe keeping – were propped against the cheque drawers. And everywhere – stuffed tight along the topmost shelves, over-flowing to the safe tops where they mingled with canvas sacks of copper, scattered in wild confusion around the strong-room floor – parcels of letters and vouchers. Over all hung the musty odour of half a century of squalor.

With his boot he stirred a half-opened parcel, out of which oozed a welter of lodgment dockets.

'McCann!' he called.

'Yessir?'

'This place is like a pigsty. Can you not spare a few minutes of your valuable time to tidy it up?'

'It's very hard ... in a two-handed office ... to find time for ... the truth is, Manager, there's no storage space left.'

'Is that so?' said Simpson. He picked up a long flabby parcel from the floor, wedged it into the narrow opening above a pile of books and commenced pounding it into place with the heel of his fist. The brown paper burst open, spilling out on the floor a batch of deposit receipt stubs.

'A nice-looking mess,' he said, dusting his hands as he shouldered his way out past McCann.

He uncovered the typewriter, changed the date-case on the counter to *Tuesday – 15 – May*, checked the time from his wrist-watch on the way out, putting the office clock forward one minute to 9.45.

McCann, who was gathering up the scattered receipt blocks stood up at the sound of the closing door. Methodically he straightened the fistful of square hard-backed stubs. Extracted the top one. Took careful aim.

'Fuck you,' he said, hurling it at the smell of breakfast coming from the air vent. It bounced back off the grill, glanced off the top of the cash reserve safe and fell spreadeagled at his feet.

Another stub followed quickly.

'And your friends in America,' he said, as it buried itself in a shelf of circular books.

A frenzy seized him. He let fly in all directions, muttering in unison with his flailing arm.

'You thick—' a whirling stub cut a train of havoc into an orderly array of gleaming home safe boxes – 'surly—' a sack of copper gave a metallic grunt – 'hulking—' a pile of pass books collapsed under a direct hit – 'unreasonable—' the case of fishing gear commenced to slither sideways to the floor. He caught it before it reached the ground. As he propped it up once more against the cheque drawers, he gave a short burst of laughter.

'Bugger him, anyway,' he said mildly. A bloke should have more sense. Getting worked up over that big slob's tantrums. Once the hangover's cured we'll be palsey-walsey again.

Moving around on tiptoe, he built up the fallen column of pass books and rearranged the scattered home safe boxes into tidy ranks, working quickly and quietly, his ear cocked for any sound coming from the air vent. He had picked up the stubs remaining on the floor when he heard the office door open.

'Blast him,' he hissed.

In two silent strides he was across the strong room and the stubs were dropped into the space behind the cash safe. He commenced to hum loudly. Barging noisily around the book safe, he collected an armful of books, letting one fall on the floor and retrieving it with a loud curse, tugging and wrenching with clumsy hands and shuffling feet. Still humming lustily he staggered out into the office, peeping over the top of the heaped-up books towards the end of the gangway.

'Oh, it's you, Annie,' he said.

He dumped his load on top of the office bookcase.

'Phew!' he said, drawing his hand across his forehead. 'D'you know you bloody near put the heart across me. I thought it was the Boss. He's in queer bad twist this morning.'

Mrs. Mahony's large pale face peered round the door jamb.

'May I come in, Mr. McCann?' she said.

Without waiting for an answer, she waddled in, folded arms shoring up the massive sagging breasts, belly and buttocks, that never knew corset, jauntily wobbling, poor tortured feet slapping along in battered old house shoes, the gaping sides of which were plugged with bunions.

She stopped at McCann's box.

'Dispatch from His Lordship,' she announced. 'Strong room in filthy state. Must be swept out at once. Tidied up before opening time.'

Her pale, almost invisible, eyebrows gave her an expression of sardonic irony.

'I'll not be in your way, Mr. Mac?' she asked.

'Of course not, Annie. Go right ahead.'

Mrs. Mahony shuffled back up the office. Turned at the door. 'It'll be all right so,' she said. 'I'll be back directly.'

The door closed. Opened again almost immediately.

'Psst!'

He looked up from the cash book he was heading. Around the door jamb, only her mop of streeling hair could be seen: dry, snuff-coloured, powdered with dandruff.

'There's no harm in people talking to themselves,' she said. 'But when they start yelling, the dear knows where it will end.'

Before he could answer, she was gone.

He whistled, a low appreciative glissando. Cripes, that's a good one. She must have heard everything. The whole bloody litany. Her ear cocked to the air vent. Drinking it all in. And then letting on she could hear the racket from the kitchen. A crazy idiot running amok in the strong-room. Yelling at the top of his voice. Oh, a right alibi. Though, God knows, it must have sounded daft enough. Echoing through the grating like a stuttering fog horn. Anyone in the kitchen was bound to hear the commotion. If the Big Fellow had been around he'd ...

McCann, lugging out from the strong-room the heavy metal cash box topped by two loaded silver trays, grimaced.

'Sweet suffering Jesus,' he pleaded, 'surely not?'

A moment's reflection reassured him. If Simpson had been earwigging, Annie, instead of taking a rise out of him, would have given him the tip-off. That was her form. A coarse untidy slut. Grumpy and stubborn and filled to the gills with prejudices. But, at bottom, a decent kindly creature. Simpson swears by her. Claims she is the best housekeeper he ever had. Discreet. Shut-mouthed. Loyal.

He commenced laying out the notes and coin on his cash desk.

Her loyalty is flexible, though. She'll scoff at the absurd antics he indulges in when he's half-jarred. Ridicule the constant hangover griping and snarling. Kick up hell about his senseless all-night guzzling. Even pass you a warning in her own devious way. As she did just now. But dare you run him down and she'll fly at your throat.

Tens, fives, singles, halves were neatly stacked against the back of the desk. The wooden baize-bottomed trays, packed tight with bags of small and large silver, placed in readiness to one side. On the floor, at his feet, a sack of copper. He had just shaken out a cloth bag of loose silver and copper and was starting in to count it when Mrs. Mahony returned carrying a worn-down broom and a dust-pan. A duster protruded from the pocket of her apron.

As she passed the cashier's box, McCann said:

'You wouldn't clean out that byre in less than a week.'

'Sure, we'll deal with the big dirt, anyway,' she said.

He followed her to the strong-room door. Lounging against the jamb, he watched her flicking the broom across the cobwebbed roof.

'They're troublesome vermin too,' she said. 'The spiders.'

The trailing webs fluttered agitatedly under the wind of her sweeping.

'Real dust collectors.'

Viciously she poked the broom into a corner of the roof.

'They'd scald you to the heart.'

She brushed and belaboured the parcels on the upper shelf.

'His Lordship's fit to be tied this morning. Nothing's right. Eggs hard. Bacon burnt. Tea cold.'

She broke into a fit of coughing. Paused to let the dust cloud settle. Sniffed.

'Doubting Thomas. Standing there surveying. You'd think I meant to plunder all round me.'

McCann coloured.

'It's ... it's just ... you might want help ... shifting things, you know.'

'Ha!' she said. She began dusting the backs of the ledgers.

'You clashed with him, eh? That's why you were showing your tantrums?' she said.

'He rounded on me for no reason in the world. The big slob.'

Mrs. Mahony faced him.

16

'Amn't I tired telling you to leave the poor man alone in the mornings. He's not in the best of form till later on.'

'But, Annie, I never—'

'You should surely know by this time that he's not at himself till he's taken the cure?'

'I know that. But, sure, he—'

'It takes two bottles of beer to rightify him. You've no business aggravating him—'

Through the grating came the sound of a faint pop.

'Eu-eu!' Mrs. Mahony's head pivoted.

'There he goes,' she said. 'I better finish before he comes out.'

She started sweeping the floor vigorously, driving all before her – dust, dockets, brown paper, bits of string, pins, rubber bands – till the sweepings were blocked by the ledge of the steel door frame.

Another pop.

'He should be on the mend shortly,' she said, laying aside the brush and picking up the dust-pan. Half stooping, half squatting, she scooped at the refuse, using the high steel ledge as a buffer.

'You'd never credit it,' she wheezed, edging her way across the door frame, scooping as she went. 'He wouldn't take time to pour out the beer in the morning .. drinks it out of the bottle like a sucking calf ... claims you get the whole virtue of the beer that way . .'

At the third pop, Mrs. Mahony straightened up painfully.

'My God,' she said. 'He must have put in a terrible night's drinking.'

'What did I tell you?' said McCann. 'He acted the weasel from the moment he set foot in the office this morning.'

Gathering up her cleaning materials, she shuffled towards the door. Paused uncertainly. Paused again. Turned back.

'Mr. Mac,' she said. 'I'm very worried. What d'you think I found when I was dusting out the sitting-room an hour ago?'

He shook his head.

Rummaging in the neck of her jumper, she drew forth and held up to view a pair of black satin panties.

'Behind a cushion on the sofa,' she said.

McCann gazed at the damning evidence.

17

'The hard man,' he murmured reverently.

He drew a deep breath.

'There must be some explanation, Annie,' he said. 'Could the laundry possibly have returned them by mistake?'

Mrs. Mahony sniffed.

'It's *to* the laundry they should be going. Not coming back. But that's not all. The ashtray was choked with cigarette butts and they smeared with lipstick.'

She lowered the panties down to stomach level.

'Two whiskey glasses were smeared as well,' she added.

McCann eyed the garment judiciously, his lips moving in mysterious silence.

'There were two fine-looking big nuns,' he said at last, 'going the rounds yesterday, collecting for the Foreign Missions. Take care but he asked them into the house for a little liquid refreshment. And one of them – maybe her drawers slipped their moorings.'

He gave a yelp of laughter.

'Oh, a right awkward situation. The Boss could hardly hold them up and say: "Which of you two ladies dropped your bloomers?" I bet you he stuffed them behind a cushion, knowing the one with the draughty bottom would be in some time looking for her loin cloth.'

He slapped his thigh in delight.

'That'd be the day,' he crowed.

'It's no laughing matter,' said Mrs. Mahony. 'I have my good name to think of. If there's any malafoostering going on I'd have to give in my notice. Or John Mahony would put me out of the house.'

'You're getting very suspicious, Annie. Sure you know the poor man has no time for women. Not while there's drink to be had.'

She sniffed again.

'It's not the first time I've known him to have women in the house.'

McCann gazed at the pale expressionless face. She has him taped, he decided. All along she must have known. Just kept her trap shut.

'You're jumping to conclusions,' he said. 'I'll guarantee you're wrong. He's unfortunate in his friends, that's about the height of it.'

18

'Whatever you say, Mr. Mac,' she said doubtfully. She made to go. Hesitated. Tapped her bulging jumper.

'What am I to do with these . . . ?' She grimaced.

'Leave them where you found them,' he said.

'Or better still,' he added, 'throw them down some place where he's bound to trip over them.'

As she turned away, he said:

'Unless you'd rather launder them and send them to the Convent.'

'I'll tell you what I'll – ' She broke off. Listening.

'Here he comes,' she said. 'I'd better go.'

Simpson was humming to himself when he returned to the office. A sing-song tuneless drone, punctuated by gentle burps as the gas from the beer erupted. Waiting for McCann to return from the Post Office with the morning mail, he checked his diary. No Standing Orders were due nor were any 'Yearly Applications to Head Office for the Renewal/Increase/Decrease (Delete as necessary) of Overdraft Facilities.' A quick run through of the Manager's Portfolio – a battered wallet whose torn compartments and their contents were secured by a jagged red band cut from a cast-off motor tube – revealed a bundle of yellowing title deeds to be sorted, listed and sent up to the Law Officer: the baptismal certificate of a deceased customer: a letter from the Bank of England refusing payment of a mutilated one pound note on the grounds that the missing portion had already been presented by another Bank: four Industrial Insurance Policies – premiums one shilling a week each – discovered to be unavailable as security: a certificate for fifteen Ordinary Shares of £1 each, Hillcrest Collieries Ltd., with a stockbroker's letter attached stating that the Company was the subject of a Court Order to wind up and the shares could be considered valueless: a long screed from the Premises Department enquiring about the adequacy of the fire precautions at the Branch: a thirty years old receipt from the Superintendent of the Civic Guards for the surrender on request of 'one Webley & Scott revolver (Automatic Pistol) together with twenty rounds of unexploded .32 calibre ammunition.' Nothing that required immediate attention.

He sat up on the high stool, resting cheeks on knuckled hands, the aftertaste of the beer still clinging to his palate. A pleasant drowsiness burdened his eyelids. He blinked himself awake.

That third beer had been a mistake. Two generally did the trick. Any more made you dopey. Still, all things considered, he felt in good enough shape. If only he could remember a bit more about last night. What time had he got home? Had he made it on his own steam? And the headache? Was it really due to drink? Perhaps he had staggered against some obstacle? Or fallen? Carefully he examined the knees and elbows of his well-cared-for grey suit. No frayed threads. No telltale stains. Maybe he had been oxtered home – completely pole-axed? Feet dragging the ground. Grunting unintelligibly. Perhaps spewing his guts up.

His half-hearted attempts to pierce the stubborn opaqueness – the hangover oyster shell protecting his cringing conscience – yielded no disclosure. Yet at the back of his mind hovered a memory – a disturbing formless ghost that refused to be laid.

Once more the car engine started up. Muffled. At the far end of the village seemingly. The same car undoubtedly. Though now it appeared to have developed engine trouble. The exhaust beat was irregular. Put-put-put . . . put-put . . . put-put-put . . put-put. Missing in two cylinders. Plugs oiled up. Or dirty terminals.

The ache at the back of his right temple began again. Faintly.

He shook his head violently as though shaking off a cloud of gnats. He muttered:

'What can't be cured, must be endured.'

He was gazing out the window, tapping the glass impatiently, whan the cashier came back with the letters.

He wheeled on him. Growled:

'What does that clown mean, running his car engine all morning without a break?'

McCann's jaw dropped.

'What's that, Manager?'

'Revving up his engine like a lunatic for the last two solid hours. Don't tell me you didn't hear it. The racket that car kicked up must have been heard in every house in the village.'

'What . . . car . . . sir?' asked McCann.

'If it wasn't a car, it was a van. Or a truck.'

McCann's lips shaped silently the words: *Car. Truck.*

'Don't you hear it now, man?' said Simpson. 'Belting away. Up at the head of the village someplace.'

Head tilted to the side, brow furrowed in concentration, McCann listened.

'I'm afraid I can't hear it, sir,' he said.

'Nonsense!' said Simpson, cocking his ear towards the window.

A lone gull cackled threateningly, finishing with a prolonged wail of disappointment: the office clock beat out a steady pulse: heads askew, eyes aslant, the two men listened.

Simpson broke the silence.

'He must have switched off his engine,' he said.

'Very likely,' said McCann gravely. He handed the letters to the manager. 'Someone must have told him he'd left it running.'

Simpson gave him a suspicious glance.

'If the Guards did their duty,' he said, 'that sort of carry-on would soon be stopped.'

'You're dead right, Manager.' McCann started back to his box.

'Come here a minute, Mac.'

Startled, McCann wheeled round. Simpson was leaning forward, head outstretched like a hissing gander.

'My forehead,' he said. 'Do you see anything?'

Slowly McCann walked the few paces back.

'I can't . . . see—'

'How can you see from there? Come in close and have a good look.'

Through fetor of stale whiskey and freshly drunk beer, past contemptuous stare of grey protruding eyes, McCann peered close.

'Over the right eye, Mac? Any bruise or bump?'

McCann surveyed the expanse of smooth healthy skin rising from the bushy eyebrow.

'Not a thing, Skipper,' he said.

'Just what I thought,' said Simpson, rifling through the mail. 'Better open up. It's after ten o'clock.'

Whilst the first customers drifted in, Simpson sorted the letters out into four categories. The unwanted. The expected. The unknown. The dreaded. They were dealt with in that order.

The unwanted – circulars from Unit Trusts, glossy reports from International combines, begging letters from missionary organizations – recognizable by the reduced postage – got the waste-paper-basket, unopened.

Envelopes whose contents could be divined were ripped open: notes, cheques, money orders, dividend warrants, verified: dockets filled out: the completed transactions slapped face down on the desk.

The unknown were dealt with to the accompaniment of a muttered commentary:

'Oh, it's you is it?' *'Please find enclosed cheque. Account a bit behind. Should be in order now. Send new cheque-book.'* So that you can plunder the till again. Without by your leave or word of warning. Back your cheque will go R D if you don't mind your step. Hullo! And what have *you* to say for yourself? *'Can't get in to sign bill. Bad with pains. Please grant spareance. Will have you right shortly.'* That's the Lay of the Last Minstrel, all right. Pains! Pains! Pains! When you wanted the money you were sprightly enough. No trouble putting the legs under you then. Well, the props had better be working shortly. Or else. Now, then, what have we here?

He raised his voice:

'Listen to this, McCann. From some place in England called Fenton Parva. *"Please may I have full information how one can obtain a loan from your Bank?"* '

McCann drew his pen sharply across the latticed wire between the two boxes, the stabbing finger of his other hand calling attention to the counter. Simpson waited till the office was empty. Resumed:

' *"and what age limit, rate of interest and date of repayments? The amount of the loan in question would range from £1,600 to £2,000. Would you require security? I am a native of the village, so don't be alarmed with my surname. Yours faithfully, Mrs. M. Szlakowicz. PS. There are no banks in Fenton Parva or I would not bother you".'*

McCann chuckled appreciatively.

'No banks in Fenton Parva,' he said. 'Would you require security? She's a cunning knave, that one. A wolf posing as a sheep in wolf's clothing.'

Simpson crumpled up the thin lined sheet and flung it in the waste-paper-basket.

'There'll be no reply to that exhortation,' he said.

Only the Head Office envelope now remained unopened.

A large bulky envelope, tattered and grimy. Strips of brown gum paper were plastered all over it. Sealing down the torn flap. Taping the worn frayed edging. Covering the original address with layer upon layer of re-addressed strips. Fragments of used and torn-off stamps pocked the upper portion of the envelope, mingling with postmarks that jostled each other like porter rings on a bar counter. He counted the postmarks. Nine times the envelope had been used. It would have fallen to pieces long since were it not for the gum straps that held it together. You'd wonder at the petty meanness of a huge enterprise like a bank, he thought.

Grabbing up the envelope, he ripped off the flap.

'That will put an end to your wanderings,' he muttered.

Two more used envelopes in little better condition were among the contents. These also he destroyed.

This act of rebellion heartened him. Briskly he ran through the batch of branch cheques, ticking them off from the remittance letter. The circulars next. A long screed from Lombard Street giving dates and instructions for the next month's coupon cutting. A dollar rates memo. Four circulars reporting lost or stolen cheque books. A police notice warning of the activities of *Carlo Manelli alias Luigi Cinthio alias Jaco Fondi who has recently cashed large numbers of stolen Travellers Cheques in Cork and Dublin. He is aged 55/65, height 5 ft., heavily built, broad face, grey or white wavy hair; he speaks little English, possesses an Italian passport, wears large diamond and gold rings and smokes heavily scented cigarettes. Usually travels in the company of women of tall and flashy appearance.'

Reverently Simpson laid down the notice.

'Everyone has their own little weaknesses,' he murmured.

There now only remained a single special letter. Gingerly he lifted it. Scanned it rapidly. Re-read it.

Gathering up the mail he pushed it into the pigeon hole between the two boxes, rattling it urgently.

'McCann?' he called softly.

'Sir?'

Simpson peered over the partition to make sure the office was empty. He said: 'Today is the day for your bow-tie and dickie. We're to have company.'

'Company?'

'Yes. Rillington, the general manager from Lombard Street

and one of our own directors, Creeth, are doing a tour of the western branches. They will be with us around three o'clock this afternoon.'

McCann gulped.

'Today?' he said. 'There must be some mistake. It's to-morrow they mean.'

'No, my friend. Today it is.'

'Sweet suffering saviour!'

'Oh, you needn't worry. It's only a social call they're making.'

'How are you so sure of that?'

'They're bringing their wives with them. An expense account excursion.'

'But what's the Lombard Street bowzie want? He has no errand in a little huxter shop the like of this.'

McCann's despairing gaze swept shabby walls, grimy ceiling, the board floor splashed with ink stains, brass and woodwork dull, unpolished.

'Mr. McCann,' said Simpson, 'these two gentlemen and their doubtless charming wives are taking this opportunity to view the magnificent scenery of the western seaboard. They are not on the inspection staff.'

'But how will you—?'

'I'll rush them straightaway up to the sitting-room. Throw a few agrarian gargles into them. Believe me, if their glasses are kept well topped up, they'll have eyes for nothing but lakes and mountains.'

'I hope you're right, Manager.'

Simpson got down off the stool.

'I want to get in a supply of liquor,' he said. 'Gin. Brandy. Scotch whisky. There's an unopened bottle of Jameson in the liquor press. Maybe I'd better get a bottle of sherry, too.'

At the door he turned slowly.

'They'd never be expecting a meal?' he suggested.

McCann shook his head dazedly.

'Not at that hour,' he said.

'Though, God knows, I wouldn't put it past them,' he added.

Simpson found the housekeeper clearing away the breakfast dishes.

'We're having visitors today, Mrs. Mahony,' he announced gaily, ignoring her averted face. 'We'll want to lay in some re-freshments.'

24

'Aye,' she grunted into the sugar bowl.

'You could run across to Billjoe's and bring back a bottle of Scotch. One of brandy. One of gin. And a bottle of sherry.'

'Another big night, I suppose?' She flicked her apron viciously across the table cloth, scattering the toast crumbs to the floor.

'We should be all right for Irish,' he said, opening the door of the wall press.

She straightened up, watching him sardonically as he poked around among the glasses and bottles.

'Where's the bottle of Jameson got to?' he asked over his shoulder.

'I'll tell you where it is,' she said. 'It's upstairs in the sitting-room. Along with the rest of the disgraceful litter your friends left behind them last night.'

'Upstairs?' He started towards the door.

She picked up the tray of breakfast dishes. Said she:

'Are you trying to tell me you don't remember scoffing off the Jameson? You must have been queer an' drunk so. I suppose the rest of the party were as bad. So seen by the state of the room.'

Simpson's eyes bugged. He blinked rapidly.

'No need to make a song and dance because I asked in . . . er . . . some friends for a night-cap. I just couldn't bring to mind if we'd finished the bottle or not.'

'Oh, it's empty all right. Your fine friends saw to that.' She sniffed. 'A nasty tribe they must have been, leaving their trade-mark on all they touched.'

She waddled to the door. Turned.

'Aye, and leaving behind more than that, as you'll doubtless find out.'

Simpson watched her go. That, he decided, is one riddle solved. Someone saw you home last night. A plural someone, if Mrs. Mahony is right. Probably as drunk as yourself. Spilling drinks and scattering cigarette ash. Leaving their trade-mark, as she put it. Wonder who it was ? Probably some gougers scenting free drink. He sighed. Oh, well, that's the way. We're only alive once and must make the best of it.

On his way back to the office, he looked into the kitchen.

'Better add a bottle of Jameson Tan to your list, Mrs. Mahony.' He addressed the rigid back stooped over the steaming sink. 'We didn't—' He raised his voice above the din of rattling delph. 'We didn't mess the sitting-room about . . . er . . . too much, did we?'

'It's everyone to his own way of thinking.' She lifted a plate and rubbed it vigorously with the dish-cloth. 'To my mind it's poor conduct in a Bank House.'

'Oh, if that's the way you're taking it!' He closed the door on the angry clatter of dishes roughly handled.

The office was full when he got back. McCann broke off checking a lodgment. Leaned out of the box. Whispered urgently: 'Old man Duffy wants to see you.'

Simpson spotted the crest of white tangled hair down at the far end of the counter.

'Mr. Duffy,' he called. 'Did you want me?'

'Could I speak to you a wee moment, Mr. Simpson? Privately? If it's not taking up too much of your time.'

The cringing subdied accent gave Simpson his cue. In a loud arrogant voice he said:

'Could you not call later? We are very busy.'

Duffy's scraggy frame shrank, seeking the shelter of its baggy tweed carapace. He sidled up the counter to the manager's box.

'It's very important, sir. I'm badly stuck,' he said, in a shrill piercing whisper.

'Very well,' said Simpson. 'Come into the inner office.'

The tense attentive silence was broken as Duffy moved down the office through a gentle litany of:

'Nice day, Ned.'

'Well, Ned, how are you the day?'

'Great weather, Mr. Duffy, for this time of the year.'

'You're looking well, Ned.'

With the key turned in the door of the private office, Duffy gave a smothered squeal of laughter. He moved about in the cramped space, skipping exultantly, head and shoulders twitching, hands stuffed deep in trousers pockets clawing and clutching spasmodically.

'Be jaykeys, Jim, you're a great man,' he said. 'A thought-reader.'

Simpson gave him a sour look.

'What caper are you up to now, Ned? Putting on an act like that before an office full of mohawks.'

Duffy jerked his head in the direction of the outer office.

'Not one of those mohawks but owes me for fertilizer. Or groceries. Or seed potatoes. Or farm implements. Be jaykeys, the only way I'll get my money is by putting on the poor mouth.'

Still jigging, twitching, shoulder-shrugging, moving his body around inside his clothes like a man with the itch, he halted beside Simpson. He lowered his voice.

'And when we're on to the subject, I want you to write me another pay-up-or-else letter. Lay it on thick, Jim. The stronger the better. Threaten law if you don't get your money.'

Simpson sat one-hipped on the office table, swinging his free leg slowly.

'Much good it will do you. Sure every dog in the street knows you're rotten with money.'

'They do not. And I'm not rotten with money. Be jaykeys, I've only the few ha'pence gathered together that'll give me decent burial and get a few masses said for my soul.'

'Who do you think you're codding, Ned? You must be the wealthiest man in the county.'

The twitchings in Duffy's limbs ceased. He stood poised on the balls of his feet, body leant forward, face expressionless. Quite still but for flicking tongue moistening dry lips. A dangerous little reptile, thought Simpson.

'Listen here now. And pay attention.' A threatening finger prodded Simpson's knee. 'You're a right fellow, James. A sensible fellow that'll give sensible advice. And you're not a blabbermouth. That's why I've told you so much. But if ever anything leaks out about my affairs, I'll know where it came from. The missus herself doesn't even know how I stand.'

He executed a jigging side-step, rubbing his hands gleefully together.

'She came to me last week, be jaykeys. Looking for a new coat. A fur one, if you don't mind. Told me it was the talk of the parish how shabby she'd got. And her tethered to such a well-doing man.'

He paused dramatically.

'Do you know what I told her, Jim?'

'Couldn't guess.'

' "Lizzie," I says. "Have you any idea what the people will say if they see you parading up the centre aisle next Sunday in a fur coat?" "No," says she. "Well, I'll tell you," I says. "They'll say," says I, "that Ned Duffy has so skinned the sick and down-trodden that he has fleeces to spare to show off his wife's big backside. And they'll say," says I, "that Ned Duffy is getting too big for his boots. And what's more," I says, "they'd be right. Couldn't you get a coat length of good heavy sensible tweed from one of the weavers," says I, "and get it run up by the dressmaker?" '

Simpson watched the rapidly moving lips and the bright, merciless, birdlike eyes. God help your poor wife, you mean little maggot, he brooded.

'And what do you think she said, Jim? You'd never guess.'

'What did she say?' Hating himself for asking the questions.

'Says she: "The coat I have is not bad at all. I'll send it to the cleaners and it'll do another wee while." Be jaykeys, did you ever hear the like?'

The heartless cackle of laughter drove Simpson to his feet.

'I'll type out the letter now for you, Ned,' he said. 'Stay here till I come back.'

As he went back to his desk he kept driving a massive balled-up fist into the palm of his other hand. I'd like to clout that cruel little weasel. He has pity for no one. Not even his own kith and kin.

He rolled a sheet of headed notepaper into the carriage of the Remington and adjusted the margins.

Edward Duffy, Esq., he began, typing two-fingered, *Grocer, Har dwa re—*

He lifted his fingers from the keys and glared at the typed address. God knows, a machine like this would put you climbing the walls. You never know when it's going to act the jibber. But what else could you expect from a battered-out recon-ditioned wreck. Complain and you'll only be told to send it off again for further reconditioning. Surprising the Head Office wonder-boys haven't issued a Staff Memorandum instructing us that all used bum fodder should be sent back to the makers for reconditioning.

Moodily he began to unroll the sheet of notepaper, changed his mind and rolled it back. Too good for the rapacious old scoundrel, he decided. He typed on:

28

& General Merchant, Glenard.
 Dear Sir,

What was to be said? Duffy wanted a letter strong enough to convince the most sceptical of his debtors. Well, Simpson smiled sourly, a letter calling up an advance should do the trick. Doctored up a little, of course. He rooted out from his desk a specimen copy. Started up again:

> *I have to inform you that owing to the unsatisfactory position of your account and your evident inability to honour your commitments* – that'll drive a grunt out of him, muttered Simpson – *it has become neces sary to suspend all operations on your current account at this office except lodgements in permanent reduction of the debt. Any further cheques issued will not be paid.*
> *I have been instructed by my Directors to call on you, as I now do, for the repa yment of your debt to the bank.*
> *Failure to comply with this request will result in legal proce edings being instituted against you.*
> *You would be well advised to give this matter your immediate attention.*
>
>

Yours faithfully,
Man ager
>

Simpson signed the letter and brought it back with him to the inner office. Here he found Duffy, one arm plunged to the elbow in the waistband of his trousers, frantically scratching his crutch.

'This heat has me scalded,' Duffy spoke across his raised shoulder, his face furrowed into a frown of intense concentration. 'The fork of the trousers are lacerating me. It's pure agony.'

'Take a look at this and see will it do.' Simpson tossed the letter on the office table. 'Aye, it's good weather all right.' He turned away towards the window, not troubling to hide the look of distaste on his face.

He glanced quickly around the Square, without really expecting to see an idling car. I'll have to go easy on the drink, he resolved, if this is the way it's beginning to take me. The pulsing stopped as suddenly as it had started. Behind him, he heard Duffy mumbling to himself:

'Unsatisfactory position of your account ... inability to honour your commitments ... suspend all operations ... further cheques will not be paid ... call upon you, as I now do, for repayment ... failure to comply ... legal proceedings.'

Duffy chuckled appreciatively.

'Be jaykeys, Jim, you've excelled yourself this time. That last bit is out on its own – "You would be well advised." It's an ultimatum that would convince an assize judge let alone the gulpins I'll be showing it to.'

Without looking round, Simpson said:

'You should show it to the Income Tax Inspectors. It might put an end to your troubles.' He formed his lips into a soundless whistle. That's a shrewd kick in the guts, Mr Cute Hawk.

'There'll be no more tax troubles. My affairs are in safe hands at last.'

Simpson swung round. Startled.

'What have you ... how have you managed that?' he asked.

'I've taken up golf. Joined a club in the city.'

Simpson eyed the small scraggy figure in the cheap reach-me-down suit. The wizened face. The hands clumsy, uncared-for, stubby-fingered. He burst out laughing.

'You're codding me, Ned.'

'Indeed I'm not. Why wouldn't I start golf when the Tax Inspector has taken it up?'

'Well ... I'll ... be – So that's it. I suppose he's a member of the same club?'

'Aye. We have an odd quiet round together. For a few shillings. He's not very good, no more than myself. But he wins most of the games. A thorough decent fellow.'

'The softening-up process before you got down to business.'

'Oh, no! We never talk business at all. Though I did mention to him once how hard it was for a man the like of me, with no education, to fill up the tax forms.'

'Oh-ho! Now we're getting somewhere. He was very helpful of course.'

'He was indeed. Told me any time I wanted help or advice not to be afraid to ask him.'

'Which, no doubt, you did.'

'I called in to see him last week. Brought the books with me. Just planked them down on his desk. "Here," says I. "There's no use beating about the bush. You know more about these matters than me. Take a run through these books and tell me what I owe you. I have my cheque book with me." '

Simpson stared at him. Awestricken.

'Do you know what it is, Ned Duffy? You're in a class by yourself.'

Duffy smiled modestly. He dug his hands deeper in his pockets, jingling silver and keys.

'The Inspector said something similar. "Ned," says he, getting up from his desk, "an honest man is the noblest work of God." He insisted on shaking hands. "D'you know," he says, "you've given me back my faith in human nature. Call back next week and I'll let you know how you stand." '

Before Simpson could pass any remark, there was a knock at the door and McCann put round his head.

'Excuse me,' he said. 'There's a document for you to sign, Manager.'

'Right,' said Simpson.

Duffy put away the letter in his wallet.

'I'll be off now,' he said.

As Simpson was unlocking the door, he leaned over to Duffy and whispered:

'I hope it was the right set of books you showed him. Not the ones locked away in your safe.'

Duffy, who had been stowing away the wallet in his hip pocket, froze into a sciatic crouch.

'It's queer and hateful, that class of chat.' He spoke in a low, whining voice. 'I wonder at you coming out with the like of that. A man in your position.'

'Come off it, Ned,' said Simpson brusquely. 'Didn't I tutor you myself into the mysteries of duplicate ledger book-keeping. You can keep your lamentations for the Tax Inspector.'

Wriggling like a fawning dog, Duffy skipped around Simpson. He looked up at him coyly.

'You're an awful man, Jim. Forever codding and joking. You had me well fooled there. Only for I know you so well.'

He sidled past the bulky figure and out into the main office. Came jigging back. At the counter, the row of heads swung round.

'You'll do all you can for me, Mr. Simpson, won't you. I'm rightly banjazed.' Again he spoke in a loud carrying whisper.

Without answering, Simpson re-locked the inner office door

and returned to his desk where he started in on the back-log of the work, signing receipts, initialling pass book entries, dealing with correspondence requiring immediate attention. Remittance cheques had begun to pile up in the pigeon hole. These had to be examined carefully for possible errors, branded with the branch brand and sorted into the three sections of the clearing system – Dublin, Belfast or London clearing centres. In each of these sections a further sub-division was necessary, grouping together and placing on listing slips, the cheques of each bank. Finally, the whole batch of cheques had to be entered, with full particulars recorded, on a loose-leaf remittance sheet.

As fast as Simpson cleared the pigeon hole, McCann kept pushing through further batches of cheques taken in over the counter in lodgments. Shortly before lunch hour a lull came. McCann settled down to sorting out the heaps of notes that littered his cash desk. Simpson, finished at last with the remittances, sat on the high stool, knuckle-propping his chin, his eyes staring vacantly at a branch progress-graph hanging from the wall. The wives of the two head-men, now what would they be like? The director's wife would be a bit long of the tooth, you could gamble on that. But the other one. The English one. She'd probably be young enough. A blonde, surely. They all are. Well toveyed up. Big assed and big diddied. A good pair of props under her. With a few bumpers of gin under her roll-ons she'll start showing a length of leg. The low armchair – or even a creepy stool – would be the place to put her sitting. Where her legs will be well cocked up. Maybe she'll . . .

As the more and more scabrous images floated before his mind a pleasant glow of desire crept over him. When McCann bolted the street door of the bank and started putting away his cash for the lunch-hour break, it was with reluctance that Simpson slid off his stool and left the office.

Simpson was frowning with vexation when he returned to the office. He tackled McCann at once.

'Were you talking to Mrs. Mahony this morning?' he asked.

McCann's eyebrows rose.

'I was. Why?'

'Did she say anything . . . Was she complaining about anything?'

'No more than usual.' McCann's manner was cool. Offhand. You'll get nothing out of me, he swore.

'Did she ... maybe she mentioned ... had she anything to say ... any complaints ... about the house, I mean?'

'She *did* say something about the sitting-room being in a bit of a mess.' Whiskey, lipstick, black satin panties. It's well she didn't find a used french letter. You'll want to watch your step, James, my lad. 'Probably cigarette ash on the floor. Empty glasses not put away. You know the way women go on about nothing.'

'She's had a lip on her all morning. Hasn't said a civil word to me since breakfast time.'

'Don't worry. She'll get over it. Did she get in the soothing syrup for the visitors?'

'She did. And I told her when she answered the hall door – they'll ring at the private door, of course – to usher them straight up to the sitting-room.'

Simpson paused. Rubbed his chin slowly.

'Do you know, come to think of it, there was an odd expression on her face when I said that.'

A banging noise distracted him. A customer was pushing at one of the swing doors.

'The other one,' he called out. And to McCann: 'They're coming here a lifetime and they've never learnt that one of the doors is blocked up.'

'The main thing,' McCann said, 'is to keep them occupied upstairs. So that they don't come nosing around down here. The two executive bowsies, I mean.'

He turned to the counter where an old man was waving a deposit receipt to attract his attention.

'All right, William,' he said. 'I'll be with you in a moment. I'm just getting out my cash.'

'It's not cash I want, young fellow. It's just a word of advice.' Simpson leaned out over the counter.

'Well, William, what's your trouble?' he said.

'It's the pension, James. The gauger's after me, I doubt. About this.' He waved the receipt aloft. 'He wants me to sign a paper. So that he can ferret out what money I have in the Bank.'

'If you don't sign, you'll get no pension.'

'But I've been getting it for going on ten years. They can't cut it off now?'

'If you didn't declare your savings when you put in for the pension, they can make you repay every shilling you shouldn't have got. Over the whole ten years.'

'My God, they'll have the very shirt off my back.' The old man thumped the counter. 'I'll not pay, I tell you. I'll do jail before I pay.'

'How much is in it, William?' Simpson pointed to the receipt.

'Sure it's only a wee trifle of money.'

'How much?'

'Something over four hundred pound. A lifetime's gathering.'

'You'd better declare it. They might let you off light enough.'

'Could you not do anything for me, James? I've known you for a long time. Maybe if I were to draw it out now, the gauger need never know a thing about it.'

The faded blue eyes fastened on Simpson.

'You wouldn't be at any loss. I'd bring the money back here when the fuss was all over.'

'Are you asking me to make a false declaration? They go back three years you know.'

'You've only to tell him that I've no money in the Bank. That's all.'

'I couldn't do it, William. It would be as much as my job is worth.'

The old man folded up the deposit receipt. He nodded his head slowly.

'Aw now,' he said. 'I might have known. You're like the rest of them, Mr. Simpson. All for the big fellow. No regard for the likes of us.'

Opening his waistcoat, he extracted from an inside pocket a wad of newspaper secured by a thick elastic band. He kept muttering to himself.

'Never get old if you can. No one has any time for you.'

The elastic band was off. The newspaper unrolled to reveal a large leather purse.

'Many's the thing I've seen in me day. I've seen all sorts and sizes of men come and go.'

He unclasped the leather purse and commenced, slowly and carefully, to fit the folded receipt into its depths.

'It was aye the big getting bigger and the small dwindling to perishing point. Nowadays—'

The click of the closing purse emphasized the pause.

34

'Nowadays the middens are rising, the mountains sinking.'
Simpson cleared his throat noisily.

'You'd be a good age now, William?' he said.

'I'll be eighty next month.'

'You're a hardy man for your years.'

The old man, busy swaddling the purse in its newspaper covering, looked up.

'It was poor health I had, the best of my days. Sure I've been stretched on the bed this six weeks. With the pains.'

'You don't take proper care of yourself. That's what's wrong. Half the sickness you hear about is the people's own fault. The other half is thought up. I wouldn't waste pity on one of them.'

Simpson straightened up. 'Look at me,' he said. 'Not a day's illness in my life.' He thumped his chest. 'Sound as a bell. No doctor ever got a shilling off me.'

'The big tree falls heavy,' said the old man, snapping the elastic band back on the wad of newspaper.

'Not till you put the axe to it,' said Simpson.

'No need to edge a blade. The wind or the weather could just as well bring it crashing to the ground.'

'You're not in a very cheerful mood, William. If I wasn't in the whole of my health, you'd be getting me worried.'

The old man was now putting away the parcelled-up purse in the inside pocket of his waistcoat. With lowered head he watched, intent on seeing that the parcel was safely stowed away. When he spoke it was as if he were talking to himself.

'I've seen men as big as yourself, Mr. Simpson. Fine big men. Strong as bulls. Bursting with health.'

With stabbing hand he forced the parcel deeper into his pocket.

'You'd find them at every Fair, winter or summer, standing all day about the Square without hat or coat or scarf.'

From the lapel of his coat he extracted a huge blanket pin with which he commenced pinning up the pocket.

'And it maybe bucketing rain the day long or blowing an east wind that would skin you. And you'd see them in the pubs afterwards and they swallowing back porter with the steam rising off their clothes like a ground fog.'

He began buttoning his waistcoat with slow clumsy fingers.

'They'd often fall into a ditch on the way home and sleep it

35

out there till morning. And damn the bit harm it would do them.'

He broke off and glanced up under his eyebrows at Simpson.

'Then there'd come a Fair day you wouldn't find them around.'

He paused. Did up another button.

'The next Fair they wouldn't be around either.'

Another pause. Another button.

'The following Fair you'd hear they were in the County Hospital. And before you had the bad news properly digested, you were paying offerings over them below in the chapel.'

He buttoned the last button and pulled down the wings of the waistcoat.

'I've seen that happen, not once, but many times.'

'I suppose it comes to us all some time,' said Simpson in a doubtful tone.

'Aye, surely,' said the old man. 'Well, I'd better be going now.'

At the door he turned. 'If there's one thing is sure and certain,' he said, nodding his head to emphasize the words, 'it's that a small leak'll sink a great ship.'

Simpson waited till the swing door settled.

'Did you hear that, McCann?' he said. 'That's a vicious old rascal. Coming out with that harangue. All because I wouldn't help him to defraud the Government.'

'You wouldn't want to pay too much attention to the poor devil, Manager. He's madly worried about—' McCann broke off as the swing door rasped. 'Good day, ma'am. Nice weather we're having.'

'Aye, this day has some sense. A wee sup of rain now would crown everything.'

'It would surely. The country is parched for the want of it.'

'I was wondering, Mr. McCann, would you take the rent from me? Or has it gone over the gale day?'

Simpson settled down to draft a letter to the Premises Department. *Fire Precautions* – he headed it.

'Now!' he said aloud. No fire escape. Inside walls of first floor sheeted with plaster board. Exposed wires in attic. No flue linings in chimneys. Wait a minute now, that won't do. Those are hazards, not precautions. Start with the fire extinguishers. How many are there? One on each floor. That's three.

36

What kind of condition are they in? Head Office will want to know when they were last serviced. And there's some instruction about buckets of water and buckets of sand. Or was that an air-raid precaution? Better look up the Book of Words.

He got out the Head Office Book of Regulations and began to leaf through it unenthusiastically. Attendance. Foreign Exchange Transactions. Keys. Mechanization. Here we are. Premises. Custody of. Safeguarding of. Damage to. The rasping screech of the swing door brought his hand up with a jerk. Must be grit under the door. A chip of gravel brought in on a shoe sole. Nasty sound. Still a couple of swings more and it will free itself. He turned the pages slowly. Should be coming to it now. Yes. Fire Precautions ... all times ... prevention better than ... locking stable ... horse gone. The rattle of the blocked-up door ruffled him.

'The other door,' he bawled, without looking up. 'Push the other door.'

McCann's whisper galvanized him.

'Jesus, it's the two buffs!' His face, pale and scared, was pressed to the pigeon hole.

Before Simpson could move there was a grinding crunch. His advice had been taken.

'My God, the bloody door has jammed, Manager!' Beads of sweat were breaking out on McCann's forehead: there was the urgency of despair in his anguished whisper. 'You'd better open it for them, sir,' he beseeched.

'If you had cleared out the grit a half an hour ago, this wouldn't have happened,' said Simpson, before starting off for the door. The grinding and rasping continued as he unlocked the inner office door.

'Sorry, gentlemen,' he called out to the two figures on the far side of the glass panelled doors. 'An unfortunate hold-up. I'll free it for you now.'

The burly man struggling with the door did not answer. He glared back at Simpson from under thick sandy brows, his face flushed with exertion. Behind him the smaller man tried to make himself heard above the screeching of the door. The only word that came to Simpson was the reiterated:

'Wait ... Wait ... Wait ...'

Unhurriedly, Simpson spat on his hands, rubbed them together and grabbed the brass door handle. Spreading his feet

37

apart, he rolled his shoulder muscles and gathered himself together for the heave. At the same instant the shoving shouldering figure, deciding, apparently, that pushing would not succeed, commenced tugging at the handle in an attempt to wrench open the door. When Simpson flung himself back with a violent jerk the stranger was lifted off his feet and swept into the office in the wake of the whirling door. If Simpson had not grabbed him by the shoulder as he shot past he would have crashed to the tile floor.

'That was a near thing,' said Simpson cheerfully, releasing his grip.

'How are you, Mr. Simpson?' said the small man, extending a hand. His face was puckered up into a smile of singular falsity that occupied only the lower half of his face, stripping the rabbit teeth back to the gums but leaving the stony grey eyes free to pass their pitiless verdict. 'Bigger and better than ever, I'm sure.'

'Game ball, Mr. Creeth,' said Simpson, shaking hands. 'Never better.'

'I don't think you've met Mr. Rillington. From our Lombard Street office. Mr. Rillington, Mr. Simpson.'

Simpson held out his hand.

'Pleased to—'

'What's the matter with that swing door?' Rillington barked.

'A chip of gravel got stuck under—'

'Not that door, man. The other one.'

Simpson pocketed the unwanted hand. His astonished gaze swung from the furious face to the swing doors.

'The other one,' he repeated.

'Yes. The one that's bolted.'

'Oh, that one. It is blocked up.'

'Might I enquire why?'

'If it is blowing an east wind the two doors fly open. Often the notes are blown off the cash desk.'

Rillington sniffed his disbelief.

'Why don't you put up a notice on the glass panel – *Out of action*?'

'I did. But I had to take it down again.'

'Why?'

'The customers used to struggle and sweat to get the door working again. Shouting is the only thing they understand.'

Rillington's rat-trap mouth clamped shut.

'Would you care to come upstairs?' said Simpson. 'A little refreshment after your journey, eh? I'll hop outside and get the ladies.'

'Do you see that, Creeth?' said Rillington, pointing. 'And that? And that?'

Simpson's gaze followed the pointing finger but could not locate its target.

'Henh?' he said.

'Those insurance advertisements, Mr. Simpson,' said Creeth. 'They should not be displayed in the office of a bank.'

'But they've been hanging there for years. I've seen them in every office I worked in.'

'All the more reason why they must come down.' Creeth flashed on his toothpaste smile.

'Tell me, Simpson,' said Rillington. 'Did you ever see an advertisement for our bank displayed in the office of an insurance company?'

Simpson tugged at an ear.

'To tell you the truth ... I never took particular notice.'

Contemptuously, Rillington brushed past him.

'Here,' he said, taking down an advertisement. 'Look at this. That company was swallowed up in a merger twenty years ago. You surely knew that?'

Simpson stared at him stupidly.

'Throw it in the rubbish bin,' Rillington continued. 'And the others along with it.'

'But ... they're pictures ... framed pictures ...'

Simpson's protest petered out under the withering stare of the butcher's-blue eyes.

'May we have a look round the office, Mr. Simpson?' said Creeth.

Bewildered, Simpson stood aside to allow the two men through to the inner office.

'No carpet?' said Rillington, sniffing at the bare boards, torn and pitted by hob-nails. 'No armchair for the customers?'

The unfairness of this attack stung Simpson. Carpets! Armchairs! If he were to apply for either of these luxuries, the Premises Department would cut the lard out of him. He said:

'A carpet would be in queer shape at the end of a Fair Day

after a score of mountainy men had trampled cow dung and tobacco spits into it.'

'Simpson, these tobacco-chewing, dung-spattered men are customers of this Bank and, as such, deserve better treatment than this.'

He hacked at the soft timber with the heel of his brogue shoe as though preparing to take a place kick.

'Creeth!'

'Yes, Mr. Rillington?'

'Indent Premises for one office armchair and one carpet, wall fitting, measurements to follow.'

There was a moment of uneasy silence. Simpson decided to try again.

'Perhaps you gentlemen would care for a little—'

'What is this?' Rillington had picked up from the table a square wooden object. He held it aloft.

'What d'you mean, sir?' Simpson stared at it stupidly.

'This thing adorning your table. You don't know what it is?'

'It's the base of an ink-stand, of course.'

'And where, might I enquire, is the inkwell?'

Twice Simpson opened his mouth to reply, before he ground out in baffled fury:

'That ink-stand has got nothing to do with me. It was sitting where you found it when I was appointed to this Branch and it has been there ever since.'

Rillington permitted himself a slight puckering of the lips.

'Well, Simpson, after long years of devoted service, shall we allow it to retire?'

Without waiting for a reply he sent the wooden stand skimming across the room where it crashed against a metal waste-basket.

'Indent for one marble fountain-pen stand, Creeth.'

'Yes, Mr. Rillington.'

'And this electric light fitting? I take it that it also was in this state when you took over the Branch?'

Simpson stared up at the dirty fly-blown light bulb, housed in the jagged fragments of a broken shade.

'I don't know,' he said. 'I never noticed it till now. We don't have much time for looking around in this office.'

'That's one explanation I never heard before,' said Rillington.

'Well, take time off to look round now.' He waved a contemptuous hand.

With Rillington's eyes, Simpson gazed round, taking in the paintwork on the walls – the dark-utility-green of a school lavatory broken out into leprous scales of crumbling plaster: the ordnance survey map of the area, so browned with age as to be quite illegible, barely sustained by its wooden rollers; the century-old photograph of the Head Office building, dour and unlovely, its steps studded with tall-hatted porters and bowler-hatted customers: the stationery press occupying a whole section of wall with its contents overflowing to floor and window-sill.

'How many branches did we visit on this trip, Creeth?' asked Rillington.

'Fourteen.'

'None of them, I might say, were up to standard. But, undoubtedly, of all these offices, yours – Mr. Simpson – is the most squalid.'

Simpson eyed the burly sandy-haired figure with loathing. This foxy gulpin meant to humiliate him. Like all big men, he couldn't stomach meeting a bigger. If only—

'Remember this,' resumed Rillington. 'The most important parts of a Bank are the frontage – take a note, Creeth, to arrange about exterior redecoration – the main office and the manager's private office. These are the only parts of the building the majority of the customers ever see. And of these, the private office is the most important. It should be better furnished than your own sitting-room.'

Despairing, Simpson tried again.

'The sitting-room. Would you ... er ... care to ...?'

'We'll have a look at the main office now, Mr. Simpson.' Creeth gripped him by the elbow and propelled him gently forward, with Rillington marching in front pointing out the defects.

'Hanging lights in a Bank office! Preposterous! You must really move with the times. Tubular lighting must be fitted. Make a note of that, Creeth. That clock – it must be a hundred years old. Get rid of it. Apply for an electric one. Your heating arrangements are hopelessly out of date. See that a modern system is installed. And make sure it is adequate on the customer's side of the counter. I am tempted to think, Simpson,

41

that you have lost your vocation. You would have made an ideal curator in a provincial museum.'

In desperation, Simpson introduced him to the quaking cashier but Rillington was not to be side-tracked. With a brutal grunt of acknowledgement, he turned away and continued his diatribe:

'Those windows. They are in a disgusting state.'

Simpson looked round. They were bad all right. Crusted with weeks of dirt. How had he missed noticing?

'When were they cleaned last? How often does the contractor clean them?' Rillington thrust his head out pugnaciously.

It was then that Simpson, staring at the scornful face a few inches from his own, placed the unfamiliar smell that had been nagging at his nostrils since this boor stormed into the office.

The whiff of recently-drunk wine, that's what it was. This bullying English swine, spawn of a jumped-up nobody, had been hogging into the table wine at lunch. Simpson's spirits rose. The man was obviously three-quarters scuttered. But how else would he be, brought up to sip port and nibble biscuits? He wouldn't survive long in an all-night session drinking whiskey and chasers.

'The housekeeper cleans them,' said Simpson. 'She gave them a good going-over a few days back.'

'She did not use much elbow-grease, judging by the state they are in now.'

Simpson cleared his throat. It was time to assert himself. He was being pushed too far.

'Mr. Rillington,' he said. 'You evidently have no experience of conditions on the western seaboard. People in these parts have long since given up trying to cope with the salt spray blown against their windows by the Atlantic storms. Mrs. Mahony does her best but it's a losing fight.'

'It strikes me,' said Rillington, squinting at the window, 'that there is a good deal of dirt mixed up with that salt spray.'

You're dead right, thought Simpson. He drew a deep breath. Here goes for the ha'porth of tar.

'Naturally,' he said. 'The Council are demolishing an old building further up the street. The dust is blowing all over the village.'

'I see,' said Rillington. 'Well, if I were in your shoes, I couldn't stand to look at those windows day after day. I would go outside and clean them myself.

'Where's the toilet?' he barked.

'Turn right, at the end of the office.' Simpson moistened dry lips. 'It's ... er ... not too ...' His voice limped to a halt as Rillington started down the office.

Step by step he followed in his mind's eye, the sandy-haired man's progress through the narrow dingy passageway with its cracked and filthy hand-basin tucked into the wall like a holy water font and crowned by a brown-stained square of mirror glass hanging lopsidedly from a water-pipe and on into the tiny lavatory whose flaking walls shed their plaster on to a floor so damp that a stranger would surely hold responsible the bad marksmanship of the pump-shippers and would now be lifting on its hinges the wooden seat he must believe to be securely fastened to the lavatory bowl ...

CRASH! At the sound of the falling lavatory seat, Simpson winced. Creeth and McCann, who had been whispering together, broke off with startled up-jerked heads. Silently they awaited the inevitable outcry.

Instead a loud whooshing commenced, punctuated by little grunts of relief. On and on it went whilst the three men listened in embarrassed wonderment.

He must have left the door open, the ignorant ape, decided Simpson. He could picture him standing over the lavatory bowl, swaying gently backwards and forwards, his squinting gaze intent on directing the steaming contents of his bladder into the fizzing bowl. What a gutful of wine he must have to pooley for such a length of time. Perhaps he'll be in more amiable form with that weight off his chest.

With a succession of explosive grunts, he dribbled to a finish and flushed the bowl. Now for the rumpus, thought Simpson.

But when Rillington came out, all he said was:

'That's an extraordinary shaft leading up to the lavatory skylight. It had me fooled for a moment. I thought it was some primitive kind of service lift.' He gave a brittle laugh. 'Curious place it would be for a lift. Beside the lavatory cistern.'

Simpson felt his face flush. There would have been no dry jokes cracked if the lavatory was for the use of customers.

'Mr. Rillington ...' he began.

43

'Did you make a note of all my suggestions, Creeth?' asked Rillington.

'I did.'

'Well, there is not much point in wasting any more time here, is there?'

'I suppose not.' Creeth turned to Simpson. 'You'll hear from Premises in due course. In the meanwhile you might get the office spruced up a little better. You know, Mr. Simpson,' the rabbit teeth were bared again in the gleaming toothpaste smile, 'everywhere we go we find the same lack of spit and polish in the cleaning and care of the Bank office.'

'None quite so slovenly as this, though,' said Rillington.

Simpson glowered dumbly at the two men – the foxy-haired Sassenach and his fawning toady. No use in sticking his neck out for another blow of the chopper. Better let them get to hell out of here at once.

'I was wondering, Mr. Rillington,' said Creeth, as they moved off towards the inner office. 'Perhaps the two ladies might like to look over some of the native hand-knit wear? We would have time enough to bring them to . . . What is the name of the firm, Mr. Simpson?'

Before Simpson could answer, Rillington growled back over his shoulder:

'If you want to spend the next hour, Creeth, pawing over women's underwear – I don't.'

They were out in the main office when the phone rang. Simpson, anxious to be rid of his visitors, kept going. Creeth stopped.

'Aren't you going to answer the phone, Mr. Simpson?' he asked.

They returned to the inner office where Simpson went to the window ledge and picked up the phone. Behind him he could hear the two men moving about. Quietly. Earwigging, undoubtedly.

'Hullo!' he said. 'Glenard two three.'

'Brian Mullen calling,' said the one voice in the world he least wanted to hear. 'Is that you, Jim?'

'Speaking.' The two men seemed to be holding their breath. Listening intently.

'How's the old head this morning? If it's anything like mine, it's as big as a pot.'

44

The voice, grating like a slate pencil, came through with alarming clarity. Simpson pressed the receiver tight to his ear in the hope that the sound could be contained in the mica shell.

'You were in powerful form last night,' the voice roared on, coming from some riotous area inside his skull. 'I never saw you better. You sang ballads, danced a jig and produced rabbits from your hat. You entertained the entire company. You're a great bloody man, that's what you are.'

Simpson's eyes rooted frantically at the corner of their sockets. On one side Creeth was examining an old letter book: on the other Rillington was writing words of doom in a small loose-leaf jotter.

'Yes,' said Simpson. 'Quite so. Where did you see it last?'

'Eh? What's that?' A parrot's raucous screech tore at his ear drums. 'Did you say where?' A sound that could have been a cough or the hawking loose of a ball of phlegm rattled the receiver. 'Is the ould memory gone? Whiskey is a hoor for leaving you mindless. You surely remember the sing-song in Snout's. The women thought you were the last word. Sure they wouldn't have travelled with us only for that.'

'This is a very bad connection,' said Simpson. On either side the two figures seemed to have closed in and were leaning towards him, listening attentively. 'Would you mind repeating what you said? Slowly. It's most important that we get the facts correct. Where did you say you left it?'

'Snout's,' screeched the voice. 'In Long Nosed McGinley's. We drank there till the street lights went off. And then you asked us all down to the Bank House for another jar or two. Myself and the two dames. You can't have forgotten that.'

The car engine started up again but could not drown out the heavy breathing of the receiver crushed to his ear. Or was it his own breathing? It certainly did not come from the two silent figures beside him.

'But have you made a thorough search?' he said.

'Come again?'

'These things turn up again when you least expect it.'

'You can say that again, Jim. I met Bee this morning. And she's very worried.'

Simpson's throat dried up.

'Who did you say?' he croaked.

'Aw, for Jesus sake, have a heart – Bee Harrington. You

45

surely haven't forgotten the bucking carry-on. She claims sh[e]
left her pantaloons somewhere in the Bank House.'

The throbbing of the car engine rose to a higher pitch. Hi[s]
eyes squeezed shut to smother the pain lancing his eyeballs.

'Before we do anything,' he said, raising his voice so that hi[s]
words would be clearly heard by Creeth and Rillington, 'you'[d]
better have a thorough search. In the meanwhile you migh[t]
give particulars of the missing—'

'Look here, Jim,' the voice cut in. 'How the hell would I d[o]
that? Jesus, I never laid eyes on them. It's all a matter betwee[n]
the pair of you.'

Simpson, squeezing the receiver tighter to his ear, gazed ou[t]
through the window at the quiet square drowsing under th[e]
scorching sun. The only human being to be seen was a retire[d]
civic guard standing on the pavement edge, legs wide apart[,]
hands clasped behind his back, motionless but for the slowly
turning head that lamped its path with the relentless scrutin[y]
of a lighthouse beam. Of the visitors' car there was no sign.

'Hold on a moment,' he said, reaching for pad and pen.
'I'll make a note of that. What did you say the serial letter
was?'

Covering the mouthpiece with his hand, he turned to Rillington.

'Tck-tck-tck!' He shook his head sorrowfully. 'The usual
carelessness. A lost cheque book. Probably turn up again in a
few—'

From the unmuffled receiver a cackling sound broke out.

'Haw! Haw! Haw! The serial letter. That's a good one. It's
Bee – for Beatrice. And a queer bloody cereal *she* would be
before your breakfast. Haw! Haw! Haw!'

Horrified, Simpson clapped the squawking instrument back
to his ear. Ignoring the babbling voice, he said:

'I'll just jot down those numbers.' He called them out as he
wrote. 'Bee ... six ... nought ... four ... seven ... one ... Is
that right?' The pain behind his eyeballs had died away but
his ear, crushed flat by the pressure of the receiver, began to
ache. The pitch of the car engine had dropped to a steady
idling hum.

'Are you gone off your rocker, Jim? Throwing figures at me
like a bingo caller.'

'Well if any cheques bearing those figures – I mean serial

numbers – are presented, we'll get in touch with you. Is that clear?'

'I don't know what you're blethering about.'

'Right. We'll do that. Good-bye for now.'

'Hey, don't hang up. This is strictly a business call. I'm ringing from the kiosk in Creevan. The car's packed up and I'm getting a lift to Dublin with Larry Gaynor. We're on our way now. By the coast road. What I want to know is . . . are you listening, Jim?'

'Yes. Go on.' What the hell is he after?

'The garage say it wants a complete overhaul. Reconditioned engine. Bodywork sprayed. New battery and tyres. A big job.'

'Yes.' The suspicion was becoming a certainty.

'Well . . . I may have to overdraw for a few weeks. Will it be all right?'

'How much?' The two menacing figures on either side seemed to be intent on the answer.

'Oh, not more than a hundred pounds.'

'A hundred pounds!' Mister Brian was putting the arm on him all right. On the strength of last night's capers. It's always the same. Drink with someone tonight and he'll be in with you tomorrow for a loan. Still . . . he's an only son. The old mother has a few thousand spogged away. And he has a good job in Dublin.

Someone plucked his sleeve. It was Creeth. His lips framed the words: 'What's wrong?'

Simpson put his hand over the mouthpiece.

'He thinks he's filled in one of the cheques for a hundred pounds,' he whispered.

'Get the particulars,' Rillington's voice rasped at him from the other side.

'Are you there, Jim?' The voice sounded anxious. 'Will that be all right?'

'Yes. What amount did you say?'

'A hundred pounds. It shouldn't be more than that.'

'For how long?'

'Och, a few months. I'll instruct the firm to lodge salary and travelling allowance direct to you each month.'

'Are you sure?'

'Dead certain. You know I wouldn't let you down.'

'All right. A hundred pounds. I'll make a note of that.'

'You're a great bloody man, Jimbo. I'll not forget you for this.'

'Righto.'

'Have to run now. Larry's getting impatient. Hey, wait! Just saw an old playmate go past. She must be on holidays. A good sort. See you around shortly. Ta again.'

Simpson cleared his throat as the receiver clicked. Commenced to write on the pad.

'Yesterday's date, is that right? ... What number? ... Oh, I see ... And you signed it? ... That's unfortunate ... Did you search everywhere? ... That's what you should do ... From cellar to attic ... Yes ... Yes ... Ring back when you find it ... Yes, I'll do that ... Good-bye now.'

He cradled the receiver, banging it awkwardly against the prongs of the stand.

'He'll find it all right,' he said. 'Probably in the pocket of his Sunday suit.'

'You'll inform us at once, Mr. Simpson, if it doesn't turn up,' said Creeth. 'A lost cheque book is bad enough but a signed cheque for a hundred pounds is a really serious matter.'

'He's searching the house from top to bottom. If he doesn't find it, I'll ring up Head Office.'

'Are you not going to ring off?' asked Rillington.

One eyebrow cocked in derision, he watched as the big man, harassed and bewildered, blundered back to the phone and reached out for the handle. He smiled with satisfaction when Simpson started back in fright at the shrilling of the bell.

'Come on,' he said to Creeth. 'We'll go. We are late as it is.'

Without a backward glance he stalked off, followed at a decent interval by Creeth, murmuring polite farewells and smiling his brittle toothy smile.

'I don't know which is the worst,' said Simpson, kicking shut the inner office door. 'That smiling Judas, or his ill-bred venomous boss.'

'Do you know what it is, Skipper? That pair of hoors struck this branch like the wrath of God. I won't be the better of it for a week.'

Simpson went back to his desk muttering:

'Carpets ... clocks ... armchairs .. tubular lighting ... finding faults with everything ... and to crown all a phone call from that young idiot, Brian Mullen.' He glanced at the clock. 'Better close. It's after three o'clock.'

McCann said when he came back:

'That English hallion is a proper nark. He never stopped cribbing the whole time he was here.' He commenced sorting his notes. 'There's a rasp to that fellow's tongue that would raise blisters. Did you hear him wading into wee Creeth? About the women's underwear?'

'Aye,' said Simpson, frowning thoughtfully. Underwear. Maybe Mullen wasn't cracking a joke about the missing knickers. He'd better have a look before Mrs. Mahony ...

Hold on, now. Perhaps it's too late. That would account for the show of temper all morning. What was it she had said in the dining-room? 'A nasty crowd. Leaving things behind them.' Bet you she has discovered something. It would be as well to investigate.

Apprehensively he started off, moving cautiously past the closed door of the kitchen, treading lightly on the creaking stairs.

The sitting-room had been tidied up. Ash trays emptied. Glasses put away. Table and carpet cleaned. The curtains flapped in the wind that had freshened the stale atmosphere of the room.

One glance was enough. They were spread out straddle-legged on the back of his armchair, the black satin showing up – as it was evidently meant to – against the white coverlet. He picked them up. Isn't she the right old vixen? Dumping them under your nose like this without saying a word. He sniffed the satin fork. Ugh! He grunted at the acrid tang. These bloody things could do with a wash. She must be a dirty bitch, that Harrington one. More powder than soap in that set-up. Hope to God she's not a walking crab hatchery. The last time he had entertained those gentlemen it had been a job getting them off the premises. His stomach had been like a slab of seed-cake. If somebody hadn't told him about blue butter, he'd be plucking them out with finger and thumb to this day. The very thought of them was enough to give you the itch. He stuffed the panties into his jacket pocket and made off for the lavatory.

There he shed trousers and shorts. With the aid of a hand mirror he scrutinized the folds and recesses of belly and crutch.

49

probing the jungle of pubic hair for signs of animal life. To his relief, there was nothing to be found. As he rebuttoned his trousers he reflected that crabs were not the only affliction a night's carousing could walk you into. At any rate nothing can be done now. You'll know for certain in a few days time if you've got the bead. It should be a lesson to you to steer clear of young scoundrels like Brian Mullen. They're the ones that get you into trouble.

He soaped and washed his hands carefully. Took out a pocket comb and coaxed back into place a couple of errant hairs. As he did so he noticed a cluster of black-heads on his forehead. Or perhaps they were soot smuts. Reaching down for the face cloth he was surprised to see the spots float down and settle on his chin. With hand outstretched to rub, his gaze flicked back to his brow to verify their dispersion. The spots sidled back once more into position. He rolled his eyes from side to side and up and down. The spots followed. Reluctantly, it seemed. As though they were being drawn willy-nilly after his shifting gaze.

He took out his handkerchief and held it up before his eyes, turning away from the window so that the white linen screen would be rendered more opaque.

It was impossible to tell the exact number of spots. They lay to the right of the point at which his gaze was directed. There could have been eight. Ten. Perhaps even more. They were all of the same colour – a peculiar murky green. Their size varied from pin-point to pin-head: their shape amorphous. They were grouped into a definite pattern. A pattern that was somehow known and familiar. By closing each eye in turn, he found that only one eye was affected. The right eye.

He rolled the eye violently from side to side in an effort to rid himself of the irritant. He knuckled and poked and rubbed. To no avail. He filled the hand-basin with cold water, plumped his face in and opened his eyes. Picked out by the white porcelain the dark green motes swam around in a green translucence that might have been the element in which they had their being.

It's biliousness, he decided, as he towelled himself dry. Biliousness causes spots before the eyes. Didn't you often hear that? And that's only another word for a sluggish liver. Exercise and a good dose of liver salts will clear up this condition.

Whistling cheerfully, he hurried downstairs, ignoring the still-closed door of the kitchen.

McCann looked up as he came in.

'What was the bould Brian ringing up about?' he asked.

Simpson began to rummage in his desk, muttering:

'Where on earth has it got to? It must be here somewhere.'

Propping up the desk-top so that it acted as a shield and still murmuring: 'I saw it here yesterday. It's around someplace,' he fished from his pocket the satin panties, folded them up neatly and slid them into a pass book envelope.

'Ah, here we are!' he said triumphantly, holding aloft the envelope. 'I knew I had left it here.'

He closed the desk, sealed the flap of the envelope with Scotch tape and, in bold flourishing script, addressed it to:

Miss Beatrice Harrington,
Poldrew,
Glenard.

In the top left-hand corner of the envelope, he printed the one word:

Personal.

Slipping the envelope into his pocket, he said casually:

'I mustn't forget to post that today. I overlooked it yesterday.'

McCann finished counting a bundle of singles. Pinned a note-strap round them. Pencilled on it the total amount.

'I see young Mullen's car in the garage,' he said. 'A right mess he's made of it this time.'

'What's that?'

'Mullen's car. He must have turned it over a couple of times. The roof's well battered.'

'So that's why it's in the garage. He never told me that.'

'He'll be in here some of these days trying to borrow money to pay for it.'

'As a matter of fact,' said Simpson, 'That's what he was ringing up about. To arrange for a temporary overdraft to get the car on the road again.'

'He has a brass neck, hasn't he?'

'You can mark up a Discretionary Authority of a hundred pounds. For ... Oh, better make it six months. That will give him plenty of time to pay it off.'

'I don't know, Manager. I'm doubtful about that fellow.'

'Where's the risk? He has a thousand a year job. With travelling expenses. He's an only child. Who else will the old biddy leave all her money to?'

'To the Foreign Missions, I'd say.'

Simpson's heart skipped a beat. There was the possibility. The remote chance. She was a pious old geezer. But still – your own flesh and blood come first.

'Aw, nonsense,' he said. 'Utter bloody nonsense.'

An obstinate frown came on McCann's face. He said slowly:
'I still think he's a slippery gent, Manager. You'd be safer handcuffed to a ghost.'

Simpson did not answer. He was checking the posting of one of the ledgers. Against the white background of the ledger pages, he became aware of a change in the dark spots floating before his eyes. They had coalesced into one blob whose colour had changed to a brilliant emerald green. The shape suggested by the spots was now better defined. It had the appearance of a bird. A perching bird. Plumed, beaked and combed. A parrot or a cockatoo, he figured out. Even as he watched, the green figure became outlined by a narrow purple margin giving precision to what had been blurred and illusory.

The powerful arched bill, the jagged points of the comb, the close packed tail feathers: all were clearly visible. As it swayed to and fro across the white pages on an invisible perch, it was even possible to detect what could be the outline of a tiny claw poised at breast level as though the bird had the one-legged stance of a wader.

Simpson found himself shaking his head to rid himself of the swaying image. It was no use. Back and forth across the lined and figured pages it swung. As he eased away the strap-marked pages, the green blob slid across the titled headings. Oscillated wildly as he compared cash book and ledger entries. Alighted on the extended balance, when he tried to check if the addition or subtraction was correct. At length he slammed the ledger shut.

'Is your cash balanced, McCann?' he asked.

'Yessir.'

'Well, bundle it into the safe and we'll get out of here. The checking can be finished tomorrow. Maybe a bathe will wash the taste of this day out of our mouths.'

'Right, Manager. I'll post the letters and get my togs.'
'The car will be at the door when you're back.'

When McCann, waiting in the passenger seat of the little red saloon, watched him swaggering across the street from the hotel, toes pointed out, towel and togs swinging from one hand, car key at the ready in the other, he knew at once that Simpson had a few rosiners in him. The sour look had gone from his face. His eyes had already developed the bird-like glitter they always had when he had drink taken. The only odd thing about him was the way he kept shaking his head as though there were something loose inside his skull that could be rattled back into position.

'What way will the tide be, Mac?' he said, as he got in and started up the engine.

'There should be . . .' McCann was cut short as the car roared off, Simpson going through the gears like a racing driver.

Not a word was spoken until Cleggan Cross was reached. There, a large black station wagon shot out from a side road to the left and pulled across their path. Had not Simpson slapped the brake pedal down to the boards, there would have been a collision. The station wagon careered on ahead, disappearing in the distance in a cloud of dust.

'Who was the raving lunatic driving that car?' Simpson asked, as he drove slowly along waiting for the dust to settle.

'Damned if I could tell you.'

'Didn't you even get the registration number?'

'How could I, the speed it was going?'

Simpson drummed his fingers irritably on the steering wheel. 'Tck! Tck! Tck! Your predecessor was more observant.'

They had reached the high ground overlooking Creevan Bay. As they topped the last hill, McCann sat up. Below them a wide expanse of ocean glowed with an insane aching blue.

This blue was intensified by the sombre towering arms of rock in which it was held captive and against which it writhed and struggled ceaselessly, lacing the base of the cliffs with a mist of steaming sweat. The reefs of rock and bare rocky islands that dotted the bay were lathered with foam. Far out on the horizon, Seal Island, a long hump-backed mass, its lighthouse and string of whitewashed cottages barely visible

53

through the spray, seemed to cringe before the battering waves.

The road wound down into the village of Creevan, a scattering of houses including a spirit grocery, a Post Office and Laurel Lodge – the doctor's house – a dingy barracks of a building set back off the road in a high-walled enclosure.

Simpson parked the car outside the pub and the two men went down the narrow path to the beach. Ploughing through the soft sand, powdered to the texture of flour by the Atlantic rollers, they made their way to the foot of the cliffs where, sheltered from the biting land breeze, they peeled off and got into their bathing trunks.

'We'll wait for the doctor,' said Simpson, squatting down on the sand, his back to a rock.

McCann flung himself down on his outspread towel. Hands clasped under his head, he let the hot afternoon sun soak the irritation and anxiety out of his system. When the doctor arrived, he had slipped into a dazed stupor. To the greeting: 'Hey there, Mac!' he mumbled a close-lipped: 'Hey!' without bothering to open his eyes. He lay, beads of sweat trickling down cheeks, chest and armpits, barely aware of the drone of talk mingling into the background of strident lark-song and grumbling breakers.

A bare foot jogged him on the hip.

'Get up, you lazy sod. We're going in now.'

'Right, doc,' he said, scrambling to his feet, dizzy with the burning sun.

They waded out through the breaking surf to the deeper water where the gathering rollers furrowed the sea. Simpson was the first down. He plunged into the base of a roller, coming up on the far side, puffing and blowing. Swimming with a slow, easy breast stroke, he ducked down his head, gulping up mouthfuls of sea water which he sprayed out noisily through nose and blubbering lips like a spouting whale. (This he considered an infallible cure for a persistent hangover.) As he opened his eyes under water, he discovered that the brilliant green object troubling his vision all afternoon was now swimming leisurely in the marbled depth below him. He lifted his head, shaking it violently so that the long lappet of hair now dangling behind the white dome of his skull, undulated like a length of seaweed.

'What's the matter with the Big Fellow?' shouted the doctor.

'He's been shaking his head for the last hour like a horse tormented by flies.'

McCann, not yet immersed, was moving gingerly forward, breasting the waves on tiptoe. He waited for the doctor to draw level.

'It's a hangover,' he said. 'The head's bursting off him.'

He moved off again.

'Hey!' the doctor called. 'Lamp this. I've been practising all week.'

He lowered himself into the water, flung himself forward and went through the motions of the breast stroke. Standing beside him, McCann watched the frantically kicking legs and threshing arms sink lower and lower without the body being carried an inch forward. Soon, completely submerged and sinking rapidly to the bottom, the arms and legs continued their appointed task until McCann, fearing a drowning, hauled him up by the bathing trunks.

For a second he stood, arms still moving, eyes tight shut, cheeks puffed out with held-in breath. Then he relaxed.

'How far did I get?' he asked, gazing at McCann with anxious spaniel eyes.

'You're improving. But don't overdo it. A few strokes at a time till you gain confidence.'

Thereafter McCann stayed in the shallow water, swimming slowly round the doctor in case he got into difficulties. When they came out eventually and towelled and dressed themselves, Simpson was still swimming around, his bald head glittering in the sunlight.

'He's a powerful ox of a man, our James,' said the doctor. He looked at his wrist-watch. 'I've a call to make. Tell him I'll be in Hannah's in an hour's time. We'll have a few jars. Be seeing you.'

McCann lay back, head propped on his rolled-up towel, and waited.

'We've time for a walk,' said Simpson, when the bathing kit was stowed away in the boot of the car.

Without looking back to see if McCann was following, he started off up the narrow cliff path. McCann knew this walk like the back of his hand – it was the only route Simpson ever took. A mile out and a mile back, mostly walking in single file except where the low boundary ditches fell back to allow them to walk abreast. When that happened, Simpson moved in, so that his companion was forced to walk on the cliff edge. At the mile-end the path debouched into a field. Round this field Simpson stalked, keeping close to the surrounding hedges. Always he travelled in an anti-clockwise direction, still holding to the inside so that he was forced at intervals to stoop under projecting bushes or step over trailing briars. Having circled the field, he led the way across a grassy headland running far out into the sea. At the extremity of this headland, bare rock fell away steeply in a series of narrow shelves. Clambering down to the first shelf, Simpson settled himself down, feet dangling over the edge, back resting on the smooth rock wall. Now the pipe was produced, filled and lit. Three puffs, a contented sigh, and the first words of the entire walk:

'That's better.'

After that, a desultory conversation would begin.

Today it was different. McCann remained silent. Gazing down in enchanted delight.

All about, the sleek Atlantic combers, homing at last after their interminable journey, reared up and pounced on the jagged outposts of rock, smothering them in creamy turbulence. Rolled on to attack the buttressed base of the headlands, where they boiled over the rocky shelves, reaching ever higher at each attempt. Charged with lowered crests at the sheer face of the cliff wall, only to be flung back in rippling pools of lime-green effervescence. All around waves nibbling, gnawing, tearing at the rocks. Hissing, gurgling, bellowing as they erupted: retreating with hungry, long-drawn-out gulps.

Directly beneath, a squat, shiny, humpbacked rock kept fighting its way to the sea-top, shaking the cream and green from its flanks as it rose. Its surface was peeled bare but for a long hank of seaweed that billowed out with each receding wave.

McCann grinned as he stole a look at Simpson, sitting hat on lap, puffing steadily at his pipe, mindless of the wind that ruffled his combed-up pigtail of hair. Why is he so sensitive about being bald, wondered McCann. Except for pride in his physical strength, he has little personal vanity. Yet he is foppish enough to waste time coaxing into position the few ribs of hair left to him in the belief that it defeats the threat of baldness.

Picking up a stone, McCann tossed it idly towards a herring-gull perched on a nearby ledge. It fell short but the gull launched itself into space, rising effortlessly on steely-canted wings. It allowed the offshore wind to whirl it away until, righting itself, it sank slowly on pinions delicately poised, alighting gently on the surface of the sea. There it floated, swaying up and down to the motion of the waves.

McCann, overwhelmed by the intolerable beauty, felt an irresistible urge to communicate. With anyone. Even Simpson.

'Jim,' he said, trying to bridge the chasm with a Christian name. 'Have you ever seen anything more beautiful?' The awful banality of this stupid question, delivered in a hoarse quavering voice, made him sick with shame. He tried again: 'Why ever did they call the island, Seal Island?' His voice rose to a squeak. 'With its long snout ... and its scaly back ... and its outstretched tail ... it could be nothing but ... a crocodile.'

Simpson took three slow puffs at his wheezing pipe.

'They're odd ducks. The Seal men,' he said, nodding towards the island. 'In-breeding, that's the cause of it. They're sib, the whole rick-me-tick of them.' He stared across at the island, frowning abstractedly. 'That and the poteen stilling. That's what has them the way they are. Do you know there are three pubs on the island. One worse than the other. But they're alike in one thing. They all sell poteen. Once in a while the Guards come from the mainland and capture a worm or a barrel of wash. There's a prosecution, headlines in the local paper, a homily from the pulpit by the parish priest. The D.J. inflicts an exemplary fine. And for weeks afterwards every still on the island is working overtime to meet it.'

The wheezing of the pipe had now changed to a watery guggle. Gripping it by the bowl, he shook it steadily till the last drop of brown spittle dripped from the stem. He gave an experimental suck. Satisfied, he resumed:

'More like jungle savages they are than common Christians. I mind during the hot summer a few years back, when stout or beer couldn't be got for love nor money and even minerals were not to be had, a kill of stout came into Hannah Murphy's below.' He pointed with the stem of his pipe. 'Before Hannah had time to tap the barrel, the boat had tied up to the slip. The twenty or so men aboard made their way the half mile to the

57

pub, running and walking for fear others would have got there ahead of them. Hannah had the zinc bath filled with stout, ready to start bottling, when they arrived. Every man grabbed a glass and they sat around the zinc bath, dipping their glasses into the stout and swigging it back for further orders. They stayed in the bottling store till they'd finished the kill. Then had a whip round and paid Hannah as much for the kill as if she had bottled it. There wasn't a local dreuth got as much as a mouthful. Now, how did they get to know on Seal Island what wasn't known on the mainland, except by some sort of bush telegraph?' He chuckled softly. 'I was down at the slip when they all came staggering up the road around midnight. Fluthered to the world. Half-pint bottles of whiskey sticking out of their pockets. They sang and danced on the half-deck of the boat till I lost sight of it in the darkness.' He chuckled again. 'Cute enough, they brought along a Pioneer to act as helmsman. They got back to the island safely.'

He looked at his wrist-watch. 'We'll go,' he said, getting to his feet. 'The doctor'll be at Hannah's by this time.'

McCann fell in behind him.

'A thick-skinned, unseeing philistine!' he muttered, under his breath.

When they reached the pub, it was to find the doctor, glass in hand, already installed on a high stool. Hannah, a little ageless woman with a rosy cheeks and frizzy brown hair, was at the grocery counter arranging soup tins on an upper shelf. She said:

'Mr. Simpson! Mr. McCann! I'll be with you directly.'

'What'll it be?' said the doctor.

'Jameson ten,' said Simpson.

'Guinness,' McCann said.

Hannah came round to the bar side and dished up the drinks.

'Did you have a nice dip, Mr. Simpson?' she said.

'Very refreshing, Hannah. Very refreshing. It tones up the whole system, you know.'

With clenched fist he struck his chest a couple of jaunty raps. Stopped. Shook his head violently.

'The salt water must have got into my eyes,' he said.

'You know,' he said, 'there are times when the sea water gets more salty. It would burn the eyes out of your head.'

'I was wondering what was wrong with you, Jim,' said the doctor. 'For the last couple of hours you've been shaking your head like a man rattling dice.'

McCann picked up his tumbler of stout and blew a crater in the froth. Took a long slow slug. Then wolfed it down in a few noisy gulps.

'Nobody changing?' he asked.

'You must be parched with the thirst,' said the doctor. He drained his glass. 'The usual, Hannah. Gold Label.'

Simpson held out his untouched glass.

'Spread another layer of Jameson on that lot, Hannah. And some fresh aqua in the jug.'

When the drinks were served and the whiskeys watered, he raised his glass:

'The first today, lads.' He beamed jovially at the company.

'Good luck,' said the doctor, over the lip of his glass.

McCann, preoccupied with the careful pouring out of his bottle of stout, said without looking up:

'Be with you in a tic. Stout's a bit high.'

He finished pouring. Lifted his glass in salutation.

'Down the hatch,' he said. Once more he drained the glass without taking it from his lips. He sighed with satisfaction.

'God save us all from a dearth of porter,' he said piously.

'You're going the right way about causing it,' said the doctor. 'You'd better buy him another, James, before he dies of the drouth.'

'Same again, so. But I don't hold with this wolfing down of liquor.'

There was a smug smile on McCann's face as he took a slug of stout out of his newly-filled glass and replaced it on the counter. He had established a lead over the two whiskey drinkers. Now he could relax.

They had three more rounds, taken so slowly that McCann was forced to swirl the remains of his stout around in the tumbler to bring back a head on it.

Though no more customers came to the bar, Hannah was kept busy at the grocery counter. Outside the wind had died down, leaving a breathless sultry heat. Each time the shop door opened some of the company would say::

'It's working up to thunder.'

Or, running a finger round inside a sweat-soaked collar:

'Bloody close in here.'

Conversation languished till they sat drinking in silence.

At length the doctor slid off his stool.

'Time for a bite of grub,' he said. 'Might see you later on if you're still around.'

When he had gone, Hannah said:

'Do you know what it is? He has put me in mind of meal-time. I'll call Delia down to look after the shop while I make myself a drop of tea.'

'What about making tracks for home?' said McCann.

'Delia?' Simpson said.

'Aye. Delia Clifden. My sister Rose's girl. She arrived from Dublin this afternoon. She's upstairs. Resting.'

'Didn't she spend a summer here five or six years ago?'

'She did. But she was only a slip of a schoolgirl then. You'll not know her now. I hardly knew her myself.'

She moved to the door.

'You might serve us a couple of drinks before you go, Hannah,' said Simpson.

'But, Skipper, it's time . . .'

'You'll be a long time dead, McCann. So cheer up.'

They nursed their drinks in silence until the kitchen door re-opened.

'Well, Delia,' said Simpson, getting to his feet. 'Come here till we have a look at you.'

Without hesitation, she gripped the two welcoming hands.

'You're a tidy slip of a girl,' he said. His gaze travelled up from the long slender legs to the flat uncorseted stomach: from the perky breasts to the intent serious face with its smoky grey eyes, generous mouth and golden casque of hair. He squeezed her hand. 'A bloody fine-looking woman,' he amended.

The drink is beginning to get him, decided McCann. From now on the language will worsen.

'Oh, flip!' she said, pulling away her hands. 'You're only saying that.'

She turned towards McCann.

'And who is your friend?'

'McCann, this is Miss Clifden.'

They shook hands. He said:

'Could we trouble you for another drink, Miss Clifden? A

whiskey – Jameson ten year old and a bottle of stout.'

'I'm Delia. What do they call you?'

'Frank.'

She opened a bottle of stout and tilted it against the glass with an expert touch.

'You certainly know how to handle Guinness, Delia,' said McCann.

'Pity I wouldn't. After working for two years in a pub in Bermondsey.'

She filled out Simpson's whiskey. Placed it before him. Said:

'And what'll I call *you*? The last time I stayed here you were Uncle Jim.'

'Augh, that was in Brian Boru's time. When the pigs were running bare-footed. You would be entitled to drop the Uncle by this time.'

Tapping her teeth with a fingernail, she eyed them:

'Jim and Frank,' she said.

'You'd be powerful butties, the pair of you?' she said.

Faces creased in smiles, they nodded their heads vigorously.

Slowly she shook her head. In pity. In sorrow. In gentle condemnation.

'If I'm any judge,' she said, 'you'd be the right pair of black-guards.'

Laughter broke and volleyed between them. In its warmth McCann and Simpson drew their stools furtively nearer. McCann discovered that his glass was unaccountably empty.

'You gobbled it up like a cormorant,' she said.

More laughter.

'We'll have another round,' said McCann.

'It's my turn to buy,' Simpson said.

McCann insisted. Simpson planked a ten-shilling note on the counter. Delia said:

'It's Jim's treat, Frank. What are you taking?'

He belched, deep and prolonged.

'I'm full to the gills with stout. I'll take a whiskey this time, Jim. A Gold Label.'

'You're a silly little fellow, Frank. Don't you know that whiskey on the top of a feed of stout will put you on your ear?'

With pouting lips, McCann puffed noisily, as though emerging from a dive in ice-cold water.

'Damn the bit harm it'll do me,' he said.

'I don't see any sense in drinking to stay sober anyway,' he added. A contentious tone had crept into his voice.

Delia put the drink down beside him.

'This'll warm the cockles of your heart,' she said.

'Water or soda?' she asked.

He topped it up with water.

'All the best. To all the best,' he said, taking a slug.

'Here's to the top, for the bottom's in danger,' said Simpson.

'Aren't we clever?' said Delia.

In no time McCann found his glass empty again.

'There'd be no harm in a fellow buying a drink this time?' he asked in an aggressive voice. Without waiting for an answer he ordered two whiskeys.

Simpson was the first to lift his glass this time in salutation. He intoned:

> Here's good fortune
> To the girls of Gorting:
> Not forgetting those that come
> From the Plumb.

Leaving down the glass she was polishing, Delia – born in the Sperrin mountains – bowed her acknowledgments.

They drank up. Simpson bought again. Two more whiskeys.

McCann discovered the room had suddenly become very hot. Though he knew he was stone-cold sober, he felt a slight dew of perspiration breaking out on his forehead. Lifting his brimming glass – she must have been leaning hard on the bottle when she was filling out the drinks – he recited slowly, with what he hoped was proper gravity and decorum:

> 'Here's to the girl from over the hill,
> If she won't do it, her sister will . . .'

A clamour of protest broke out. As if the quiet bar was now crammed with angry critics.

'Hush! Hush!'

'Pipe down!'

'Language, Frank. Mind your language.'

'Keep the party clean, sonny.'

McCann gathered himself together. Lifting his glass high in the air, the contents scattering in all directions, he bawled at the top of his voice:

> 'So here's to her sister.'

With a final flourish he drained whatever was left in the glass, replacing it on the counter with exaggerated care. He heard Delia's laugh and in an embarrassed cough:

'Would you like a nice cup of tea, Mr. McCann?'

'Are you back, Auntie?' Delia asked.

He discovered Hannah standing beside him.

'Well, the Lord bless you, Hannah. I'd love a whole pot of tea and a couple of hard-boiled eggs and a hunk of cheese and about half a loaf of bread.'

'Foolish little fellow,' a voice said.

The next thing he was seated at the kitchen table with Hannah fussing over him.

'You must be starved, you poor man,' she was saying, as she poured out the tea. 'Don't you know well you shouldn't take drink on an empty stomach.' Slices of buttered toast appeared on his plate. 'It's all very well for a big man, the like of Mr. Simpson. But we're not all like him.' A cup was placed before him, brimming with a savoury mess. Still stirring it, she said: 'I mashed the eggs up in a cup with a bit of butter. You told me once you liked them that way.' She pushed plates nearer to him. Plates of white bread, home-made brown, curranty scones, oat cake, sliced cheese, 'You're to eat everything up, young man. I don't want to see hilt nor hair of you till you've cleared the table.'

She was gone and he was eating voraciously. With greedy abandon. Spilling tea, cheese flakes, buttered egg, breadcrumbs, over pants and shirt. At length he sighed, pushed away the dishes, spread his elbows on the table and rested chin on knuckled hands.

It was dark when he woke up. His neck was stiff, his head muzzy, his mouth dry, hot, foul-tasting. A fierce thirst gripped him. He pawed his way to the door. Switched on the light.

Someone had cleared away the dishes but the milk jug still remained on the table. He finished the heel-end of milk left in it. Taking a mug from the dresser, he filled it from the cold tap of the sink. Twice more he filled it before the edge was taken off his thirst.

He stood by the kitchen sink, listening to the hum of conversation muted by the twin doors of bar and kitchen. At last he decided to venture back to the bar.

The shop was crowded. Customers lined both counters. Hannah tended the bar counter. Delia carried trays of drinks round to the grocery one. The babble of noise was incessant as each group of drinkers strove to make themselves heard above the general din. Tobacco-smoke was so thick in the low-ceilinged room that McCann was forced to stand at the door coughing and spluttering before he got used to the atmosphere.

Simpson was drinking at the grocery counter. Along with him the doctor and two local farmers, Clancy and Vereker. There was much banter and laughter – directed at Delia. Simpson spotted him almost immediately.

'The hard man himself,' he shouted. 'do you feel better now? Didn't I tell you, man, that whiskey and stout don't mix?'

'What are you drinking, Frank?' asked Clancy, a squat fat man with a head so swollen that the pink skin was stretched across it, tight and shiny as a drumhead. He spoke in a low wheezy voice that had exhausted itself in its passage through the layers of fat.

'A stottle of bout, Pat. I'm parched with the drouth.'

He drank it down rapidly.

'Top them up again, Delia,' he said.

'Take it easy,' said Vereker. 'There's no bleeding rush, chum.'

Small, dapper, moustached, he had worked in England for some time. When drunk he acquired a bogus accent to remind his listeners of this fact. Vereker was not the only one under the weather. The doctor, frowning and glassy-eyed, watched closely as Simpson took matches from an open box and arranged them in a geometrical pattern on the counter. Clancy swayed gently on his heels, a foolish smile on his face.

Like a thimble-rigger Simpson shifted the matches, re-arranging them into new patterns, his stubby fingers moving smoothly and swiftly.

'That's how it's done,' he said at last.

'Isn't he wonderful?' said Delia. There was more than a hint of proprietorship in her voice.

'Show her what you can do with a deck of cards, Jim,' Clancy said.

'The very thing,' said the doctor.

'Away and get a pack of cards, Delia,' Vereker said.

64

Simpson called after her:

'An old pack will do.'

When she came back with the cards, Simpson was standing in the middle of the room with his jacket off. His shirt sleeves were rolled up to the shoulders. With outstretched arms he was displaying to the admiring company his control over the muscles of his biceps. Under his authority they rose in swelling tumescence or fell back, limp and flabby. They leaped and twitched and danced. They squirmed and undulated. It was as if beneath the fallen canvas of a circus tent, the clowns and tumblers, the acrobats and wire-walkers, still continued to perform.

He took the cards from her, holding them delicately in the finger and thumb of his right hand. Fanned them out expertly. He held them up, turning them back and front, for all to see. Flicked them together again. Blew on them long and lovingly. Paused.

In the silence, Delia's voice could be heard whispering:

'What's he going to do?'

Suddenly he gripped the pack of cards with both hands. Slowly, inexorably, he twisted one hand against the other in a clothes-wringing motion, to the sound of ripping cardboard. A final jerk and the pack of cards was ripped apart. Triumphantly he held up in either hand a raw white-edged portion of the torn deck.

'Goshhh!' breathed Delia. Reverently she picked up the torn cards when Simpson left them on the counter.

'Thirsty work,' he said, rubbing his hands together. 'Same again all round.' He tendered a pound note. 'And take the price of the cards out of it.'

'Indeed I won't,' she said. 'I'll hold on to them as a keepsake. If you don't mind, Jim?'

'Of course not,' he said tolerantly.

They drank, and the doctor bought. This time Simpson, to McCann's surprise, changed to stout.

From the bar counter a voice called:

'What about lifting the half-hundreds, Mr. Simpson?'

A pleased look crossed Simpson's face.

'If you'd like me to,' he murmured modestly. 'Perhaps we could arrange a match.'

The men at the bar counter gathered in a whispering group.

At length one of their number was pushed forward, a burly dark-skinned man.

The spokesman of the group said:

'Ned the Mines here is back from South Wales. He'll match you.'

The weights were brought in from the store. The two contestants finished their drinks. Ned the Mines peeled off and rolled up his sleeves. They tossed for priority. Simpson lost.

Ned the Mines hitched up his trousers. Spat on his hands.

'Single lift. Free style,' he said. 'Drinks each lift. Loser pays all.'

'Agreed.'

Ned stooped, gripped the half-hundredweight by the ring. Raised it, bent-armed, to shoulder-height. Paused. Pushed it aloft to the full length of his arm. Held it there, steadily poised. Lowered it to shoulder-level. Paused. Let it gently down on the ground.

He gazed inquiringly at Simpson.

'A stout,' said Simpson.

Ned called for a stout and a beer.

They drank in unison, placing the empty glasses side by side on the bar counter.

Now it was Simpson's turn. He gripped. Lifted. Hoisted. Lowered. Straightened up.

'Repeat the dose,' he said.

Once more they drank, replacing the drained glasses carefully on the counter.

'Double lift. Free style,' said Ned.

He gripped the two weights. Steadied himself. Shouldered them. Steadied himself once more and hoisted. A cheer went up from his supporters.

'You're a dinger, Ned.'

'Good you-boy-you.'

He lowered the weights and called:

'Same again, Hannah.'

They drank. Slower this time but finishing together.

Effortlessly Simpson went through the same routine.

'A slight similarity,' he said when he straightened up.

The drinks finished, Ned called:

'Single lift. Stiff-armed.'

Gripping the weight, he straightened up with the half-hundred dangling at his thigh. A long pause. Then with a grunt he swung the weight up sideways, his arm poker-stiff. At the tip of the hoist, the swaying weight thumped against the back of his forearm, sending a shudder down through his whole body. Almost immediately he lowered the weight, still stiff-armed, and grounded it carefully. The sweat was breaking on his forehead. His breathing was heavy.

'Another couple of scoops,' he said.

He gulped his beer down noisily, banging the empty glass down clumsily on the counter.

Relaxed and unstraining, Simpson performed his task and called:

'Two more restoratives.'

Ned frowned at this order but said nothing. He dealt with his drink slowly and cautiously.

'Double lift. Stiff-armed,' he said.

He stood, the two weights held in either hand, his chest rising and falling as he sucked in the air needed for the lift. At last he moved.

'Aaaaaaaaaaahhhh!' he roared throatily, urging on his tired, unwilling muscles. The outstretched, burdened arms rose slowly to shoulder height where they stayed, quivering violently with the strain of keeping them aloft. While you could count five, he remained in that position, a tortured sweating figure impaled on a cross of his own construction. Then:

'Aaaaaaaaaaaahhhh!' he roared again, his whole body coming to furious violent life. Thighs, belly, torso: all combined with his outraged arms to push, to thrust, to impel upwards their numbing load. His knees began to buckle under the strain, his body to crumble and shrink as though the two half-hundredweights were squeezing his body together like a concertina. His mouth sagged open, the breath whistling and snoring through his parched gullet. His pain-racked unseeing eyes bulged from their sockets. Sweat rolled down his face and arms: his shirt clung dripping to his body.

But the weights rose slowly, jerk by convulsive jerk. When they were above the level of his head, he paused for perhaps the space of a second. Then with a last despairing grunting effort he swung the weights up until they thudded together like cracked and discordant cymbals. Before his friends had finished cheering, his tired arms fanned out under their intolerable burden, sweeping down rapidly till the weights clashed again at knee level. Wearily he dropped the half-hundreds to the ground.

'Aw, jasus,' he sighed with relief. He rubbed his aching hands together. 'Thirsty work.' Suddenly, he smiled. 'Pints, that's what we'll have. Two long creamy pints of double.'

As he gurried into his own drink, he watched Simpson let down the pint, taking it cool and easy, till he had emptied the tumbler and left it back on the counter.

As casually as before Simpson drew the back of his hand across his mouth. Stooped. Picked up the weights.

Almost at once he hoisted, sweeping the weights up in two wide arcs, as though he were lifting cardboard dummies. He held them aloft while the crowded bar cheered and McCann clapped till his hands smarted and Delia cried:

'Oh, lovely, Jim! Lovely!'

Slowly he lowered his stiffened arms, never allowing the load to dictate the speed of the descent. At last he eased the weights gently to the ground.

'We'd better stick to the pints,' he said quietly.

He nursed his drink while the argument became more and more heated, some claiming that Ned the Mines had lost the match, others that it was clearly a draw. Ned sipped his pint and said nothing.

In a lull, Simpson broke into the argument.

'Would it be in order,' he asked, 'if I were to call the next lift?'

There were no dissenters.

Simpson finished his pint.

'Double lift. Free style. Varied,' he called.

He lifted the weights. This time he made careful preparations, working the soles and heels of his shoes around on the floor to get better purchase, rolling his shoulders and flexing the muscles of his biceps. At length he shouldered the weights. Counting aloud and treating the half-hundreds as though they were dumb-bells he went into the ordinary drill routine. Hoisting the weights aloft. Thrusting them ahead. Shooting them out to either side. Up. Down. Forward. Back. Out. In. Down. As if he were in a drill hall. Repeating smartly: 'One! Two! One! Two!'

A great cheer went up.

'Good man, yourself!'

'There's no holding you!'

Above the din, Delia's treble rang out:

'Keep it up, Jim! That's the style! Show them how it's done!'

Porter sweat dripped from his face. Steam rose from around the brim of his correctly positioned hat. His heaving chest kept pace with the piston motion of his arms. But his mouth was closed and he breathed easily through flaring nostrils.

'One! Two! One! Two!' Like a demented drill sergeant, he barked out the tally, urging himself on and on until Ned the Mines shouted:

'Give over, Boss! The best man wins!'

He planked a pound note on the counter.

Simpson grounded the half-hundredweights with a sigh of relief. Mopped his forehead with a handkerchief. Tucked the damp and flapping shirt back into the waistband of his trousers. As he was trying to re-insert the gold links into the cuffs of his rolled down shirt sleeves, Delia rushed across.

'Let me do that, Jim,' she said.

She stooped over the massive forearms, lingering over the simple task, apologizing for the clumsy fingers that brushed his skin so tenderly. So deftly.

At last the cuff links were secured. She lifted his jacket from the counter.

'I might as well earn sixpence,' she said, holding it up outspread. He slipped his hand into the proffered arm-holes.

'Maybe you'd take it in kind,' he said over his shoulder.

As he fumbled about, looking for the other arm-hole, she leaned towards him and whispered:

'That's for you to find out, Mr. Universe.'

He faced around slowly, shrugging his jacket into place. There was a smug smile on his face. His eyes, bugged with drink and desire, stared down at her avidly.

'No time like the present, Delia,' he said.

'Hush, Jim,' she said. Gripping his arm, she edged him back till they stood on the outskirts of the crowd.

'Buy a drink, honey,' she told him.

Obediently he called for drinks all round. The doctor followed suit. And soon the company were mingled together in constantly changing groups, with rounds of drink materializing before them, coming from who knows where. Paid for by who hell cares. The hum of conversations rose to a clamorous up-roar, each man listening only to his own inspired utterances. Fists were thumped on the counter. Backs were slapped. Drinks were spilled. An odd snatch of song would rise above the din. A group of men at the top of the bar called out:

'Quiet! Quiet!'

And when the noise lessened:

'Patrick John for his pleasure.'

An old man was pushed forward, the crowd backing away to give him room. He put a cupped hand to his mouth and commenced to sing in a high reedy voice:

'I went down to a hiring fair, in a place they call Strabane,
And there I hired for six long months with Brady of Killann.
He promised eggs and bacon and sugar in me tea,
He gave me Da the money and then shook hands with me,
Saying: "Welcome to you Johnnie, you're with a decent man."
But little I knew what I had to do for Brady of Killann.'

There were shouts of:

'Rise her, Patrick.' 'Soften him up with porter, somebody.' 'Quiet! Quiet!'

A drink was thrust into the singer's free hand. A couple of hasty slugs and the song was resumed. Verse after verse detailed the life of a wretched Donegal labourer bound on a six months' contract to a strong farmer in Tyrone.

The old man reached the last verse:

'So, to conclude and finish, take this advice from me:
Stay away from wealthy farmers with their bacon, eggs and tea:
And when they tell you: "Hurry" do as little as you can,
For they'll break their bounden promise like Brady of Killann.'

As was the custom, he did not sing the last few words but spoke them into his cupped hand in a hurried shame-faced manner.

A storm of cheers, whistles and catcalls greeted the end of the song. Soon another singer was on his feet and before long the whole company were bawling patriotic songs. With dull eyes and faces stupefied with drink they sang of murder and vengeance, thwarted love and bitter hatred; hardship, injustice, exile. By this time all were well under the weather. The doctor sat at the grocery counter, staring wretchedly at four untouched whiskeys. Beside him Clancy sat, no drunker than before, contentedly lapping up stout. Vereker, staggering drunk, wandered around aimlessly, muttering incoherent greetings to those he bumped against, a trail of beer spatters marking his passage. Of Simpson there was no sign. And Delia?

McCann, drinking at the bar counter with two fishermen, peered around the crowded, smoke-laden room. She was not to be seen. On the pretext of being in need of a leak, he went out to the kitchen, glancing into the empty drinking-room on the way past. The kitchen, too, was empty.

A sour ball of anger and disappointment rose in his throat. He hurred back to the bar where he ordered a fresh round of drinks.

'And I'll have a Gold Label this time,' he added. 'A large one.'

Hannah was very distressed.

'You've a right to stick to the Guinness, Mr. McCann,' she pleaded. 'You know the way whiskey affects you after stout?'

'Give the man his pleasure,' one of the fishermen said.

'It's all right, Hannah,' said McCann. 'It was the empty stomach sickened me before. I have a gutful of food in me now.'

She served up the whiskey. He threw it back and ordered another round.

'Och, Mr. McCann!' she protested. But she dished up the double whiskey nevertheless.

McCann took longer over this drink. He swirled the whiskey round in the glass, relishing the feeling of warmth and well-being that pervaded him. With each sip the clamour in the room lessened until at last – his glass emptied – the mouthing, wild-eyed, gesticulating figures made no more noise than the subdued, conversational hum of a cluster of feeding dung flies. When he spoke, his own voice sounded muffled. Disembodied.

'One more large whiskey, Hannah, and I'll go back to the stout.'

With a reproachful look, she filled out the drink. She said:

'You've a right to take the stout first and leave the whiskey for later.'

'Pull a stout, so,' he said.

As she was pouring out the stout, he downed the whiskey, puffing noisily after each mouthful.

'You're making a bog hole of your poor stomach, Mr. McCann.' She shook her head disapprovingly as she placed the tumbler of stout at his elbow.

Her moving lips added no meaning to the muted buzz going on all round him. It was as if, stunned and stricken by the heat, he rested for a moment, head hanging like an exhausted beast, while around him the irrelevant murmur of insect life rose and fell in a ceaseless dirge. The heat was intense. Beating down on skull and shoulders. With little hope of bettering his lot, he took a long slug of stout. Sighed deeply. Replaced the glass. The walls of the room had closed in. The ceiling had become depressed and threatening. Smoke swirled and eddied around dim moving figures.

He started to mop his teaming forehead and smarting eyes but the handkerchief slipped through his nerveless fingers and fluttered to the floor. Stooping to retrieve it, he felt a warning spasm of nausea rise in his throat. He straightened up, gripping the swaying counter.

'Must . . . go . . . out,' he explained to the heedless company in noiseless fishlike gasps. Air . . . Air . . . Want . . . fresh . . . air.'

He plunged towards the door.

'Are you all right, Mr. McCann?' Hannah called after him.

Outside on the road, he began to feel better. The threatened nausea did not recur. Soothed by the cool night air, he set off up the cliff path, walking silently on a grass verge – moonlit, calcified, alien. When a cloud slid across the moon, he stopped, suspicious of the perilous half-dark. In fits and starts he reached the cliff-top where he flung himself down in the long grass.

He lay there – supine – head pillowed on forearms, savouring the safety of solid earth. Not till the night sky had ceased swaying and plunging did he lift his head to look around.

A cloud darkened the moon, casting its shadow far out to sea – a shadow frilled with the delicate lace of moonlit water. Even as he watched, the shadow fled headlong – put to flight by the foaming torrent of moonlight sweeping towards the shore. It overtook the gorged and portly rollers polishing their bald crests with glittering silver. It swept over rocky spine and jutting islet exposing bared treacherous fangs. It broke on the shore, scouring the sand to a bone-white pallor. It flowed up the strand, over wrack and shingle and crushed shell, past nets staked out to dry, piled up lobster pots and empty fish-boxes and into the high-walled secrecy of the Hermit's Cove where it betrayed and unmasked the two figures outstretched on the sand.

Simpson had removed his hat. With scrupulous precision it was placed in the centre of his neatly folded jacket. His trouser legs were hitched up in a provident and seemly manner above sock level. His bald head, bowed piously to the ground, swung from side to side like a dog nuzzling for a hidden bone. The frieze of nape hair had the effect of twisting the face back to front so that it gazed up at the sky from the hunched-up, elbow-propped back with whiskered featureless anonymity. But for the rude thrusting buttocks he could have been mistaken for a tired business man saying his night prayers.

Of Delia nothing could be seen but the arms clasping Simpson's neck and the legs splayed out on either side of him.

Even as McCann watched, the splayed legs coiled and locked round the constraining figure. Smothered groans. Animal grunts. Tiny birdlike cries. A wild rushing gabble of sound as the locked figures rolled and tossed in twitching tormented epilepsy.

He saw and heard nothing more. With a groaning bellow his tortured stomach voided its contents on the grass. Again and again he retched and spewed, sobbing and crying with rage and humiliation. Cold sweat poured down his face. His body trembled. His eyes bulged with every spasm of sickness. His gaping mouth, scoured with bile, drew no comfort from the cool night air.

When at last the retching stopped, he wiped away the sweat and tears with a shaking hand. Cautiously he raised his head.

The Hermit's Cove was empty. Only the ploughed and trampled sand glazed by brilliant moonlight, bore testimony to its recent tenancy.

Stumbling on rubber legs, McCann made his way back to the pub, to find Simpson prancing up and down the bar, singing. Of Delia there was no sign.

'In the evening by the twilight you could hear those darkies
singing,
In the evening by the twilight, you could hear those darkies
sing.'

Simpson sang in a nasal voice, twisting his head from side to side, impaling the unwary with a compelling glare. His jacket hung neatly: his tie was carefully knotted: his hat angled correctly.

He is putting on a bloody act, decided McCann, edging unobtrusively towards his glass of stout. Damn the bit drunk he is. Just covering up.

'A little nonsense now and then is relished by the wisest men,' declaimed Simpson, holding aloft his glass of whiskey. Spotting McCann, he swaggered across.

'Your hand in mine, Mac,' he said, reaching out his hand. 'What'll it be, pal?' He retained McCann's hand in a vice-like grip. 'What's your poison?'

'I . . . I . . . I think I've had enough.'

'A glass of brandy, Hannah, for my young friend.'

'But, Mr. Simpson, he's—'

' 'Twill settle his stomach. Nothing like a drop of brandy to heat up the innards.'

He raised his glass.

'Now,' he said, clinking McCann's glass at rim, at base, at midriff. 'Never above you! Never beneath you! But always with you!'

They drank, McCann savouring the warm assuaging glow.

'How's that?' asked Simpson.

'It helps.'

'I think another is called for.' Simpson rapped the counter. 'Two more, Hannah.'

In a pleasant alcoholic daze, McCann sipped his brandy, paying little heed to his surroundings. Only once did he surface.

Simpson was leaning towards him. Speaking very low and confidential.

'Man – know thyself,' he said. 'The first law of nature.'

Dramatically he paused. Leaned closer.

'And women – do thou likewise.'

He chuckled softly.

'Eh?' said he, giving McCann a knowing, a painful dig in the ribs.

'Aye,' said McCann, lifting to his mouth a glass that, fed by some celestial spring, remained always three-quarters full.

It seemed only minutes after this that he heard Hannah say: 'No, Mr. Simpson. No more. It's much too late.'

To his surprise McCann discovered the bar deserted. Without protest he finished his drink, bade good night to a yawning Hannah and followed Simpson out to the car.

On the way back he huddled down into the passenger seat, watching, with indifference, the hedgerows hurtle past: flung from side to side on corners: jolted into awareness by a clumsy gear change or the screech of locked tyres.

Uncaring, he accepted Simpson's offer of a final nightcap, stumbling upstairs after him on leaden feet. Stretched in an armchair he watched him pour out the drinks – two tumblers of whiskey so lavish that McCann's queasy stomach lurched in horrified anticipation.

Simpson raised his glass.

'The first today,' he said, throwing back the whiskey with such obvious relish that the words might well have been true.

McCann took a distasteful sip.

'Happy days,' he mumbled into the bottomless depth.

His own glass refilled, Simpson gazed inquiringly across at McCann.

'Ready yet?' he asked.

Hurriedly McCann covered his glass with the palm of his hand.

'I'll stick,' he said.

'Well,' said Simpson, raising his tumbler once more. 'Ong-she-wong.'

McCann left his barely touched drink carefully on the carpet. A wave of drowsiness broke over him. He closed his eyes.

Beyond the lowered lids Simpson's voice rose and fell with the soothing murmur of distant surf. Grumbles. Growls. Complaints. The meaningless moaning complaints of swooping gulls. A sudden shout awoke him.

'McCann!'

'Whah?' His jerking limbs sent the tumbler of whiskey flying. 'Whazzat?'

'Open the fucking window!' shouted Simpson. Sprawled out

in the armchair opposite, his flushed face clenched into a frown of anger, he emphasized his instructions by pointing dramatically his slopping glass. 'Open it fucking full!'

'Do you feel all right, Manager?' asked McCann.

'Open the window, I tell you,' repeated Simpson.

McCann pulled down the upper sash.

'Lower,' ordered Simpson. 'That's better.'

'Now,' he said. 'Put a record on the radiogram. A loud record. A bloody brass band or the like.'

McCann did so. And soon the strains of *Colonel Bogey* played by the band of the Coldstream Guards resounded in the room.

'Full volume,' ordered Simpson.

McCann turned the knob of the volume control as far as it would go. The ornaments on the mantelpiece shook and jangled, wincing from the brassy blare that reverberated from wall to wall.

Above the clamour, Simpson roared:

'This'll give the spying bitches—' he pointed triumphantly to the open window '—something to talk about.' He put down his glass. Got to his feet. 'The parcel of gabby old hoors.' With tight-shut eyes, he quacked wide-mouthed. 'Yap! Yap! Yap! All day long. Everybody's business but their own.' He waved his arms widely. 'To buggery with the whole damn crew.' He commenced to dance, capering wildly with uplifted kicking legs, singing in time to the music:

> BAL-LOCKS
> *To the whole damn crew.*
> BAL-LOCKS
> *And the same to you.*

Wilder and wilder grew his capers as the drums thumped out the rhythm: ever louder rose the jeering cry of 'Bal-locks' under the urgent summons of trumpet, trombone and crashing cymbal. The floor shook under his pounding feet. Pausing only to roll up his trousers to the knee, he danced on, cannoning from wall and bookcase and chair-back, his eyes glaring madly in the direction of the open window. When the music stopped, he staggered across to the mantelpiece where, after a final taunting 'Bal-locks', he rested his arms on the ledge.

'That was my Argentine dance,' he said, speaking into the

mirror. 'I learnt it when I was pearl-diving in the Sea of Azov.' He grinned and grimaced at his own reflection. 'Dangerous job that. Big fellow attacked me once. Hammer-headed gentleman. Would have nipped the danglers off me if I hadn't kicked him in the teeth.' He winked slyly at his leering image, nodding his head in approval. 'Couldn't have afforded to lose those yokes, could we, pal?' he asked the crafty knowing face.

McCann, staring dazedly at the back of Simpson's head, saw once more the hulking white1skulled figure threshing around in vicious ecstasy on the moon-blanched beach. Once more his stomach heaved. Swallowing back the bitter cud, he moved away to the bookcase, a gaunt glass-fronted skeleton, bare-ribbed but for one shelf. As he stooped to investigate, Simpson said, still addressing the mirror:

'What do you think of her? Fine bit of stuff eh?' Again he winked – a slow, conspiratorial wink.

McCann slapped the wooden frame.

'Sound timber,' he said. 'Well constructed. Where did you get the set of Shaw?' He indicated the blue limp leather volumes ranged along the lower shelf – the only books to be seen.

'Daly's Auction Rooms. Fifteen quid – with the books thrown in. They make a fine show, don't they?' said Simpson.

'It wasn't the bloody bookcase I was talking about,' he added.

McCann opened one of the glass doors. Swung it gently to and fro.

'You made no mistake there,' he said. 'You'd go further and fare worse.'

He took out a volume – *Man and Superman.*

'Could I borrow this?'

Simpson finished his drink.

'Where's your glass, McCann?'

Retrieving the overturned glass, McCann held it up.

'You're a foolish little fellow,' said Simpson, pouring. 'You'll only fill your head with silly ideas wading through the like of that. Don't you know that reading never got a man anywhere?

'Take it with you if you want it,' he said.

McCann pocketed the volume. He watered his whiskey and took a wry sip. He was tired. Sleepy. Sober. Leaning against the mantelpiece. Simpson scowled into the mirror with ill-concealed distaste and impatience. He, too, appeared to have drunk himself sober. The party was at last over.

'I'm bursting for a leak, Manager,' he said. 'If I don't go soon, I'll wet my pants.'

He placed his brimming glass beside Simpson's on the mantel-piece – an unequivocal pledge of his imminent return.

'I'll use the office lav,' he said, making for the door.

Simpson did not answer.

Closing the sitting-room door after him, McCann, humming gaily, went downstairs. At the foot of the stairs he opened and slammed shut the office door. Then he tiptoed across the hall to the street door, opened it gently and just as gently eased it shut. Off up the darkened street he went, still tiptoeing cautiously, until, rounding a corner, he was beyond sight or sound of the Bank. With a sigh of relief he settled back on his heels, and heel and toe stepped it out up the hill towards his digs.

'Bugger him for an ignorant hoor-hopper,' he muttered.

Simpson woke early next morning. No hangover. Sound as a bell. He rolled over on his back and began to assemble the jig-saw memories of the previous night.

McCann's desertion rankled. Clifford would never have done a thing like that. He would stand by you till the last drink. But McCann. Making out he was going to the lavatory and sneaking off to his digs instead. A dirty trick that. Wonder what he wanted with that play of Shaw's? Couldn't make head nor tail of that mohawk. *Back to Methuselah* with its he-ancients and she-ancients and children hatched out of eggs and Adam and Eve appearing on the scene at the rear; a lot of nonsense, if you ask me. If that's the stuff he's reading he'd bear the watching. Slipping up on his drinks and his nose forever stuck in books and his nasty sneaking habits. Which reminds me. It was Mister Nosey McCann that was on the cliff top last night. Watching the whole carry on. Would never have been taped only he started puking his guts up. Must have followed the pair of us out from the pub. The ungrateful little scut. That's the thanks you get for taking him out for the evening. Still ... He should have sense enough to keep his trap shut. The job teaches you that virtue. And from what Annie says, he's a right young rip. Smelling after women like a tom cat. Young country

78

ones, mainly. That hardly know what they have it for. But of course doing everything very hidden and cute. Confiding in no one. A lone bird. But you can't keep anything hidden in this parish. They could tell you the colour of your cack before you had loosened a button. You'd be as well to broadcast everything you do, for they will get to know of it anyway. Wonder was he able to distinguish much at that time of night? With the moon out he would probably see plenty. When the puking started we were hard at it, too. It nearly made a hames of the whole caper. Only for the wee Clifden lassie was too far gone to stop, there was every danger of a short-arm shrinkage. God knows, a shock like that would drive all notions of hoorology out of anyone's head. You must hand it to Delia. She kept belting away. Ignoring everything. If the Primate of Ireland was standing over her, poking at her with his crozier, I'd swear to God she wouldn't miss a stroke. She's fond of what she likes, all right, the bould Delia. And she knows how to dish it up.

Stretched out on the bed, Simpson let the waves of desire break over him. Heart hammering, head buzzing, limbs weak, he was so lust-ridden he scarcely heard the house-keeper's knock.

'Eight o'clock, sir. Time to get up,' she called.

'Aye,' he growled.

Reluctantly he crawled out of bed. Stood up. Stretched himself, rolling his head from side to side to loosen out the neck muscles. As his eyes swung round, taking in the familiar landmarks of the room, he noticed a curious flatness about everything. Nothing stood out. Each object – wardrobe, dressing-table, chest of drawers, bedside table – fitted into the background of cream wall paper as though it were screwed in flush with its surface. They could well have been coloured illustrations of furniture that had been pasted on the walls during the night. A trick of the morning sun, Simpson reflected, noticing the moted sunlight shafting in the window.

There was something odd, too, about the floor surface when he crossed to the bathroom. It seemed to have become uneven, causing him to pick his steps carefully to avoid stumbling. In fact he did stumble against the jamb of the bathroom door on his way in. Caused probably by his dressing-gown catching in the door handle.

As for the upset tooth glass and the jar of shaving cream knocked to the floor, these mishaps were undoubtedly due to sheer clumsiness. Or carelessness.

But the shaving debacle was a different matter. To lose overnight your skill with a cut-throat razor. To find yourself pecking timidly where once you shaved with bold sweeping strokes. To gash yourself on cheek, chin and neck, so that your face sprouted cotton wool cists. To give up at last and finish the job with an electric razor. These things added up to something more than clumsiness.

Stripping away the wisps of cotton wool, he bent over the hand-basin, lathering, scrubbing and splashing his face. He dipped his head into fresh-run cold water, rubbing his smarting eyes to rid them of soap.

He turned away from the basin, water dripping from face and hands. Grunting and puffing energetically, he pawed about with tight eyes in search of a towel. Failing to find one, he knuckled his right eye free of soap and opened it cautiously the merest slit. He squinted around in puzzlement. Once more he sought to clear the lather from his eye, rubbing it vigorously, poking into the socket with prodding finger-tips. Satisfied at last that all traces of irritant were removed, he again opened the eye. This time there was no doubt about it. Something more fundamental than soapsuds was obstructing his vision. For one startled second he was convinced that complete blindness had descended on him. He stood motionless, staring wildly before him with the one wide-open eye, frightened to move a muscle lest worse misfortune befall.

When at length he gathered courage to open the other still-smarting eye and saw the shocked face staring back at him from the mirror, a flood of relief swept over him. How easy it was, he reflected wryly, for even the soundest and most sensible person to panic over some unfamiliar symptom of a harmless, every-day complaint.

He leaned closer and studied his image in the mirror, goggling wide-eyed, rolling his eyes from side to side, dragging at each lid of the affected eye in the effort to discover the obstruction.

Nothing was to be seen. Both eyes appeared exactly the same. Clear. Healthy. Vigilant. Both stared back at him as shrewdly, as keenly watchful, as ever.

Still, when he closed the left eye, no vision remained in the other one. All was darkness, as if the lids of both eyes were opening and closing in unison.

But it was not complete darkness. Light – a barely perceptible glimmer – seemed to be seeping through. He found that by holding his hand over his open right eye, the quality of the darkness changed. Became a deeper darkness. The rapid movement of his hand, swung close against his face, could be discerned as a flickering shadow. When, as an experiment, he tried switching the bathroom light on and off, he could clearly distinguish the shuttling from darkness to gloom, just as he would have from behind closed eyelids.

Another super hangover, he decided. An aggravation of the biliousness that had set in yesterday. First noises in his ears. Then spots floating before his eyes. And now this. He would really have to lay off the drink. Cut it out altogether. It was time to stop when it affected you this way. Of course, there could be no harm in having a few scoops at night. Before going to bed. Or maybe a jar or two after a dip. But these big nights took too much out of you. A fellow got far better value taking a girl out, throwing the few gargles into her and hammering a job in the back of the car. That would be the stratagem from now on. Less drink and more dick. That Delia lassie, for instance. She'd be an inexpensive jaunt. You would save enough to change your car taking *her* out for the night. Besides keeping your weight down and getting to bed earlier. He would fix up a date with her tonight.

He towelled himself slowly, letting his thoughts linger on Delia. The infinite variety of whens and wheres and hows that her active co-operation made possible, unfolded before him in a brilliant Technicolored trailer. He licked his dry lips.

'Your breakfast's ready, Mr. Simpson,' the housekeeper's voice interrupted.

He finished dressing without further mishap and went down to the office, where he signed the attendance book and turned his key in the manager's lock of the strong-room. His breakfast was on the table when he got back to the dining-room. Mrs. Mahony seemed to have recovered from her previous day's bad temper. She hovered around the table, inquiring solicitously if the eggs were too rare, the tea strong enough, the bread properly toasted.

'Is it a crick in the neck you have, Mr. Simpson?' she asked, as she watched him reach around awkwardly for the teapot. 'Wait now and I'll fill your cup myself.'

Head still turned sideways – a prisoner to his one good eye – he watched her pour. 'I think it's one of those bilious attacks I sometimes get,' he said.

'Biliousness, how are you! It's a hangover you have. What were you drinking last night, is there any harm asking?'

'Floating spots. In the right eye. Can't see too well out of it. The old liver, I suppose.

'All I had was a few stouts and a whiskey or two,' he added, in an aggrieved voice.

'Tck! Tck! Tck!' clucked Mrs. Mahony. She wiped her hands on her apron. 'Turn around and face the light.' She stooped over him, her lips pursed. 'Open your eye wide. Wider still. Shift it from side to side.' Hands on his shoulders, wheezing and grunting in concentration, she studied the glaring, rolling eye. 'Nothing to be seen there,' she said at length. 'Whatever it is, it'll probably clear itself before long.' She straightened up. Dusted her hands together. Shuffled to the door. 'It's a fret to man,' she muttered over her shoulder, 'the way you acquit yourself. It's a wonder you have an eye in your head at all.'

Impatiently he pushed away his empty plate. She's getting a bit above herself, the old bitch. Forever lecturing and giving out the pay. You'd think she was the boss of the house the way she goes on. I'd give her her walking papers only there's no one else to be had.

He contented himself by necking a single bottle of beer before returning to the office. McCann was waiting for him. Triumphant.

'I got it open,' he said, indicating the strong-room door. 'There's a knack in it. You give it a hoist when you're pulling it towards you. There's nothing ... to it ... really.' His voice trailed to silence under Simpson's baleful glare. He cleared his throat. 'The head's fairly flying off me with the effort, though,' he said apologetically.

Simpson brushed past him without a word. Unlocked the cash safe. Brought out a ledger from the strong-room. Settling himself on the tall stool, he commenced to check the posting of the previous day's cheques and lodgments.

Almost at once he stopped. Squeezed his left eye tight shut. Stared down at the ledger page. Bewildered. Against the white paper the impairment in vision of his right eye was at last apparent.

Between himself and the ledger page there appeared to be draped fold upon fold of curtain material. It was dark green in colour, changing here and there to a lighter green, where loops of the material had been caught up, allowing a tiny trickle of light to filter through. When he rolled his eyes, these loops changed shape and position, as though a strong breeze were sending the curtains flapping inwards. This billowing movement did not alter in any way the totality of light admitted by the curtains. It only emphasized the effectiveness of the frayed and tattered hangings and the impossibility of penetrating their clinging folds. By steadying his eye and gazing intently at the open ledger, he could discern – or fancied he could discern – through the rents in the green fabric the rapid movement of his hand across the surface of the page. But of the outlines of his hand or of the ledger itself, much less of the letters and figures in their coloured columns, he could distinguish nothing. He opened his left eye and blinked rapidly to clear his vision.

'Mr McCann,' he said.

'Yes, Manager.'

'How did you find the whiskey last night? There was no chance of it being laced with poteen? You've no bad hangover, have you?'

McCann grinned ruefully.

'Only for my puking up the greater part of the cargo, I don't doubt but I'd have a worse head than I have.'

He shook his head slowly in reluctant admiration.

'You're a great bloody man, Manager. Eyes clear as a baby's after a night's gargling that would make history. I don't know how you do it.'

'If it wasn't poteen it was cheap whiskey of some brand or other. They're all the same, the publicans. When you've a few jars in, they dish you up the rot-gut. Proper dynamite. Stuff that would give you a hob-nailed liver. As it stands, I can hardly see out of one eye over the head of it.'

'Which eye?' asked McCann, peering over the wooden partition.

'The right one.'

McCann came around to Simpson's desk.

'Isn't that the one you were complaining about yesterday morning?' he asked. 'Maybe it's a bit of grit that's got into it.'

'Grit be damned,' exploded Simpson. Then, dropping his voice: 'Take a look, anyway. Maybe *you'll* find something.'

Once more he rolled the eye around, holding the eyelids apart, so that McCann could scan its depths.

'Nothing there,' announced McCann at length. 'It's probably a mild attack of astigmatism.'

'A great bloody help *you* are,' said Simpson, 'with your grit and your astigmatism.'

He turned back to his ledger-checking, working with head tilted to the side and right eye squeezed shut. McCann lingered uneasily.

'Would it not be better if you wore an eye-shade?' he said, hesitantly.

Without bothering to reply, Simpson went on with his work. But when McCann came back from the Post Office and left on his desk, along with the day's mail, a flesh-coloured celluloid eye-shade, he slipped it on at once. All day he wore it, taking it off for interviews or when he suspected someone thought he was hiding a black eye. Ignoring the customers, he stayed stooped over his ledgers, working his way through the constant flow of remittance cheques and overseas drafts with few interruptions.

Only once had he to leave his desk. An old man, deaf and unlettered, wanted advice on how to escape death duty on the £5,000 he had on deposit at the Branch. In the inner office, with his mouth to the old man's whiskered ear, he hissed out the information that if £1,000 were deposited in five separate Branches in the joint names of himself and each of his five children – the receipts, of course, to be held by himself – no estate duty would be payable as each receipt would, on the old man's death, be payable without question to the surviving depositor.

When Simpson, squinting one-eyed, was filling out requisitions, the old man said in a smug voice:

'I see you're like myself, Mr. Simpson. Getting no younger. When the eyes start giving trouble, it's time to put your affairs in order.'

Simpson glared at him.

'It's only a blast,' he said. 'It'll be gone by tomorrow. Sign your name on each of these forms.'

When he left the completed forms on McCann's desk so that new deposit receipts could be issued, he muttered:

'That old cod should be put away. He's doting.'

At the end of the day, when McCann was locking up his cash, Simpson said:

'I was wondering should I take a run over to Creevan to see the Doc. He might be fit to give me a bottle. Or maybe some eye-salve.'

'I'd say it's the best thing you could do,' said McCann. 'It's maybe nothing serious but it's as well to take no chances.'

During the journey to Creevan, Simpson drove carefully. He found he had continually to check a tendency to drift across the road as though the car was at the mercy of a strong side wind. Parking outside Hannah's bar, he misjudged his clearance and bruised the rim of his front wheel against the pavement edge. Cautiously he reversed and got out to examine the damage. A hub-cap dinged. A section of the rim buckled inwards. Blast that, he muttered.

The beach was deserted. On the soft sand he stretched out, hands under his head, hat tilted over his eyes. He lay there without movement till the crunching sand and the doctor's voice aroused him.

'Have you been in yet, Jim?'

Simpson sat up. Tipped his hat back. Screwed up his eyes.

'No,' he said. 'And I don't know will I.'

The doctor sprawled out beside him.

'Are you feeling that bad?' he asked. 'You were fairly knocking them back last night. Still at it when I left. Without a bite to eat, I suppose. Don't you know a man can't drink properly unless he eats properly?'

'You could be right. But I'd be more inclined to blame the drink. Bad drink, I mean.'

'You're wrong, Jim. It's rarely the quality of the drink that causes the hangover. It's more often the quantity. What are the symptoms this time?'

Simpson moistened his lips.

'It's like this.' He spoke carefully, in a dry, detached manner. 'One of my eyes – the right one – appears to be giving trouble. It's not functioning properly.'

85

'In what way?'

'There seems to be some slight obstruction ... urr ... something hampering the vision. Oh, nothing serious, I'm quite sure. A liver symptom probably.'

'Just how bad is it? What degree of vision have you?'

'As a matter of fact ...' Simpson hesitated. Ashamed. 'Not a whole lot.'

'As bad as that?'

'Actually I can see bugger-all out of it.'

The doctor got to his feet.

'I better look into this,' he said.

When they reached the parked cars, he asked:

'Can you handle the car all right?'

'Of course I can.'

'Well, come on so.'

They drove – each in his own car – to the surgery where the doctor seated Simpson facing the sunlit window. 'Hold your handkerchief over your good eye,' he said, moving to the window. He lowered the blind half-way. Noisily. 'Now,' he said. 'Any difference in the quality of your vision?'

Simpson hesitated.

'Yes,' he said deliberately. 'It's dimmer. Of course I heard you draw the blind, Doc,' he apologized.

Soundlessly the doctor lowered the blind to the full.

'Now?' he asked.

Frowning, Simpson directed his one-eyed glare at the lowered blind.

'There's no difference that I can see,' he announced at last.

'One more try,' said the doctor, flicking the drawn blind noisily up and back to its original position.

'How is that?' he asked.

'That's better,' said Simpson. 'At least ... I think so ... though it's hard to be certain ... as a matter of fact, I'm only guessing.'

'That's what I thought,' said the doctor.

'Don't move,' he said. 'Keep your good eye covered.'

From his bag he rooted out a pencil-type torch. Held it close to the staring eye.

'Any difference now?' he said, switching on the torch.

'Oh, yes. Much brighter. You're using a torch, aren't you?'

'Yes.' He released the pencil clip. 'And now?'

'You've switched it off.'

Moving around the surface of the eye, he directed the slender beam into pupil and iris and into the bloodshot corners of the eyeball, switching the torch on and off intermittently and drawing from Simpson a droning litany of: 'On. Off. On. Off.'

'Nothing the matter with the optic nerve, at any rate,' said the doctor.

'Hold on a moment,' he said. He drew back the lighted torch a little and passed the forefinger of his left hand rapidly back and forth across the surface of the beam.

'How about that?' he asked.

'There's something moving.'

'In what direction?'

'From side to side.'

The doctor held his finger motionless in the beam of light.

'Any idea what shape or size?'

'No. I can make out nothing now.'

'What about this?' The doctor wagged an admonitory finger.

'Something is moving again. Up and down this time.'

Again the motionless finger.

'Still no idea of its appearance?'

'No. It's gone again.'

The doctor crossed the room and pulled up the blind.

'All right, Jim. You can put away the handkerchief.'

Simpson blew his nose noisily.

'How long will it be before it clears up?' he asked.

'I'm afraid that's a question for a specialist to answer.' The doctor sat down at his desk. 'I'll ring up an eye-man in the city. A good friend of mine. First-class man at his job. This is his address.' He scribbled out a note and handed it to Simpson. 'Be there tomorrow afternoon. He'll fit you in without an appointment. As an emergency case.'

Bewildered, Simpson stammered:

'B-b-b-but . . . there's surely no need . . . the-the-there's nothing wrong . . . no emergency . . . that is . . . there's not much wrong, is there?'

'It looks to me as though you have ruptured a blood-vessel in the eye. Probably due to that weight-lifting act of yours last night.'

'Ruptured blood-vessel,' Simpson's voice rose to a horrified squeak. 'That's impossible. I've been hoisting the half-hundreds for the last twenty-five years and damn the bit harm it ever did me.'

'You were a different man twenty-five years ago, Jim. Never forget that. Antics like that don't suit a man of your years.'

Simpson fairly gobbled with rage.

'I-I-I'm a better man than I was then. Never a day's illness in my life. I'd stand up to any hardship. Sure you saw how I dealt with that miner last night?'

'I know, I know,' the doctor soothed. 'Just take it easy till you see the specialist. Go straight home from here. No bathe. No drink. Go to bed early and have a good night's sleep. And remember, don't drive to the city. Take the bus. It will be some time before you get used to mono-vision.'

'It would be as well if you wore an eye-shade over the bad eye,' he added as they moved to the door.

'I have one,' growled Simpson. 'but I don't like wearing it outdoors. It's too conspicuous.'

'Better put it on, Jim. It will ease the strain on the eye.'

Reluctantly, Simpson adjusted the eye-shade and moved out to the street. As he was letting in the clutch of the car, the doctor tapped on the partly rolled down window.

'Don't forget now,' he called in. 'Straight home.'

Simpson slowed down coming to Hannah's. He needed a drink. Badly. One large whiskey. Possibly two. With a pint chaser. He could fix up a date with Delia for the week-end. A bit of relaxation after all this fuss was just what the doctor ordered. He peeled off the eye-shade, changed down to third gear and swung round the corner. As he was pulling in to park, he saw the scarlet motor-bike propped up beside the window sill, its chrome work gleaming in the sun. Simpson swerved out, accelerated and raced through his gears. God's curse on that prying little bastard. Is he on the prowl again? He's the right little ferret. Always on the go. With his nose wrinkled up for the smell of scandal. There's not much *he'll* miss. Well, this is one time he's lost out. Take care but I recommend him for transfer. That'll soften his cough. But then, what kind of a galoot will they send in his place?

He eased his angry foot off the pedal until the speedometer read a steady forty. God knows you could get worse than him. He's a fast accurate worker. Pleasant to the customers. Does what he's told. Perhaps I'm wronging the poor little devil. He could have left his motor-bike outside Hannah's and gone down to the strand for a dip. At any rate he couldn't have guessed I was going to pull in for a jar at that time. He knows by now that I never drop in to Hannah's until six o'clock.

Assuaged by these deductions, he pulled in at Hannigan's of Cleggan Cross, where, sitting moodily at the end of the counter, he sank, before leaving at ten o'clock, six large Jamesons and six bottled stouts. An hour later he was coiled up in bed, hands crossed, in ritual fashion, across his pyjama jacket, right cheek buried deep in the pillow, so that when he woke in the morning, the acknowledgement of disaster could be postponed.

Simpson, eye-shaded and glum, was first to appear in the office next morning.

'I'm taking a day's discretionary leave,' he announced, when McCann arrived. 'No need to inform Head Office. A few signed forms will keep you going till I resume duty.'

'Is the eye giving trouble still?' asked McCann.

'The doctor's sending me to a specialist in the city. Did you ever hear such bloody nonsense?'

'I don't know. The doctor's a sound man. He takes no chances.'

Simpson glared at him.

'I'm as sound a man as *he* is, any tick of the clock,' he said, as he hauled open the strong-room door. 'Get out the Forms Signed in Blank book. I'll sign four Deposit receipts and two drafts. And the Head Office letter. That should keep you right.'

An hour later he was sitting crouched up beside the window in the front right-hand seat of the city-bound bus, hat pulled down over shaded eye, shoulders hunched away from the aisle, gazing moodily at the sun-lit countryside. When he arrived at the bus depot there was time for three quick beers, a glass of whiskey and a club sandwich in a city pub before calling to the specialist. After only a slight delay he was ushered into the consulting room where Doctor Roche – small, spruce, ageless – got up and shook hands with him.

'Mr. Simpson?' he asked and when Simpson nodded, went on:

'My great friend, Doctor Madden, rang me up last night. He seems to think very highly of you.' He waved Simpson to a seat. Sat down himself. 'A very gifted man, John. Admirable material for a G.P., I would say.' He picked up a silver-mounted pen and held it poised over a record card. 'Now, if you don't mind, a few particulars. Pure routine of course.'

Full name. Address. Occupation. Previous illnesses, if any. Simpson wondered where it would stop. Parents – are they alive or dead? What was the cause, in each case, of death? Any record of hereditary disease in the family? He'll be wanting to know next if one of your grandfathers was poxed or if poor Aunt Sophie perished of the plague. When were you last medically examined? Was it a complete medical check-up? At length he paused, flung down the pen, sat back in his chair with hands clasped across his chest.

'And now,' he said, 'what seems to be the matter?'

In the name of God, Simpson fumed, has that idiot Madden not explained things to him? Of all the . . .

'It's just a little trouble, Doctor, I'm having with my right eye. Doctor Madden thought you should have a look at it.'

He took off the eye-shade. Tilted his head back. Waiting. Maybe this will put the skids under him. Half a bloody hour wasted in silly questions. A little action is called for.

'I see,' said the specialist placidly. 'I see.' He picked up the pen. Rolled it around in his finger-tips. Commenced tapping with the base of the pen on the blotting pad. Softly. Patiently. As if he was beating a muffled drum behind your coffin. He'll start whistling the Dead March next. Better, anyway, than piping that refrain of his: 'I see. I see.' It would be a poor thing if he couldn't. With the job he's undertaken to do. I suppose he thinks he's soothing you. Putting you at your ease.

'Well now, Mr. Simpson,' came the quiet, compelling voice. 'Perhaps you would explain – in your own words, of course – what this trouble consists of? And how it came about? The background to these troubles is very important. So tell every little detail, no matter how trivial.'

He reached across to a cabinet, picked up an eye-dropper and dipped it into a bottle.

'And while you are talking,' he got up and crossed to the back of Simpson's chair. 'Hold back your head. Eyes wide open.' Quickly, expertly, he used the dropper. 'The atropine will get time to react.' He moved back to the desk. 'It dilates the pupils. Enables us to investigate the interior of the eye.'

Once more the soft insistent tapping of pen on pad. 'Now, Mr. Simpson.'

Like a stubborn penitent, coaxed and harried by the whispered exhortations of the confessor, Simpson told of idling car engines, lancinating headaches, vision mysteriously impaired, whilst the specialist murmured a litany of: 'I see, I see, I see.'

When the last dribble of disclosure had ceased, the specialist asked:

'Had you any violent exercise prior to this occurrence?'

Reluctantly, Simpson told of the weight-lifting contest.

'But,' he explained. 'I've practised weight-lifting for a good twenty-five years or more.'

'I see,' said the specialist.

'Anything else?' he asked.

Simpson stared at him bleakly. Is he waiting for you to say: 'Yes, Father,' as if you were at confession. He's a bloody humbug. Sitting there behind his grill waiting for you to confess the sin he thinks is sticking in your gullet.

'Nothing that I can recall,' he said. How often had he stalled a persistent confessor with this ambiguous phrase – fruit of the discovery that 'recall' had a secondary meaning – 'annul.'

'I see,' said Doctor Roche. He selected an instrument from the cabinet, made a rapid adjustment and came around beside Simpson's chair.

'Keep your eyes wide open and stare straight ahead,' he said, raising the instrument to his right eye as though he were socketing a monocle.

There was no time to make out more than the outlines of a stubby gleaming object before Simpson found a beam of light directed into his affected eye from a distance of less than an inch. Shallow, tobacco-scented breathing warmed his cheek and, remembering the large whiskey and the three beers, he sucked in his breath, flinching back involuntarily.

'Hold steady. There's nothing to worry about,' the soft voice reassured.

Simpson strained wide open his eyes and pressed closer to the dazzling beam. Does the little tomtit think you're scared of being hurt? Show him you're bloody well not. He glared madly ahead, seeing for the first time the full extent of the obstruction to his vision. The folds of green material were now bathed in a light so strong that they took on the appearance of theatre curtains with house-lights and foot-lights lowered but the stage lighting full on. The thick curtain folds changed colour as they swayed back and forth but nowhere did the smallest glint of bright light penetrate. Yet Simpson knew that somewhere behind the brilliantly lit screen he was being spied upon.

In retaliation, he concentrated the unimpaired gaze of his left eye on the side face looming so close, noting the black-head on the flare of the nostril, and the minute green particle caked to the end of one nostril hair.

As if he sensed what was happening, the specialist suddenly leant across and focused the beam of light on Simpson's questing eye.

'Hold it,' he said.

Simpson could now see nothing – one eye being blinded by darkness, the other by glaring light. He shifted uneasily in his chair. At last he said:

'There's nothing the matter with that eye, Doctor.'

'We had better make sure, hadn't we?'.

The specialist took more time examining the good eye than the other, directing the beam of light into the dilated pupil from every possible angle.

When the ophthalmoscope was switched off, Simpson was so dazzled that he could scarcely make out the figure of the specialist crossing back to his desk. He sat in silence, staring at the hazy, featureless face. Waiting.

'Now, Mr. Simpson,' said the specialist, 'I think you should take it easy for a little while. Stay off work for . . . let's say a fortnight . . . or better still, three weeks. No need to stay in bed. Just sit around and avoid violent exercise.'

'Go on sick leave, you mean?'

'Call it that, if you like. I prefer to term it a rest period. On no account must you indulge in violent exertion. You may take a short stroll every day. No great harm in that. But no hurry or bustle. Go about everything in a leisurely manner. Don't run up or down stairs. Or take them two at a time. *Festina lente*, that's the motto.'

'But I've never been on sick leave since I entered the Bank.'

'Another thing to be avoided is stooping. If you have to pick up something, squat down on your haunches.'

'My God!' muttered Simpson.

'Coughing and sneezing, too, tend to make the eyes bulge, so do your best to abstain from both. Do you swim, Mr. Simpson?'

'I do. As often as—'

'Well, I'm afraid swimming is out of the question for the present. Though, if you are a great lover of the sea, there should be no ill effects from paddling.'

'Paddling! Are you serious, Doctor?'

'Of course I am.'

'But ... but ... but what's the matter with the eye? You haven't said—'

'You have sustained a retinal haemorrhage, Mr. Simpson. A serious defect. But one that, I haven't the least doubt, can be cleared up. With your help, of course.

Simpson swallowed noisily.

'What exactly is a retinal haemorrhage, Doctor?'

'It's a ruptured blood vessel in the retina of the eye. Caused probably, by over-exertion. A considerable amount of blood has leaked into the interior of the eye-ball, causing the loss of vision you complain of. It is to be hoped that in a few weeks time this blood will be absorbed by the jelly-like substance that constitutes the core of the eye-ball, giving you back perfect sight once more. Provided, of course, that you do nothing to provoke a further haemorrhage.'

There was a prolonged silence, during which Simpson stared miserably at the specialist with eyes containing black grapes instead of pupils.

'And now for your certificate. I'll make it out for three weeks. You should be able to resume work by then.'

Simpson accepted the certificate in silence and in silence walked to the door. As he was leaving, the specialist said:

'Your sight may be a little blurred by the drops, but that should wear off in a few hours.'

Outside in the street the bright sunlight flooded the swollen defenceless pupils, causing his eyes to smart and water. He moved along uncertainly, bumping into people and tripping on kerb stones. Surrounded by a hostile world of pushing, hurrying people, he peered ahead with dazzled, blinking eyes, striving to avoid the hazy figures that rushed towards him.

He was too busy dealing with the physical handicap of distorted vision to give thought to the implications behind the specialist's disclosure. It was when he was crossing the bridge spanning the river, where he was forced to walk in the full blaze of the sun, without street buildings on either side to protect him from its glare, that he became aware at last of his predicament. Creeping along slowly, hugging the railings of the bridge and peering ahead painfully into the rays of the afternoon sun, he had half the journey completed when, without warning, he found himself in a monochrome world. All the primary colours had become fused in a single colour. Violet.

The hostile faces hurrying towards him were violet. So were their hats and clothes and dogs and prams and cars. His hands, as he steadied himself on the parapet of the bridge, were violet also. When he looked up-river, it was a lavender flow with violet shipping etched against a lilac sky. The sun itself was a shimmering livid ball against which he was forced to close his eyes.

He leant against the bridge, eyes closed, heart pounding with fright. The specialist had never warned him about this symptom. Could this possibly be the onset of total blindness? Would he open his eyes eventually to a blind man's world? He squeezed his eyes tight shut to hold back the darkness washing against the lids. What had he done to cause this? He had not sneezed nor coughed. Of that he was almost sure. Nor had he stooped. As for violent exercise, he had been shuffling along like an old man. Perhaps he had gone to the specialist too late. With the damage to his eyes too far gone for treatment. At this thought he squeezed the knuckles of his thumbs into his eye sockets as though to plug them against invasion. What had possessed him to attempt that weight-lifting contest? Showing off before a crowd of country gawms. Trying to impress them that he was tougher than they were. As if it mattered a damn one way or the other who was the strongest. Why not own up that you were trying to impress Delia? Demonstrating what a fine parish bull of a man you were. You should have had more sense. That little hot-bellied bitch required no priming. Fingernails clawing your neck. Arms and legs pinioning your body. Wild whispered obscenities. No wonder when it was all over you were lying back gasping, with the blood pounding in your ears and the sweat blinding you. You didn't tell Doctor Madden about that piece of violent exercise when he was questioning you. Oh, no! Well, now look where it has landed you. In danger of losing your eye-sight.

Oh, God, he prayed, don't let it happen. Please, *please*, don't let it happen. I swear I won't touch that bitch again. Anything you ask, I'll do. Drive out the bad thoughts. Say my night prayers. Try to go to daily Mass. Anything. Only don't let me open my eyes to a world of darkness.

Cautiously, fearfully, he opened his eyes.

Green scummy dung-dappled water slid past the black hulls of cargo boats and the grey elegance of two coupled corvettes tied up to the quayside. Sunlight gleamed on highly-polished brass and scrubbed brown decks. In the wind gaily coloured flags and pennons fluttered at the mast-heads. Against the delicate blue of the sky, the tall red gasometer stood out in reassuring ugliness. Across the bridge the traffic flowed and on the pavements the crowd pushed and jostled. All displayed in glorious realistic Technicolor.

In chastened mood, Simpson, hat pulled down over his eyes, continued on his way through a world of kindly sympathetic people who murmured apologies as he bumped into them. In the bus he sat once more beside the window in the front right-hand seat. Every so often he would glance at his wrist-watch to see if the dilation of his eye pupils had ceased. The bus had almost reached Glenard before his blurred vision had cleared sufficiently for him to read the time.

In the Bank House he left the medical certificate on the cashier's desk with a note instructing him to phone Head Office for a relief hand. Tired and depressed, he drank a tumbler of whiskey and, though it was still daylight, went to bed.

He was almost asleep before he remembered his promise. It took many attempts before his jaded but scrupulous wits could complete to his satisfaction three embarrassed Hail Marys.

CHAPTER TWO

For a fortnight, Simpson led a life of monotony and boredom. He rose late and retired early. He avoided violent exercise or the lifting of heavy weights. Each day he drove to Creevan Bay, parked the car at the entrance to the strand, and walked slowly back and forth along the half-mile of beach, keeping to the firm sand at the water's edge. Even at the slow pace he held himself to, he managed to retain the sinuous boxer's swagger. Sometimes he would stop and watch, without particular interest, the prowling gannet as they circled tirelessly, waiting for the sudden dip that brought one plunging down on outstretched wings that were tucked back at the instant it struck the water. Or the cormorants hurrying from nesting rock to fishing ground, flying low over the water with watchful, craning heads. Or he would stand on the high bank of the river as it entered the sea, watching the fish swim up the river with the incoming tide.

When the doctor arrived for his swim, he would join him, standing at the shore-line shouting advice and warning to the bobbing head as it sank in four feet of water. Always he reported meticulously to the doctor his eye condition which began to clear up rapidly after the first few days. The dark green curtain lightened in colour and texture until he began to perceive, first the outline of moving figures, then the outline of stationary objects and, at last, only scattered fragments of light green material remained to distract his vision and to remind him of threatened disaster.

Under pressure, the doctor agreed to allow Simpson to resume duty before the three weeks certificate had expired, warning him that he must still obey the instructions of the specialist. But Simpson, once the office routine had become re-established, drifted back to his old habits. Soon, in spite of Mrs. Mahony's pleadings and protests, the morning cork-popping had recommenced.

'You're a terrible man, sir,' she would say. 'Wouldn't you think you'd take heed of the warning you got and take it easy.

But here you are – at it worse than ever. What time were you home last night? All hours of the morning, I'll warrant you.'

'Mrs. Mahony. Whatever time I came home is my own affair. It's no business of yours. The specialist never told me to put up the Pledge Pin. He knows damn well an occasional drink never hurt anyone.'

'An occasional drink, how are you!' and she would waddle away disgusted.

The afternoon bathe at Creevan, the walk along the cliff tops, the evening session in Hannah's pub: all these had been resumed. Before long he was taking Delia out in the car for innocent spins that finished up in gasping sweating exhaustion on the foreshore of some remote and lonely beach or in the echoing gloom of one of the many caves that pitted the cliff-lined coast. Hannah, scenting romance, encouraged these outings, chiding her niece:

'The city has you destroyed, Delia. You're so pale, you'd think you were sickening for something. God's good sunshine – that's what you want. Away off with you up the road for a wee bit of a dander.'

Inciting her suitor:

'D'you know what it is, Mr. Simpson, that wee girl eats no more nor a canary. A pick of this and a pick of that. She should take more exercise, that's what I'm always telling her. The wheen of times you took her out did her more good than any bottle of the doctor's.'

'We'll have to do something about that, Hannah. Tell her to root out her bathing gear and we'll go swimming in Bally-garrow.'

Dry-cleaned and dressed a couple of hours later, they would dip the unused bathing suits in the tide, wring them out conscientiously and return to Creevan, to be greeted with un-disguised approval by all in the bar.

'Had you a nice dip, Delia?'

'That's a grand wee cuddy you have there.'

'You'll be giving us the big day yet, Mr. Simpson.'

'I'd say you could do with a little tonic, James. What'll it be?'

'Oh, the usual, Doc. A Jameson ten.'

And so it went on till one morning he discovered, when going through the morning mail, two cheques of Brian Mullen's

– one for ten pounds, the other for five. Both had gone through the London Clearing. Both had been cashed in a Fulham Road Bank. The ten pound cheque was made payable to 'The Stag's Head Inn'. The other to 'The Quarterdeck Club'.

Simpson's head jerked up.

'Mr. McCann!'

'Yessir.'

'How does Brian Mullen's account stand?'

Ledger leaves rustled frantically. Ceased.

'Debit seventy-four pounds odd.'

'WHAT—? That couldn't be.'

'A few cheques came in while you were on sick leave.'

'Was there no lodgment? Didn't the firm he's working for credit his account with salary and travelling allowances for the month?'

'No, sir. Should they have?'

'Of course.'

'You didn't tell *me*, Manager. I'm certain of that. And there's no note of it in any of the books.'

Simpson grunted contemptuously.

'Get Mullen's cheques out, Mr. McCann. We'd better call off his account. I'm going to return these cheques unpaid.'

McCann leafed through the lodgments and cheques, calling out the amounts to the Manager, who ticked them off with red ink in the Accounts Current ledger. Dismally, Simpson noted the string of small cheques that brought the balance of the account up to its present figure.

'Let me look at those cheques,' he said.

Just as he expected, all were payable either to 'The Stag's Head Inn' or to 'The Quarter-deck Club'. The date the first cheque was cashed and branded by the London Bank was the twenty-fifth of May. Simpson thrust out the offending cheques.

'Mr. McCann. These cheques have all been cashed in Fulham Road boozers. Did it not dawn on you that Mullen was drinking the piece out in London?'

'I never suspected ... How could I know ... What could I do anyway ...?'

'You were in charge of the Branch in my absence. It was your place to examine these cheques carefully. If you had done so, you'd have spotted what was happening. As acting Pro Manager, you should have exercised more care.'

98

'Look here, Manager, that's just too bloody much. I warned you at the time that Mullen was a slippery customer. Yet you marked up an authorized overdraft for him of a hundred pounds. What else could I do but honour his cheques up to that amount?'

'You could have spun them when you began to suspect that he was on a bender.'

'And have that crook sue the Bank for breach of contract? I'd be in poor odour with the Directors if I were foolish enough to do *that*.'

As the awkward silence lengthened, McCann shuffled his feet in embarrassment.

'Will I ring up the company, Manager?' he said. 'We could find out did he cash his pay cheque.'

'I'll do it myself,' said Simpson, the sour taste of anger and frustration curdling his mouth.

When he came back from the inner office, eyebrows furrowed, pursed lips white with rage, McCann knew it was disaster.

'Of all the nerve! D'you know how things stand? He's out of his job. Sacked. I didn't ask them why but no doubt it was for drunkenness or debauchery or similar rascality. But what sticks in my gullet is the young ruffian had the neck to touch me for an overdraft when he was actually sacked out of his job.'

'Sweet suffering duck,' McCann whispered. 'Out on his ear and still bluffing his way.'

'Wait a moment,' he added. 'What about the car? Would it be possible to impound it in some way? Will I ring up the garage, Manager, and see what shape it's in?'

Simpson's face brightened.

'Do so, Mac, like a good chap.'

Through the partly-closed inner office door he tried to make out how the conversation was going but McCann was speaking too low and he could not reconstruct the missing fragments.

'What do they say it's worth?' he asked when McCann returned to the outer office.

'It was in poor condition.' McCann spoke in a dazed, bewildered fashion, as though he had not yet grasped the full import of the message.

'I know. I know. He told me that. But it should still be worth seventy or eighty pounds. No matter what condition it's in.'

McCann gulped. Squared his shoulders.

'He sold it to the garage for twenty smackers. Cash.'

Face flushed with rage, lips twitching convulsively, Simpson strove for words.

'He couldn't ... surely not ... twenty lousy quid ... after putting the arm on me.'

Reaching for the red ink pen, he scribbled viciously across the top left-hand of each cheque the legend: *Refer to Drawer*. He tossed the two cheques on to the cashier's desk.

'Flog them back to London by today's post. That young thug will have to be taught manners.'

He uncovered the typewriter.

'I'll write him a snorter.'

Brutally he banged the carriage back and set the margins.

'*Dear Sir,* he wrote, '*Two cheques totalling fifteen pounds have been presented for payment here today. These cheques will not be paid until your liability to the Bank has been liquidated and your account put in credit. The overdraft facilities granted to you under promise of repayment from sources now known to be—*' What hell is the word? False? Not strong enough. Fraudulent? Won't do either. Wait now. It's on the tip of my tongue. Yes. '*Spurious have been determined by the withholding of the relevant facts.*' That will put him reeling against the ropes. Now I'll give him the works about proper. '*I would strongly ad vise you to bend your attention to the wiping out of this debt or I will be forced to hand the matter ov er to the authorities so that they can proceed with a charge against you of—*' Just what could he be charged with? Not fraud. Not issuing worthless cheques because he was actually granted accommodation. It's ... It's ... I have it. '*obtaining money under false pret enc es. In the meanw hile post ba ck your che q ue book by retu rn.*'

Simpson glared at the typing flaws. The curse of Christ on the wretched thing. Just when you wanted a proper job done it starts leaping around like a bloody antelope. Well, I'm damned if I'll retype it.

Savagely, he plucked the sheet of paper from the machine. As he was about to sign the letter, it happened.

He saw it happen. Against the white paper it showed up as

though on a cinema screen. For a moment he could not grasp the significance of the scarlet column rising like a volcanic eruption and, like an eruption, mushrooming at its peak. Only when he remembered that the retina inverts all reflected images did it dawn on him that he was witnessing the onset of another haemorrhage. Fearfully he watched the mushroom cloud swell and thicken as the small steady trickle of blood kept leaking out of the ruptured blood vessel.

He closed his eyes. I will count ten, he resolved, before I re-open my eyes. By that time the haemorrhage will surely have ceased. Pen still in hand, bowed head held rigid, he waited. Counting. At ten, stricken with panic, he decided to count on. Till twenty, perhaps. Or even the half minute might be better. Less chance of being disappointed.

Motionless, he waited, suspended in a void where only sound existed. The chink and rustle as McCann busied himself with his cash. The hesitant tick of the office clock. The soft pad of hoofs as a herd of cattle were driven leisurely to pasture. Sea birds wailing. Blood thudding in straining ears. Creak of leather as anxious breathing stirred the wallet in the inside pocket of his jacket. Cautiously he raised his head, till his chin rested on his fisted hand. Perhaps this position might help to staunch the flow of blood. His face was turned towards the window through which the morning sun had begun to blaze. Through his closed eyelids he could detect the different texture of darkness. To his horror he found that he could see against the mottled background a slender pillar of darkness surmounted by a cloud of deeper darkness. The cloud had settled lower. No doubt of that. Soon, if the haemorrhage continued, the sinister cloud would sink down till all was engulfed.

Dear God, he prayed, as he had prayed before, please stop this awful thing. I know I have broken my promises to you. And I ask for mercy and forgiveness. But I was not wholly to blame. The woman tempted me. With pleading eyes and lustful words she led me on. But I will try again. And this time, with your help, I will succeed. I will stop drinking, for it weakens my will. I will go to the sacraments seeking grace to strengthen it. I will stay away from Delia altogether. All these things will I do if only you will ...

He heard the swing door open.

'Having a little nap, James?' It was a soft voice. A mean oily,

101

hateful voice. A voice that had grated on him, day in, day out ever since he had taken up duty in Glenard.

Without pause for thought, he shook his head – shaking off both sleep and sneer.

'You're early on the job this morning, Michael,' he said swinging round on his stool. Open-eyed.

Through frosted glass, smeared and spattered with blood he glared malevolently at Michael Vincent McArdle, grocer publican, hardware and general merchant, special rate depositor, devout member of the St. Dominick guild of the Sacred Heart sodality, jealous guardian of the first shilling he ever earned and purveyor of the meanest measured half-one of whiskey in the village.

'You can go back to sleep, James,' McArdle said: 'I'll not be disturbing you.'

Horrified, Simpson stared at him, seeing only the spreading turbulence as the blood stirred and shifted with every twitch of the eye-ball. Already the bright scarlet was changing to a murky green. The shifting colours were running together, swallowing up the few remaining patches through which light was still admitted. He suddenly remembered standing at his mother's elbow watching her crack raw eggs into a basin, sprinkle them with tomato juice, pour in a measure of milk and start stirring. Under the whirling fork, the kaleidoscope rapidly changed to a single colour – dark yellow. He had wondered at the time how it was that the milk and the egg-white could be swallowed by their much smaller adjuncts. It had seemed to him unjust that the little should be devoured by the less. Now this was happening inside one of his own eyes. He groaned.

'You seem to be seeing things this morning,' said McArdle.

Simpson gazed with loathing at the plump little figure, its perky cock-robin head tilted to one side quizzically.

'I could do with seeing one less,' he said, wheeling around and stalking to the house door. As he was opening the door, he heard McArdle say to the cashier:

'What's eating him this morning? Sure it's only change he want.'

Next day, Simpson once more travelled to the city. Again it was beautiful weather with the sun blazing down from a cloudless sky. This time he took no chances. Not only did he wear the eye-shade but underneath it a square of cotton wool to make sure that no sun rays could penetrate.

Dr. Roche made no secret of his disappointment.

'This is most frustrating,' he said. 'Your eye trouble was almost certainly caused by abnormal physical exertion. Are you sure you obeyed my instructions?'

'Yes, Doctor.'

'You took things easy? No violent exercise? No swimming? No excessive drinking?'

'Well ... er ... I had the odd bottle of beer. Nothing more.'
How lucky he had decided to take nothing till after he had seen the doctor.

'I suppose one – or even two – bottles of beer could do no great harm. You might sleep better after them. And plenty of sleep is most important. But remember – no more than two.'

'Yes, doctor.'

'Now we'll have a look at the culprit.'

Again the eye drops in both eyes.

'It is essential that the sound eye be always carefully watched. The organs of vision often act in unison. If one goes on strike, the other takes sympathetic action.'

For a long time he examined the two eyes.

'There is no sign, so far, of any defect in the left eye. With the other one, we are back, I fear, to where we started.'

On the desk top he tapped out a little tune in jig-time with nimble finger-tips.

'I'll put you on calcium,' he said. 'One tablet every three hours. And I would like you to see a blood specialist. There is a good man across the road from here. Doctor Savage. Come down again this day week. I'll arrange for you to see him.'

As they shook hands at the door, he said:

'Remember now, forbearance in everything.'

Simpson spent a depressing week, mooching around the house, with Annie shuffling after him, clucking:

'You shouldn't be galloping up the stairs like that, sir. Two at a time. You know what the doctor told you?'

or:

'It's bad to be stooping down to tie your shoe-laces. Put your foot up on a chair like you were told to do.'

Or, if she heard him pulling a cork:

'Now Mr. Simpson. That's the fifth one you've had today. They'll be packing you off to the eye and ear hospital if you don't do as you're told.'

Simpson would turn on her. Enraged.

'Would you, for God's sake, give over. You never stop harping from dawn to dusk. If I'd known you were going to act like a clucking hen, I'd have kept my trap shut and told you nothing.'

It was a relief to slip after hours into the office where he could check up on the day's work and read the correspondence. McCann, in charge, with a relief cashier under him, was glad of the chance to seek advice.

'Brian Mullen's cheque is in again this morning, Manager. The one payable to the London club.'

'Did he lodge to meet it?'

'No, but there's a letter from him.'

'Let me see it.'

Simpson held the letter at arm's length while he read it, a look of disgust on his face.

Dear Jim, it read. *I would be grateful if you would cover the cheque which you returned to the Quarter-deck Club, as they are rather inclined to take a poor view of a transaction of this nature. I told them that there had been some sort of misunderstanding and that it would be met if it were sent on again. I hope you will help me out this time. The Stag's Head Inn can wait for their money – they got enough of mine in their time. And their drink is as bad as any you would get in Glenard. This includes Snout's 'Best Old Irish' rotgut. Kindest regards. Brian.*

The reference to the bad drink, with its hint of shared experience, tempted Simpson to relent, but he hardened his heart.

'Not a word of apology or explanation. No mention of a lodgment. Fire back the cheque again, Mr. McCann.'

'He's evidently well-scared of the boys in the Quarter-deck joint. It must be a haunt of gangsters and thugs.'

'It might be no harm if he got a few strokes of a razor. It might bring him to his senses. He's been acting the candyman for too long.'

'What'll I say in reply, sir?'

'Oh, just type out a few lines saying the cheque will be paid when provided for. Nothing else.'

All week, Simpson never stirred out except at night. When darkness fell he would slink out, coat collar turned up, hat pulled well down over his eyes so that the eye-shade was hidden. He always took the back road into the hills, a narrow stony road, little frequented after dusk. As far as the metal bridge he would go – a good Irish mile from the village. He sauntered along, trying to give the impression of a person deep in thought. Hands clasped behind his back, head bent in meditation, he was sometimes greeted with the salutation:

'Nice night, Father.'

A wordless growl was his only acknowledgement. Back in the house, he would drink a few beers and go to bed.

At the end of the week he went up again by bus to the city. He went first to see Doctor Roche who expressed himself satisfied with the progress of the affected eye.

'It's a slow, delicate business, dealing with ocular complaints. But if *you* do your share of the work, we'll have you right in no time. In the meanwhile we'll keep you on the calcium. You seem to be reacting well to it. I'll give you another box of tablets.'

As he was filling the box, he said:

'I've arranged for you to see Doctor Savage. You can go across to him now.' He hesitated uncertainly, twisting the lid of the box back and forth. 'He is a first-class man, Savage. I have great faith in him. But ... er ... don't pay too much attention if he starts theorizing. He is one of the up-and-coming men in his branch of the profession. Full of new-fangled theories. You know the type?' He waved his hand airily. 'Good fellow, though, knows his job.'

Doctor Savage turned out to be a burly young man in his early thirties. Crew cut. Leather skinned. Tweedy. Framed photographs of rugby and golf teams hung around the walls of the consulting room. A glass cabinet full of cups and medals stood against one wall.

'Now, Mr. Simpson,' he said. 'Doctor Roche has provided me with the full facts of your case. But I would like you to describe, in your own words, the onset, symptoms and subsequent course of your complaint. I find that sometimes a fresh fact emerges even after constant reiteration.'

When Simpson had finished, Doctor Savage said:

'We will concentrate first on stopping the haemorrhage. When that has been done, we can commence tracking down the causation.'

Going to a sterilizing cabinet, he took out a syringe and a needle.

'Your blood is not coagulating as it should.'

He fitted the needle to the end of the syringe barrel.

'Take off your jacket and roll up one of your shirt sleeves.'

He looked up.

'Tell me, when you cut yourself shaving, do you have any trouble staunching the blood?'

From a shelf of bottles, he selected a squat rubber-capped one, containing a milky fluid.

'Not that I've noticed,' said Simpson.

The doctor plunged the needle through the rubber cap. Eased up the plunger gently.

'We'll pump calcium into you. That should do the trick.'

'But Doctor Roche has already put me on calcium treatment.'

Doctor Savage looked at him quizzically over the needle tip.

'Orally, I suppose?'

Simpson stopped rolling up his shirt sleeve.

'Orally? I'm afraid I don't get you, Doctor.'

'Through the mouth. In pill or tablet form.'

'Oh, I see. Calcium tablets, that's what he's put me on.'

Fumbling in his jacket, he produced the box.

'These. Two every three hours.'

The doctor crossed the room, glanced casually at the box, straightened out Simpson's bared arm.

'Hold it steady. It will only be a pin prick.'

Gripping a fold of upper arm flesh, he deftly inserted the needle and commenced to ease down the plunger.

'Don't you think,' he said, 'that this lot will go through your system quicker than swallowing a tablet and waiting for your digestive organs to process it?'

He withdrew the empty syringe.

'Don't move,' he said.

He dabbed the tiny puncture with a wisp of cotton wool soaked in iodine.

'Now you can roll down your sleeve.'

As Simpson pulled on his jacket, the doctor said:

'You'll be seeing Doctor Roche this day week, I suppose?'

'I will.'

'You'd better call in on me after you've finished with him. I'd like to see how this injection has taken.'

'Do you play golf?' he asked, as they moved to the door.

At Simpson's look of surprise, he corrected himself.

'*Did* you play golf?'

'No, I never took it up. Just as well, as it's turned out.'

With hearty gesture, the doctor slapped Simpson's back.

'Look here, old man. You don't want to take Roche too seriously. He is like a P.T. Instructor who calls for twenty press-ups to get ten. Exercise in moderation won't do you a bit of harm. But go easy on the liquor.

'And other allied frolics,' he added, with a short bark of laughter.

All the way back to Glenard, Simpson pondered over the two interviews. One doctor advising tablets, the other injections. One counselling austerity, the other moderation. The one thing they had in common was disapproval of the other's method. Of the two, Simpson decided that he preferred Savage. A much more sensible man. Did not ask the impossible. But what did he mean by that last remark? *Other allied frolics.* Was it crumpet he was hinting at? Hardly. He must know that it was injurious to a man's health to be too long without his rations. It would bring on wet dreams. Depression. A nervous breakdown. God knows what else. Look what it does to the clergy. Go into any hotel in Ireland and you'll be out of luck if you don't see one of them surrounded by a squad of young things hanging on his words and murmuring: 'Yes, Father' and: 'No, Father' and: 'You'll take another wee drink, Father' and them blind to the sickness staring out of his poor wretched eyes. Well, they couldn't be any worse than yourself stiting here with eyes a damned sight sicker and no one to cosset and console you. At this thought a flood of self-pity overwhelmed him and he crouched lower in his seat, bewildered, despondent, lonely.

It was still daylight when he stepped off the bus at the foot of the village. He squared his shoulders. Tipped back his hat. Settled the eye-shade firmly into place. Don't let these pisshawks know how you feel, he adjured. It would be as good as a week's holiday to them if they got the chance to gloat over your misfortune.

Jauntily he swaggered up the village street, nodding his head casually to the murmured greetings, the statement machine inside his skull clicking up their Bank balances as he passed.

Twitcher Hogan – long string of misery, standing sentinel outside his empty shop, blood-shot eyes winking out frantic messages in Morse. Debit: £1,275. Authorized overdraft: £1,000. Security: Deeds of Licensed Premises (dirty, run down, poorly stocked). You're running too high, chum. If you don't stop drinking the shelves bare, you're going to walk the plank. Coo Reilly – slinking along with his shoulder brushing the walls and his shifty eyes forever sliding away from your gaze. Pro. Note: £27. Reducing by £1 every three months on renewal date. Your bailsman will have to pay up if you don't do better. And how are we this fine morning, Miss Po-Face Post Office? Your nose flattened to the window for fear you would miss something. At your time of life – and you'll never see seventy again – it's time you stopped raddling your ancient dial. That little personal loan of yours to buy the T.V. set is two instalments overdue. When are you going to come across? It wouldn't look so good, would it, if we had to take steps to re-possess the bloody set. Och, is it you, Mr. Patrick Hames Aloysius Galvin, sitting out on your garden seat, airing your paunch. Would you ever stoop down and bare your high-class draper's, milliner's and haberdasher's backside till I run my tongue reverently round its grooves and creases, in honour of the £15,000 you keep on deposit in the name of yourself and your estimable wife, Sarah Anne (from whose lacerating tongue. Oh Lord deliver us) to be payable to them or either of them. Well, glory be to God, if it isn't the Master, taking the middle of the road, as usual. Sure, who would blame you? In your exalted position it would be asking too much from you if you were forced to rub shoulders with the commonalty. Still, you keep a nice credit balance and a good account is surely worth a nod of the head.

At the private door of the Bank he turned round and surveyed the village. It seemed to him that every head was turned in his direction. The evening hush spoke of straining ears and pent up breathing. Eyes sparkled in happy anticipation. Tongues dried up with urgency of disclosure.

Simpson turned his key in the lock, glanced back over his shoulder.

'Buck the lot of you,' he said, quite loudly, 'for a crowd of hungry corbies.'

The slamming door disturbed two seagulls, perched on one of the chimneys of the Bank house. With complaining cries they rose on barely moving pinions, circling twice before whirling away seawards in the grip of a made-to-measure current of wind.

Now began for Simpson a cycle of events that, by their regular recurrence, came to assume the inevitability of Greek tragedy.

For perhaps ten or twelve days of depression he observed, in his own fashion, the precept of moderation urged on him by his doctors. He avoided heavy physical exertion, abstained from swimming, squatted instead of stooping, rationed his drinking down to perhaps a half-dozen bottles of beer and a beaker of whiskey a day.

Above all, he kept away from Delia. Austerity, he figured out, would be ineffective if he indulged in bouts of fuckery.

Not that he could get the thought of her out of his head. Far from it. The longer he stayed away from Creevan, the more she occupied his mind. Huddled up in bed at night, a prey to violent desire, her image materialized before him. Obedient to his will, she performed the most abstruse contortions, twisting herself into ever more original postures for the satisfaction of her lord and master. Even in daylight he would fall into reveries during which he performed incredible stallionlike feats on a swooning passion-drunk Delia.

Always these fantasies ended in an invocation for the grace needed to overcome his impure thoughts. Three Hail Marys would be reeled off and a quick Act of Contrition. The respite gave him time to realize the desperation of his plight. Depression would descend once more on him, quenching the last spark of lust.

During this period, Annie fussed and fretted over him, giving unwanted advice, feeding him with invalid dishes, suggesting various infallible cures.

Gruel, beef-tea, egg-flip were daily provender. Carrigeen moss boiled in milk and boiled sloak – regular fare. She even tried to persuade him – unsuccessfully – to sup a huge plate of nettle soup.

'You don't know what's good for you, sir,' she said. 'In the old days these were the only remedies to be had. And look at the grand healthy eyes they had. You'd never see a body wearing specs if you walked the length and breadth of the parish.'

The climax came when she tried to persuade him to drink a cup of mare's milk every night.

'A notorious cure for weak eyes. Many's the time I heard the old people talk of it when they'd be sitting round the fire at night. Oh, a deadly cure for man or beast.'

'Annie, for the love of God, have sense. Mare's milk! You'll be feeding me on ass's piss before you've finished.'

Undiscouraged, she continued her exhortations, pressing him to call in a healer – the seventh son of a seventh son – an old and infirm man living in lonely squalor on a small farm high up in the hills.

'Ah, you should give him a trial, Mr. Simpson. There's great power in his hands. I seen him meself once put a wriggling worm on the flat of his hand. As God is me judge, didn't it give a great shake and stiffen out straight as a rush. Struck dead with the power in his hand. It was a dread to see it. A total dread.'

'Are you gone clean mad, Annie? Surely you don't believe that that old fool has a cure for eye trouble? Don't you know that he's been drawing the blind pension himself for years past?'

'I don't care, sir. You should give him a chance.'

So it went on till one morning Simpson would find the haemorrhage clearing up and normal vision nearly restored.

His spirits rocketed. At last, he decided, the calcium treatment was taking effect. Whistling tunelessly through his teeth, he swaggered into the kitchen.

'You can chuck out the remainder of that wretched kelp, Annie. It won't be needed any more.'

'Now, Mr. Simpson. You've said that before. You're only tempting Providence talking that way.'

'It's different this time.' He squinted, one-eyed, at the sun-gleaming window. 'There are only a few little pockets of blood left unabsorbed. I'm as right as a going clock.'

'Till the next time. That's all I say. And if you *are* cured itself, it's the sloak and the carrigeen moss that can take the credit. I always said the old remedies were the best.'

He stretched his arms, yawning widely.

'Bacon and eggs this morning, Annie. No seaweed.' Two-fisted he drummed on his chest. 'Make it two eggs. And don't spare the bacon. Lazarus was never as hungry coming back from the dead.'

'You'll be careful, won't you, sir? Don't be rushing off, doing what you were told not to, just because things have taken a wee turn for the better.'

'You're not a great comfort to me, Mrs. Mahony. It strikes me you've enjoyed brewing those foul concoctions so much that you're sorry to see me on the mend.'

'Oh, you shouldn't say things like that, sir. Every night I offered up a decade of the rosary for you.'

'Well, between the boiled kelp and the praying, you've done a job on me.'

Back at work in the office, the cashier found him tolerant, easy-going, cheerful. He approved of McCann's action in sending off the faulty typewriter for repairs. He praised the replacement machine sent down for temporary use. He found no fault with the running of the office during his absence. Even the Mullen fiasco failed to irritate him. When instructed by Head Office to seek the assistance of the Edgware Road office of the Bank in the recovery of the debt, he only jeered mildly as he typed out the letter.

'A fat lot of use this will be. Just picture one of those London blokes – hard hat, striped trousers, rolled umbrella – trying to bring Mr. Foxy Mullen to heel. It's sending a boy on a man's errand. Brian'll throw a few jars into him and spin him the tale. When your man gets back to the office, he'll find he's minus the contents of his wallet. If he's not minus his striped pants as well.'

When the reply came, he could hardly read out the letter to McCann for the laughter.

'Listen to this, Mac. It's rich. *Dear Sir, I have received your letter of 2nd inst. concerning your customer, Brian Mullen. I have ascertained that he is still in residence at Gladstone Mews and is in Flat No. 3*. Wait till you hear what comes next. You'll break your arse laughing. *After three visits* – he's a persistent bugger, anyway – *I have been unable to reach him, the*

111

excuse being given by a lady – polite gentleman he is, too – *also living in the flat* – a pure coincidence, of course – *that he is out on business*. Isn't that a good one? "Out on business." The bould Brain was probably curled up in bed with the pillow stuffed in his mouth to stop the laughing. Listening to Hard Hat at the door, passing the time of day with the mott. "Yes, Moddam. I quite understand, Moddam. Perhaps if I call again, Moddam." Instead of putting his shoulder to the door and bursting it in. Listen to the way he winds up. *Obviously I will call again to see Mr. Mullen and I have also written to him to-day asking him to write to me immediately concerning his account*. Brian won't pay much heed to his letters. He'd get better results if he made a pass at the mott – it might bring Slippery Tit out from under the blankets to protect his property.'

At the end of the day, Simpson was still chuckling to himself and murmuring portions of the letter.

'*Out on business*. Queer bloody business that would be, if Master Brian was taking part in it. *A lady also living in the flat*. That should get a prize for the best understatement of the year. *Obviously I will call again*. Take care but he's trying to beat Brian to the inside track. That 'obviously' must mean that he's proper horn-mad and means to have a rattle at the guardian angel at all costs. There'll be the queer commotion in Flat No. 3, Gladstone Mews, before this offensive is called off.'

In spite of all his protestations and promises, no sooner was he on the mend than he took up once more with Delia.

This time, however, there was a difference. What had previously been a casual, though pleasant enough, diversion, had now become an imperious necessity. Delia provided the last remaining claim to the virility of which he was so proud and which was being filched from him by his doctors.

For her part, she fussed over him in the same fashion as the housekeeper.

'This can't be good for you, Jim,' was her worry, as, spent and panting, they lay sprawled in a deep nest high up in the furthermost recesses of a hay-barn, their clothes scattered about in wild abandon. 'Your heart is going like a trip hammer.' She pressed her ear to his heaving, sweating chest. 'And there's a shocking wheeze to your breathing. Did you ever tell your

112

doctors about this carry-on? It might be aggravating your poor injured eye.'

'For God's sake, catch yourself on, girl. What harm could this do anyone? If we were married, wouldn't we be at it night and morning?'

'Maybe so. But all the same it worries me a lot. I'd feel responsible if something happened to you.'

But Delia's pity was spiced by the intuition that their bouts of furious love-making were now become necessary to his self-esteem – a means of propping up a sagging ego. Through this knowledge, she acquired a mastery over him that began to show itself more and more as time went on.

No longer did she submit meekly to his urgent demands. She stalled.

'Light a cigarette for me, will you, darling?' She pushed him away. Gently, but firmly. When it was lit, she lay back. 'Now, tell me something nice, Jim. You never say nice things to me any more.'

'What would you like me to say?'

'That's a silly question. When we started going out together, you were never done paying me compliments and making much of me. I must have disimproved a lot since then, for you to have become so sparing of words.'

'You've heard that old plawmaus a thousand times. Surely you don't want me to rehearse it all again?'

'And why not? Compliments never get stale. They mean more, the oftener they're repeated. It's the people themselves that get stale. Ashamed to say nice things too often for fear they'll be thought insincere. How long is it, d'you think, since you told me how sweet my hair smelt or how soft my lips?'

'If that's the line of chat you want, Delia, I'm your man. You've the best pair of props in the village. Slender ankles. Pretty calves. Thighs that are—'

'Keep your groping hands to yourself, big boy.' She sat up, smoothing down her rumpled skirt over her knees. 'Can you think of nothing else but one thing? Your mind must be a proper cesspool.'

Sometimes she would walk out on a date and he would be left sitting on a high stool in Hannah's bar, throwing back whiskeys and chasers until such time as she chose to return.

113

A glance at his wrist-watch. A long, squinting, significant glare at the bar clock.

'What kept you? Where were you till now?'

Delia ignored him.

'It's a grand night out, Aunt Han. You should take a wee stroll before you go to bed. I'll look after the bar while you're gone.'

'It's hardly worth while, Delia. It's gone closing time. I'll just put on the shutters and ramble off to me bed. I'll leave you to look after Mr. Simpson.'

When the stairs had stopped creaking and the bedroom door had clicked shut:

'How dare you cross question me like that! It's no business of yours where I was or what time I got home. You'd think I was some class of a criminal being asked to account for my movements.'

'I only asked you a civil question. And you might give me a civil answer. I've been waiting here for you for the last three hours.'

'I said I would see you tonight. I didn't say when.'

'But keeping me waiting three—'

'You should be thankful that I turned up at all. Instead of girning and growling like a pampered mongrel. I have you properly spoiled, that's what's wrong. Giving in to you over everything.'

'Hush, Delia. She'll hear you upstairs. Come here till I tell you.'

'I will not. Fine well I know what you're after. You can have one more drink and that's the finish. You'll keep to your own side of the counter too, I'll thank you.'

But sometimes she relented. Whipping off her knickers, she would fling them at him, urging:

'Come on, buster, you win.'

On an old overall, spread out on the wooden floor behind the counter, they grunted and moaned and threshed about, kicking over empty bottles, rolling against chinking cases of stout, one or other of them muttering: 'Be careful or she'll hear you,' and neither of them caring, their heedless bodies bruised by used corks and tintops, whilst the oppressive fumes of stale porter and spirits from unwashed glasses set their heads reeling, until, gasping and assuaged, they staggered to their feet – bleary-eyed, bedraggled, tousle-haired.

114

Often she said, pointing and giggling:

'Why do you keep wearing that silly old pigtail? It's dreadful-looking when it gets tossed. Some day when you're drunk I'll come creeping along and I'll . . .' Two-fingered she clipped in demonstration, 'Whip it off.'

Carefully he combed back over his forehead the dangling strands of hair.

'That'll be the sore day for you,' he said, as he replaced the comb in his breast pocket.

Picking up his glass, he tossed back the remains of the whiskey and started for the door, growling:

'I don't like that class of talk.'

She followed, grabbing him by the arm.

'I'm sorry, Jim. Don't you know well I didn't mean it? You've become shocking touchy this while back. You can't take a joke any more.'

Mollified, he allowed himself to be dragged back. Accepted the bumper of whiskey she poured out for him.

'Take something yourself, Delia,' he insisted.

'I suppose a little sherry wine would do me no harm.' She poured a liberal measure. 'Well, here's to our better acquaintance.' They clinked glasses.

Another round of drinks. And another.

'You're getting a terrible gamey look in your eyes, Jim. I wonder—' She reached over her hand. 'Tck. Tck. Tck. You're a dreadful fellow, d'you know that?'

'You're gamey enough looking yourself. Take a gawk in the mirror.'

Together they gazed at the flushed faces and tell-tale eyes.

'Well,' she sighed, 'I suppose there's nothing else for it but the floor.'

Thus, with a judicious mixture of liberality and prudence, did she hold him ever more tightly enchained whilst her ego, raw and tender from his early selfishness, began to grow a carapace of callous indifference, so that she could accept or repel at will his importunities.

It was driving back from Creevan in the early hours of the morning that the next haemorrhage occurred. He nearly ditched the car with the fright. One moment belting along at speed, tired, contented, satiated, watching his headlights mow down wide swathes of darkness as the car swung round the

115

bends in the tortuous road, whilst he dwelt happily on the notion that he would be in his bed in ten minutes' time; the next finding himself staring at the erupting column of blood gleaming scarlet against the white beam of the lights. He clapped on his brakes and pulled up the car with its off-wheels on the grass verge. Horrified, he gazed at the windscreen, watching as the blood appeared to seep up the glass, trickling in spurts, just as rain-drops gather speed and bulk as they pick up other rain-drops on their journey down the glass.

This seemed to him the worst haemorrhage so far. The flow of blood was swifter and heavier than ever before. It seemed impossible that it would become absorbed eventually and normal vision restored. The immediacy of this calamity to the debauchery that had gone before, had an appalling significance. It was undoubtedly a Divine judgement for his obstinate and continued breaking of the Sixth Commandment. Not only was he being punished for committing the sin of impurity but for breaking his sworn and solemn promise to amend his ways. There had been two – or was it three? – warnings already. But just because a haemorrhage did not come on the heels of an offence, he had chosen to ignore it. It was a gesture of defiance as surely as if he had snapped his fingers in the face of Providence. What was it the missioner had said, years ago, in the hushed, crowded, incense-laden church? Folded hands tucked into the loose sleeves of his brown habit, he stood erect in the pulpit, his pale, bearded face cold and aloof. His voice, too, cold and aloof.

Woe to the fornicator, for he shall not see God. The silence in the church became absolute. No one moved. Or breathed. Even the flickering candles seemed to wait motionless.

Half-way down the church you sat, cowering behind Lofty Logan, protected by his bulk from the dreadful searing revelation of your activities. Only once did he move – but it was enough. He stooped to pick up the rosary beads fallen from his trembling fingers and left you staring back at the calm, accusing eyes of the missioner.

And now, my dear people, he addressed you, *what of the lecherous brute who persists, night after night, in the destruction of his own soul and the soul of the unfortunate creature that he seduces. By his confessor, by his frightened victim, by his own conscience even, he has been warned and admonished.*

116

But it is of no avail. The lusts of the flesh must be satisfied: the law of God set aside!

The bearded brown-clad figure placed both hands on the plush-topped ledge, leaned far out over the pulpit. He addressed you personally. Softly. So that no one else could hear.

Let him take heed, I say. The time for repentance is short. And remember . . .

He spoke in a whisper that deafened your ears.

God is not mocked.

How did he know? Amongst the young and old and older again people thronging the church, why should the missioner have picked on him. There was only one answer to that. Cassie had spilled the whole bloody beans to this brown-robed fanatic in confession. Told him of the nightly sessions in the turf-shed, stretched out together on the thick carpet of turf-mould, lights left on in kitchen, scullery and washhouse so that no one – unsuspecting parents or inquisitive strangers – could chance upon him riding the maid. Told of the stolen nerve-wracking moments spent in her tiny eyrie high above the kitchen floor, reached only by a rickety creaking ladder and smelling and smelling and smelling in a choking tingling randy way of dirty underwear, unemptied slops and rancid sweat. Or of the hurried couplings on mattresses newly-turned during her morning bed-making. Or of all the other dangerous occasions of sin they had frequented so often and so gaily.

The missioner raised high his two clenched fists and, shaking them in frenzy, shouted to the rafters:

GOD IS NOT MOCKED!

Those frightening words still rang in his ears. Why had he been so foolish as to imperil, not only his immortal soul, but the very sight of his eyes, in the pursuit of a lustful intimacy that he had known in his heart to be wrong and sinful? Never had he believed that the punishment for his offence would be so immediate or so condign. But that was no excuse for the laxity of his conduct.

He sat motionless in the car, staring down the beam of the headlights, his eyes wide open, fixed, unblinking. By now the haemorrhage had almost filled the eye and was already beginning to change colour. Thrown into relief by the glare of the lights the bright scarlet could already be seen darkening into a sombre green. Cautiously he closed his left eye, the better to judge the extent of the haemorrhage, but even this slight movement churned up the stagnant blood so that the last glimmer of light was swallowed up in swirling gloom.

Frantically, he commenced to pray, muttering aloud the Act of Contrition.

'*Oh my God, I am heartily sorry for having offended Thee and I detest my sins above every other evil because they have offended Thee and I detest my sins because they have offended Thee and I detest my sins above every other evil and I detest . . .*'

The words of the prayer eluded him. Caught up in the starting phrases he found himself repeating endlessly a gabbled gibberish. Once more he started:

'*An Act of Contrition,*' he mouthed slowly, as though he were announcing from the stage the title of a recitation.

'*Oh, my God, I am heartily sorry for having offended Thee and I detest my sins . . . I detest my sins . . . I detest my sins . . . I detest my sins.*'

Still the words escaped him. What came after *sins*? Wait now! *Because they* something or other *evil. Cause? Produce? Are the occasion of evil?* Hold on now! *And because they they they offend Thy gracious majesty. And most of all.* What the hell comes after that? *Most of all. Most of all, because . . . because . . . because . . . they deserve Thy dreadful punishment . . . because they have crucified my gentle Saviour and most of all . . .* no, that was said already. Better start again. *An Act of Contrition. Oh, my God, I am heartily sorry for having offended Thee because . . .* It was this *because* that was making a hames of the whole thing. You keep coming back to it the same as that line in some poem or other. *The same old wheaten biscuit that we had met before.* Where had he heard that poem? It wasn't heard. It was read. Read in an illustrated book. With a picture of the biscuit in the exact centre of a plate. It was a small biscuit. Though it could have been a large biscuit on a larger plate. Rough and grainy it was. With a flat bottom and a curved top. Like a Nissen hut. That's exactly what it was like. And the people kept coming back to it all the time. They couldn't get away from it. One of them straddling something like a broom handle with a horse's head at the top and a small wheel at the bottom. Another strutting along beating a drum.

118

The third one, a girl, blowing a toy trumpet. The book was heavy and the lettering large and when you humped your knees in the bed you could prop up the book against them and turn the pages to and fro like the Mass book on the stand that the Mass servers carry back and forth from each side of the altar, bowing politely to each other when they happen to meet at the foot of the carpeted strip of the marble stairs and lifting the priest's vestments so that he would be free to lift the chalice that the altar boys fill with the wine and water from the little glass jugs and pour water over the priest's extended hands and hand him a cloth for drying them and, most important of all, strike with a gong-stick the bell for the Elevation and the Sanctus and the *Domine-non-sum-dignus* that goes throbbing on and on and on like a dinner gong and you can stop it any moment by just touching the edge of it and Mother says next year perhaps they'll let you serve Mass and you'll be able to ring the bell yourself instead of giving her headaches practising with the dinner-gong and that the nuns were to blame for encouraging you to play at saying Mass when you should have been playing games like normal children and what's more it was a sacrilege allowing youngsters to ape the holy sacrifice of the Mass with their toy vestments, toy chalice, toy altar vessels and even a toy Mass book complete with markers of coloured silk and actually the window ledge of the cloakroom laid out as an altar and the older boys taking turns at acting as celebrant and the younger ones squabbling about whose turn it was to ring the Mass bell and Mother says it wouldn't have been so bad if they had derived any benefit from it but once during Holy Week a convent boy was clerking at first Mass in the parish church and he didn't know any better than to use the draped-in-purple gong instead of the whirling rattler and never would she forget it to her dying day for it sounded for all the world like clods thudding on a coffin lid—

Thud! Thud! Thud!

Simpson jerked awake. Someone was tapping on the car window beside him. A light shone. Behind the light a voice.

'Are you all right, Mr. Simpson?'

He rolled down the window, painfully conscious of the idling engine and blazing headlights.

'Is that you, Sergeant? Nothing wrong, I hope?'

A smothered gasp registering – surprise? Derision? Anger?

119

'Oh, no. Just out on patrol. I saw your car pulled up on the grass verge. Lights on and motor running. I thought it as well to investigate. You never know what you'd find.'

'As a matter of fact, Sergeant. I just pulled in for a few minutes to rest my eyes. You know of course, I've had a bit of eye trouble recently.'

' 'Deed we were all sorry to hear of it, Mr. Simpson. Will you be able to get home all right, d'you think? At this hour of the morning a man's not at his best.'

Blast him to hell with his sarcastic cracks.

'I'll just put on this eye-shade, Sarge.' He rummaged in his pockets. 'I seem to have left it in my other suit. Ah, well, I'll have to manage without it.' He revved up the engine. 'Good night, Sergeant.'

'Good night, sir.'

The torch was switched off. Above the noise of the engine he heard the sing-song Kerry accent.

'Take it easy, sir. And try to keep between the ditches.'

Simpson was so rattled that he bungled a gear change, wincing at the rasping give-away sound. What a rotten bloody bit of bad luck. On top of all your troubles, meeting up with the Sergeant. Still it could be worse. If it had have been the new Guard, you might have been pulled in for being drunk in charge. That would have made nice reading in the paper. *'Bank Manager sleeps it off. Sole occupant of ditched car. Pleads eye strain. Attracted by the glare of headlights and the sound of a running motor, Guard Spencer at –* he glanced at his wrist-watch – Good God! is that the time it is? Four o'clock in the morning! No wonder the Sergeant heckled you.

Carefully he drove home, sitting stiffly upright, his head askew as he squinted one-eyed at the slowly swinging, dipping, lifting beam of the headlights.

His next visit to the city was most depressing. The vision of his right eye was still completely obscured by the haemorrhage. Both doctors were of the opinion that the eye condition was steadily worsening.

Doctor Roche – a gentle, kindly, worried hobgoblin – accompanied his words with a slow-swinging pencil that tapped the table-edge softly, emphasizing his message with the crisp assurance of a metronome.

'There is no need to worry, Mr. Simpson. Your complaint is following the classical lines of all retinal disorders. It may sound a platitude to say that things must get worse before they get better. But in this case—' The pencil hesitated in mid-air, a prudent, cogitating metronome. 'How shall we put it . . .' The metronome started ticking again, its problems solved. 'It is not enough for us to stop the haemorrhage occurring. We must go a step further and discover what is causing these effusions. For undoubtedly . . .'

Simpson listened in dismay. Damn the hair I care what is causing the bloody trouble. All I want is to have it stopped. Sitting up there on your toadstool like a leprechaun hammering the sole of a shoe and telling me that I'll have to go on suffering these bloody haemorrhages until such time as you can get round to finding out what hell is causing them. A fine specialist you are.

'. . . in the meanwhile, we will put you on to a fresh course of calcium tablets. Kalzarin. An entirely new prophylactic. More potent than the calcium treatment you have been already undergoing.'

He rummaged in his desk drawer. Broke open a packaged bottle. Unstoppered it.

'Now, let's see,' he said, glancing at the label. 'Oh, yes. They are in capsule form. Take one after each meal. You can wash it down with a glass of water.'

He shook out a generous handful. Popped them into a tiny envelope on which he scribbled a few words.

'You will be seeing Doctor Savage, of course? He rang me up last week to put me in the picture. He is giving you a course of injections. I believe, Calcium, he tells me.'

There was a dry smile on his face.

'Well . . . er . . . I believe . . .'

'He has a bee in his bonnet about injections. He is probably pumping calcium lactate into you.'

'He didn't say . . .'

'It can do no harm and may do good.'

They reached the door.

'But remember, Savage is a sound fellow. If your trouble stems from a blood deficiency, he will pinpoint it. He is the best blood man in the city.'

Doctor Savage wasted no time. A quick examination of the

already dilated pupil with the ophthalmoscope. A purposeful jingling of instruments. At last:

'Roche phoned before you arrived. He is troubled about the continuing haemorrhages. I am inclined to agree with him. There is evidence, in fact, of a worsening of the haemorrhage condition.'

Simpson gulped.

'A more drastic treatment is indicated. Roll up your shirt sleeve, please. Higher still. That will do.'

Round the bared upper arm he wound a length of rubber strapping.

'A massive dose of calcium injected intravenously. That should do the trick.'

From the glass-topped instrument table he picked up a large syringe, its glass barrel already filled with a milky fluid. Poising the needle point over the bulging vein in the crook of the elbow, he said:

'Keep still now. This is a tricky business.'

Cautiously he inserted the needle. Withdrew the plunger ever so slightly.

'Good!' he said, at the sight of the little slobber of blood in the base of the barrel. He glanced up at Simpson.

'One must be careful to penetrate only one wall of the vein. If no blood shows in the syringe, both vein walls have been pierced and the needle must be inserted anew.'

Stooping once more over the bared arm, he murmured:

'Hold tight now. Here we go.'

Swiftly, smoothly, he pushed down the plunger.

For perhaps four heartbeats the molten mass raced through his veins. So fast did it travel that it seemed to reach every part of his body at the same instant. His toes and finger-tips burned: his skull crackled with bubbling lava, scalding the back of his eyes and twisting his stricken features into a lunatic grin: his chest was a seething, scorching congestion of flame: his guts writhed in agony.

Normalcy returned before his loosening bowels had given way.

'That dose has gone straight into the blood stream,' the doctor said proudly, as he loosened the strapping. 'If anything will staunch the blood leakage, it is this treatment.'

He glanced at Simpson.

122

'Are you feeling all right?'

'Game ball, doctor. It was just that I thought for a minute you'd given me the wrong dose. It went through me like boiling oil.'

'You won't notice it the next time.'

As Simpson was rolling down his shirt sleeve, the doctor asked: 'You are observing all the injunctions laid down for you, of course?'

'Oh, yes, doctor.'

'No violent exercise? No heavy drinking? In fact, no extremes in anything?'

'No, doctor. I'm taking things very easy.'

'Good.'

'Just one thing more.' He cleared his throat. 'If you were a married man I would be forced to ask if you were having intimacy with your wife. But, of course, as you are a bachelor ...'

He paused. Waiting.

Simpson leant forward, on his face – he hoped – an expression of guileless innocence. What's behind this feeler? Does he suspect anything? Or is he just chancing his arm?

'Yes?' he urged.

The doctor resumed, his voice lowered confidentially.

'As a matter of fact, the sexual act could quite easily cause a haemorrhage. That is, of course, if the person was suffering from a retinal complaint. There is a certain amount of stress associated with this ... er ... activity.'

He rubbed a judicious forefinger against the wing of his nose.

'Actually, Mr. Simpson, it could be classified as a particularly violent form of physical exercise. One to be undertaken – I am sure you will agree – only by someone feeling in the whole of his health.'

Eyes closed, mouth gaping, the doctor laughed – a muted, wheezing laugh.

'Huh-huh-huh-huh-huh! Did you get that, old man? Feeling in the whole of his health. Bloody good, what?'

At Simpson's puzzled expression, he burst out laughing again.

'Don't you get it? Feeling in the whole.' With right forefinger and loosely-circled left fist, he prodded out an explanation. 'The hole. Get it? Came out of me without thinking. Strange, eh?'

123

Simpson joined in the renewed laughter with a surly cackle. The bloody idiot. What does he take me for? A shagged-out old man no longer fit to screw a woman? I'm as good a man as he is any tick of the clock. There's more fat than muscle on that carcase of his. Put a pair of fifty-sixes into his mitts and see what he can do. I'll bet he couldn't shoulder them. Let alone hoist. And that's the hallion's making out I'm a class of a fucking invalid. Unable to mount the dickey. Well, Delia could tell him otherwise.

Depression gripped him as he remembered that his last session with Delia was more than likely the direct cause of the present haemorrhage. The doctor was right. That kind of carry-on, with the sweat rolling off you and the blood battering away at the backs of your eyes and you trembling and gasping for breath: that could be the whole cause of your trouble. He would have to cut it out, once and for all. That was the only solution.

The doctor was talking once more. He tried to concentrate.

'. . . and in many cases, where the haemorrhages have gone on unchecked, the trouble may spread to the sound eye. This sympathetic reaction is one we must try to avoid. The further danger is that, with the continued deterioration of the retina, displacement may occur.'

'What exactly does that mean, doctor?'

'The retina becomes detached, with resulting loss of vision.'

'Complete blindess?'

'I'm afraid so. But this would be the result of wilful neglect. Of the continued failure to observe the restrictions imposed on him for his own good. In short, of the complete breakdown of the doctor-patient relationship.'

Once more he paused, examining, with every appearance of interest, the fingernails of each hand.

'Of course, a case can arise where a patient of abnormal physique, accustomed to strenuous exercise and the consequent ingestion of more than the average quantity of food and drink, mistakenly believes he is complying with his doctor's injunctions.'

Polishing the nails of one hand on the palm of the other, he looked up.

Simpson stared back at the shrewd, calculating eyes. He's a cagey gentleman, all right. Waiting for you to commit yourself. Buck all information he'll get. Not if he probes from now till nightfall. He's too bloody ikey altogether, Doctor bloody Savage.

'That situation could very well apply in your case, Mr. Simpson. You are a man of great physical strength, a devoted athlete and like all athletes,' he smiled winningly, from one athlete to another, 'able to stow away a considerable cargo of liquor.'

Simpson was not to be drawn.

'Tell me, now, how many drinks would you have had last night in the local? Roughly?'

That's a good one! *Roughly*. He's got his eye on the ball, all right.

'I haven't been in a pub since this last haemorrhage occurred.'

'But you are not on the water wagon?'

'Oh, no. I take a few gargles each night before going to bed.'

'No great harm in that. The night before the haemorrhage did you move out for a few drinks?'

'As likely as not, I did.'

'Did you have many?'

'No more than any other night.'

'Six, shall we say?'

'It's hard to tell.'

'A dozen.'

'I never keep count of drinks. It's a mean class of a habit.'

'Three dozen.'

'What do you think I am? A swill bucket?'

'Well, at least we know you had more than a dozen and less than three dozen. Did you do any heavy lifting or hauling?'

'Not that I remember.'

'No exertion? Of *any* kind?'

Ho-ho! What the hell is he hinting at now?

'Nothing that would cause you to sweat or breathe heavily? Or set up an abnormal pressure of blood on the retina of the eye?'

Did you get a load of that? Now he's coming out into the open. *Sweating and breathing heavily. Abnormal pressure of blood*. Isn't he the dirty-minded blackguard? And the persistent one, too?

125

'It was a quiet night. I drank up my few drinks and cleared off home like a solid citizen.'

It's true enough, too. Nobody was roaring. And you walked out the bar door sober as a judge.

'Mr. Simpson,' said the doctor. 'I have revised my earlier opinion. I believed it possible to clear up this retinal condition without having to alter very much your normal way of life. Now I fear we will have to take more drastic measures.'

Critically he examined each individual fingernail, polishing it gently with the thumb of the opposite hand.

'The injection you have been given just now is very powerful. In my opinion it is quite capable of halting these haemorrhages. But it cannot be effective without complete relaxation on your part.'

The nails of one hand were now polished. He turned to the other.

'You have been an active man all your life. It is understandable that you find it difficult to relax. But relax you must. There is only one way, in your case, to achieve relaxation. And that is—' he glanced up, 'the bed.'

He brushed invisible fragments of cuticle from his hands and got up.

'I think it advisable – in fact, essential – that you spend at least a week in bed. A fortnight or three weeks would be better but I fear you might find that too rigorous.'

'A week in bed! Surely, Doctor, that's not necessary.'

'It certainly is. These haemorrhages are becoming heavier and more frequent. It could be a very serious matter for you if they are not curbed.'

'I know, but—'

'This is not a matter for argument, Mr. Simpson. If I do not get co-operation, I shall be compelled to drop your case.'

'I am sorry, Doctor. I will do as you say.'

'That's better.'

The ugly frown melted into a comradely grin.

'And it might be no harm to cut out the night-caps. What do you say?'

Under the soothing, encouraging, patting hand Simpson was propelled to the door.

Out in the street, he held in till he had rounded the corner. Then:

'You goddam son-of-a-bitch!' he snarled, glaring at a bowler-hatted oncomer, who promptly stepped off the pavement saying:

'Excuse me.'

It was the housekeeper who bore the burden of the ensuing week. Up and down the stairs she panted, a score of times a day, at the shouted summons from the bedroom. More often than not, it was merely company Simpson wanted. So Mrs. Mahony sat wheezing in a chair at the foot of the bed, gasping out answers to his endless questions.

'Are the County Council ripping up the pavement at the head of the town? I hear the sound of drilling.'

'Is the creamery manager on the beer? I'm nearly sure it was his voice I heard shouting outside the hotel last night.'

'Who's ringing the Angelus bell now? It was twenty minutes late this morning. And he didn't give the full dozen strokes for the *Let us pray*.'

'Any more word of that young Dillon blackguard who poled the three Ballybawn ones? I'll bet he makes tracks for Omagh to join the *Skins*.'

Mrs. Mahony always waited for the bumbling too-guileless questions to reach their goal.

'Was Morty Ryan round with the fish-lorry this morning? Did he say what the fishing's like in Creevan?'

'You didn't see Dr. Madden in the village recently? There's talks of him applying for a dispensary in Galway city.'

'They say Hannah Murphy's doing a great trade in the bar these days. Open till all hours of the morning. It's well for her she has the niece staying there to help her. Or has she gone back to England?'

Mrs. Mahony's stock response was to sniff, shift from one huge hip to the other, and say:

'Is it that one?'

Back in the kitchen, delft rattled and chinked, pots were banged down, cupboard doors slammed shut. Sometimes she stopped, saucepan in one hand, steel wool scrubber in the other, staring into space.

Then a shout from upstairs.

She dried her hands on her apron. That's His Lordship now.

127

Wonder what it is this time. Up the stairs she waddled, puffing and grunting.

Through the half-open door she saw him sitting up in bed, a handkerchief held to one eye. Stricken, she stood there. The fingers of one hand plucking at her lower lip.

'What's keeping you, Annie?' he called.

She shambled into the room.

'Nothing the matter?' she asked.

'Haven't you eyes in your head?' he said, sourly.

'Och, no!' She lifted her hands in a small gesture of panic. 'Another haemorrhage. It's not possible. Not when you're lying resting, surely?'

He glared at her.

'Is the dinner ready yet?'

'I'll bring it up to you in ten minutes.'

'You'll bring me up a freshly laundered shirt out of the hot air press and I'll be down in ten minutes for dinner.'

'Don't tell me you're getting up out of your bed and you after bursting a blood vessel?'

'Stop blathering, and fetch up the shirt. Mightn't I be as well up on my feet as lying here bleeding like a stuck pig.'

'But, Mr. Simpson, dear, you must do what the doctors—'

'Fuck the doctors!' he roared. 'BRING . UP . the BLOODY . SHIRT.'

'You'll get the shirt without using all that bad chat. And I still say the doctors told you to stay in bed and stay in bed you should.'

'Look here, Annie,' he said patiently. 'These two doctors have been treating me for weeks past. Stuffing me full of damn all else but ground limestone. And it's only worse I'm getting. It strikes me very forcibly I'd get better value and more results having an occasional office read for me.'

'You should try Father Fletcher. They say he has a powerful office. But I still think you should do what the doctors tell you. Didn't they warn you—'

'The SHIRT!'

Annie brought him the shirt and returned downstairs, where she laid the dining-room table and got the dinner ready for dishing up. As she worked, she kept up a continuous muttered litany:

'God keep us from all harm. It's a terrible thing, too. Burst-

128

ing blood vessels. The poor fellow. It's a terrible affliction. God protect us from the like. It's a fret to man what'll happen. You can't tell from one day to the next. Everything is in the hand of God. Sure we can only pray to Himself and His blessed Mother.'

When Simpson came down, she fussed over him, pleading:

'More meat? A spoonful of peas? Another potato? You're only picking at your food. Sure, you must eat something. Maybe a wee helping of custard and prunes? I made it specially for you today, Mr. Simpson. They say custard is very beneficial for the eyes. What about an egg-nog, then? I could whip up one for you in a few minutes.'

Simpson refused to be tempted. He ate sparingly. Spoke but little. Made no attempt to conceal his depression.

Dinner finished, he moved out to the hall. Picked up his hat from the rack.

'Don't stay back for me,' he said. 'I may be late.'

'Are you going motoring?' she called after his retreating steps.

'Yes. Have you any objections?'

She heard the scrape of the back door opening.

'I'll leave the tea in the oven for you. You'll drive carefully?' she begged the closing door.

Worried, she stood at the kitchen window. Listening to the car start up in the garage. Watching him park it at the pavement edge whilst he closed the garage door. Shuffling rapidly to the front door as the car started off.

Cautiously she peered round the jamb of the half-opened door.

It's not hard to tell where he's heading for. Aye! There you are! He's turned off for Creevan Bay. That's a journey'll do him a power of good. Drinking till he's half stupid and then tackling that young Delia one. No wonder his blood vessels won't stand up to it. Sure, it would kill an iron man. What's Hannah Murphy doing that she doesn't cop on what's happening? Maybe she thinks she's going to make a match between them. Well, she has her porridge. Mr Simpson's been going the roads too long to fall for that kind of knavery. He's put too many through his hands. Though, God knows, with the men you can be sure of nothing. They'll stick it out like soldiers till they begin to come up in years. Then they'll get stuck on some young chit of a thing that'll run them into an early grave with ravening and roistering. And you could be all wrong. He's maybe going down to Creevan to see Doctor Madden. Didn't you hear him say he had lost all faith in the other pair. Bet you for anything that's his errand. They're great pals, the pair of them. Always were. They used to drink together a lot. You'd never see them out of Hannah Murphy's. Perhaps that's where they'll finish up. The pair of them. If they do the Big Fellow will be sniffing after a bit of tail when he has the few jars in. And he'll have Delia Clifden cocking it up for him.

Mrs. Mahony closed the door and went back to her housework, muttering and gesticulating in anger at the thought of Simpson leaning over the bar counter, glass in hand, pouring out his troubles into the shrewd, cunning, contriving ear of the bould Delia.

The housekeeper was wrong. When Simpson got to Cleggan Cross, he bore left instead of taking the Creevan road. Half a mile up this side road, he stopped the car at Cleggan church – a grim, T-shaped building, without steeple or other adornment, sited in the middle of a graveyard overgrown with weeds, out of whose depths emerged a rabble of reeling, bedraggled headstones. Glancing furtively around, he swaggered self-consciously up the cement path to the main door, dipped a perfunctory finger into the turbid contents of the grimy holy water font and tip-toed up the bare wooden stairs to the balcony, where he knelt down on the front bench, his elbows sprawled out on the ledge of the timber barrier. The church was empty, though four candles still flickered in the candelabra before the High Altar. Sunlight slanting down from stained glass windows made pools of colour – red, green, blue, gold – on the white marble of the altar steps. The peaceful quiet was only emphasized by the arthritic creakings of ancient timber and the scurry and squeak of tiny unseen creatures.

Simpson, trying to collect his thoughts into some form of invocation for help, sought inspiration from the statuary. From Saint Peter, his bearded features stern and intolerant: from the bland, black countenance of Saint Martin: from the sugary smile of The Little Flower: from the replendent mummery of the Child of Prague. He prayed to the life-size statues of The

130

Sacred Heart and the Blessed Virgin on the two side altars. At last he sought aid from the Presence behind the bronze door of the Tabernacle.

As he prayed, he noticed the trickle of people beginning to occupy the pews alongside the confessional box. For a moment he was puzzled. Then he remembered. Tomorrow was the first Friday of the month. There were afternoon confessions. This undoubtedly was the answer to his prayer. He would get the pot scraped, go to Holy Communion tomorrow morning and begin a new régime.

He tried to remember how long it was since his last confession. Ten years ago. Fifteen. Twenty. Thinking wildly back, he decided that it could not have been more than twenty-five years. But nearer than that he could not go. Perhaps it would be best just to tell the priest he wanted to make a general confession. They helped you out in that case. And probably were more lenient than if you were a regular. Still, you'd have to make some sort of preparation before you went into the confessional box.

The priest came out of the sacristy, bowed toward the High Altar and padded down the aisle of the church. The curtains of the confessional box had hardly fallen into place, when two penitents entered the stalls on either side.

Simpson bowed his head between the palms of his hands as though to squeeze out, like toothpaste from a tube, the dreadful tally of a generation of sinning. Before his closed eyes appeared the prayer book heading: EXAMINATION OF CONSCIENCE (for those not in the habit of frequent confession). Vainly he tried to bring to mind the list of sins so exhaustively catalogued. All he could remember was: *Did you make your Easter duty?* The answer to that one was, obviously: *I missed making it twenty-five times.* Certainly not a very good start. Maybe he should leave that one out altogether. He could start, as he did in childhood, with the small sins and work up gradually towards the ones that bring the priest's ear right up against the wire grill. A shiver went through him at the recollection of the sharp whisper: 'What's that, my child?' Of course, if you were in luck, you might get a confessor who would keep on saying: 'Yes my child. How many times?' until the job was finished. And probably send you away with only a decade of the Rosary to say for penance.

He squeezed his head harder. How used he start his roll-call of sins? *Disobedience. Telling lies. Cursing and swearing.* Yes. *Stealing?* Better include that one. The definition is very wide. Takes in the amount of work knocked up each working day. If you're not punctual in the morning – it's theft. *Missing Mass on Sundays.* That's a useful sin to tell. The priest always kicks up stink about it. Blames all your moral backsliding on not attending Sunday Mass without fail. Quite often gulps down the rest of the story without a cough. *Drunkenness?* I don't know. The definition of drunkenness is the complete loss of your senses. You'd have to be lying stocious on the side of the road to qualify for that one. If you can creep home on your own steam, damn the much is wrong with you. Whether you remember it or not. *Anger. Bearing malice.* I suppose so. *Did you? Did you?* How on earth did it run. *Did you . . . do anything wrong . . . against purity or modesty . . . by thought, word or deed?* That was the sin they all really went to town on. Scraping and rooting and nosing at it till they'd unearthed at last the shameful cache. His skin crept as waves of recollection broke over him. The disgrace. The humiliation. The teenage confusion. Once more he was kneeling in the confessional box. Head inclined towards the wire grill behind which loomed in the not-dark-enough-darkness the white, whispering, too-clearly-seen features of the priest. Whispering back – conscious of the many attentive gloating ears – the parrying answers to the ruthless interrogation: 'I can't remember, Father.' 'I'm not sure, Father.' 'I couldn't say, Father.'

To no avail. The scrupulous scouring of the pot went on. And the soundless obligato of protest.

'These bad thoughts, my child, did you take pleasure in them?' Such a silly question. What are bad thoughts for but to gloat over?

'How often?' All day long would be the answer to that one.

'Did they lead to impure actions, such as touching yourself immodestly?' Of course, they did.

'Did pollution occur?' You're damn right it did. Till the tank ran dry.

'How often?' Is it monthly, weekly or daily you want the score.

'Coarse conversations and the retailing of smutty stories, were they indulged in?' Surely to God, man.

'*How many times?*' Once a day, all day.

'*This impure converse, was it ever held with any member of the opposite sex?*' Indeed and it was.

'*Did it lead to unchaste actions? Such as touching each other immodestly?*' I suppose it might have.

'*Outside or inside the clothes?*' Look here, have a heart.

'*Did pollution occur?*' Jaykers!

'*How many times?*' Stop it, will you?

The stream of penitents was slackening. Simpson was horrified to discover that the time had come for him to move down into the body of the church and take his place at the end of the file of kneeling figures. His terror-stricken thoughts fled headlong.

'*Out of these unchaste actions, did intimacy ever take place? Was she married or single. Did you defile her virginity? Did she agree willingly? Or did you wear down her resistance? Are unlawful methods of preventing conception being used? Have you been going with this girl for long? Is it your intention to marry her? Do you intend to keep up this sinful association? Absolution cannot be granted if you do not promise, with the help of God's holy grace, to break with this girl once and for all.*

With flaming face, Simpson got up and tip-toed to the stairs, not daring to breathe until he was down them and the swing doors eased carefully shut behind him. A bloody big drink was the order of the day after that carry-on, he decided, as he started up the car and headed for Creevan Bay. In any case it might be as well if she were warned that there'd be no more nookery till the eye was completely healed. It would be madness to continue the caper knowing its consequence. Sunk in depression, he drove on, hugging his own side of the road and perring anxiously ahead in one-eyed concentration.

Six stiff Jamesons later, he was strutting up and down Hannah's bar, wearing the black eye-shade given him by Delia ('It makes you look so distinguished, Jim. Like a pirate.') and singing:

> '*Fifteen men on the dead man's chest,*
> *Yo-ho-ho, and a bottle of rum!*
> *Drink and the devil had done for the rest,*
> *Yo-ho-ho, and a bottle of rum!*'

'And, indeed, it's a rum you'll have,' she said, splashing Jamaica into his empty whiskey glass.

Simpson picked up the glass, eyeing it doubtfully.

'A bad mixture,' he said. 'It doesn't lie well on the malt. Still—' He held the glass to his nose and sniffed. 'One little golliogue can't do much harm.' Tilting the glass back, he drained it in two slow appreciative swallows.

'D'you know,' he said, 'I think I'll make that do me and beat it back home.'

'Are you not going to take me out for a run in the car?' she asked. 'It's a slack night and Aunt Hannah can manage by herself.'

'You'd be better employed tending bar. Your poor aunt could do with a rest.'

'Listen to what's talking.' She raised her voice to a higher key. Mimicking *'Your poor aunt could do with a rest!'* She leaned across the counter. 'Look here, Buster. It's me's been having the rest. We haven't had a session together for over a week. If you're thinking of schooling me for a Mother Superior, you can give over. See?'

'You know perfectly well, Delia, that Doctor Savage forbade any activity of the sort.'

'Is it that idiot? He'll stop you eating your breakfast next.'

'He claims it's that's causing the haemorrhages. The carry-on we indulge in, I mean.'

'Sure, we can take it easy. We needn't devour each other. Anyway, I think it's the drink that's the cause of it all.'

'Wasn't I lying on the flat of my back all week. Without sup nor smell of a drink. And I got a haemorrhage at the rear.'

'You got ne'er a naughty either, big boy. Remember.'

'I . . . I . . . I . . .' He stopped. Lifted the empty glass to his mouth. Went through the motions of sipping.

'Ho-ho!' she crowed, as he replaced the glass on the counter. 'Is that the way of it?'

'Pull me a bottle of stout,' he said. 'I'm thirsty.'

She made no move.

'You were thinking of me, isn't that it? And your poor head was filled with nasty, bad thoughts. And you—'

'Will you pull me that bucking bottle?'

'You're sweet, Jim.' Lightly she stroked his cheek with her fingertips.

'The bottle.'

'You'll get no such thing from me. The very idea of it! A bottle of stout. You'll get a big glass of brandy—' She took down the Hennessy bottle. '—to build up—' She uncorked it '—your lost energy.' She poured. Glug. Glug. Glug. Glug.

'Go easy, Delia.'

Glug. Glug. Glug.

'Will you stop.' He jerked his glass against the neck of the bottle, sending splashes of brandy over the counter. 'D'you want to put me on my ear?'

'What are you worrying about? It's on the house. A restorative, we'll call it.'

With a flourish, she replaced the bottle.

'Call it whatever you like, it'll do a job on me if I take it.'

'You'll take it. And it's on me it'll do a job. With your kind assistance, of course.'

'There'll be no jobs done tonight. I want to get back early to Glenard.'

'What for?'

'To be in time for confession in the parish church.'

'Are you serious, Jim? What need have you to get confession? Sure you've nothing to tell.'

'What about all the flailing we were doing night after night. Would you not tell that in confession?'

'I would not. Those were only venial sins. Don't be looking at me like that as if I'd two heads on me. Don't you know that a naughty isn't a mortal sin if the two people love each other. Isn't that common knowledge?'

'Look, Delia. For two people – unmarried people, like ourselves – to practise what the catechism calls fornication, is a mortal sin. No doubt in the world about it. And it has to be told in confession.'

'I don't believe it. Fornication is what hoors and prostitutes do. Not the like of us. Anyway, I won't have you running off to the priest, blurting out the whole thing to him. Rehearsing, for his benefit, every little detail of all we said and did for the last God knows how long.'

'It's not like that at all—'

'It won't be. I have great plans for you tonight. Drink your drink and I'll tell you.'

Simpson took a slug of brandy.

'What are you planning?' he asked.

'You're spending the night here,' she announced. 'In the spare room. Won't that be nice? And if you're good, you'll maybe have visitors.

'Look at him now,' she jeered. 'Licking his chops. No more words of confession.'

'How will you work it?' he asked.

'Dead easy. It's a wonder we never thought of it before. I'll tell Aunt Hannah you got no sleep last night with the pain in your eyes. That I'm worried about letting you off home, weighed down with drink and drowsiness. And you driving a fast car. A kind of racing model.'

He raised his glass in tribute.

'You're a walking bloody marvel, Delia. That's what you are. A credit to your sex.'

'Take your drink down with you now to the room. Before Aunt Hannah gets up. When you hear her stirring above, you can let on to be dozing in the armchair. Leave the rest to me.'

So when Hannah came down after her evening nap, it was to find Simpson sprawled out in the armchair, pulled in to the kitchen range. He was snoring gently. An empty glass at his side.

Soon the whispering voices, the soft footsteps, the heat of the room, the effects of the drink, turned pretence to reality. The snoring thickened to a throaty grunt. His head fell forward to his chest. His dangling hand knocked over, unheeded, the empty glass.

He woke to find someone going through his pockets.

'Whozzat?' He jerked upright. In the darkness Delia's face loomed over him.

'Where's the switch key?' she whispered urgently.

'What?' he muttered.

'Wake up, you big baboon.' She shook him roughly. 'I told Aunt I'd get the car keys. So you couldn't start the engine.'

He came awake.

'Here.' He reached them to her. As she moved off, he hissed: 'Pull a stout for me, for Chrissake. I'm parched.'

She was back almost immediately.

'Drink up,' she said, thrusting the tumbler of stout at him.

'The doctor's below in the bar. He could be in on top of you any minute.'

As he gulped back his drink, she said:

'I'm supposed to be persuading you to stay the night. How am I doing, d'you think?'

Putting down the empty glass, he got to his feet, yawning and stretching.

'D'you know what it is, girl. I think I'll throw myself on the bed for a wee moment. I'm properly jaded.'

He followed her to the foot of the stairs.

'You'll be well and truly jaded before I'm through with you,' she whispered over her shoulder. 'And don't take the stairs two at a time. You're supposed to be drunk.'

With exaggerated caution he mounted the stairs – leaden-footed, stumbling, breathily heavily. At the end of the corridor she opened a door and switched on the light.

'In here,' she said, dodging past him as he made to grab her. 'Aren't you the saucy article. Can't even wait till we get to bed.'

She pushed him before her into the room. Backed out again.

'I'm away,' she said. 'It would look suspicious if I stayed up here too long.'

The door closed. Reopened almost immediately.

'There's a half-pint of Jameson in the wardrobe,' she whispered. 'A jerry under the bed. And leave the door ajar.'

As she was easing back the door, she said:

'Let you not fall asleep this time.'

But he did. When she crept into the room two hours later it was to find the light on, the empty half-pint on the floor and Simpson stretched out sound asleep. Shaking and whispered pleading failed to rouse him: he merely clutched the bed-clothes tighter round himself and rolled over on his side, whimpering.

As she turned away in disgust, her attention was caught by the tangled pigtail coiled upon the pillow. Her face broke into a smile.

'It's time you were taught manners,' she murmured, tip-toeing to the dressing-table where she picked up a pair of scissors.

Back at the bedside, she gathered up the lappet of hair, grasping it as close to the skull as she dared. Slowly, cautiously, silently, she squeezed tight the blades until the shorn hair came away in her hand. Stuffing scissors and hair into her dressing-gown pocket, she moved to the door. Finger on the switch, she looked back.

'You'll thank me for this some day, Jim,' she said to the bald befringed skull.

She switched off the light and returned to her room.

He was awake when she called him in the morning. Very lovely and fresh and desirable she looked, fair hair tousled, face still flushed with sleep, slim figure emphasized by the long dark-red dressing-gown.

'Good morning, wretch,' she said. 'No need to ask did you sleep well. It's a wonder you didn't shake the slates off the roof with your snoring.'

'You didn't come back last night. What happened?'

'D'you hear this?' she asked of the ceiling. 'You didn't come back! And me spending the better part of the night trying to waken you.'

'You're codding me?'

'Indeed, I'm not. If you hadn't been such a gulligut, swallowing back the whole half-pint of whiskey, you might have stayed awake.'

'God, the bloody half-pint! I'm sorry, darling.'

'Forget it. I'm going to start the breakfast. What would you like?'

He eyed her hungrily.

'I'll give you three guesses,' he said.

'Knowing you, one would be enough. But it's breakfast I'm talking about.'

'Forget the breakfast and come in here.'

He tried to grab her dressing-gown but she ducked back out of reach.

'Aunt will be getting up any moment now,' she said.

'Come on,' he pleaded. 'Please.'

She looked over her shoulder, in a hunted manner, listening intently.

'It's too chancy,' she said.

'Come on.' He edged in towards the wall. Patted the vacant space encouragingly.

'Well.' She slowly unfastened the sash of her dressing-gown. 'We'll have to hurry, though.' She let the loosened robe fall to the floor. 'Aunt's an early riser.' She slid cautiously into the bed, huddling in beside him.

'Aren't you the right little fraud,' he said, running a hand down a cool naked flank. 'Letting on to be worried about the breakfast when you were all geared up ready for nookey.' The springs of the bed creaked madly as he rolled over on to elbows and knees. Beneath him he felt her body stiffen in alarm.

'Hush!' she whispered.

There was a sound of a door opening gently. Then soft, shuffling steps down the corridor. Towards the stairs. Soon the clink and rattle and sizzle of cooking came up from the kitchen.

Delia stirred. 'I better go,' she said.

'Not now, you can't.' He felt the protest leave her body as desire awoke.

'You'll hurry, won't you, darling?' she murmured, clutching him frantically.

Face buried in the pillow, he grunted an incoherent reply. Engulfed in passion, they strained and struggled, all caution abandoned. But for a creaking stair, they would never have noticed Hannah's approach.

'Listen!' he urged, lifting his head. The shuffling steps came to the door. Paused. A timid rap.

'Mr. Simpson.'

He tried to quell Delia's passionate squirmings.

'Yes?' he gasped.

'Will I bring up your breakfast when it's ready?'

Eyeballs bulging, head thudding with surging blood, Simpson had still enough self-control left to try to release himself.

'Don't you dare!' Delia hissed, grinding herself against him. Sweating fear and passion, he tried to steady his voice.

'I'll ... come ... down,' he squeaked in a fluty, trembling, utterly unnatural voice that seemed to proceed, not from himself but from beneath and around him, where the uproar of sighs, groans and creaking bedsprings had assumed horrid proportions.

'Are you all right, Mr. Simpson?' The handle of the door turned, gently, tentatively.

Simpson's heart missed a beat. Is the fucking door closed? Did the silly bitch leave it open behind her? How will I stop Hannah from coming in? What am I to say? His reeling, uncontrollable thoughts steadied for one invaluable second.

139

'Cramp!' he squawked. 'Leg . . . muscle . . . balled-up.'
Before Delia's mounting frenzy could sweep away all power
of speech, he managed to squeal:

'Near . . . better . . . NOOOOOOOWWWWWWWW.'

He buried the drawn-out groan in the sweat-sodden pillow
and gave himself up to the final paroxysm, heedless of the rattle
and clang of the tortured bedsprings.

When the final spasm had ceased, he rolled over on his back.

'It's better now, Hannah,' he said in a dull listless voice. 'I'll
be down directly.'

Without waiting for the departing steps, he swung himself
out of bed and padded around the room, picking up underpants, shirt and trousers from where they had been pitched the
previous night. He was murmuring irritably:

'Silly bitch! Stupid, horn-mad, careless bitch! You might
have had us both destroyed.'

A sound from the bed caused him to turn. She was laughing. Sheet stuffed into her mouth, she was breaking her heart
laughing.

'What hell's the joke?' he asked.

She took the sheet from her mouth.

'Cramp!' she wheezed. 'Leg balled up. Which one, pray?'

Another gale of quickly smothered laughter swept over her.
She pointed.

'What's eating you now?' he asked.

'Look in the mirror,' she said.

He gazed at the naked, burly, irate gentleman clutching the
garments to his hairy paunch as though he were adjusting a
sporran.

Puzzled, he turned back to the bed.

'I don't get it,' he said.

Silently she indicated, with pointing finger, the back of her
head, tapping the skull noisily.

He looked into the mirror again, turning his head sideways.

'In the name of God, you didn't—'

Choking with laughter, she nodded her head vigorously.

'You . . . You . . . You . . .' He dropped the clothes he was
carrying and advanced on the bed, his clawed hands extended
before him.

Cool, unflurried, she held up a warning hand.

'If you touch me, Jim, I'll scream the house down.'

He hesitated. Took an uncertain step forward.

'I mean it,' she said, her voice level, matter-of-fact. 'And you know what'll happen if Aunt comes up?'

Baffled, he turned away. Once more he examined, with head askew, the shorn fringe of back hair. In the mirror he could see her leaning forward. Watching him. A frown of anxiety on her face.

'I did it for your own good,' she said. 'Honestly. It looks much better now.'

'Why don't you mind your own bloody business, you meddling trollop?' he growled at the mirrored image.

Horror-stricken, he watched her nose wrinkle in distaste. Distaste verging on disgust.

'Cross-patch!' she said, leaping out of bed and pulling on her dressing-gown. At the door she turned.

'You're in the way of becoming a dry, bitter old stick,' she said, before she flounced out of the room, head high and robe fluttering defiance. She had not yet come down when he left, after breakfast, for Glenard.

When he looked back afterwards, it seemed to him astounding that he had not realized the ominous disclosure Delia's mirrored expression of disgust signified. Perhaps he was already too infatuated to accept the warning. But surely he should have grasped the implications of their changed relationship. The casual and unexplained breaking of dates. The increasing contempt for his views and susceptibilities. The switch over from fussy sympathy to irritable doubt.

'You know, Jim,' she would say. 'I really believe your whole trouble is mental. You have yourself convinced that all this commotion is going on inside your eye. Sure anyone in his right mind would know after one look that there's not a thing the matter with it.'

'But the doctors—'

'Don't talk to me about doctors. They're only codding the folk. Those two play-boys in the city are making a right idiot of you.'

'What about Doctor Madden? Didn't he—'

'Doctor Madden, is it? He knows as little as the rest of them.'

'You're very pack with him, at the same time.'

141

'And why not? He's a nice little fellow. But do you think I'd pay heed to a word he'd say or do a thing he told me?'

'Well, all I know is I can only see out of one eye at the moment. And for weeks past.'

'Stuff and nonsense, Jim. You've only to try hard. Just concentrate. If you do, you'll find you have the use of your two eyes before you know where you are.'

'You silly bitch, would you have some bloody sense?'

'There you go again! Weren't you told by the doctors it was bad for you to get excited or angry?'

'How the hell can I keep my temper when you start preaching concentration? And, anyway, what's it matter whether I get angry or not when you claim that the fucking doctors are only codding me? Such balls I never heard—'

'Would you listen to the bad chat? You never used language like that when I knew you first. Now you only have to lose an argument and you're into the cursing.'

And so another row was in the making.

In spite of Delia's jeers and his own waning confidence, he still travelled to the city once a week to see the two specialists. The routine remained unchanged. Oral treatment from one doctor: intravenous injections from the other: mutual recrimination from each. Their only common ground their certainty that a calcium derivative would eventually stop the haemorrhages. Proprietary nostrums – many of them sample products – were tried out, one after the other, without success. But still they persevered, Roche – tapping out with pencil on pad his messages of advice and sympathy: Savage – questioning, always questioning, his hearty booming voice edged with suspicion, his plump manicured hand ever on the alert for an encouraging shoulder-squeeze.

Only once did the routine vary. Savage had always, at the first attempt, succeeded in piercing with the syringe-needle the single vein-wall so that the calcium could be injected into the blood stream. On this occasion he jabbed the needle through both walls of the vein. Discovering no blood in the glass barrel of the syringe when he lifted the plunger, he said: 'Queer,' and thrust the needle once more into the distended vein.

Again and again he jabbed. No result. In desperation he grabbed Simpson's wrist, steadied the forearm against the

142

table-edge and slowly, gently, very very cautiously, eased in the needle, ignoring the steady trickle of black, stomach-turning blood spreading across the pale hairless flesh.

Simpson saw the sweat break out on the bronzed forehead as the plunger was thumbed up slowly.

'Bloody odd,' the doctor said, frowning at the milky contents of the syringe. Unloosening the rubber tourniquet, he wiped away the mess of dark ugly blood with a wad of cotton wool.

'Hold that,' he said, as he pressed the stained wad against the many punctured vein. 'Don't move your arm till I come back.'

He returned, carrying two balloon glasses.

'Drink up,' he said, handing one to Simpson. 'Doctor's orders.'

He raised his own glass chalicewise. Sniffed. Swirled the contents and drank.

'Salignac Napoleon.' He smacked his lips delicately. Drained the glass. Leaned forward confidently.

'Sorry, old boy,' he said. He watched Simpson toss back his drink.

'Feel better now, old chap?' he asked. 'Don't know what the blazes went wrong. Blunt needle maybe. Or vein walls knocked up.'

He left down his glass.

'Well,' he said, adjusting the syringe. 'Here goes. New needle. New arm. Roll up the other sleeve like a good chap.'

Warmed by the brandy, Simpson watched in detachment the needle slide in and the plunger draw up its token issue of blood. As the plunger went down, he clenched his anal muscles against the inevitable loosening of the bowels when the fiery warmth coursed through his body.

'That's better,' said the doctor, dabbing iodine on the puncture mark.

Simpson rolled down his shirt sleeves and pulled on his jacket, heedless of the flow of sporting gossip about hunters (equine), second row forwards and drunken golf dinners.

Delia was right, he conceded. These specialists were a shower of bloody banjaxers. Chancers every damned one of them. Good enough for treating crabs, piles or strictures of the flute. Maybe even good pox doctors. But let them loose on a complex organ like the human eye and they were up the creek. They didn't even know where to begin. Stuffing you full of anti-this and anti-that without ever digging up the source of the trouble. Instead of telling you straight out that they can do nothing for you, they keep you dangling on, week after week, with the bloody trouble getting worse all the time till it will be too late to do anything. And now babbling away about sport when the bastard knows you might never again lift a half-hundred.

A dreadful lassitude seized him. He stood, hands dangling at his sides, head drooped forward, legs sagging at the knees whilst the energy drained out of his limbs leaving flabby muscle and flabbier flesh. For the first time the full extent of his predicament was made manifest. This large, powerful, co-ordinated body, always obedient to the driving force of his will might become overnight a shambling useless hulk that stumbled about in unending darkness, a burden to be clothed and foddered and brought to bed by souring, dissatisfied helpers. At last pawing his way alone round a house suddenly become unfamiliar and unfriendly, his very bulk a handicap, to be somehow constrained from crashing into fixtures or furniture. Not knowing whether it was day or night, morning or evening, so that life became a grey desolation marked out by chiming clocks and rattling delft.

A hand squeezed his shoulder soothingly.

'See you next week, old chap?'

'Yes, doctor.'

'And remember – no brandy without a medical certificate.' The doctor chuckled softly.

For a moment Simpson hesitated. Should this silly clown be told to shag off for himself? Cracking jokes to cover up his own clumsy botching. Making a proper idiot out of you, as Delia said.

Simpson turned away. Ach, what's the use of rising trouble? Maybe in the end he'll hit on a cure. You never can tell.

'Good-bye, doctor,' he said, trudging wearily to the door.

Simpson's increasing lethargic dejection was unconcealed. McCann noticed it first in the deterioration of the manager's appearance. The squared shoulders had begun to droop: the arrogant, thrust-out chest to buckle inwards. Gone was the boxer's graceful swagger: the jaunty resilient stride. Instead he

144

shambled along on flat, hen-toed feet, shifting around a body become too clumsy and heavy for its means of locomotion. His dress, too, had become careless. Pants unpressed: collars worn a second day: shoes unpolished: handkerchief grimy and grey.

Annie, the lazy bitch, must be having the time of her life, McCann decided. She seems not to care how the poor bugger's turned out. Goes about now with his hat on all the time. Sometimes he even forgets to shave. It is hard to believe that only a few short months back he would have lacerated you if you turned up in the morning with a hair out of place. Of course, he's not working. But even so, Annie should not let him go to pieces like that. It's a bloody shame. For that matter, what about Delia Clifden? Why doesn't *she* smarten him up? You'd think she'd be ashamed to be seen out with him. But you wouldn't know what her little game is. Maybe she thinks when he's far enough gone in self-pity, he'll drop into her lap like a wind-fall. Well, she's in for a sore shock. The boss is no marrying man. He's a nookey merchant. When some other useful unit comes along, the bould Delia will be dropped – plonk – on her plump little wriggling backside. And a pleasant heart-warming sight that same backside is. I wouldn't mind a couple of fistfuls of it myself. On the quiet. But it's too danger-ous with the Boss-man on the job. There'd be hell to pay if he found that a junior official was treating his little nookey-bird to a rub of the relic. Though, according to Annie, the whole town and country bar myself are riding the arse off her.

Annie, too, noticed his despondent aspect. Like a man that's turned his face to the wall, she considered. He's given up hope. The sin of despair. He visits the church and goes to Mass but he hasn't been to the sacraments since the Lord knows when. For-ever praying and fingering his beads but dam the bit of religion he's got when you study him up. Relics? He'll have no truck with them. Didn't I beg and beseech him to bathe his eye in Lourdes water? He wouldn't give in to it. Says it is ordinary tap water. Peddled to pilgrims by atheist Frenchmen. Even the relic of Matt Talbot. A link of the chain that touched his holy flesh. He wouldn't hear of it touching his eye. Claims he was a scab who wouldn't join a union. As if that had anything to do with it. He wouldn't see Father Fletcher – a wee man with a notorious Office. And right go wrong, he refused point blank to go on a pilgrimage to Knock or Gerrytown. Swindles, he called them. What can you do with a person like that? If he only would have faith in something – let it be a stone on the side of the road – there'd be hope for him. But he jeers and sneers at everything. How does he expect God to pity him in his affliction when he turns his back on everything holy? And to crown all, isn't the poor man still running round after that young rip, Delia Clifden. No good will come of that. In this world or the next. She'll have the two eyes out of his head before she's through with him.

As for Delia, she was continually upbraiding Simpson.

'What's the matter with you, Jim?' she would say. 'You're letting this thing get the better of you. You have yourself worked up into such a state that you nearly believe you're going blind. Well, *I* don't notice you getting shortsighted. There's nothing much misses you – be it far or near, large or small. But there's one thing sure and certain, if you don't stop worrying you'll finish in an early grave. Look at the cut of you now! A trembling, frightened creature. Old before your time.'

God knows, she thought, looking at him, it's true enough. All right to pass a few weeks of the summer. No more than that. Already he's beginning to stake a claim on you. A person of your age isn't going to be tied down.

Though Simpson was now on continuous sick leave, due to the frequency of the haemorrhages, he still took an interest in the work of the office and liked to go through the incoming mail each day. This never failed to provide him with sardonic comment.

'Listen to this,' he would say, after opening the Head Office letter. 'It refers to the Gilroy conveyance. *Holder does not appear to have successfully divested herself* – maybe the knickers got stuck to her welt – *of her interest in the event of her demise* – not her death, you'll kindly note – *The habendum* – he's coming the hound with that one, all right – *The habendum in the last deed would appear to pass only a life interest* – that would be poor bowel movement, wouldn't you say? – *As the authorities have it, if the estate declared by use is a larger estate than the estate of which the grantee to uses is seised, the cestui que use only gets an estate equivalent to the estate of which the grantee is seised.* —Isn't he the great wee man to hold all that in his head? But wait! *Orme's Case, L.R.* 8c. *p.*

281 – which translated into the vernacular means: if you don't believe me, look the fucking thing up. And hold it! Hold it! Hold it! – there's a habendum here that'll go down in history – *I hope this clarifies matters.* – Be Jesus, that remark would take a lot of beating.'

Certain phrases in letters drove him frantic.

'*I desire to say.* Why hell can't he say it and have done with it? Is it that he can't speak because he's dumb? Or has he some disability like a hare lip or a stoppage in his speech? Even the worst gancher in the world willl make some attempt at making himself understood.'

'*I beg to advise.* Get up off your benders, you cringing hoor. If you think you're going to get any better treatment by begging and craving, you're far mistaken. You'll get the same kick in the arse from the Heid Yins as the rest of us.'

The Brian Mullen saga still irritated him. The Edgware Road office had written again:

'*Since my last letter further calls have been made to your customer but to no avail. As you will appreciate, it is always difficult to obtain access to a flat, particularly when the tenant is obviously trying to evade the Bank. If you wish me to continue to attempt to see Mr. Mullen, perhaps you will kindly let me know.*'

Simpson instructed McCann to tell Edgware Road Branch that they might drop their attempts to contact Mullen. Instead the latter was to be bombarded with more and more threatening letters, each one demanding a lesser reduction of the debt until, it was hoped, something would be forthcoming. No replies were received. A calling-up letter under registered post was dispatched.

'This generally brings some sort of result,' explained Simpson. 'There's an official look about it that scares the shit out of them. And, if nothing else, it is proof of delivery.'

There was no reply.

The postal authorities were now requested to provide the registered receipt. When it arrived it was found to be signed 'E. C. Wingate' in handwriting other than Mullen's.

'I'll lay odds,' said Simpson, 'that E. C. Wingate never threw a leg over the bar of a bike.'

By the same post came a letter from 'The Stag's Head Inn':

Dear Sir,

Mr. Brian Mullen changed the enclosed cheque for cash in my licensed premises and although it was subsequently represented for payment it was returned R/D on each occasion. I would be grateful if you would say whether it has now any chance of being paid. Failing this, could you, perhaps, contact Mr. Mullen and ask him to do something about it before it expires. I am unable to contact him myself as he is no longer welcome as a customer in my house and I do not know his address in London.

Yours sincerely,
Patrick Brady.

On being shown the letter, McCann said:

'I meant to tell you that there's great talk in the village about the grand job Brian has got with a London bookie. There's probably not a word of truth in it. That's why I didn't tell you before.'

'I heard a whimper myself. If it's any kind of a shady job there's every possibility Master Brian is in it up to his neck. I'll put this Brady fellow on his track anyhow. Maybe he'll have better luck than the Edgware Road manager. If nothing else, he might give him a few slashes with a razor.'

He rolled a sheet of letter paper into the typewriter.

'Here goes,' he said.

Dear Sir,

re: Brian Mullen

I return unpaid cheque for £10 issued by above. I regret that this cheque has not yet been made good. There appears to be little hope that Mullen will mend his ways. From his behaviour I am forced to the conclusion that he is a malingerer – not a person temporarily out of luck but a deliberate chancer.

His address is: Flat No. 3, Gladstone Mews, Edgware Road. The flat is guarded by somebody by the name of E. C. Wingate, who repels boarders with the slogan: 'Mr. Mullen is out on business.' Guile or physical force would be needed to effect an entrance. Though, once in the flat, I believe Mullen could be pressurized into coughing up the ten-

148

*ner. He is definitely not broke. Let me know how you get on,
as I have my own troubles with this scoundrel.*

Yours sincerely,

James Simpson,
Manager.

'Don't you think that's going a bit too far, Manager?' said
McCann, when he read the letter.

'Nonsense. If you can point to a single phrase that's not
justified, I'll tear up the letter and write another.'

'What about: "Guile or physical force would be needed to
effect an entrance"? Isn't that a direct incitement to violence?'

'Ha-ha, my young friend. You forget that we know the sex
of the guardian angel at the gate. The kind of physical force
I expect Mr. Brady to use might well be gratifying to E. C.
Wingate. The bould Padraig might effect an entrance in more
ways than one.'

McCann slowly shook his head.

'Tck! Tck! Tck! You're a terrible man. You might be responsible for the loss of an innocent young girl's virtue.'

'After she's been through Mr. Mullen's Academy for Young
Ladies, her virtue will be in flitters. Any more questions?'

'How about the suggestion that Mullen could be pressurized
if once Brady got into the flat? Isn't that as good as telling the
Stag's Head gent to bring along his knuckles, bicycle chain and
gully knife?'

'Of course it is. Isn't that what I want? The only way
Brady will ever get his money is to scare the daylights out of
Mullen.'

'But, Manager, if an inspector ever comes across that letter
there'll be hell to pay.'

'Do you think I'm such an idiot as to sort past a carbon
copy? This correspondence is strictly personal and private.
If the Bank benefit anything by it, the directors won't be worried by the methods used.'

Three weeks later the reply came.

It was a Saturday. The mail did not arrive until after the
office was opened. All morning the counter was lined with
customers – teachers with their pay cheques, shopkeepers for
small silver for the week-end, the late summer visitors with
Travellers' Cheques to be cashed and, of course, at one minute

149

before closing time, the inevitable Michael Vincent McArdle, grocer, publican, hardware and general merchant, special rate depositor, devout member of the St. Dominick guild of the Sacred Heart sodality and general bloody nuisance, slinking up to the cashier's box with an apologetic glance at the clock, a thick bundle of cheques in his hand, and the usual greetings:

'Sure, it's only change I want.'

Only when the Bank closed for the half-day did Simpson get the opportunity to read the letter to McCann.

'Get a load of this, Mac,' he said. 'It's good.'

'*Dear Mr. Simpson,*' he read. '*Thank you for your letter regarding Brian Mullen. Your assessment of him is accurate.*'

Simpson raised his locked hands aloft in a victorious boxer's salute.

'*I am sorry to say,*' he read on, '*that I have not had any further luck in the matter of the R/D cheque. Nor do I expect to have, indeed. The address that you have, i.e. Gladstone Mews, Edgware Road, is not his but that of one of his girl friends.* D'you get that? *One* of his girl friends. Evidently Master Brian must have been blowing his coal in the Stag's Head about all the women he can get. *For all her apparent lack of discrimination in her choice of boy-friends, E. C. Wingate is quite a nice lassie but naturally uncooperative in helping anyone to locate Mullen. He stays at her flat only on odd occasions, I am told, and has no permanent address there.* Fly boy, Brian He'll pay no rent if he can avoid it. The mott must be feeling sore about that or she would hardly have told Brady. Now here's an interesting part. *E. C. Wingate – or Evie as I finished up calling her – was circumnavigated with the aid of a ball of malt or two but little good it did me.* Apparently he got nothing. Neither ride nor rumour. The silly yob gave up too easily. Sure a naggin of whiskey wouldn't rock a Child of Mary. He should have poured the stuff into her till it came out of her quim. *I shall keep my eye out for Mullen and if I have any success I will certainly let you know. If you are ever in these parts at all, come in and have a dram.* He sounds a decent class of a chap. God knows, I believe I'll call there if I'm ever in London.'

'He seems to consider Mullen a blue duck egg. It looks as if you'll have to transfer his account to the Bad and Doubtful Debts list.'

'You'd be a bit previous. If I know my man he'll be back here some of these days, strutting around like a conquering hero, moving from pub to pub buying drinks for all hands.'

'How are you so sure of that?'

'Calling drinks for the house in a London pub would be more liable to earn you a belt with a blackjack than the esteem of the congregation. In a village like this, a few judiciously spent ponds will buy you a popularity out of all proportion to the amount of porter drunk. He'll be back all right.'

Simpson tucked the letter away in his wallet and left the office.

It was about this time that Delia conceived the notion of using the Bank House as a rendezvous. She had already wormed out of Simpson that the car could be driven into the garage and entry achieved by means of the back door of the house.

'There's no need for me to be seen at all,' she argued when he pointed out the risks – the chance of the house-keeper return-in, or of a caller who would have to be admitted. 'Once in the bedroom, we're safe and sound. We can do whatever we like. And, anyway, you promised me the use of the bath sometime. You know there's none here.'

Her conspiratorial smile breached his defences. Reluc-tantly he agreed to call for her the next night. They would start out after dark. Get back to Creevan before midnight. Hannah would not have gone to bed. A few jars and he'd say: 'I must be off. It's getting late.' A night's innocent enjoyment would be over.

Next day he warned Annie to keep up the fire as he intended to have a bath before he went to bed.

'Will you be out late?' she asked.

'I couldn't rightly say,' he said. Stalling.

'You'd better be back early if you want the water warm. I'm leaving at six. It'll be gone cold at eleven.'

'I'll be back long before that.' He tried not to sound pleased. Tea finished and Annie gone, he placed the newly-purchased bath salts and toilet soap in the bath rack, left a bottle of Jame-son and two tumblers in the wardrobe of his bedroom, and started off for Creevan.

He pulled in to Hannigan's of Cleggan Cross for a quick snort. To steady his hands, twitching with excitement. One glass of whiskey he would have. No more. The night could be banjaxed by too much drink. The glass was at his lips for the last slug when the car pulled up. No time to escape. Maybe they're strangers. Or won't notice you if you don't look round. You can duck out as they're calling their round. He stared into his glass as the door opened.

'Would you look at who's here? The bould James.'

'Long time no see, old chap.'

It was Clancy and Vereker, the latter already putting on his phony accent. Thinking the quickest way to get out of the company was to buy a drink and go, Simpson asked them to join him. He took only a small whiskey himself. Gulped it back. Straightened up.

'I'll be on my way,' he said.

'Faith and you'll not,' said Clancy. 'A bird never flew on one wing. You'll have one from me before you go.'

Clancy's round drunk up, Vereker stood. Then Simpson stood again – on the general principle that it is always easier to break away from the company on your own round. Finishing his drink rapidly, he replaced his glass on the counter. Firmly and finally.

'No more for me, lads. Doctor's orders.'

'That for a bloody yarn. I never seen you looking better. What's your hurry, anyway?'

'Cheese it, Pat. Asking a bloke a question like that. Have you no manners?'

Clancy wheeled round, his eyes almost invisible under frowning folds of pink, shiny skin.

'What are you getting at, Vereker?'

'A bird, chum. He's meeting a bleeding bird. That right, Jim?'

'Surely to Jesus she'd wait five minutes till we finish our drinks?'

'This is no ordinary bird, mate. She's a proper eye-dazzler. Take the sight out of your ruddy squinters. Am I right or am I wrong, James?'

Simpson had picked up his glass again. He rapped it on the counter. 'Same again.'

'It's not your round, Jim,' said Clancy. 'We'll keep the ship on an even keel.'

'Take a pew, boss, within sight of the high altar.'

With his foot, Vereker hooked a tall stool and drew it over. Simpson sat down between them. The two men had been at the fair of Garton. Soon Simpson was caught up in the flow of talk about cattle and sheep, the iniquities of tanglers, the scarcity of fodder, the high price of con-acre, the trickery practised at cattle-marts. Drinks appeared, were paid for and swallowed up. When next he looked at his watch it was nine o'clock.

The two men, both well drunk by this time, were arguing about the type of dog best suited for driving cattle.

'A Collie dog,' wheezed Clancy. 'That's your man. He'll herd cattle against any dog in the land.'

'Too long of the leg, mate,' said Vereker. 'Get gored easily. For cranky cattle there's naught to beat a Corgi. Proper cattle dog, he is. So stumpy the bleeding horns can't get under him. Nippy little bastard, too.'

'A Collie,' insisted Clancy. 'Or even an ould mongrel shepp. Handle cattle anywhere. No use arguing. Just look round you.'

He swept his outside arm in a wide arc. Belched. Deep and sustained.

Quietly Simpson slipped off his stool, leaving his drink untouched.

'I'll let *my* dog off the chain,' he said, low and confidential. He moved off towards the yard door.

The two men, spluttering with laughter, shouted after him.

'Mind he doesn't get away on you, Jim!'

'You want to muzzle the blighter if you're meeting the bird tonight, chum!'

As he picked his way through the littered yard with nothing to guide him but the light from the kitchen window, Simpson muttered to himself:

'You're too bloody smart, Mister-my-fucking friend. Some day you'll go too far, and I'll paste you to the wall.'

He kicked open the door of the dark dilapidated jakes and proceeded to relieve himself in the general direction of the squalid wooden seat, trying to ignore the stench of ordure and the buzzing of disturbed flies.

Delia will raise hell, he brooded, as, swishing, he strained and grunted. Three hours late and well lit. A bad start to the night's activity. It was the fault of those two bowzies. Nothing would do them but drink. And more drink. You'd think they weren't

153

scuttered enough as it was. Without making beasts of themselves. That little Vereker scut. With his air-force moustache and English twang. *He's meeting a bleeding bird.* How did he guess that? Of course, he's in and out of Hannah's all the time Bound to tape what was happening. Wonder how many know the score. They're a cute pack of gets around here. Bloody little misses them. Still they're only guessing. Unless? No, that's impossible. We always kept a look-out for spotters. What about the time you hammered a job on the beach? Below the cliffs? Where all and sundry could see you? McCann spotted you. Why not Vereker?

He shook off the last drop. Stowed away with jutting rump and crouched back. Buttoned up. On his way out the yard gate to the car, inspiration came to him. Without giving Delia time to reproach him, he would move into the attack himself.

Humming cheerfully, he started up the engine, switched on the lights and pulled out from Hannigan's, accelerating slowly so that he might escape undetected. On the way to Creevan he drove furiously, stooped over the wheel, intent on the swinging beam of the headlights.

He pulled up at Hannah's with a squeal of brakes. Jumped out. Stalked through the crowded bar without acknowledging the chorus of greeting. Took his stand with his back to the kitchen range.

Delia came in from the bar, glowering angrily.

'What's the idea of—'

'Do you know what I'm after hearing? Flung up to my very face?'

She stared at him. Open-mouthed.

'By that little scut, Vereker. I'll be dug out of him yet.'

'Vereker? Who is he when he's at home? And what has *he* got to do with it?'

'He has all to do with it. He's one of your aunt's customers. A small man with a moustache.'

'Oh, him! Sure no one pays a bit heed to that little banty cock.'

'They will if he goes round spreading the story he told me.'

'What story? For goodness sake, come to the point, Jim.'

'Bring down a ball of malt, Delia. I want it badly.'

'All right. All right. Don't rush me.'

154

As she turned back to the bar, he tried to keep the smile of triumph from his face. The trick had worked. She was thrown off balance. Now, in her anxiety to discover his news, she would forget her own resentment.

'What story has Vereker been spreading?' she said, as she came back to the kitchen with the drink. 'Is it about us?'

He splashed in some water. Drank slowly. Placed his glass on the table.

'It is.'

'Oh!' She moved closer to him. 'What had he to say about us?'

'Plenty.'

'Such as?'

'I'd as soon not repeat it. It'll only annoy you.'

'You might as well tell me. You have me half told already.'

Right you are, he decided. Here goes.

'Vereker saw us. From the cliff top.'

'Well?'

'Don't you understand? He was spying on us.'

'I'm sure he's not the only one, if I'm any judge.'

'You don't know this Vereker gentleman, apparently. He'll go round town and country, telling everyone.'

'What harm if he does?'

'Are you gone clean cuckoo? Do you mean to tell me that it means nothing to you that that little rattlesnake is spreading it about that he saw the pair of us hooring at the foot of the cliffs?'

'That's right. And stop shouting. And don't use that word — I don't like it.'

'What word?'

'You know quite well.'

'All right. He'll say he saw me screwing you below on the beach. Is that any better?'

'Yes. And who'll believe him? Everyone agrees he is a notorious liar. Let him repeat his filthy gossip. We can afford to laugh at it.'

Baffled. Bewildered. At last in admiration, he stared at her.

'Why?' he asked.

'Because from tonight on, we do our—' She hesitated. Smiled, 'our screwing,' she said primly, 'in the Bank House.'

'Jaymedy Mike!' he whispered.

'So finish your drink and we'll be on our way.'

He drank up and followed her to the side door. Getting into the car, she suddenly asked:

'Where did you meet this fellow, Vereker?'

He switched on the self-starter. Revved up loudly.

'Was it in Hannigan's?' she shouted.

Letting in the clutch, he roared off up the long steep hill leading out of the village.

'Take it easy,' she said. 'We'll be in bed soon enough.'

Dry-lipped, breathless, he tried to concentrate on the road.

'So that's what kept you! You were in Hannigan's. Me waiting for three solid hours while you were drinking with your pals. And then making up this story about Vereker to excuse you being late.'

'It's true enough. What Vereker said.' His voice was strained. Hoarse.

'Do you know what you'll do? You'll turn the car right now and drive me back home.'

He slowed down.

'But, Delia,' he pleaded, 'you can't do that. I got the housekeeper to put on a roaring fire. So that you'd have plenty of hot water for your bath.'

She sniffed.

'All right. But you're taking me straight home after I've had my bath.'

As the car picked up speed again, she stretched across the steering wheel and sounded the horn.

'Did you hear me? Straight home after the bath.'

His mouth opened and closed several times before he said: 'I heard.'

At Cleggan Cross, he whirled round the corner, glimpsing the car still outside Hannigan's. He heard Delia sniff once more.

'Vereker,' she muttered.

On the outskirts of Creevan, he stopped the car, reached over to the back seat and pulled across a rug.

'You'd better squat down on the floor. I'll throw the rug over you.'

Without protest she crouched down, facing the seat, head bowed on fisted hands. Carefully he spread the rug, trying to give it the appearance of having slipped casually to the floor.

'Here we go,' he said, starting off again. He reached down to pat the shapeless hummock. 'Steady the Buffs.'

As they drove along, he kept up a running commentary.

'We're turning off the main road now. Swinging left. Soon we'll be going under the old railway arch. There now! In another moment we'll be topping the hill. Yes, there's the lights of the village. Never thought they were so bright. Here's the first one. Not many folk about, thank God. Just the odd straggler. Hawker Dempsey, of course. Prowling along looking for a fogey. A soft mark to touch up for a wet. Poor chance tonight, by the look of it. And there's Snout, standing at the door. Rubbing his feelers together like a hungry spider. Better salute him. "Good night to you, Mister McGinley." God help the poor bugger gets a feed of your whiskey this holy night. Now we're wheeling round into the Square. We'll be home and dry in a couple . . . God above, what's this?'

The car jerked to a crawl.

'There's a light in the frigging office. McCann must be back working. Better if I drive on past. I can take you home the back road.'

The rug stirred.

'You're bringing me in for a bath. As you promised.' The muffled voice was peremptory.

'But I can't while McCann—'

'If you don't, I'll disgrace you.'

Simpson changed down. Swung the car into the Bank entry. Drew up outside the garage door.

'We're at the garage. Don't stir till I tell you.'

She heard the car door click. Steps crunching on gravel. The rasp of a heavy door swinging open. Then he was back in the seat beside her. The car eased forward again. Stopped. As he was closing the garage door, she flung off the rug and got out.

'Don't move or you'll bang into something,' his voice came from the darkness.

She stood motionless while he brushed past her. Another door opened. Just enough for her to see Simpson's bulk against a background of night sky. Cautiously she moved over beside him. Looked out.

The light from a ground-floor window shafted across a small scraggy lawn. There were no blinds on the window and she could see into the brilliantly-lit room as though it were a stage

157

set. Desks and office furniture were placed like unreal stilted props. Even as she watched, an actor, sawn off at the waist, moved across the stage, throwing a long shadow over the patch of lawn.

'It's McCann all right,' said Simpson. 'I'll hunt him home.' As he made to close the door, she said:

'Leave it open. I don't want to be left in the dark.'

She watched him go down the path and in the back door. A few moments later he, too, passed across the lighted window.

On an impulse, she stepped out on to the lawn. Keeping to the edge of the shafted light, she worked her way towards the window, until the two figures were in view.

McCann was seated at a desk on which was an open ledger. He was sifting through a sheaf of correspondence, picking out letters which he handed to Simpson standing beside him. Simpson read. Pointed an angry stabbing fore-finger at the quaking letter. Mouthed silent vicious curses. Picked up another letter.

Delia waited impatiently while the two characters mimed their roles with gesture and action. At length, disgusted, she turned away and made for the back door. Easing up the latch, she slipped in. Closed the door. Took off her shoes.

Without taking much precaution, she padded up the hall-way. Scurried, like a scalded cat, up the stairway and crouched down behind the banisters.

Soon the two men came out from the office, talking in under-tones. 'He's a first-class bloody chancer,' she heard McCann say before the hall-door closed. Simpson started up the passage-way to the back door. Leaning out over the banisters, she sig-nalled:

'Psst!'

As if he had tripped on an unexpected projection on the floor, he stumbled to a halt.

'Who's there?' he called hoarsely.

'Who do you think, stupid?' she hissed.

He climbed the stairs, muttering to himself:

'Shagging women! You couldn't trust them as far as you'd throw them.'

'What's that?' she asked sharply.

'Why didn't you stay outside when you were told? You might have stumbled into McCann when he was leaving.'

158

'Fat chance of that with the two of you colloguing away together like hanging jurymen. What poor devil were you disposing of, tell me?'

He led the way towards the bathroom.

'A prime blackguard that keeps issuing dud cheques. He'll finish behind bars if he doesn't watch. I'll run the bath for you now.'

Forcing down the bath plug, he turned on both taps.

'You can regulate it yourself.'

He straightened up.

'Bath salts,' he pointed. 'Sponge. Soap. Fresh towel.'

Awkwardly he stepped back. Lolled against the closed door.

'Just what are *you* waiting for, buster?' she said. 'Do you think I'm going to undress with you gaping at me?'

'Aw, have a heart, Delia. You'd think I never saw you before with your clothes off.'

She opened the door.

'Out!' she said. 'Out! You take too much for granted.'

Pushing him out, she slammed the door. He heard the bolt click shut.

For a moment he listened outside but nothing could be heard above the sound of gushing tap water. Moodily he crossed to the bedroom. Got out the whiskey. Poured himself a glass. He was stretched on the bed, sipping his drink, when he heard her call. At once he put down the glass. Rushed to the bathroom door.

'What is it?' he asked.

'The bolt's off,' she said. 'What kept you?'

When he opened the door he could see nothing for the thick cloud of steam. Against this white mist, the green scum of unabsorbed blood obscuring the vision of his eye showed up with startling clarity, shifting and swirling as he looked around. A cud of bitterness rose to his throat. What was he doing here anyway? Acting the penny-boy for a chit of a girl no more than half his age. Running to her if she cracked her fingers. Wasn't there a score of girls in the area, better built and better mannered, to be had for the picking? Girls that would be damned glad to have a leg thrown over them. That wouldn't be treating it as a class of a compliment if they let you mount them. That would be cute and close-mouthed and not disgrace you with a public display of intimacy. God knows, half the countryside

159

could have seen the shameless, brazen antics of her on the cliff tops or deserted beaches or even, so help me, the grass verge of the bloody highway. What was he thinking of, anyway, bringing her to the Bank House? Fouling his own nest. Let this get out and he might as well pack up and go. If she doesn't drive the eyes out of your head with her unbridled craving for cock. Surely to Christ you should know by now that this randy scuttling after a rutting bitch will only bring on another haemorrhage? Have you forgotten, you sore idiot?

From the cloud of steam, her voice nagged:

'Are you deaf? Why are you standing there like a mutton dummy? Can't you answer a civil question?'

'What do you want to know?'

'What kept you? I've asked you a dozen times.'

'Sorry.'

'Come here and soap my back.'

His heart clenched in anguish as he stood beside the bath looking down at her. She was sitting up straight, hands clasped around raised knees. Beads of water glistened on her shoulders. Trickled erratically down the smooth back. Her skin glowed, as though life – fierce, urgent, resolute – seethed and bubbled under a thin envelope of flesh. A lock of hair dangled foolishly over one eye. Her thumbs tapped out upon her left knee the rhythm of a dance number. Young, guileless, terribly vulnerable she looked. An intolerable wave of tenderness overwhelmed him. An urge to comfort. To caress.

He touched her shoulder gently.

'Here,' she said. 'The soap.'

Over her shoulder she handed it to him.

Gravely, conscientiously, he lathered and rubbed, rubbed and lathered, while she complained:

'Go easy, will you. You'll take the skin off my back the way you're scouring it.'

Once, to steady her swaying body, he cupped a hand against one of her breasts. She pushed it away immediately.

'Now-now! No monkey business or out you'll go.'

At last she lay back in the bath, eyes closed, muscles slack, savouring the scented warmth. Dry-mouthed, jaw muscles aching, Simpson stared at the brown nipples rising provocatively from the soapy, scummy water.

At length, she roused herself.

160

'Get the towel. You can dry me.'

Wrapped in the bath towel, she stamped around impatiently whilst he tried, with a show of nonchalance, to towel down the moist and yielding flesh. She shrugged him away.

'I'll do it myself. You'll be all night at it.'

She dried herself briskly, flung the wet towel on a chair and commenced to dress. Desperately Simpson sought ways to detain her.

'There's no need to ... to rush off so early. It's only—' he glanced at his watch. 'It's just gone ten.'

Head emerging from the waist-band of her skirt, she paused, eyeing him with cagey stare.

'We could have a jar before I drive you home,' he said, wincing at the blatancy of the excuse.

She tugged the skirt down. Pulled and patted it into place.

'If you're planning any hanky-panky,' she said, 'you're wasting your time. I'm going home after one drink.'

She finished dressing and followed him across the landing to the bedroom. Watched as he got out the glasses and the whiskey bottle from the wardrobe.

'You had everything nicely planned,' she said. 'Pity it's too late for me to stay.'

At the dressing-table, back turned to her, he filled out the drinks. One a half-tumblerful. The other a normal measure.

'Water?' he asked over his shoulder.

'Yes.'

Into the smaller drink, he poured from the carafe. Poured till the two measures were level.

'That should do the trick,' he said. 'And a little tincture for myself.'

He tilted a driblet of water into the second glass.

'Here we are,' he said cheerfully, crossing his hands as he picked up the drinks. As he swung round, his hands uncrossed and he passed her the larger drink. Grasping his own glass so that the contents could not be seen, he raised it.

'Bottoms up,' he said, clinking glasses with her.

He drank. Three long slugs.

'That's better,' he said, putting down his empty glass.

Delia was coughing and spluttering.

'Did it go down the wrong way?' he commiserated.

Tears in her eyes, she wheezed:

'Where did you get ... that whiskey? ... It's fierce strong.'

'Up the town some place. Why? Nothing wrong with it, I hope. Tasted all right to me.'

He filled himself another modest measure. Topped it up with water. Sipped.

'Nothing the matter with that whiskey, as far as I can see. Maybe I put too much water in yours. It's a mistake to drown it, you know.'

She took a cautious sip. Grimaced.

'Awful. Tastes of linoleum.'

'Probably too young. Not manured ... I mean matured properly.'

'It seems to be hitting *you* fast enough. You're stuttering already.'

'I am not.' He drank. A quick gulp. Smacked his lips appreciatively. 'I'll swear it's not a day younger than ten year old. Drink it up and stop acting like a schoolgirl.'

She drank standing, puffing loudly after each swallow.

'You get to like it, don't you?' he said.

'Lino. New lino. Just unrolled. Smelling of cat.' With a final puff of relief, she put down her empty glass. 'Come on now. We're for off.'

'What's your hurry? It's early yet. Plenty of time for another gargle.' He held up the bottle invitingly.

'I don't know. It's dreadful stuff.'

'Tell you what. I'll bring up some milk. That'll kill the taste.'

When he came back, she was sitting on the bed.

'You're very comfortable here,' she said.

He collected the glasses and commenced to mix the drinks as before. One large. One small. A compensating quantity of milk in each. As he crossed his hands he had to look closely to detect which held the most liquor.

'Now,' he said, as he reached her the glass. 'See if that tastes any better.'

She sipped.

'Ummm. Much better.'

She kicked off her shoes. Plumped up the pillow. Stretched her feet out on the quilt.

'Much better.'

She sipped the whiskey and milk, whilst Simpson strove to make small talk. As was his wont, he ran through the alphabet,

eking a topic. *A* is for *amorous*. Too revealing. *B* is for *bunk*.
itto. *C* is for *cheesecake*. Jesus, I can't get away from it. *D*
for *drunk*. We bloody well hope. He burst out laughing.

'What's so funny?' she asked.

'I was thinking of Vereker.'

'Nothing funny about that little squirt.'

'Ach, it was just something he said. About muzzling a dog.'

Come to think of it, it was a damned good suggestion. There
ust be one left in that package in the dressing-table drawer.
'll do away with this withdrawal racket. She'll never know
e difference. Queer how she thinks *that* a worse sin than the
b itself.

'D'you know. I'll take 'nother drink. Just a teeny weeny
e.'

She demonstrated with all-but-joined thumb and fore-
nger.

She's showing signs of wear and tear, he decided, as he filled
r out another huge bumper of whiskey, colouring it with a
ttle splash of milk. This one should work the oracle.

Without shuffling the glasses, he handed her the jaundiced-
oking mixture.

'Down the hatch,' he said, throwing back his own watered
hiskey.

He stood for a moment, watching her lower the drink in small
t steady gulps. Satisfied, he turned away to the dressing-
ble and commenced to hunt through the drawers. Just as
came across the package, she called:

'Jim, it's getting very hot.'

He pocketed the package. Crossed to the bed.

'Why don't you peel off some of your clothes? You'll feel
oler then.'

Obediently, she commenced to pull off her jumper. With
ailing arms she struggled to get it over her head. At last, in
muffled shout, she begged:

'Help me off with this thing, will you?'

He eased it off. She lay back on the pillow, hair tossed, cheeks
otched, eyes glazed.

'Take me home, Jim. Please.'

He bent down and flicked his finger gently across her sweat-
aked forehead.

'Give,' he whispered. 'Don't be nasty.'

163

'All right. A quickie.'

Blood thundering in his ears, he tore off his clothes. (out a french letter. Adjusted it with frantic, fumbl fingers.

'I don't feel so good. What's keeping you?' Leaning on elbow, she peered. Blinking.

'What have you got there? Come here.'

He shuffled nearer.

'Is that what it is? One of those filthy, wicked things?'

She reached out. Ripped it off. Flung it across the room.

'Are you trying to make a hoor of me?' she cried.

Rolling over, she buried her face in the pillow. Sobbing.

'Ooooooooh,' she wailed. 'What am I to do?'

He stood over her, appalled at the wild sobbing. Awkwar he patted the writhing, twitching shoulders.

'It's all right,' he said. 'We'll go home now.'

She wriggled away from him.

'Don't touch me,' she screamed. 'You tried to make a h of me.'

Whirling over on her back, she strove to push herself right.

'What will I do?' she moaned. 'I feel awful. Ooooooooh!

As he bent to comfort her, she opened her mouth wide a puked all over him. She continued to puke as he padded to the bathroom to sponge himself clean. She was still puk when he came back with the wet bath towel. But by this ti it was dry, convulsive retching. The green gawks, he diagnos noting the saliva stringing from her mouth. Too much dri the greedy bitch. She was hogging it down like a bloc cormorant.

'Ooooooooh!' she groaned. 'This is terrible. I'm going die. Oick! OICK! O I C K!'

Once more a fit of retching attacked her. Doubled up, e bulging, face contorted, she sought to void the contents her by-this-time empty stomach. A trickle of green bile flov from her gaping agonized mouth.

Simpson pulled on his clothes and got to work with towel. God blast her, he raged, she has boked over everythi Quilt, sheets, pillows, his pyjamas, the carpet: all were sp tered with puke. His own stomach began to get queasy as swabbed up the rancid mess. He poured himself a dri

164

Gulped it back neat. Picked up once more the stinking towel.

'Move over,' he growled, pushing her roughly away. 'I've a mind to rub your nose in it.'

At last, satisfied that the worst of the mess was cleaned off, he went back to the bathroom and flung the towel into the unemptied bathwater. Half-heartedly he attempted to rinse it off but soon gave up and left it to steep in the bath. There'll be a nice how-do-you-do when Annie sees this mess and the puke stains in the bedroom. You'll have a job convincing her that you were responsible for it all yourself. She knows no matter how drunk you are you never cat. Better blame it on the retinitis. Anything to do with the eye trouble she's prepared to believe. And God knows if you don't have a haemorrhage after this night, it'll be a miracle. Depression settled on him. He stared at his reflection in the bathroom mirror. Rolled his eyes slowly. Closed first one eye. Then the other. The left eye was still sound. The right one encumbered with unabsorbed blood.

These curse of God women. The cause of every trouble. A man should never get tangled up with them. I swear to God from this day out, I'll stay clear.

He turned away from the mirror. Home she goes. This minute. As he entered the bedroom, he called:

'Up you get. I'll run you back to Creevan now.'

There was no answer. For a moment he thought she was gone. Then he saw she had crept under the clothes and was now sound asleep.

He stood, looking down at the flushed face resting on the knuckles of one hand. She breathed with the shallow, rapid breathing of a child. Once more it was brought home to him how vulnerable she looked. Perhaps inside the tough carapace of brazen shamelessness, there lurked a shrinking cowering spirit, fearful of hurt.

Better let her sleep it off, he decided. It would be criminal to bring her back home, the way she feels now. He looked at his watch. It was only eleven o'clock. He would let her sleep for an hour. She'd be all right by then.

He stretched himself beside her on the quilt. Stared up at the ceiling, trying to ignore the smell of puke and the ragged green curtain of blood shown up by the white of the ceiling.

Yes, he resolved. Tomorrow I will go to confession. The longer a person stays away, the harder it is to get the courage to go. After all, what is there to fear? Isn't the priest instructed to go easy on a penitent who has not been to confession for a long time? All well and good, but there's the odd scarifier. An old embittered man. Rancorous with the long celibate years. Taking it out on others for what he's missed desperately himself. Wading into you for details so that he can get a kind of second-hand satisfaction. It must surely be that. What other reason could he have for delving into the minutiae of sin? After all, the number of times and the methods used are merely another aspect of the sin itself. Could there be any great difference between doing a woman three times in the course of a night and doing a quick job on her on three occasions during the lunch hour? It was all very mixing. Well, he would go through with it this time. No more back-sliding.

He shivered. Pulled the quilt over himself. Might as well keep warm while I'm waiting. Think I'll close my eyes for a few minutes. They're very hot and tired. The rest will do them good. He sighed. Snuggled down under the quilt.

The housekeeper's knock aroused him.

'Righto!' he answered. And then: 'Good Jesus!' as he came fully awake.

'Nothing the matter?' she enquired anxiously.

'Oh, no,' he said, sliding the bedclothes cautiously over Delia's head. 'I'll be down in a jiffy.'

When he heard the kitchen door close, he shook her awake, holding his hand over her mouth.

'Don't make a sound,' he said.

She shook her head.

'That was the housekeeper,' he said, releasing her. 'It's eight o'clock. You've got to get out of here.'

He jumped out of bed.

'Get your clothes on quick.'

'They're on,' she said crossly. 'Except my jumper.' She commenced to slip it on. 'My God, look at it!' She held it out. Gobbets of puke were dried into it. 'I can't go out in that thing. You have it ruined.'

The injustice of this remark infuriated Simpson. He gripped her by the shoulders. Shook her roughly.

166

'You puked on it yourself,' he hissed. 'So put it on and get out of here.'

'But how—'

'Turn it inside out. No one'll be a bit the wiser.'

'But—'

'The main thing is get out of here. As quickly and quietly as you can.'

She stopped picking off chips of spew.

'Look, big boy,' she said. 'When I do get out of here, how do I get home? And what fairy tale do I tell Aunt Hannah? You know I've been away all night with you.'

The enormity of the disaster dawned on him. Not alone was he stuck here with this girl on his hands but he'd have to leave her home and convince Hannah that everything was above board.

'I'll go down first. Go into the kitchen. Keep Annie in chat. Make as much noise as possible. While you steal downstairs and out the front door.'

He rubbed his unshaven chin.

'Hold on now. I'd need to leave the front door ajar. So that you could slip out quickly. You could go on out the Creevan road and I'll pick you up as soon as I can get away.'

'Have you no sense at all? Sure the whole village would know before lunch time that I'd spent the night here. Why not go as I came? Out the back. No one need see me leaving if I keep under the rug.'

'Good, you girl you. I can go out to the garage for something and leave the two doors open coming back. Come downstairs as quiet as you can. I'll find some way of making noise to cover the creaking steps. Are you right now?'

She nodded. Held up her two hands with fingers crossed.

'Good luck.' She smiled encouragement.

This was the moment it was at last borne in on him that he loved this infuriating trollop. Needed her more than aught else in life. Found unbearable the thought that he might ever be forced back to an existence in which she had no part. Discovered how his heart lifted at the smallest sign of encouragement or regard.

'I'm off,' he said gaily.

Down the stairs he tramped. Into the kitchen.

'Well, Annie, how are the bones this fine morning?'

167

She looked at him with a keen, a shrewd eye.

'No better than your own, I'd say. And the morning's nothing to shout about either.'

'Which reminds me. Doctor Madden gave me tablets to take. I must have left them in the car.'

He bustled off out to the garage. Rooted around in the car. Came back, leaving garage and back door ajar.

'Can't find them. Must be up in the bedroom.' He slammed shut the kitchen door.

'Tablets,' she muttered into the sink. 'Them things.'

He lifted the poker. Rooted between the bars of the range. 'Poor-looking coal, I'd say. Where did you get it?'

She'd be starting off now. Creeping down, balanced on tiptoe. Her heart in her mouth. Nervous of a creaking stair. Or a loose board. Watching the kitchen door for fear 'twould suddenly fly open.

'It was got in McArdle's. Why?'

'There's no last to it. No more than there's in that little get himself.'

He poked viciously at the fire. She would be two steps down now. Swaying from side to side. Clutching at the banister rail for support. Her face caught up in a frown of concentration.

'Where else would I get coal but in McArdle's? There's none to be had anywhere else in the village. And well you know it.'

'Maybe. But don't let him push muck like this on you. That craw-thumping little maggot would sell you road-metal for firing. And then stand up in the choir every Sunday singing—' he beat out the rhythm with the poker on the range.

> *'FAY-hayth-AW-AWF-our-FAH-ha-THERS-HOHly-FAITH*
> *WE-WILL-UHL-be-TRUE-to-THEE-till-DEATH.'*

That would surely take her half-way down the stairs. If she makes a quick run of it. But no. She'll be teetering down. Biting her lips. Muttering *hush* to herself at every sound. Wondering should she take off her shoes. Or would she be handicapped carrying them. She should be getting near the creaking stair any minute now.

'You're in queer form this morning, Mister Simpson. You'd fight with your own shadow.'

168

It should be the next step. Now!

With a flourish he jammed the poker into the slotted plate covering the fire box, yanked it off and sent it clanging across the top of the range. He pointed down into the burning coals.

'Look!' he roared. Stabbing, gouging, churning the coals, he demonstrated their inferior quality whilst smoke and smuts rose around him. 'Look at McArdle's coal! Look what that miserable scraggy little piss-hawk sold you for coal.'

Angered beyond endurance, Mrs. Mahony shouted back:

'Would you stop interfering with me kitchen!'

Startled, he hesitated. It was in that split second of silence that the stair creaked. Loudly. Unmistakably.

'What was that?' head to one side she asked.

Flinging the poker down on the range, he strode to the door. Turned, hand on the door knob.

'If you didn't see those tablets around, I better have a look upstairs in the bedroom.' He spoke in a loud, arrogant voice, head turned sideways so that his voice would carry.

She waddled towards him, a couple of steps. Whispered:

'There's someone out there on the stairs, I'll swear to God.'

'You didn't, by any chance, come across them, Mrs. Mahony? The tablets, I mean?'

In exasperation she shot forward an anserine head. Hissed!

'Would you stop craking and listen? I hear someone moving outside.'

'Can you not answer a simple question? Did you see any sign of my tablets?'

She waddled forward another step.

'Och, you and your ould tablets. I tell you THERE'S SOME-ONE OUTSIDE!' She mouthed the words in a loud carrying whisper.

'McCann, probably. He told me he was coming in early this morning. The work's got behind.'

With an air of determination, she resumed her advance.

'Whoever it is, they'll not be left skulking there for long.' Her threatening voice had risen to a shout.

A defeated expression on his face, Simpson moved away from the door.

'Wheest!' Mrs. Mahony hissed.

Outside there was a step. Firm. Purposeful. A double knock on the door.

'May I come in?'

Without waiting for an answer, Delia entered. Glanced coolly from one to other of the silent pair.

'I hope I'm not intruding?'

Mrs. Mahony's pent-up breath was released in an explosive puff.

'It's about my handbag, Mr. Simpson,' Delia explained, serene and at ease. 'I must have left it in your car last night. You weren't a minute gone when I missed it. I got the chance of a lift over from Creevan this morning, so I thought I'd call and collect it.'

'Handbags. Tablets,' Mrs. Mahony muttered.

Eyebrows raised, Delia's casual glance was welt-raising. She moved closer to Simpson.

'I wasn't worrying about whatever few shillings were in it. It was the letters. Personal letters that I just couldn't bear the thought of someone reading. You know how it is, Jim?' She lingered tenderly over the Christian name.

Folding her arms over her enormous bosom, Mrs. Mahony glared at Delia.

'Do you usually come into houses through an upstairs window?'

Delia ignored her.

'Do you know, Jim, there would have been a most frightful row if one of your Bank inspectors had called this morning. The private door was lying wide open. An invitation to all and sundry to walk right in.'

She laughed gaily.

'Actually, that's what I did,' she said.

Choking with rage, Mrs. Mahony spluttered:

'Are you ... are you suggesting ... do you mean to make out ... that I left ... you wouldn't dare ...'

Hurriedly, Simpson cut in:

'It's all my fault, Mrs. Mahony. I must have left the door open behind me when I looked out to see how the weather was doing.'

'Mr. Simpson, you can't—'

'Look, Jim. I've got to get back to Creevan. There's a day's work ahead of me. Let's collect the handbag and hook it. If you don't leave me home, I'll have to wait for the post van.'

Like a dog enticed by two joint owners, his head swung from side to side. At last he said, apologetically:

'I shan't be long, Annie.'

'Come on, Jim. I'll cook you a bit of breakfast when we get to Creevan.'

Stunned, agape, Mrs. Mahony watched them go.

Delia's aunt was easier to hoodwink than Annie. Told the lame story of a car breakdown and an enforced stay in a hotel, Hannah said:

'You had a right to come back in the post van, Delia. Not to be dragging poor Mr. Simpson over here at this hour of the morning.'

But if Simpson's foolish escapade escaped the humiliation of public opprobrium, retribution was exacted in a way he had come to expect.

On the way back from Creevan, after leaving Delia home, he was forced to stop the car twice with the onset of a completely new symptom of eye disorder. A sudden stab of pain behind the eyes; a glitter, bright and eye-narrowing, as though the morning sun, warming the side of his face through the open car-window, had shifted position and was now dazzling the windscreen: a distortion of vision that forced him to slam on the brakes and pull in to the side.

The glitter persisted. Not the gleaming clarity of sunlight, drenching the whole field of vision with light, but two snuff-coloured streaks, above and below the centre of vision, glittering balefully with every movement of the eyes. These streaks, pulsing with menacing light, changed position constantly, causing the kind of distortion seen in Fun Fair mirrors or through flawed and bubbled window glass. Objects writhed and buckled and forked and straightened. Things in the foreground – trees, telegraph poles, paling posts – undulated crazily. The road ahead quaked and quivered. The far-away sweep of mountain rose and fell like a tossing sea. The whole landscape lit by this threatening brown glitter.

Although Simpson gazed ahead with glaring motionless eyes, still the shift and sway of distorted vision continued. Fearful that a haemorrhage would break out in both eyes, he sat immobile, white-knuckled hands gripping the steering wheel. Even when the glitter and distortion ceased – as sud-

171

denly as it had started – he sat on, terrified that the smallest movement might bring on another onslaught.

At last he started off again, driving slowly and cautiously, striving to avoid the jolt of pot-holes, the jerk of carelessly-changed gears. But before he reached Cleggan Cross, he had to pull in once more to the side of the road. This time he closed his eyes and relaxed so as to avoid any strain on the muscles of the eyes. In the turmoil of fear and anxiety, one thought kept recurring – could this be the prelude to something more serious than a haemorrhage? Could this be a loosening – a kind of shifting – of the retina before complete detachment and the onset of blindness? Instinctively he opened his eyes. Normal vision was restored except for the almost unnoticed background of unabsorbed blood.

He got home without further incident but in the days following similar onsets of distorted vision occurred with increasing regularity. Beset with worry and dismay, he now began to dread the thought of sleep when blindness could pounce on him unawares. When he did doze off, it was only to reawaken in an hour or so, staring wildly into the darkness, unable to decide whether or not he had been robbed of sight. At last he reached the stage where he left the light on all night and stared for hours at the ceiling, until – overcome by exhaustion – he would drift into an uneasy slumber.

During the day he moved about, tired and distraught. The mounting fear of eventual blindness forced on him the need to examine minutely and to memorize everyday objects that, up to this, had passed unnoticed and unvalued. He would stand for minutes on end staring at the figure of a cow outlined against the evening sky, given grace and beauty by the sleek darkening background. Or watch a horse, tormented by flies, stamp hoofs dramatically and shake mane and tail in unconscious splendour. The ever-changing colour of sea and sky were borne in on him for the first time, so that he would gaze in wonder at the infinite variety of something as familiar as his own face in the mirror.

This, too, became an object of study. But it was the eyes alone that he examined. The cowardly, treacherous eyes. He leant close to the mirror. Moved his head from side to side. Pulled the lower lids down gently. Looked deep into the pupils of these curious commonplace grotesques that could connive, without struggle, at their own destruction. Nowhere was there any evidence of treachery. Pupil, iris, cornea: all had the appearance of normality. No sign of sore or lesion. And yet, in the interior of these healthy-looking organs some canker was at work, undermining their efficiency. Eventually quenching their vision, so that the rest of the healthy body would become nothing but a tub of guts.

The continued lack of sleep began to tell on him. His hands, arms and the back of his neck crawled with invisible insects. Continually he rolled up his sleeves, examining the skin minutely. Nothing could be seen. Even a magnifying glass failed to reveal anything. They were tiny midges, he decided. Or gossamer spiders. At bay he kept the thought that they might be algae or some form of plankton floating about in his blood stream. Or crawling about under the skin.

It was when his eyes and the corners of his mouth started twitching that he took Delia's advice and asked Dr. Madden for sleeping tablets. The doctor refused.

'You're under the care of two specialists. First-rate men. If they recommend soporifics, I'll give them to you, surely. But not otherwise.'

'How the hell am I to get to sleep, so?'

'There's one infallible sleeping draught. A raw onion. Take one every night with a bottle of stout. You'll sleep the clock around.'

'Bugger you for a pal, John. Do you think I'm an idiot?'

But he tried the raw onion, And the stout. Two raw onions. Two stouts. It was no use. Hannah boiled onions in milk for him. Onions with garlic. Onions steeped in cider. She plied him with hot milk and pepper. Hot lemon and cloves. Hot milk and porridge. All to no avail.

Aching with tiredness, he would stretch out in bed, letting his limbs relax, till he lay flaccid as a jelly-fish. And then, just as he felt himself slipping into merciful darkness, he would be jolted violently awake, arms threshing, back arched, legs kicking madly. Once more he would lie staring at the lighted ceiling, guarding jealously each minute of vision.

His only sources of relief from insomnia were drink and Delia. The two vices most to be avoided.

It was a vicious circle. Weak from lack of sleep, let him

decide to drink himself into a sodden stupor. From pub to pub he would travel, sinking balls of malt and chasers of stout, until at length, pissed to the world, he would stagger out of Snout's or Smiler's or Humpy Daly's at closing time, to claw his way back to the Bank House. There he would reel upstairs and fling himself down on the bed, shedding only his boots and jacket. But though he slept long and deep, he knew what would greet him, come morning, when he opened his eyes. The ragged green curtain that betokened a haemorrhage or the brown glittering distortion that Dr. Roche had warned him was the prelude to a retinal detachment.

If he sought sleep in Delia's arms after a bout of sweating wrestling crumpetry, it was only to encounter the same symptoms as he drove back to Glenard or lay in bed listening to the Angelus bell next morning.

Delia, quick to grasp the significance of the sprawling figure snoring in her lap, grew impatient.

'Look here, Jim.' She shook him awake. 'We can't go on this way much longer.' They had taken the cliff path at Creevan and were lying on a grassy headland projecting far out into the sea.

Dizzy, bleary-eyed, he sat up.

'Wha's-a-matter?' He yawned and knuckled his eyes. 'Couldn't I have a few minutes' sleep itself?'

With prim, set face, she brushed and straightened out the wrinkles from her skirt.

'That's what's wrong. It's ages since you got a proper night's sleep.'

He yawned again.

'I know. I know. We don't have to go over all that again. Haven't I told you the way the eyes are acting up? It's hard to sleep when you don't know whether you'll wake up blind or not.'

'Listen, Jim, will you?' She spoke slowly, patiently, as though explaining something simple to a stupid child. 'Haven't I told you, as often as fingers and toes, that if you set yourself at it properly, you'll sleep till dinner time. It is just a matter of concentration. Concentrate hard enough and you'll sleep, I'm convinced of that. Of course, you must ask for help. Pray to the Blessed Virgin. Keep saying Hail Mary's. Say the Rosary. Say the fifteen decade one, if you have to. Do you know, I can't

174

say my few night prayers without falling asleep. So why shouldn't you . . .'

He listened to her voice rising and falling like the slow swell of the moonlit sea stretched out beneath them. Nibbling, gnawing, eating away their love with the sharp little teeth of pity.

'I read somewhere that if you imagine yourself lying on a cloud. Instead of in bed – you know what I mean. And you pull the fringes of the cloud round yourself like bedclothes, tucking them in at the back of your neck and over your shoulders till you are warm and comfy and settle deep down into the cloudy fluff with your eyes tight shut and . . .'

The moon was low in the sky. A harvest moon – sleek, lemon-coloured, half-grown. From it there poured a broad stream of glowing rippling lava that hissed and crackled as it came in contact with the beach. Rocks floated on its surface, their outlines distorted as though by rising steam. On either side were dark stretches of sea, margined by the darker line of cliffs cutting across the dimly-lit skyline. Straight out to sea, wallowing in the flood of moonlight, was Seal Island. On the end of its snout Thunder Light glowed intermittently, a thin finger of light flicking the water as it revolved. Along the humped back and long outstretched tail, tiny lights of cottages were strung out – phosphoresence gleaming on the scaly armour of some ancient sea monster.

The hiss and crackle of the sea, the faint put-put of a homing fishing-boat, the lunatic splendour of the harvest moon, the pleasant murmur of the girl's voice, gripped him suddenly with an aching intolerable hunger. A hunger that had to be put into words.

'Look, darling!' His wide-sweeping hand gathered in all the beauty of the night to lay at her feet. 'Isn't this . . . Never have I . . . Did you ever see . . .' He groped for the words that must be said.

'I knew you weren't paying attention. That's what is wrong with you. You're all the time woolgathering. You'll have to pull yourself together.'

He made one more attempt.

'See, dear! Out there. Seal Island . . . and . . . and . . . the bay.'

'Oh, flip! You'd think you never saw it before. If you had to look at it every night like me, you'd have proper cause for

175

complaint. That old lighthouse flashing away all night long into the bedroom. If I wasn't a good sleeper, I'd be as bad as yourself.'

'It's not the lighthouse. It's just ... the whole thing ... the ... the ...'

'I'll tell you what it is. It's just your own stupid invincible thickness. Look at the state you've got yourself into! Rambling away like a raving madman. All from pure lack of sleep.'

'You're wrong, Delia. It's—'

'You've taken to using me as a kind of a sleeping draught. You've no sooner had your oats than you're coiled up, snoring like a stuck pig. It's no compliment to me, I can tell you. But it'll stop. From now on there'll be no more love-making till you've caught up with your sleep.'

'But you can't—'

'Can't I? You'll see.'

She kept her word. Threats, entreaty, persuasion, nothing would make her relent. Instead, she added a new condition to her capitulation terms. He must try another doctor. A Dublin doctor this time.

Simpson, working on the assumption that the doctors you know are better than the one you don't know, held out. Roche and Savage, though worried at the onset of the new symptoms, had not suggested calling in a further consultant. Both seemed to feel that continued massive calcium treatment would halt the continued deterioration. Savage, emphasizing the importance of co-operation from the patient, continually warned against excess.

No one knew better than Simpson the truth of this admonition. Along with his other worries he had to carry the knowledge that he was almost certainly the author of his own mosfortunes. For this reason he told neither doctor of his continued insomnia. Too well he knew that it would be dragged out of him that its cause was due not alone to worry but to enforced abstinence. The corollary that drink and debauchery – twin causes of his complaint – were now become indispensable for sleep, would not be lost on the two specialists. It was impossible, therefore, to ask either of them for sleeping tablets.

For a few days he managed to achieve uneasy drunken slumber. But the hangover and the anguish of waiting for the resultant symptoms became too grievous to bear. He decided to cut the drink out altogether. After all, sleeplessness was to be preferred to blindness.

Now he stayed up as long as possible. Reading. Or listening to the radio. But always boredom and exhaustion drove him to bed. There he would lie, tossing from side to side, bones aching, nerves screaming for sleep. Plunging down into nightmare-ridden stupor, only to be jerked back into terrified wakefulness.

Soon, dream and reality became indistinguishable. The figures that stalked his dreams could be sensed waiting outside the locked door. Their cautious steps could be heard padding on the landing floor. Doors closed gently. Stairs creaked without reason. Whispered voices spoke words that straining ears could not catch. Sometimes, wakened by a shattering explosion, his ears still ringing with its fury, he was convinced that inside his own skull something terrible had happened. The warning symptoms of a tumour or the sudden impact of a brain haemorrhage. For minutes he would lie, scared to move, for fear movement was impossible. Once, finding a threatening figure stooped over the bed, he lashed back with clenched fist, not moving the rest of his body so as to take his assailant unawares. When he plucked up courage to roll over and face his adversary, he would not have believed in its existence were it not for the damning evidence of his torn and bloody knuckles. Until daybreak he lay, facing the closed door, breathing warily through open mouth, the only sound, his thumping heart.

Annie worried about him.

'I don't know what's come over him,' she told McCann. 'This last week or so he's gone to pieces. He tells me he can't sleep. And I believe the light's on in the sitting-room till all hours.'

'Take care but he's entertaining company. Long-haired company.'

'I wouldn't say so, Mr. Mac. He's had a sickener of all-night parties.' She grinned sardonically. 'I'd say the last one near did for him.'

McCann looked at her quizzically.

'Would that be the night you found the bloomers – the mourning ones – stuffed into the springs of the sofa?'

'Behind a cushion they were. 'Deed, it might be.'

'He was in better form then than he is now, begod. That was the night he drank rings round him, set me on my ear, put Vereker, Clancy and the doctor mouldy drunk, beat the lard out of Ned the Mines at lifting the half-hundreds and finished up by hammering a job—'

'He's off the booze altogether.'

'You're codding me, Annie?'

'I'm not. He hasn't had a drink for a week. That's what has me worried. I think myself he should have eased off gradually.'

'No wonder the poor devil can't sleep. No drink and no—'

He paused. Pursed his lips. Rubbed them gently with his forefinger, frowning thoughtfully.

'What about the Creevan lady? Has he dropped her, too?'

'Och, that affair is wound up long since. She had no time for him since he got the eye trouble. The thankless little trollop.'

'Are you sure, Annie? I've a notion he still calls out to Creevan.'

'The car hasn't left the garage since I don't know when. There's no other way he'd get to Creevan. And why, if I may ask, are you so curious about what the boss is doing?'

'I was just wondering.'

'You were, were you? You'll be taking up where he left off, I suppose? Keeping it in the family, as it were?'

Gazing at her with admiration, McCann said gravely:

'Do you know what it is, Mrs. Mahony, you're a woman of great discernment. I'd think very little of taking your advice.'

He turned back to the open ledger. With poised pencil, he started to add the long columns of interest decimals – rundowns whose total was due for carrying forward to the next page.

Mrs. Mahony picked up mop and pail. Waddled off towards the door.

'Much good may it do you,' she said over her shoulder before she slammed the door.

Passing the foot of the stairs, she heard the grandfather clock on the landing strike. A single chime.

It can't be the half hour, she thought, quickening her pace to check the time with the kitchen clock.

Half-way across the hall, the chime sounded again. At the

same time she heard Simpson hurry across the landing to his bedroom, closing the door behind him.

She counted the strokes of the clock. Ten. The clock's mad fast, she decided.

Almost at once the bedroom door re-opened and Simpson walked back across the landing.

She waited. The clock struck the half hour. Then commenced to strike again.

Once more Simpson hurried back to his room. The door closed. What on earth is he doing, she wondered.

At the last stroke of eleven, he emerged again.

'What's wrong, Mr. Simpson?' she called, as he hurried along the landing.

He stopped.

'Come up here a moment, Annie, will you?'

He waited whilst she puffed her way upstairs. Went ahead of her to the bedroom door.

'Stay here,' he said. 'I'll be back directly.'

She heard him go back up the landing. Again the clock struck. A pause. The hour commenced to strike. He's gone off his rocker completely, she decided.

At the third stroke he was back, with the door closed.

'Now, listen,' he commanded.

She looked at him, mouth agape.

'Not there,' he said. 'Over here.' He crossed to the bed.

Reluctantly she followed him.

'Now,' he demanded, 'what does it sound like from here?'

'What does what sound like?'

'The clock, of course. Can you hear it chiming?'

Through the adjoining wall, the sound of the striking clock could be heard distinctly.

'I can, surely.'

'It's not too loud? Listen carefully.'

'How do you mean – *too loud*?'

'Is it louder than it should be?'

'Och, Mr. Simpson dear, how on earth would I know? I'm just an ordinary working woman. How would I know anything about a complicated machine the like of a clock?'

'Would you, for Christ's sake, stop chattering and listen to the fucking clock.'

In silence, the furious and the affronted stood together. Heads cocked to one side. Listening.

At length Simpson crossed to the door.

'Tck! Tck! Tck! I'll have to start the chimer going again.'

'You needn't bother your barney, Mr. Simpson.' She had her hands clasped across her stomach. As she spoke, her elbows beat against her body like the wings of an angry bird. 'To get from in here,' she nodded towards the sitting-room, 'to here before the clock'd stop chiming, you'd want the agility of a cricket.'

'What on earth are you talking about, woman?'

'It's after striking twelve o'clock.'

Baffled, he paused. Then flung the door open.

'I'll just have to keep putting on the clock till it reaches—'

'You'll do no such-an-a thing. You'll stay right here where you are and tell me what all the commotion is about.'

He went across to the window, jerked the blind up and kept toying with the cord as he gazed out on the Square.

'Something went wrong with the clock last night.' His back was turned stiffly towards her.

'Aye.'

'It was striking too loud. Much too loud.'

'Well, Lord bless you, many's the night I've lain in bed and heard the clock striking the hours and I thought it would deafen me. It's just the quiet of the night that makes it sound so loud.'

He swung round.

'You don't understand, Annie. It got louder. All the time louder.'

'I know. I know.' Her voice was soothing. 'In a big, empty house like this, any class of a noise is like—' She searched for a simile. '—like in a railway station.'

'I had to put my head under the bedclothes in the end. It got so loud.'

'Would you listen to him, the poor angashore. It was nightmares you had. That was all. Sure, you've had no proper sleep for days.'

About to say something more, he stopped. Nodded his head slowly.

'You're probably right, Annie. It was all a nightmare.'

'I'll make you a hot drink the night. A rum punch that'll set you snoring till dinner-time.'

'I'll take a hot drink. But no rum.'

'You're a terrible man. Really you are. It's either a feast or a famine with you. Nothing less.'

She started for the door.

'Well,' she said. 'I'll make you some class of a hot drink. But without a sup of rum or whiskey—'

She went out, shaking her head sadly. Almost at once, she re-opened the door.

'Don't forget to re-set the clock. We'll not know where we are if you don't.'

He nodded dumbly.

Mrs. Mahony came back at eleven o'clock that night. Brewed from herbs and hot milk a foul-smelling, foul-tasting potion. Stood over Simpson till he drank it to the lees. Refused to leave till he went to bed.

'Even if you can't sleep,' she maintained, 'you're getting your rest.'

When she had gone, Simpson switched on the lights again. Rolled over on his right side. Settled down to sleep.

So tired was he that his head had scarcely stopped burrowing into the pillow than he was plunged into deep, dreamless sleep. He seemed only to have slept an instant when he was jolted awake by the chiming of the clock. His ears ringing with the sound, he lay, frozen into stillness, awaiting the second chime.

When it did not come, he tried to sink back once more into sleep. It was no use. Eyes tight-shut, fists clenched, body tensed, he strove with the compulsion to discover the time. At length he gave in. Held up his right wrist to the light. Squinted through narrowed eyes.

Twenty-five minutes to wait for the hour to strike. Fifteen hundred seconds. An unimaginable period. The only respite was to count off the seconds. Perhaps it might even bring on sleep.

He started to count. In sixties. Doubling down one finger of his left hand for each sixty. When the hand was completely fisted, he checked on his wrist watch. Only four minutes had passed.

He took up the count again. Deliberately slowing it down

181

so that the closed fist would amount to even more than five minutes. Half-way through the third minute he found that his concentration was slipping. Ten or even twenty seconds were being dropped from the count. A glance at his watch showed a lapse of only two minutes.

A new idea came to him. He would conjure up before his eyes the image of the clock on the landing. Watch through the glass panel in its belly the swing of the pendulum. Count in time to its beat. In this way the tally of used-up seconds could be reckoned correctly.

Against the backcloth of his closed eyelids, he strove to project the image of the clock, as he had seen it a score of times a day for half a lifetime.

Like ectoplasm, amorphous, wavering, it began to take shape. The clock-case first, rising tall and slender, from its broad-based plinth. It was a mahogany case – one of the few objects upon which Annie lavished attention. Its highly-polished surface, laced with bright yellow scrollwork, glowed warmly. The glass panel, too, was decorated with scrollwork but not so closely grouped as to obscure the gleam of the swinging pendulum. As it swung back and forth, he sought not only to catch the rhythm of its motion but also to hear the tick of the escapement.

At last his straining ears caught and held the faint sound of the clock. Once more he commenced to count. As he did so, the sound became clearer, so that he was able to transfer his attention to the clock face.

It read nineteen minutes from the hour. By pressing his face to the glass he could actually see the jerky movement of the minute hand as it nibbled at the seconds.

Soon he found there was no need to reckon up the passing seconds. All he had to do was watch the minute hand eat its way up the clock face until, with a final bite, it registered the hour.

The three-quarter hour was scarcely passed when he was stunned to hear the muted clamour, the rattling, clanking, groaning that preceded the striking of the hour.

When the sound ceased, he could picture the striker poised, quivering, ready for the first chime. And then, before he had time to buttress himself against it, the first stroke of the hour was upon him.

There was nothing abnormal about the sound. It was no louder than usual. Perhaps a little more penetrating. But then, it had always had a harsh, discordant note.

The second and third chimes carried a similar strain. It was when the mechanism was whirring, preparatory to the fourth chime, that Simpson suddenly realized the difference in the quality of the sound.

It had nothing to do with the volume of the note. Or its pitch. Or resonance. It was its penetrating power. The waves of pulsing sound that, in the daytime, broke impotently against the stubborn barrier of his ear-drums, had managed, under cover of the night, to breach these defences. Like surf bursting its way into a deep rocky cavern, chime after chime swept into his cringing skull, to swirl and churn around the bony cavity, smashing against its walls with dull, aching clangour.

At the last stroke of the clock, he lay weak and shaken, his ears still ringing with the echoes of the din.

It was many minutes before he could steel himself to quit the warmth of the bed and do what must be done. At last he crept out, switched on the landing light and padded his way the length of the corridor. Opening the door of the clock case, he stood, body swaying wearily, eyes half-closed, trying to decide which of the weights controlled the striker.

'Blast it, anyway!' He shut the glass-panelled door. Wrenched back the frame of the clock face. Wrapped his handkerchief round the striker, knotting it securely.

'That'll keep your trap shut, you noisy bastard,' he muttered, as he started back to his room.

But it didn't. Till daybreak, he lay sleepless, listening to the thwarted whirring of the striking mechanism, fearful lest the handkerchief would unloosen and the racket re-commence.

Next morning, the first thing he did was to unhook the chiming weight and bring it down to the kitchen.

'Here, Annie,' he said. 'Put this away. It'll not keep me awake any more.'

Mrs. Mahony took it from him.

'What's this?' she asked, turning it over in her hands. 'Oh, it's the clock weight.' She nodded her head approvingly. ' 'Deed and your right. You'll have a good sleep the night.

'It never kept the best of time, anyway,' she added.

Simpson went to bed early that night. It was the first time for many days that his mind was free from worry. The haemorrhages had eased off since he had gone on the dry. Abstinence had muzzled his desire. The possibility of at last cleaning his slate in confession had begun to appear possible. The handing over of the clock weight to Mrs. Mahony had seemed in some way symbolic.

He coiled up, gathering the bedclothes tightly round himself, luxuriating in the thought of the hours of deep reviving sleep that lay ahead, sensible only of the quiet ticking of the landing clock – slow, soothing, wonted.

The words sank slowly into his consciousness, drawing him down to black satiny depth where words spun slowly. And spinning, sank. Sloooow. Soooothing. Woooonted . . .

He jerked awake. WONTED. Why, he shouldn't be hearing the sound of the clock at all. It's at the far end of the bloody landing. The sound couldn't possibly carry from there. And even if it could, why had he never heard it till now? It was true he had heard the ticking of the clock last night. But that was his own doing. He had made audible his own mental images. By sheer effort of will. Surely to heaven he was not now to be afflicted with poltergeists of his own creation.

He listened. It was no figment of the imagination. Faintly the beat of the pendulum came to him. Faintly – but quite distinct. It had the same quality of penetration as the bucking chimes.

Soft, insistent, it invaded his skull, tapping lightly behind eyes, ears, forehead. The premonition came to him that these tiny hammer blows were but the probings, the testing out of his defences, by an advance guard. The main body of his tormentors had yet to launch its attack.

Appalled at this thought, he sat up. At once the ticking ceased. Ah, now I know what it is, he decided. The blood pounding in my ears. All this worry and excitement has caused the blood pressure to rise. Naturally the sound of the beat is different. And, of course, when you lie down this sound becomes more apparent.

Satisfied, he lay back. Sure enough, all that could be heard was the steady throbbing of the blood in his ears. A normal reassuring sound. Aren't you the right bloody idiot, he chided. Getting yourself worked up into such a pitch over nothing.

He pulled down the pillow till it met his shoulder, burrowed his head in deeply and prepared to sleep. But now he was beset by a new phenomenon. Someone had told him once of a cardiac condition that produced what was known as a diastolic heart beat. A double beat of the heart. This was the latest misfortune to befall him.

Tick-tick. Tick-tick. Tick-tick. Like a time bomb, his heart was ticking out a warning message. At any moment the explosion could come.

He sat up again. If his ticker was going to burst, he'd prefer to die sitting up. There was some chance of fighting back in that position. If you stayed lying down, you had no hope of survival. He took a deep breath, expelling it slowly through his mouth. Then he allowed himself to listen.

The double heart beat had ceased. Instead the ticking of the landing clock had recommenced. Loud and clear. As if the grandfather clock were standing in the corner of the room. The wretched thing had never stopped ticking – that was the explanation.

For a moment the relief of knowing that he was not suffering from some murderous form of cardiac trouble, banished all his other worries. Then the steady inexorable thudding inside his head gave notice that the full force of his tormentors was now deployed.

He tried plugging his ears with his fingertips. This merely had the effect of reversing the direction of the sound. Now it tried to force its way out, fomenting inside his skull, where it swelled up in enormous bubbles that burst steadily and painfully against the tender interior of his eardrums.

Pulling the bedclothes over his head served him little better. The sound seeped through, its volume increased, it seemed, by the claustrophobic atmosphere.

Driven beyond endurance, he leaped out of bed, flung open the door and switched on the landing light. At the far end of the corridor the grandfather clock stood – grave and dignified – the sound from its mechanism, the accustomed discreet whisper.

Enraged still further at this sight, he strode along the landing, pulled open the door of the clock case and stopped the swing of the pendulum. That should do the job, he calculated.

In the silence that ensued, he stayed, eyeing dubiously the

motionless pendulum. Suddenly he reached into the case, unhooked the remaining weight and left it down on the passage floor.

That's better, he decided, slamming the clock case door. On his way back up the corridor, a steady dripping sound caught his attention. It came from the kitchen. Cursing softly under his breath, he went downstairs.

The kitchen door was open. From inside came the rustle of a thousand tiny scuttling feet. Like a jeweller's shop with its whispering ranks of watches and clocks. It was the curse-of-God cockroaches. He had forgotten all about them.

Shuddering with disgust he stopped at the foot of the stairs. Nauseated. Unmanned.

Above every other sound rose the measured tick-tock of the water dripping into the steel sink. If he were to get peace to sleep, this must surely stop. Steeling himself, he walked to the open door. Switched on the light. Waited.

The rustle of feet rose to a frantic scramble. Died away slowly. Had ceased completely by the time he ventured into the kitchen, empty but for two cockroaches, plump and polished – the last of the many – that scurried to the safety of a cracked flagstone at his approach.

He turned off the tap. Tightened the other one. Turned to go. The deep throaty tick of the wall clock gave him pause. It seemed to him a much louder tick than the landing clock. No reason why it wouldn't force its way into his bedroom. The staircase well would act as a sounding board and increase the volume of noise. Better take no chances. He could explain to Annie in the morning.

He opened the front of the clock and stopped the pendulum. Stood back and listened. Nothing could be heard except his own breathing. At last the house had been silenced.

He closed the kitchen door and started back up to his room, comforted by the thought that the office clock was electric and quite soundless.

Back in bed, he settled himself down once more to sleep, taking the precaution this time of rattling off three perfunctory Hail Marys.

At last he slept. For how long, he did not know. Except that it was still dark when he awoke to the ticking of the wristwatch against his ear. He had placed it, as usual, under the pillow, but it had slipped down during the night. Now it prattled away cheerfully into the lobe of his right ear. He was about to stuff it back under the pillow when he changed his mind. No use looking for trouble.

He held the watch at arm's length. Strained his ears. Not a sound could be heard. Satisfied, he reached out, left the watch on the bedside table and coiled up contentedly once more.

Not for long. Hardly had he drawn the first breath that was the prelude to slumber when the chattering of the watch jogged him awake. The solemn beat of the pendulum clock was hard enough to bear. This inane prattling was much worse. It was as if, inside the watch case, a metal cricket toiled, hind legs pedalling, metal knees rasping, in the frantic effort to produce the dry, distasteful, rattling chirp that passed muster for merriment.

Wearily he got out of bed and shifted the watch to the dressing-table. He stood looking down at it uncertainly. Even from here, the sound of its mechanism was inaudible. Still . . . better to be sure than sorry. Picking up the watch, he left the room and went to the bathroom where he hung it on a cup-hook beside the mirror. He closed the door of the bathroom, rattling the door-knob to make sure the watch was safely closed in and could not escape. Then, shame-faced, he slunk back to bed. Until daybreak he lay awake, rolling and tossing in the bed, unable to relax sufficiently to fall asleep. With the morning sunshine breaking into the room, he switched off the light and managed to doze uneasily until breakfast time.

Red-eyed, unshaven, irritable, he cut short Mrs. Mahony's inquiries.

'How do you think anyone could sleep in this house, with taps dripping all night and that wretched clock in the kitchen twanging away on the double-bass.'

She nodded her head understandingly.

'I was just thinking it was hardly run down. Was it keeping you awake?'

'It makes more noise than that wooden monster on the landing.'

'Let it stay idle so. There's no great need of a clock in the kitchen anyway.'

'Here,' he said, taking the wristwatch out of his pocket. 'You can use this. I don't want it at the moment.'

187

She gazed at him incredulously.

'You're not going to tell me that the watch—' She stopped. He's in a bad way all right, she thought. Even the sound of the wristwatch is getting him down. 'It'll do me very nicely, Mr. Simpson. I'll hang it up on the dresser.'

She went out to the kitchen, shaking her head and muttering to herself:

'Tck! Tck! Tck! The poor fellow. In the name of God, where will it all end?'

All day long, Simpson moved aimlessly around, unable to remain for very long by himself, anxious for someone to bear him company.

In and out of the kitchen he wandered, trying to engage Mrs. Mahony in conversation. Only to be driven out when she made it plain that he was keeping her back in her housework.

He slipped into the office when he surmised it was free of customers. McCann hardly bothered to hide his impatience.

'Do you want anything, Manager?'

'No. Not particularly. I was just wondering—' What could he say to start up a conversation? 'Any word of that ruffian Mullen at all? Did that fellow Brady from The Stag's Head ever write again?'

'It's funny you should mention Brian Mullen. Wasn't the old hen herself in this morning. Bubbling over with the news that her little darling is coming home for a holiday.'

'What's that?'

'She says Brian is coming over for a holiday. He's been working too hard. Needs a rest.'

'It's a rest he'll get if he ever shows his nose in the village. The Civic Guards'll pick him up ... What's the use of talking nonsense? He'll not come home. He'd never have the neck.'

'You're wrong, Manager. I'll gamble you that he turns up, large as life. Going from pub to pub like a conquering hero. Buying drinks for the boys everywhere he goes.'

'He'd never dare. He must know bloody well that I'd put the dogs on him if I ever got the chance.'

'They still talk about him, you know. He has become part of the folk-lore of the village. Any company you're in, you've only to mention his name and the saga starts. The night Brian sucked his way through a case of eggs. The time Brian won the pint-drinking competition. Brian's reputation as an arch-hoorsmaster. It always finishes up with someone saying, in a reverent sort of way: "He was the rare duck." '

'Oh, he's a duck all right. You couldn't keep track on him for ducking. But he'll not duck out of his debt to the Bank, if I've any say in it.'

'Can I speak to you for a moment, Mr. McCann?' A worried-looking woman, with a pale face and purple hat, was waving an Income Tax Assessment form in a frantic effort to attract his attention. 'I got this latty-tat in the post this morning. What's it all about, d'you think?'

'Excuse me, Manager.' McCann moved over to the counter. Simpson stood uncertainly, shuffling his feet. The relief cashier was busy in his box: it was going to take some time for McCann to persuade the poor frightened woman that the sledge-hammer thickness of tax inspectors is best ignored. At last Simpson left the office.

All evening and far into the night, he kept on the move. Seeking company. Dreading the hour when he must go to bed. At two in the morning he staggered blindly to his room, flung off his clothes and rolled into bed. Before falling asleep he did a mental tour of the house to assure himself that every clock had been duly stopped. Satisfied, he plummeted into a stupor of sleep.

He awoke to the certainty that there was a clock in the room. Even though there was no present evidence of it, he felt the room to be full of latent sound. Sound that had awakened him and that would recur again.

Tense, expectant, he lay waiting. The house was drained dry of all sound. You could actually hear the stillness. It was as if every room in the house, every brick and timber, waited, like himself, with bated breath. When he moved, the creak of the bedsprings brought an avalanche of noise. He settled himself down once more, now on the flat of his back, his two fisted hands pressed tight against his thighs, his ears straining to catch the first whisper of sound.

When, at last, it came, it was the sound he expected. The ticking of a clock. Not the slow pendulum variety but the rapid chatter of a watch. Or rather, judging by the volume of the sound, an alarm clock.

189

He tried to place the direction from whence the sound was coming. But it seemed to change position. Now coming from the wardrobe. Now the dressing-table. Now the mantelpiece. Sometimes the ticking faded, only to return once more, loud and clear. There was no doubt at all about it. Somewhere in the room was hidden a watch or clock, a thing long forgotten, probably with mainspring or balance wheel broken, intended to be sent away for repair but in the meanwhile put away. But where?

Simpson pushed back the clothes and swung out of bed. As his feet touched the floor, the sound stopped. It did not die away into silence. It stopped instantly. At full pitch. Sitting on the side of the bed, he waited for the sound to recommence.

It did. From the direction of the chest of drawers in the corner of the room. He moved over to it and pulled out a drawer. The ticking stopped immediately.

Drawer by drawer, he went through the contents, spilling out shirts, socks, ties, underwear, sweaters, scarves. As he was working on the last drawer, the ticking started up again. This time from the wardrobe.

He straightened up slowly, eyeing the wardrobe with a cagey look. No use trying the cupboard part of it. Nothing would be found there, except perhaps in the pockets of an old suit. He would do the drawer first.

On tip-toe he crossed the room. Stooped down carefully. Eased open the drawer. Once more the ticking stopped.

It was a linen drawer, packed tight with blankets, sheets, table-linen, towels, pillows and bolster slips. Methodically he took them out, one by one, placing them carefully on the floor. The drawer emptied, he started packing them all back again. By this time the ticking had broken out at the dressing-table.

Ignoring it, he opened the wardrobe door and went through all the pockets of his suits. Not a sign of a watch.

The chattering of the watch mechanism still sounded from the dressing-table. Quietly he approached it. Bent down and listened intently at each drawer in turn. Stopped at the lower left-hand drawer, from which the sound plainly emerged.

He wrenched open the drawer. The sound stopped. But, tucked away amongst a jumble of letters and bills, newspaper cuttings and photographs, the accumulated junk of a lifetime, was a silver pocket-watch – keepsake of an uncle long dead, who had stood sponsor at his christening.

Triumphantly, he picked it up. Opened the back. Examined the works. By dint of violent shaking the balance wheel could be persuaded to sway languidly to and fro. Otherwise there was not a tick left in it.

He stayed studying the useless mechanism, trying to figure out what had set it in motion. A mouse, he decided. Must set a trap tomorrow. In the meanwhile this bloody yoke must go downstairs.

He left it in the wall press of the dining-room and started back up the stairs again. Scarcely had he reached the stairhead than he heard, through the open door of the bedroom, the dry, monotonous ticking. Still coming from the dressing-table.

There were four drawers unsearched. One by one he emptied each of them. Poked about amongst the contents. Jumbled everything back in again.

He hauled out the dressing-table. Searched behind it. Underneath. He shifted the wardrobe, the chest of drawers, the bedside table. Under the bed he crawled, feeling around in all directions. He rolled back the carpet from each wall, investigating gapped or loose floor-boards. He pulled out the fender. Examined the grate. Reached up inside the chimney, pawing blindly around the flue.

His soot-stained hands and the begrimed state of his pyjamas brought the search to an end. In the bathroom, getting cleaned up, he tried to reason out the implications behind this mysterious phenomenon.

If there was no watch or clock in the room, he was suffering from hallucinations. Cracking up. A person who heard imaginary noises was – not to put a tooth in it – nothing but a raving lunatic. A proper nut.

'If, on the other hand, the sound was external, he could learn to live with it. What matter where the wretched watch was concealed? Up in the rafters or under the floor-boards, it counted for nothing against his sanity.

So, back once more in bed, he tried to visualize the watch. Not in any particular part of the room – that would call for more fruitless rummaging. No – against the screen of his closed eyelids, purpled by the dazzle of the naked light bulb, he would project the image of the undiscoverable timepiece. Undiscoverable timepiece. He rolled the words around his mouth, savouring their strutting pompous gait. He kept repeating them, like an incantation, until there was conjured up the hazy outlines of a watch.

It appeared to be a pocket watch, like his Uncle Willie's. The back was hinged open so that the mechanism was exposed to view. Nothing moved. The balance wheel hung idle and behind it the bank of cog-wheels that loomed larger and larger until swallowed up in the shadows, was motionless.

Even as he watched, the mechanism came to life. The balance wheel glittered as it flickered back and forth. The cog-wheels commenced turning. Levers rose and fell. All in time to a harsh implacable ticking. Underneath this sound rose a constant clank and rattle and creak as the cog-wheels meshed one with another in an imperceptibly dwindling twitch that died out finally in the huge cog-wheels in the background. This gradual change from motion to immobility fascinated him. He decided to start at the small, stuttering, impatient cog-wheel – the first to receive impulse – and follow the jerky movements down the long reach of wheels until he pin-pointed the exact wheel where motion ceased.

He had hardly covered more than a dozen wheels when the whole mechanism came to a sudden grinding halt and he was left with the darkened screen of his eyelids and the silence of the room.

Still unwilling to give in that he was suffering from delusions, he clung to the belief that somewhere hidden in the room was a watch that went intermittently.

As if to prove him right, the next time the ticking started his eyes shut automatically and the watch materialized. Once more he tried to track down, wheel by wheel, where motion ended and stasis began. This time he got a few wheels further on before the mechanism stopped.

But now he found himself a prisoner of his convictions. Let the ticking start: the watch mechanism be evoked: and he was condemned to travel from wheel to wheel in his impossible task.

Sometimes he sought to ease his burden by starting at the cog-wheel where last he had finished. It was of no avail. The peremptory ticking – the wagging of an admonitory finger – would allow no cheating. It insisted he make certain he was

really starting where he had left off. By the time he had
checked and re-checked, the wheels had come to a stop. At
length the futility of this endless toil forced him to make
another effort to find where the watch was concealed.

Once out on the floor, everything returned to normal. The
ticking, when it came, was merely the humdrum sound of an
ordinary watch. He commenced to hunt around. Starting with
the drawers, he investigated minutely. Loose boards were lifted
once more. Carpet ends rolled back. On the assumption that
it could be a tiny wristwatch, he stood on a chair and examined
window ledges, door lintel, picture rail.

Dreading the thought of returning to bed, he prowled back
and forth across the bedroom floor, trying to figure out the
possible whereabouts of this wretched nuisance. It must be in
the rafters, he at last decided. He was trying to remember
where the torch was, so that he could investigate, when the
ticking restarted.

Instantly he was caught in the rhythm, as though obeying
the commands of a drill sergeant.

Left! Right! Left! Right! Up and down the room he
marched. In time with the beat. Wheeling smartly at each
wall.

He had now become a working part of the clock itself –
for it had grown in stature as it had in beat – a cog-wheel
meshed to a powered cog-wheel and himself meshed to and
powering a third. One of a series of ever-larger – or ever-
smaller – wheels, bustling along like himself at an ever-slower –
or ever-faster – speed. What position he occupied in the system
of wheels, it was impossible to tell. All he could be certain of
was that he was neither first nor last. All around him he could
hear the thud and rattle and creak of moving parts. Just as his
own feet thudded on the rattling, creaking, carpeted floor-
boards.

When the sound ceased abruptly, he came to a halt – dizzy,
trembling, soaked in sweat. He crept back to bed. But not to
sleep. The rest of the night was spent either counting cog-
wheels or tramping the floor.

When Annie was questioned next morning, she was unable
to help.

'God knows, Mr. Simpson, you could be right. There's been
a constant pilgrimage up and down that trap-door to the attic

since I came around here. If it wasn't plumbers or electricians or tradesmen of some sort or another, it was one of yourselves with books or parcels. It would be a wonder to heaven if there was nothing left behind with all the coming and going.'

'If there's something up there, I'm going to find it.'

'Do you mean you're going to go up there, poking around, looking for a going clock? Who in the name of God would leave the like of that after them? Not to mention keep it wound?'

'It could be a battered out alarm clock that the mice are tricking at. It's been known to happen before.'

'What d'you think your doctors would say if they knew a man in your state of health proposed to plouter around lifting big heavy ledgers and bulky parcels? In a filthy old attic. Sure you might hit your head off the roof timbers and do more damage to your eye. Or maybe even slip off of one of the rafters and come down through the ceiling.'

'Would you stop prating and get me the step-ladder.'

When he lifted the trap-door and climbed into the attic, he flinched at the enormity of his task. The attic occupied the whole extent of the Bank roof. It was lit by one small skylight, located near floor level and about mid-length of the roof. Little light penetrated to the far side of the room and the two gable-ends were pools of gloom. But there was enough light to discern the heaped-up mass of wooden boxes packed tight with books and documents: the parcels each containing a half-year's collection of dockets, vouchers and requisitions: the tattered, broken-backed ledgers labelled with the dates commenced and finished. The bulk of this dusty, mildewed accumulation should have been sorted out and lorried off years ago to the nearest foundry for destruction if Simpson and his predecessors had not dodged a tough unrewarding chore.

The room was baked with heat. He took off his jacket and hung it on the spike of the window fastener. Reluctantly he removed his hat, already sticking to his forehead with sweat. He hung it on top of the jacket. Took out a pocket comb. Patted and carefully combed the nearly-fully-regrown pigtail into place. Looked around. Sighed. A start must be made some place. Best to work along the rafters, clearing before him as he went.

All morning he worked. First shifting books, parcels and boxes into even higher heaps to expose the spaces between three or four rafters. Then he walked the length of every rafter, examining minutely the sections between each, lifting up rags, papers, bits of broken board, cardboard boxes, empty bottles. With a pointed stick he poked into crevices in the brickwork and the corners of timbers where cobweb-encased dust had lodged. Gingerly he lifted coiled wires and searched underneath, fearful of chancing on a stripped wire. Poked around and under the pipes leading from the tank.

One section done, he heaved across another load of obsolete material, to lay bare a further section of rafters. He began to take pleasure in the heavy, sweating work, ignoring the heat and the dust, stepping up the weight of the lift as he found his long-unused muscles answering to the strain. Soon he hardly knew or cared for what purpose this massive labour had been undertaken. The satisfaction of physical exertion: the delight at finding his body still a willing servant: the knowledge that skill and strength had not forsaken him; these sensations kept him toiling on till the last stretch of rafters was cleared and examined.

Sweating, dusty, breathless, he stood – a puzzled expression on his face. Then it dawned on him that all this labour was wasted. Nothing had been found.

Depression softened his limbs. His shoulders drooped. His arms, tired and aching, hung listless. When he crossed the rafters to the skylight, to collect his hat and coat, the spring had gone from his step.

That night and the next night, the ticking of the clock tormented him until at last, weary and dazed from lack of sleep, he was forced to admit that it was an hallucination. As though his tortured nerves welcomed the surrender, he dropped off at once into a deep, dreamless slumber.

He slept late, waking up dizzy, stupefied, unrefreshed. And to the recognition that he was on the verge of a nervous breakdown. Listlessly he shaved and dressed, thankful for the knowledge that, so far at least, his delusions were confined to the hours of darkness.

His hands seemed to have become clumsy, the fingers slow-moving and unreliable. He nicked himself repeatedly with the razor, the soap kept slipping from his grasp, the buttons of his trousers would no longer fit the button holes. When he began to make the knot in his tie, he found that he no longer remembered how it was done. Again and again he tried, going through all manner of complicated movements, until it was borne in on him that he did not even know how to begin. Whether from the left or right? Which end of the tie should be pulled down furthest? Almost weeping from chagrin, he stared at the frowning, blotchy face and the stupid nerveless hands holding the ends of the tie.

It was at this moment that the ticking started up again.

Horrified, he listened, aware at last that his delusions must now be borne both night and day. At this thought, the scream that had been bubbling in his throat these last three nights threatened to erupt. By clamping tight his mouth he contained it, knowing well that if he started to scream, he would not be able to stop.

Opening the bedroom door, he shouted:

'Annie!'

'What is it, sir?'

'Come up here a minute. Quickly.'

He waited impatiently as she lumbered up the stairs. Before she reached the landing the ticking had stopped.

'Well, sir?' She waited at the door.

'Socks,' he said. 'Clean socks. Where are they?'

'Tck! Tck! Tck! Clean socks. Did you drive me up all those stairs to tell you where the clean socks are? Don't you know right well they're here?' She pulled open a drawer. 'Look at them. There's enough here to do you till Christmas.'

'But where's the brown ones?'

'Brown ones?'

'Yes. Don't you remember? I bought them in Dublin the last time I was on holiday.'

'Brown ones?' Pair by pair, she took them out, leaving them on top of the chest of drawers. The drawer empty, she wheeled around. 'I told you there were no brown ones. Grey or black – that'll all you ever went in for.'

She began replacing the socks. In a few minutes she would be gone. There was only one way to detain her.

'Are you trying to make me out a liar, Mrs. Mahony?'

She turned round slowly, a pair of socks in either hand. Eyebrows lifted, jaw dropped, she gaped at him.

196

'My goodness,' she said. 'What's biting His Lordship this morning? He must have got out of the wrong side of his bed.'

'That's a poor class of a joke. Making a mock of somebody because they can't sleep. Through no fault of their own. You can surely do better than that.'

Confused, crestfallen, she looked at him appealingly.

'Och, Mr. Simpson, sure you know fine I wouldn't—'

His upraised hand cut short her apologies.

'Ssh,' he whispered. 'D'you hear it?'

The clock was ticking, loud and distinct. It could have been sitting on the bedside table, so clear was the sound.

Mrs. Mahony did not hesitate. She waddled over to the head of the bed. Inclined her ear for a second towards the wall. Reached out her fisted hand and rapped. Once only. Very, very gently.

The ticking stopped immediately.

'An end'll be put to *your* gallop, you ill-begotten whelp.'

She made the Sign of the Cross on the spot where she had rapped. Put her lips against the wall. Spoke a few indistinct words.

'What do you think it is, Annie?'

She turned round, her face grave, worried.

'It's an insect, sir. A class of an ould beetle that burrows in timber.'

'How does he make the ticking noise?'

"With his head. He batters it against the wood. In a fit of temper. They say he's the most cantankerous insect in the whole universe.'

'He's welcome to batter his brains out. I was beginning to think I was suffering from delusions. Hearing that yoke at his capers night after night. With not a clock around anywhere. Think of it. A beetle. An insignificant bloody beetle. That's the best bit of news I've heard for many a long day, Annie.'

She shook her head.

'I wouldn't say that, Mr. Simpson. There's ill-luck attached to them. They're no asset to any house.'

'Why?'

'They're called the Death Watch. You get people to say—'

She broke off and started to waddle to the door.

'What do they say?'

Over her shoulder, without stopping, she said:

197

'Och, 'tis an ould pishogue. Nobody believes it.'

'But what is it?' he persisted.

She turned at the door.

'They say it's a warning ... a warning of death ... for some person in the house ... sure, it's all a lot of nonsense.'

'Look, Annie. We're well used to cockroaches in this house. And your Death Watch is just another sort of cockroach. So don't worry.'

As she turned to go, he asked:

'What kind of a curse were you laying on the poor beetle when you spoke into the wall there now?'

'You'd only laugh at me if I told you. You don't believe in cures ... or charms ... or anything that's handed down by the old people.'

'Tell me, Annie,' he pressed.

'I will not, then. All the good would go out of it if I did. But I'll engage it'll help. Even if it'll not do the trick.'

'How do you mean?'

'Sure, if a thing's laid down, there's no deferring it. All you can do is, wish it away some place else.'

'And that's what you did?'

'What else could I do?'

The glow of relief and tranquillity that was welling up inside him, spilled over.

'Annie,' he said, 'you're a terrible person, that's what you are. You have me properly spoiled.'

'Ach, hould your tongue. It's little enough to do for anybody.'

She left the room. With rapid accustomed fingers he knotted his tie, slipped on his jacket and went down for breakfast.

That night he went to bed early. For the full round of the clock he slept, waking at ten o'clock, to find the sight gone completely from his damaged eye.

CHAPTER THREE

IT was some time before the full impact of this new disaster smote him. In fact, while he was shaving and dressing, it appeared that the loss of sight in one eye was compensated by clearer vision in the other. Up to this the combined vision of both eyes had suffered from the continual cloudy blur affecting one. Now there was no unabsorbed blood whatever to hamper the sight.

At breakfast he read the paper without difficulty, instead of peering at the print through the green scum that always floated before his eyes. It was many months since he had enjoyed such comfort.

In a vague way he recognized that something of significance had happened but he never thought to connect it with the threatened detachment of the retina. This calamity, he knew from experience, would be ushered in with terrifying glitter and distortion. It would happen after physical or emotional stress; not whilst the body was stretched out, supine and relaxed, the eyes closed in slumber.

Only when he closed his left eye – the sound eye – did he realize the completeness of the loss of sight of the other one. This was absolute and impenetrable darkness. Limitless. Stretching to infinity. It cowed the spirit. Quenched all hope, Brought anguish and despair.

The blood specialist's warning words came back to him. *Retinal displacement. Most serious. Results in complete and incurable loss of sight. Danger of sympathetic blindness in the remaining eye.*

The unfairness of this new blow after the weeks of abstinence embittered him. If this was the reward of virtue, he would have been better employed in vice and villainy. It would seem that sobriety and decorous behaviour paid no dividends. Maybe a fellow would be better off battering it out the best way he could. Regardless of God or man.

At this bleak prospect he flinched. A man must believe in something. No doubt about that. Though it was hard to ac-

199

cept that his present misfortunes had been planned and laid down by Divine Providence. You'd be no better than a beast in a slaughter house waiting patiently for the butcher to roll up his sleeves and spit on his hands before splitting your skull with the pole-axe.

Still, there was no knowing. Maybe this whole calamitous business might have been avoided if you had gone to the sacraments as time and again you swore you would. But no. You had other ideas. You put your faith in the medicine-men. Now you see where it has got you.

The safe thing was to have a foot in either camp. See a doctor but get confession as well. He would contact Madden this evening. Get him to fix up an appointment with the best specialist to be had in Dublin. He should have done this long since. Instead of attending for months past two quacks who could think of nothing better than stuffing him full of calcium. The inside must be nearly burned out of him by this time with all the quick lime it had been fed.

If he had only heeded Delia when she warned him about those two chancers, he would have two working eyes in his head instead of one. He would call in to see her on the way back from Dr. Madden's. Tell her of his decision. She'd be delighted. Things would be back again on the old footing.

Then, on his way back home, he would stop off at Cleggan church and get Confession. If there was no one in the church, there'd be nothing for it but the Parochial House. Though he had never been very keen on that caper. Telling your sins in the dark anonymity of a confessional box was one thing: a very different matter barging into the priest's sitting-room, saying a few words about the weather and the crops and the next minute kneeling at his feet, asking to have your pot scraped. Too cold-blooded altogether. Nothing would convince him that a priest would not remember all the sins he was told under *those* circumstances. And the name of the penitent. Though they would like you to believe that the sins you tell a priest are wiped from his memory a few minutes after confession. As though he has built-in windscreen wipers. Well, that hare won't sit. Granted that on a Saturday night with a constant stream of penitents shuttling out and in for hours on end, the priest's only recollection would be of the boring lack of inventiveness shown by the customers. It was a very different

200

kettle of fish pretending that he would forget what you told him man to man in the quiet of the Presbytery. Still, it's better to get the job done when you're in the mood for doing it. So you're going to get your skillet cleaned this evening, my friend, and no more shilly-shallying.

A decision come to, he felt happier. After all, he still had perfect vision out of one eye and the specialists could be wrong about retinal displacement. A really first-class man would surely know of an operation to replace the retina. It hardly seemed more difficult than other eye operations he had heard of.

Dr. Madden, after examining the eye, did not hold out much hope. Though he admitted that, with his limited knowledge, he could not positively diagnose a retinal detachment.

He agreed with Simpson that it might be better to get the advice of a really-first class Dublin specialist, in case there was any danger of loss of vision in the sound eye.

'Tell you what I'll do,' said Madden. 'I'll ring up Dr. West-wood. He's the best man in general practice in Dublin. And what's more important, he's in touch with the top medical brains in the country. If he can't do anything for you, no one can.'

An appointment was arranged for Simpson at three o'clock on the day after next.

'It would be as well if you went to Dublin tomorrow,' Madden advised. 'You'd be in better form for a medical check-up.

'And Westwood said you were to be prepared to stay for a week,' he added. 'He must intend to give you a proper going over.'

He saw Simpson to the door.

'Better stay off the drink in Dublin, or Westwood will pack you off to John of God's. He's a real sergeant-major, they say.'

He patted Simpson's back. 'Good luck, Jim.'

Simpson stopped off at Hannah Murphy's on the way back through the village. The bar was empty. He rapped on the counter.

'Well, look who's here,' said Delia, when she came in from the kitchen. 'I thought you'd given us the go by, it's so long since you called.'

201

'I was in poor shape these last few weeks. Hardly stirred out of the house. Up the bloody walls I was going. The old nerves, I think.'

Elbows on the counter, chin knuckle-propped, she gazed at him.

'Up the walls, eh? Did you miss me that much? Maybe now you'll take my advice and see a proper doctor before those two quacks have you ruined.'

'As a matter of fact, I've just seen Madden. He has arranged for me to see a Dublin specialist.'

She straightened up.

'About time, too. God knows, I was never as glad to hear anything. This calls for a little drink.' She turned to the shelves. 'A Jameson Ten if I'm not mistaken. And for myself ... let's see now ... I think on this special occasion ... a little brandy ... there we are!'

She handed him the glass. Raised her own.

'Here's good health, Jim. You'll be on the mend from now on.'

'Good luck, Delia.'

Slowly he drank, savouring the familiar prickling tang.

'I'd need to be on the mend,' he said. 'The sight has gone altogether out of the right eye.'

'The right eye? That's the damaged one, isn't it? I thought there was something queer about it.' She leaned over the counter. 'Close the good one. Tight.' She stared into the open eye. Cold, heartless, inscrutable, it met her gaze. She drew back, shivering.

'You'd be surprised what these Dublin doctors can do. They'll probably graft on a new retina. When do you go up?'

'Tomorrow. I may have to stay for a week or more.'

Her face lit up.

'A week?' Her lips moved rapidly. Counting silently.

'Yes. This Dr. Westwood is going to give me a thorough medical check-up. Madden has a very high opinion of him.'

'Well, that's great news. But you must put up a fight yourself. You lose heart too easily. Try and be cheerful, that's what you must do.' She stopped. Snapped her fingers. 'I'll tell you what we'll do. We'll have a celebration tonight.'

'A celebration?' He smiled wanly.

'That's right. We'll go to the "Glass and Bottle". That new roadhouse opened a few weeks back. You remember the big splash in the newspapers?'

'Is it not a bit far?'

'Twenty miles. That's all it is.'

'It's nearer forty, if you ask me.'

She stamped her foot impatiently.

'Don't be quibbling. Are you taking me or not?'

'If you're all that keen, I'll take you surely. But I had intended to get confession at Cleggan on my way home this evening.'

'Confession! What do you want going to confession for? And you not out of the house these months past. You and your old scruples. I told you before, if you as much as breathe a word, I'll ...'

'All right. All right. We'll go. But we'd want to start fairly soon.'

'I'll tell Aunt Hannah. She must have washed up by now.'

Simpson chatted Hannah in the bar until Delia was ready to leave.

'Don't wait up for us, Auntie,' she said when she came down from her room. 'We may be late.'

'Good night, dear. Good night, Mr. Simpson. Enjoy yourselves.'

On the journey, Delia refused to allow him to stop off any place for a drink.

'You can have all the drink you want when we get to the Glass and Bottle. If we're late, there won't be a table to be had.'

There were already a score of cars drawn up in the parking lot when they arrived. Over the entrance, a huge illuminated bottle poured a brilliant stream of light into a tilted, partially-filled glass. Delia hugged herself in ecstasy.

'Gorgeous!' she said. 'Makes you feel thirsty. And excited.'

Inside, people were milling around between the bar and the ballroom.

'Let's push through and book a table,' she said. 'We can have a look round afterwards.'

Simpson booked and paid for a table. A three-piece band – Hammond organ, guitar and drums – was playing desultorily. Picking up a theme, tossing it around from one to the other before flexing their muscles on something else.

'The dance hasn't started yet,' said Delia. 'Let's have a drink in the main bar.'

They secured two high stools at one end of the long counter, its glass front lit by rainbow lighting. Three white-jacketed barmen moved around smoothly, efficiently – taking orders, serving, polishing glasses. Never idle.

'What'll it be?' asked Simpson.

'Something queer, I think. Something . . . unusual.'

'Will I mix you the house special?' the hovering barman asked. 'A Green Dragon?'

'Please do. That would be lovely.'

'And you, sir?'

'Jameson Ten. Large.'

As the barman mixed the cocktail, Simpson looked around. He knew no one amongst those sitting around at the scattered tables. Nor in the friendly cluster round the big open fireplace with its smouldering logs. Nor amongst the stony-faced group watching on the telly the frenzied, majestic but completely silent movements of a symphony orchestra. No familiar face stared back at him from the highly-polished mirrors at the back of the bar. Just as well, he thought. His friends would never stop twitting him if he was discovered in a joint like this.

The barman placed the drinks before them. Was paid. Moved away. Simpson leaned across to Delia.

'You should have stuck to brandy,' he said. 'These cocktails hit you like a sledgehammer if you're not careful.'

'I don't care. It looks delicious.'

A green effervescence pounded to spume by the battering Atlantic rollers, it lipped the top of the frosted glass. Cherries, olives, slices of mandarin orange, impaled on cocktail sticks, rose from its surface. Mint leaves swayed slowly to and fro like fronds of seaweed.

She sipped the drink. Nibbled at the fruit. Gazed about her happily. These were the people – the handsome, well-dressed men, the elegant, sophisticated women – that Jim should be mixing with. Instead of the scruffy, foul-mouthed, noisy creatures you find in village pubs.

'Another of those yokes?' Simpson asked.

'Yes, thank you,' she said primly. Why must he be so vulgar? Always saying something out of place.

At the far end of the bar somebody belched. 'Better out than your eye,' a deep, whiskey-soaked voice avowed.

Of course in every company you'll find one hallion. It's probably someone – she drank deep, savouring the cool, mint-flavoured taste – with a little too much taken. You'd only to look around to see how well-mannered everybody is. Gentlemen leaning forward talking intently. Ladies smiling demurely over the rims of their lifted glasses as they acknowledged the compliments. Each person paying attention only to those in his own group.

A swarthy sardonic-looking young fellow, seated at a table with an elderly lady and gentleman, caught her eye and winked – knowingly. Unthinkingly, she smiled back. Picked up her glass. In embarrassment drank.

'Finished already?' said Simpson. 'You're fairly mopping them up, girl.'

She dabbed her mouth delicately with her handkerchief.

'They're really delicious.'

'You'll take another so?'

'I believe I will.'

Watching and listening, she sipped. It was hard to sort out the babble of voices but once in a while a message came through.

A man's voice:

'It's just one of those things, Lena. Can't you stop harping about it?'

From the other end of the room, a woman drawled:

'But, darling, you didn't see her. She was footless. Absolutely and completely plastered.'

A voice growled:

'I don't give a canary's feck and that's a mean enough article.'

Suddenly, over the hum of voices, the Hammond organ thundered out a volley of rolling chords. Sank into silence. Broke out again into throbbing melody with guitar and drums beating out the rhythm.

'Drink up, Jim,' she said, gripping his arm. 'They've started dancing. We'll go into the ballroom.'

Their table faced the orchestra. The organ was now glowing

with light and Delia watched, fascinated, as the fingers of the organist squeezed the melody from the keys of the two manuals while his feet trundled from pedal to pedal trampling out the rumbling bass.

Her own feet began to tap out the beat.

'Come on,' she said. 'Let's dance.'

'With only three couples dancing. Not on your life.'

'Don't be stuffy, darling. Come on.'

'Wait till the floor gets crowded.'

'Here!' He called over a waiter. 'Bring us . . . What will you have this time, Delia?'

'Oh, I suppose I'd better go on to brandy,' she said listlessly.

He turned back to the waiter.

'A large Jameson Ten and one of those Green Dragon cocktails.'

'Thanks, Jim, but I'd rather a brandy.'

'Very good, madam. A brandy and a double Jameson Ten.'

By the time the waiter had brought back the drinks, the floor had filled up with dancers. The sound of shuffling feet, the tremble of the floorboards, the urgent beat of the rhythm, set Delia jerking impatiently. She swallowed down her drink and jumped to her feet.

'Get up, you lazy loafer,' she said.

'Wait till I finish my drink,' he pleaded.

'Oh, flip!'

Reluctantly, she sat down again. At once the young man who had been watching her from amongst the crowd standing at the door, crossed to their table and bowed stiffly to Simpson.

It was the young brat who had winked at her. Talk about nerve. This was colossal impudence.

'Do you mind if I dance with your partner, sir?' he asked, smiling persuasively.

Of all the cheek. The two Lords of the Universe are to settle between them who will dance with you. You're to have no choice at all in the matter, apparently.

'Not at all. Go ahead, old chap.' Simpson sounded relieved.

My God, do you hear that. 'Go ahead, old chap.' You'd think the big lunk-head wanted rid of you. It would be the price of him if you went off and didn't come back. And the other twirp. Treating you as if you were something of no consequence. *'Can I borrow your evening paper, sir?'* *'Go ahead, old chap. I'm finished with it.'* Surely Jim must know what this young rooster is smelling round after.

'May I?' The stranger was stooping over her.

Without a word, she got up.

'I'll bring her back safely,' he called, as they whirled off into the wheeling, jostling crowd.

He's a good dancer, at any rate, she decided, matching her step to the long, raking stride. He holds you firmly. His balance is perfect. He's never in any doubt about what he's going to do. A conceited young pup, more than likely.

'Nice band,' he said, cutting in expertly between two wallowing couples.

His hands are dry. That's one thing in his favour. How she hated damp, sweaty hands that ruined the back of your dance frock and stuck to everything they touched.

'Floor's good.' He swung her out from the milling crowd on the centre of the floor into the calm periphery. In the mirrored walls she watched them dance – lithe swarthy man and tall willowy blonde. They moved with the smooth precision of a clockwork toy – back and forth, fast and slow, twirling and twisting as they went. He smelt good, too. Of toilet soap and shaving lotion with, underneath, the faint smell of flesh. Firm, warm flesh.

'Big crowd.' The music had stopped. In the mirror she could see him standing beside her – elegant, graceful, foreign-looking. She clapped for an encore. Perfunctorily, and, clapping, saw the bored, sophisticated blonde tap the fingers of one hand against the palm of the other. She had made no mistake in choosing white. It was *her* colour, all right. Emphasized her slimness. Gave her a look of poise and refinement. Such a simple little frock, too. No frills or fuss. High-necked. Sleeveless. Severely cut. And how right she had been to wear only her little gold ear-rings. Nothing else. What need had she of jewellery whose hair was burnished gold?

The music recommenced and they moved off again.

'You don't have much small talk, do you?' he said. 'Though, God knows, my own supply has run out.'

In silence they danced the length of the ballroom. Under

the bandstand, with the organ sobbing out a blues, he hissed in her ear:

'What's your name?'

'*Sugar and crame,*' she flung back at him.

He gave a whinny of laughter.

'*And if you ask me, mine's the same,*' he quoted. 'Though my friends call me George.'

A beefy, red-faced man, using his partner as a battering-ram, ploughed into them. He glared at them angrily.

'My fault,' said George. 'Sorry.'

He whisked her away to the anonymity of the crowded mid-floor. Tucked safely inside the heaving mass, he said:

'Now you know what I'm like. Instead of reefing that big, clumsy ape, I grovelled. As if it was my fault. Do you know, if you were to batter out my brains with an iron bar, I believe I'd apologize for the thickness of my skull.' He sighed. 'Ah, well. Anything for a quiet life. What did you say your name was?'

'My friends call me Delia,' she said. 'And don't worry about that ignorant gulpin. You'd only be wasting your time trying to hammer manners into him.'

The music stopped.

'Next dance,' announced the guitarist.

As they walked back to the table, he said:

'We'll have another session before the night's over.'

'Good-oh.'

Simpson made a movement of disengagement as they approached – leaving down his glass and hoisting himself up, hands on chair seat, a few begrudging inches. He did not speak.

'Thank you,' said George, nodding at them both.

'Thanks,' Delia said.

He was hardly out of earshot when Simpson growled:

'I'll swear to God, he's a half and half, yon fellow.'

'What's that?'

'Hey!' Simpson called to a passing waiter. 'A Jameson Ten and a brandy.'

'How do you mean he's a half and half?'

'A rig. Neither this nor that. Neither fish, fowl nor good red herring. As sure as God made little apples, that gent's a rig.'

'You mean he's not a proper man? That he's a . . . a . . . a maphrodite?'

'For all he'd be capable of doing, you'd be as safe sleeping with your great-grandmother, peace rest her.'

'And how are you so sure, he's—' She balked at the word.

'Wasn't I watching him shaping and play-acting round the floor. And that cackling high-pitched laugh of his – *that* never came from someone with the full equipment. Oh, it's easy enough to guess he never lifted his leg to a lamp-post.'

'Here we are,' he said, as the waiter arrived with the drinks.

Filled with resentment at Simpson's malicious taunts, she watched him clumsily picking out coins from a handful of silver.

He's fairly well jarred, she acknowledged. While we were dancing he must have had a few more large ones. Still . . . it would be the price of him . . . if I were to . . .

She tossed back her drink.

'And what's tickling you?' Simpson tapped the hand holding the empty brandy glass. 'There's a self-satisfied grin on your face, as though you had raided the larder.'

'Maybe I'm planning to.'

The orchestra struck up again.

She put down her glass. Jumped to her feet.

'Up you get, buster,' she said. 'We're dancing this dance.'

Reluctantly, he heaved himself up. Grumbling.

'All right! All right! All right! Anything for a quiet life.'

Startled, she stared at him.

'Did you think I would renege?' He straightened his shoulders. 'Come on,' he said, buttoning his jacket. 'We might as well get this over and done with.'

'Hold on,' she said. 'You're surely not going to dance with your hat on?'

'Why not?' he growled.

'Not with me, you're not.' With a quick movement, she reached up and plucked off his hat, pitching it down on the chair.

'Now we'll—' She broke off, peering at his head. 'What's going on here? Don't tell me you're growing it again?'

'Now, what's wrong?' he muttered guiltily.

'The fringe. Mr. Know-Nothing! The fringe! You've stayed away for weeks past so that you could grow the wretched thing in peace.'

'I did not. You know perfectly well it was the nerves.'

209

'That'll do now, sly-boots. You're fooling nobody. Making out he was laid up with an attack of nerves, when he was all the time nourishing this silly-looking pigtail.'

'Dry up, will you?' he hissed. 'Don't you see everybody's gaping at us?'

Gripping her by the arm, he dragged her out on to the dance floor.

To her surprise, she found he could dance quite well. Not as enterprising as George but, within his own limits, as proficient. The wall mirrors told her he carried himself erect and with a curious grace for one so tall and heavy. The methodical way he progressed in turn round each side of the ballroom reminded her of a polar bear she once watched in the zoo. Huge, shaggy, clumsily-built, it yet conveyed, as it padded back and forth across the bare stony platform of its pit, an impression of controlled power and menacing loose-limbed grace, more awesome than lion, tiger or leopard, until one tumbled to the fact that its constant to and fro prowling never once deviated from a well-known and well-trodden path so that upon reaching either wall of the pit, it brushed its snout against the smooth stone, tossed its massive head in the air and wheeled round with clicking scraping toenails to the right – always to the right – padding back to the other wall to repeat this manoeuvre in every monotonous detail. It was as obstinate, as cautious, as set in its ways as her partner. In fact if Jim were to throw back his head and sniff at each corner of the ballroom, the illusion would be complete.

Simpson's orderly progression round the dance floor had one useful result. It enabled Delia to conduct a reconnaissance in depth of the shifting pattern of the dancers.

At last she spotted him. Dancing with a little red-head at the far end of the ballroom. He was overtaking them rapidly, helped considerably by Delia's sudden onset of leaden-footed fatigue. Soon he was just behind them, his right hand raised with fluttering fingers, trying to attract her attention.

Lifting her hand cautiously from Simpson's shoulder, she waved a greeting.

He mouthed a silent question. Only two words. Single syllabled. The first with straight lips. The second pouting. Again and again he repeated the mimed question but now with forefinger pointing first at her. Then at himself.

It was quite plain what he was trying to convey. 'Next dance?'

She nodded her head. Held up her fanned-out fingers. Emphasized the message with bent wrist and brandished watch.

He nodded, smiling. Counted off five minutes by bending, successively, the fingers of his uplifted hand.

Just then the music stopped. Clinging to his arm so that he could not turn, she whispered urgently:

'Do you mind if we don't finish this dance, Jim? I have to spend a penny.'

'What a shame. I was enjoying it so much.' He could not conceal the note of relief in his voice.

In kittenish fashion, she hung on his arm as they went back to their table. Then, hat once more cocked at a jaunty angle, he swaggered with her to the door.

'You didn't notice the powder-room as we were coming in?' she asked, looking anxiously to either side as they stood at the entrance to the ballroom.

'Oh, I see it now,' she said. 'I'll meet you in the bar. Keep a seat for me.'

As he turned away, she called after him:

'Order up a Green Dragon for me, will you, darling?'

Squaring his shoulders, he walked with bouyant step to the bar. Secured two high stools at the counter. Ordered.

'A Jameson Ten and a brandy.'

He watched the barman take up the Jameson bottle.

'Make it a large Jameson,' he said.

Four drinks later it began to dawn on Simpson that he could not for much longer hold a vacant seat at the crowded counter with the more and more unlikely plea that it was in use. Already a man standing at his elbow, and shifting irritably from one foot to the other, was giving him nasty glares.

Blast her anyway, Simpson raged. Where hell has she got to?

He finished his drink and got to his feet, ignoring the untouched brandy. Outside the bar he stood, uncertainly, eyeing the constantly shifting crowd. At last he decided that the obvious place to start off his search was the 'Ladies' – right at the end of the corridor.

Purposefully he stalked off, ignoring the clusters of loud-mouthed aggressive drunks. At the entrance to the ballroom he hesitated. Perhaps some drunken gouger had bullied her into dancing with him. It might be worth investigating, as he could hardly go into the ladies' bloody lavatory looking for her.

He pushed his way through the mob lounging round the door. To his astonishment, the floor was now packed tight with a mob of barely-moving dancers. To allow more space, the tables had been shifted and the chairs lined round the walls. Every chair in view was occupied. As well look for the queen in a swarm of bees.

For twenty minutes he stayed, carefully scanning the stream of dancers. Convinced at last that she was not in the ballroom, he left and moved down the corridor, slackening his stride as he approached the lighted sign. A steady trickle of patrons tittuped into the rose-lit interior, glimpsed with each swing of the door. No one seemed to be leaving.

It must be an enormous joint. Or else, like the dance floor, it was bursting at the seams with sweating humanity. God knows, poor Delia could well be trapped in a horde of hefted females. Or maybe she was crouched in a cubicle, overcome by a sudden weakness. Or perhaps while he had been wasting his time looking for her in the ballroom, she had returned to the bar to rejoin him.

At the thought of this possibility, he turned and hurried back the way he had come.

The bar, too, was crowded. He peered, with smarting eyes, through the haze of cigarette smoke. She was not at the counter nor at any of the nearby tables. A tall fair-haired girl, sitting at the far end of the room, caught his gaze. The back of her head seemed familiar. He worked his way through the throng of drinkers until he caught a glimpse of her profile – an arrogant, hawk-nosed woman of mature years.

He decided to have a drink and try to figure out where Delia could have gone. He shouldered his way up to the counter, ordered a Guinness and retreated with it to a quiet corner of the room where he could lean against the wall, sip his drink and keep an eye on the entrance to the bar.

Before long he got uneasy. What if something really serious had befallen Delia? A heart attack? A bad fall due to weakness or to drink? Maybe she had struck her head on the tiled floor when she fell. She could be lying there now, unconscious, with the blood pouring out of some fearful gash. She could even be—

He finished his drink, left the empty glass on a table and started off once more up the corridor.

The whole length of the corridor he went, stopping at a door marked *Private*, a few yards beyond the ladies' lavatory. He stayed there for ten minutes but no one entered or left. Slowly he walked back up the corridor, trying to nerve himself. He stopped opposite the hen house. It should be dead easy. March boldly across the few steps, barge in through the door and then rush down the line of cubicles, kicking in the door of each as he passed. Then out again like a bullet. With any luck at all, he'd get away with it – the toilet was a long distance from the ballroom.

He was about to move forward when he suddenly remembered. The bloody cubicles would be penny-in-the-slot affairs. He was properly bunched.

Pulling out his loose change, he extracted the pennies. Eight of them. Surely to Christ there'd be no more than eight loose boxes. If there were, he was done. Even as it stood, he'd have to work damn fast to get the job done before someone butted in on him.

He took a look up the corridor. No one to be seen except the loungers outside the bar. He squared his shoulders. Clutched the pennies in his sweating hand. Eased the choking collar from his neck. Now, he urged, starting forward.

The door opened before he reached it.

'Excuse me!' he said to the pale, foxy-haired woman facing him.

'My God!' She put her hand to her mouth.

For a full second they stood staring at each other in embarrassed silence, before she brushed past him and fled up the corridor, glancing back to see if she was followed.

Blast it to hell, he muttered. What was that bitch doing in there all that time? I'd gamble a pound to a penny she was squatting on the lavatory seat in a drunken stupor, the way Delia is probably doing this very minute. God's curse on the whole lot of them for a shower of bloody clifts.

Back he marched to the bar. Squeezed in to the counter.

Bought himself a stout. And drinking, brooded. This night had turned out a real stumer. And it was supposed to be a celebration. Queer old celebration this was. Drinking porter on his owneo. And tomorrow heading off for Dublin for another round of quackery. Depression settled on him. The drink tasted flat and insipid. Around him the cheery buzz of drunken banter ebbed and flowed. Backs were slapped, quips bandied, deadly secrets whispered loudly into drunken ears. Only Simpson stood sober and isolated. If Delia were here it would be different. Where on earth had she got to? More than likely while he was going from Billy to Jack looking for her, she was doing the same thing. When he had been out searching for her, she had returned to the bar. Not finding him she had tried elsewhere. He should have stayed put in the bar from the word go. But it was too late now to make amends. All he could do was to keep on hunting for her. He could try the ballroom again.

This time, after satisfying himself she was not on the dance floor, he decided he had better make the round of the ballroom to make certain she was not sitting out a dance.

He started off, following the flow of the dance, stepping over outstretched feet, dodging couples swooping like minnows across his path, sidling past wedges of stationary dancers blocked by a pair of slobbering love-birds, alert for a glimpse of blonde hair or white frock.

Half-way round the ballroom, he was knocked off balance by a couple charging into him from behind. He stumbled forward, steadying himself by gripping the shoulder of the man dancing ahead of him.

'Excuse me!' he said.

The man, a small man with rabbit teeth, looked over his shoulder.

'No cutting in,' he growled. Then, seeing Simpson towering over him: 'Sorry. I didn't hear them announce a "Gent's Excuse Me".'

He relinquished his partner and backed away. Simpson found himself facing the foxy-haired inmate of the ladies' lavatory.

'My God!' Again her hand flew to her mouth.

Rabbit and unwitting stoat, they stared at each other until, caught up in a crush of dancers, she was pushed into his arms.

Reluctantly he grasped her lifted hand, settled the palm of his other hand firmly on her back and shuffled forward. He made no attempt to dance. Just kept making his way round the fringe of the dance floor. Watching out for Delia.

Neither of them spoke. He could feel her trembling in his arms. Whether from delight or apprehension, he neither knew nor cared. Maybe it was a bit of both. She'd be the type of begrudging bitch who prays every night for a sex maniac to make up her mind for her. So that she can have all the fun, a fair share of sympathy and no condemnation. She must feel she has chanced on an iron-framed, over-strung, tuned-up-to-concert-pitch model. One that would be capable of bursting into a ladies' lavatory and ravishing the helpless squatters. Probably expects to be hurled to the floor and ridden to death before the eyes of the shocked dancers.

At this pleasant fancy, he shook with silent laughter. At once his partner's trembling ceased. He could feel her body tensing. Surely to heaven she doesn't think you're getting sexed up. Seems to be something eating her all right. She clutched at him avidly, squeezing tight against him. Begod, this is the queer carry on for holy Ireland. The bloody woman's mad a'horsing. If you're not careful, it's yourself will finish up on the ground with the arse being ridden off you. His laughter was rapidly becoming uncontrollable. With red face and bulging eyes, he strove to contain it, whilst he jerked and heaved and grunted with the effort, realizing – to make it even more ridiculous – that he was giving a life-like imitation of someone in the throes of passion. As the violence of his pent-up laughter increased, his partner's breathing became more shallow and agitated. She's in a bad way, he decided. Better get off the floor before she explodes.

By this time they were a few paces from the door. He stopped. Broke away from her. Said, in a wheezing, gasping whisper 'Sorry, ma'am. Must take the dog off the chain. Maybe we'll be fit to find the right place this time.'

He turned away abruptly and hurried to the door, sobered by the astonished stare from the humiliated, hurt and reproachful eyes.

Rushing back to the bar, he found the crowd had thinned out. There was no sign of Delia. Seated on a high stool at the counter, sipping a large whiskey, he tried to figure out what his next move would be.

His brief appearance in the role of sex maniac had left a sour taste in his mouth. He was disturbed. Even slightly worried.

Mocking is catching, he reminded himself. You read about these crimes every day in the paper, without really believing that they happen to actual flesh-and-blood people. Under ordinary everyday circumstances. In parks and quiet cul-de-sacs. In lonely plantations and on the verges of busy motor-ways. In a three-up, two-down council house, a luxury flat or a farm-house in the heart of the country. Among the rhododendrons lining the avenue of a great estate. If, in all this variety of places, why not at a drunken gathering in an isolated road-house?

Now thoroughly alarmed, he finished his drink and left the bar. The most likely place to try, he decided, was the car park.

Outside the main entrance, he stood appalled at the magnitude of the task ahead of him. Row upon row of cars filled the entire parking lot. Beyond, on the county road, he could see the parking lights of cars lined along each side of the highway. A constant coming and going, with doors banging, headlights switching on and off, cars pulling out and backing in, created an impression of utter confusion. Worse still, from many – too many – of the parked cars came the glow of lighted cigarettes.

The car park, illuminated by the huge neon sign, proved a relatively easy chore. The occupied cars could be passed with a quick side glance. For those unoccupied, he had merely to slow down and scrutinize each one closely as he sauntered past.

Out on the road it was different. The cars with parking lights on were, of course, a great help. They created a small island of light – enough to investigate not only the car itself, but also, where the parking was close, the ones in front and behind.

But in the stretches of darkness in between he was forced to examine each car closely, face pressed against the window glass. In one car – an old-fashioned, sinister-looking monster – a figure stretched out limp on the back seat, one arm dangling on the floor, set his skin tingling with dread until a lighted match held to the window disclosed a carelessly-flung rug and overcoat.

At last, every car examined, he walked back up the road slowly, pondering the next move. There seemed to be nothing for it but the Ladies' Lavatory again. This time he would give the girl in the cloakroom ten bob to have a search. Or he could get someone from the Reception Office to ... My God, why hadn't he thought of it before? He would get them to page her. 'Would Miss Delia Clifden please come to Reception! Would Miss Delia Clifden please come to Reception!' He could hear the bland, carefully-modulated voice calling over the Tannoy as he had heard it many times that evening.

He smartened his pace. A quick drink was indicated. Then the Reception Desk.

The bar had filled up again. To get to the counter he was forced to push his way through a rabble of swaying, shouting customers. On the way back, his attention centred on the gingerly balanced glasses of stout and whiskey held in either hand, he was hailed from a nearby table.

'And where have you been hiding away all night?'

It was Delia. Sitting, bold as brass, tucking into one of those bloody Green Dragons. And along with her that half-and-half get, George – a big, welcoming smile on his blackguardly face.

'Pull up a chair and join us,' he said.

Simpson placed the two glasses on the table and seated himself, without saying a word.

'We were looking for you everywhere,' said Delia. 'We searched the ballroom and the car park. And the Lord knows how many times we were in here.'

That for a bloody yarn. Wherever they were, they managed to keep out of the flow of the traffic.

'What are you having?' George asked.

'Nothing. I have my own drink here.'

'Nonsense. You'll have a drink with us.'

We and *Us*. To listen to the pair of them, you'd think it was a couple of reigning monarchs you'd stumbled upon. Much more of this kind of chat would be hard to put up with.

George cracked his fingers imperatively.

'Waiter!' he called. He cracked his fingers again. 'Damned

217

poor service here,' he remarked to Simpson. 'Waiter!' he called again.

Delia was gazing at him spellbound. Surely, thought Simpson, she hasn't been taken in by this puffed up little bull-frog.

'A large whiskey for this gentleman,' said George, when the waiter arrived.

'Jameson Ten,' Delia prompted. Oh, the pair of them have it all worked out. Soften the lug up with drink and there'll not be a bit word about it. They're sorely mistaken then.

'Any time I was in the ballroom I didn't see you, Delia. Or your friend, Mr. What's-his-name.'

'Dinsmore,' said Delia. 'George Dinsmore. And George, this is my friend, Jim. Jim Simpson.'

'Pleased to meet you,' said Dinsmore, leaning over and reaching out his hand.

Simpson, busy fishing out a piece of cork from the froth of his stout with a nail-file, did not appear to notice the gesture.

'We weren't all the time in the ballroom, of course,' said Delia. 'We were in the cocktail lounge, too.'

'Though most of the time we were in the coffee-room, Delia,' George said, a little too quickly.

'That's right. When we weren't hunting around trying to find you, Jim.'

'Aye.' God help them. They're to be pitied. Run off their feet trying to locate you.

'You know there's a hellish mob here tonight. There's people wandering round all night looking for their partners. It's a ruddy shame. Set yourself up as a roadhouse and you can get away with murder. The Guards should enforce the dance-hall act.' He clucked indignantly into his gin and lime.

'If you become separated at all, you have a poor hope of finding each other again. Isn't that right, George?'

'Not a hope.'

'Aye.' They were keeping the ball nicely in play.

The waiter arrived with the whiskey.

'Will that be all, sir? Very good, sir. Thank you, sir.'

He left, soured by a tanner tip.

Dinsmore lifted his glass, levelled an ingratiating look at Simpson, raised the tumbler in salutation.

'My best respects,' he said.

Deliberately Simpson pushed the fresh glass of whiskey away from him.

'What's wrong, Jim?' asked Delia. 'Is it not Jameson Ten?'

'I said I had my own drink with me.' He picked up the whiskey glass he had brought over to the table. Filled it half and half with water from the carafe.

'I suppose, like myself, Delia,' he said, holding aloft the glass to scrutinize the whorls of fusel oil swirling in its depths, 'you found the dance floor a bit too crowded for dancing?'

With slanting gaze, he watched her telegraphing frantic appeals with raised eyebrows.

Dinsmore answered, cool and unperturbed:

'The few times we danced, there weren't very many on the floor.' Simpson's fingers tightened on the glass. 'Of course, people keep all the time surging out and in to the bar. The floor could be packed one minute and empty the next.'

Simpson sipped his whiskey. He's playing it safe all right. Marking time when he doesn't know the answers.

'That was a queer rig Dr. Madden's woman had on her.' He addressed himself to Delia. 'You could bloody near see the cheeks of her arse, it was so low in the back. She should have been ordered off the floor.' He sank the butt-end of the whiskey and left down his glass. 'She's from Galway direction. A schoolteacher, they say.'

'I didn't notice her,' said Delia.

'Dammit, you must have. Madden says he hailed you.'

'Maybe he did. But you know the way you miss people in a crowd. I mean ... with the band playing ... and all that ... we mightn't have heard him ... you know the way it is ...'

Dinsmore cut in:

'Good little combination, that band. The organ bloke is just about first class. Chap with the guitar isn't bad either. Drummer a bit monotonous, but as good as you'd get in any country outfit. Are they a resident band?'

'Of course, he could have seen you in the coffee room, Delia. Or in the cocktail bar. Or, God knows, maybe out in the car park.'

In the silence that followed, Simpson took a long slug of the stout. Wiped his lips with the back of his hand. Placed the glass back carefully in its own porter ring.

'Did you notice how many Glenard ones turned up?' he

219

said. 'You'd be tripping over them every place you went. McWilliams and the wife, the two Higgins girls, Attorney Coyle. All the quality.'

He finished his stout. Got to his feet.

'We'll have another drink,' he said.

He started off towards the counter. Stopped and came back.

'Do you know who I had a couple of jars with? And him well scuttered? You'd never guess.' She shook her head slowly. 'The *Meenagunogue Herald and Tribune*. Dicky Vereker. Drunk he was, he was lamping everyone coming or going. There's not much that little ferret misses. It's God help the poor bugger who has anything to hide, when he's around.'

He chuckled softly. And still chuckling, moved away.

While the barman was filling the drinks, Simpson caught a glimpse through the press of the pair of them with their heads together. Colloguing. They've got plenty to talk about. Do you think will they have the neck to bluff it out that they were the whole time looking for you? Delia's too shaken to put up much of a show but that bastard Dinsmore might brazen it out. He's as cool as a cucumber. The only thing to do is to keep insulting him till he loses his rattley.

Simpson brought back the drinks and as he was placing them on the table, Delia said:

'Was it in the ballroom you saw all the folk from—' She broke off. 'Haven't you made a mistake in ordering up that round?'

'How? Wasn't it brandy you wanted?'

'Yes, but there's only,' she pointed, 'a brandy and a whiskey here. You didn't bring George's drink.'

'Why should I? I didn't take his drink. He doesn't have to take mine.'

You could call that a proper toe in the hole. Surely he'll take the hint and clear off.

'Don't be rude, Jim. Get George his drink and stop acting the maggot.' Her voice strove to be firm but didn't quite succeed.

'It's all right, Delia,' soothed Dinsmore. 'I'll buy my own.'

He called over a passing waiter and ordered a gin and lime. No one spoke till it was brought back. Then Dinsmore lifted the glass and said in a conciliatory manner:

'Cheers, everybody.'

'An old woman's drink, if ever there was one,' said Simpson.

Dinsmore left down his glass untouched.

'Really?' He raised his eyebrows in interested inquiry.

'Good for flushing out the kidneys. Nothing else.'

'Is that so?'

'People say it has a depressing effect on your man. Takes the bone out of him altogether. Filleted Fagan would be a poor dish to set before a queen.'

'Now, Jim!'

'It's all right, Delia. Don't get excited. Naturally this does not apply to your friend here. He can drink all the gin he likes without it doing him any harm. And we know why. Don't we, Delia?'

Dinsmore, watching them warily, said nothing.

'George works in the Department of Agriculture.' Delia broke the silence at length.

'How interesting,' said Simpson. 'Would he be an artificial inseminator, by any chance? That would seem to be the sort of job would suit his reproductive powers.'

Before Delia could protest, Dinsmore cut in:

'I work in the laboratory. Research work, you know.' His tone was mild. Placatory.

'Research,' Simpson mused. 'There was a great opportunity tonight for a bit of quiet research work. Isn't that right, Delia?'

She glared back at him.

'Don't be taking it out on Delia,' Dinsmore said quietly. Ignoring him, Simpson leaned over towards Delia.

'Tell me,' he said. 'Has he anything at all in the fork of his trousers?'

'He has more than—'

Before she could finish, Dinsmore interrupted:

'You're spoiling for a row, aren't you?' He spoke in a level voice.

'It's about time you discovered that.'

'Well, I want no trouble. See?'

'Get to hell out of here, so. Nobody wants you in this company.'

'Is that the way you feel, Delia?'

'Of course not, George. Don't mind him.' She nodded her head towards Simpson. 'He has a few too many taken.'

'If you don't go on your own steam, I'll take you by the scruff of the neck and throw you out.'

'How dare you, Jim?' Delia burst out. 'You've no right to threaten a friend of mine like that. Your language all evening has been disgraceful. A corner-boy would not use such coarse, vulgar abuse.'

'All I want to know is, does this half and half get intend to sit on here till he's lifted out of it?'

Dinsmore looked at Delia appealingly.

'Maybe I'd better—'

'Don't stir, George. We were sitting here before he arrived. He has no right to order you out.'

'All right,' said Simpson dispassionately. 'If that's the way you want it, that's the way you'll get it.'

Pushing back his chair, he got to his feet. The people at the adjoining tables were by this time sitting in rapt and silent expectancy.

In two strides he was round the table. Grasped the lapels of Dinsmore's jacket. Hauled them together. As the seated man stared at him in fascinated horror, Simpson transferred his grip to one hand.

'Up off your seat, Prince Charming,' he said. 'You're on your way.'

With a sudden heave, he had Dinsmore clear of the seat and was holding him up kicking and squirming.

'Stop it, Jim! Stop it at once!' Delia screamed, tugging at Simpson's free arm.

Ignoring her futile intervention, he made for the door, carrying at arm's length the struggling figure, followed by a throng of curious onlookers. Dinsmore's eyes were bulging in his head with the strangling grip of the jacket collar. His head was tipped back. His gaping mouth gasped for air. His lunging feet – now high in the air, now trailing the ground – strove to kick. His flailing arms to strike.

Simpson disregarded the wild glancing blows. With Delia swinging off one arm and Dinsmore hefted by the other, he was back in the old weight-lifting days that he had thought were gone for ever. Only for the danger of choking his victim, he would have given him a few straight arm hoists.

Through the hall and out to the entrance porch, he carried his burden. There he set him down. Gave him a push that sent him reeling.

'Into your car,' he said. 'And away off home with you.'

Delia rushed over.

'Are you all right, George?' she asked. 'Did that big ape hurt you?' She fussed over him, helping him smooth out his rumpled jacket. Straightening his tie. 'Will you leave me home in your car? I'm not going back with that brute.'

Clawing at his collar to loosen its grip, he gasped:

'But . . . I've got no . . . car.'

'How are you travelling so?'

'I got . . . a lift . . . from friends.'

'How do you expect me to get home?' Delia wailed. 'You led me to believe you had a car.'

Dinsmore glanced at the crowded porch, where Simpson stood amongst the interested spectators.

'Would you lower your voice, for God's sake. You don't want the whole countryside to know your troubles, you silly bitch.'

'Don't talk to me that way, George Dinsmore. You're like all the men. You'd bite the hand that feeds you. Once you get what you want, you—'

He caught her by the shoulders and shook her roughly.

'Dry up, will you?' he hissed. 'You don't want to wash your dirty linen in public, do you?'

'But how am I to get home, George?' She was crying now. Drunken, maudlin tears.

'Go home the way you came. And leave me alone. You've brought enough trouble on my head.'

He turned away and walked off through the parked cars towards the roadway.

'Where are you going, George?' she called after him, miserably.

He did not look round or answer.

From the porchway, Simpson called:

'Are you coming, Delia?'

He moved off towards his car. Slowly she followed him, snivelling wretchedly into her handkerchief, heedless of the few watchers left on the porch.

For the most of ten miles, neither spoke. At length Simp-

223

son growled in a tone of exasperated resignation:

'Queer celebrations, as the old lady said when she broke her leg.

'I wouldn't mind so much,' he continued, addressing the silence, 'only that this whole bottle of smoke was brought on by a bloody little bobtailed runt not worth wasting powder and shot on.'

'He's no bobtailed runt,' said Delia sulkily.

'You could hardly describe him as a parish bull, could you?'

'I know what you're after, Mister Curiosity Box. But you'll worm nothing out of me.'

She wriggled deeper into the seat.

'Except that he's far from being a half and half,' she murmured, settling herself down to sleep.

Simpson drove on, his mind detached from the swinging beam of the headlights gulping up voraciously white lines and dotted lines: tarmac and potholes: road signs and hurtling hedgerows. It was hardly possible, surely to heaven, that he had been mistaken in his diagnosis of that Dinsmore gawm. His squealing laugh and effeminate gin-drinking, the elegance of his clothes, the way he danced and, above all, his craven lack of spunk in allowing himself to be publicly humiliated without putting up some sort of a fight: all these symptoms added up to the only conclusion possible – that he was some sort of a queer-hawk. A nancy boy or something of that sort. And yet what did Delia mean by that crack of hers that *he was far from being a half and half*? Was she taunting him? Or did she really mean that the little rat had hammered a job on her? As this suggestion took root Simpson tramped on the accelerator, flinging the car at each corner and wrenching it round with screaming tyres. It was a horrifying thought. She had never met the fellow before. In fact she was only a pick-up. And yet ... she would ... the very first time they met ... let him ... He put the boot down to the boards and glared ahead, while the car pitched and lurched.

'Go easy!' Delia complained. 'You're after banging my head off the window.'

He slowed down. But of course that was all nonsense. What girl in her right mind would tell the bloke who brought her out for the night that she had been shagged by a complete stranger. No. She was only gibing at him. Striking back at him

224

for calling the fellow a half and half. But sure that's all he was. A bloody nancy-boy. Hadn't he heard somewhere that girls have a soft spot for them? That they like their company and understand them better than men do? Probably they feel safer with these queers. They can relax, knowing there's no danger of being screwed when they're well plastered. Oh, she'd be safe enough in the company of that gent. Though now that he thought back on it, the pair of them looked properly shagged out when he met them in the bar. Delia's eyes – with mourning bands under them – were so far back in her head that they were scraping the sockets.

'Would you, for pity's sake, ease up! You'll have us in the ditch if you're not careful.' She was sitting up straight in the seat, staring anxiously ahead.

He slowed down the car to fifty. Maybe it would be as well to forget the whole affair. After all, she'd had a good few jars aboard. People – the steadiest of them – did unpredictable things with enough drink taken. And it was really possible that the pair of them *had* been looking for him. If he had just stayed put in the bar instead of drifting around like a fart in a snowstorm.

He changed down and pulled in to the verge to avoid a batch of straying cattle milling around on the road. Clumsily they backed away from the advancing car, bumping into each other and staring at the headlights with blind frightened gaze. Once clear, he went through his gears rapidly, booting up the speed to sixty-five. It was getting late and he had to be up early to start off for Dublin.

He glanced across at the passenger seat. Delia with head in hands and shaking shoulders was weeping her heart out. Great God, what next?

'What's the matter?' he asked. 'What are you crying about?'

'I'm not crying. I'm laughing.'

'What the hell is there to laugh about, I'd like to know?'

'I'm laughing—' Once more she started off into a fit of hysterical laughter. 'I'm laughing ... at you carrying George ... like you'd carry a cat ... by the scruff of the neck ... that was after dirtying the carpet ...' She let out another squeal of laughter. 'Holding ... Holding it well away from you ... because ... because ... because it stank.'

Simpson, too, began to laugh. And soon the pair of them were screeching and choking with laughter. Simpson was forced to pull up the car as he could not see properly out of his streaming eyes.

Each time the laughter would ease off, someone would start it off again by a word or a phrase.

At length Delia gasped:

'Come on, Jim. We'd better be getting back. It's late.'

'What about a naughty before we start? Just to show there's no ill feeling.'

Delia pushed away the pawing hands.

'None of that, you big baboon. You'll serve out your penance first.'

'Aw now, Delia—'

'Aren't you for Dublin first thing in the morning? And weren't you told to abstain from drink and women if you wanted to preserve your sight? Start the car up, Jim, and no more nonsense.'

When they reached Creevan, she was still adamant. He was allowed into the bar for a drink. A single drink. Delia refused to join him and when his whiskey was drained she hooshed him out.

'Call in when you're back from Dublin,' she whispered, before she shut the door. 'There's no knowing what I'll have for you.'

Next morning Simpson drove up to Dublin, booked into a quiet hotel near Fitzwilliam Square and was asleep in bed, after a couple of nightcaps, before the bar closed down.

At half-past two next afternoon he was prowling the pavements of Fitzwilliam Square, scanning the fanlights of the Georgian houses for Dr. Westwood's number. Soon he was mounting well-scrubbed steps to a newly-varnished door with a gleaming brass fox-head door-knocker. The receptionist who answered the door ushered him into the waiting-room – a vast, high-ceilinged room – round whose cream-coloured walls sat a frieze of patients – stiff, silent, protected from unwarranted intrusion by disdainful eye and arrogant chin.

Simpson sat among them uncomfortably, crossing and uncrossing his legs, swallowing noisily, fleeing their unseen gaze by leafing through copies of *Punch, Dublin Opinion* and the *atler* or by studying the hunting prints lining the walls, epicting faithful ape-like grooms, whey-faced gentlewomen, apsized and bedraggled riders, stiff-legged galloping orses.

Every so often the receptionist would open the door and all a name. Leisurely, almost reluctantly, a lady or gentleman ould rise, move nonchalantly across the room and go out, ithout evoking a turned head or a sidelong glance.

The atmosphere of decorum and reserve had such an effect n Simpson that, when his turn came, he jumped to his feet nd marched to the door, only to discover to his chagrin that e was still clutching *Dublin Opinion*. He stalked back, flung ne magazine on the table, then startled at the sudden noise in ne stillness of the room, muttered 'Excuse me!' to the circle f cold withdrawn eyes.

When no murmur of forgiveness came, he wheeled about nd strode to the door, his face flushed with rage and mor-fication. So angry was he that, when Dr. Westwood rose to reet him, he grasped unthinkingly, the extended hand in his xtra-special bone-crushing grip. At the smothered whimper f pain, he released his grip immediately.

Ignoring his blanched and mangled fingers, the doctor re-umed his seat. In a dry voice he commenced the customary atechism.

Name. Address. Occupation. Age. Previous medical record. 'amily history. Any deaths from hereditary complaints. The sual old hat.

As he quizzed, thin lips giving each word its due and only neasure, Simpson studied him.

He was young. In his early thirties – at most. Tall. Lean. legantly dressed. Hawk-nosed and cold-eyed. An egg out of ne same clutch as the Biddies in the waiting-room.

'We needn't delve too deeply,' he said at length. 'Dr. Mad-en sent me a comprehensive report on the course of your omplaint.'

He riffled – unseen – through papers in the open drawer of is desk, glancing at them without much interest.

'What we must first do is to discover exactly the extent f impairment to the sight of each eye.'

He got to his feet.

'I have arranged an appointment for you with Dr. Robin-

227

son, the best eye-man we have in town. For—' he glanced
his wristwatch, 'half past three.

'Robinson,' he repeated. 'Harold Robinson. Just five doc
further up from here.'

He bowed a dismissal.

'You can call back here afterwards with the report,' he sa
as Simpson moved to the door.

Dr. Robinson turned out to be a larger, more boistero
and better-dressed Dr. Roche.

'A little atropine in each eye. Open wide. Therrrrre we ar
Now the other. Steady now. Don't flinch. Therrrrre we g
Now relax and tell me the history of this eye trouble of you
How did it start? What was the first abnormal symptom y
observed?'

Once more Simpson recounted the onset of the fir
haemorrhage. The stabbing headaches. The olive-green clust
of spots. The coalescence of these spots into one vivid gre
whole.

'What aspect did it have?'

Simpson hesitated. What the hell did the shape matter?
all the silly bloody questions. Still ... this man should kno
his job. Here goes.

'It was shaped like a bird. A parrot, to be exact. The com
The beak. The tail feathers. All outlined in purple.'

'A parrot?' He was writing. 'Green with a purple margi
Most extraordinary. Go on.'

Simpson continued to rehearse the progress of the malad
while the doctor took down notes, occasionally murmurir
an inaudible remark. Once, when Simpson described the fir
occasion he actually saw a haemorrhage occur, the doctor sa
triumphantly:

'Like a volcanic eruption, eh? A classical symptom. Tl
retina inverting the image. Yes, go on.'

When Simpson had finished his description, Dr. Robinse
picked up the ophthalmoscope.

'The pupils should be sufficiently dilated now,' he said, mo
ing around from behind his desk. 'Yes. I thought so. No
head back. Open wide your left eye. Thaaaat's the ide
Steady!'

Again the stooping head, the blinding beam of light directe
into his left eye, the shallow preoccupied breathing.

228

'The light now, please. Turn your head a little more towards me. That's better.'

With his good eye, Simpson saw the beam of light switched on, felt the warm breath fan his cheek, smelt the faint aroma of shaving talc or lotion, heard tiny sighs and grunts, that reminded him of the urgent excited snuffling of a terrier at a rat hole, as the doctor positioned himself anew. He tried to convince himself that he could see faint gleams of light in the appalling darkness contained in his right eye. As he rolled his eye from side to side at the bidding of the doctor, there appeared to be a pale luminosity creeping in from somewhere. At the corner of the pupil, he thought.

Experimentally, he closed his left eye. All was darkness. He kept the eye closed, swinging the other one from side to side, striving with straining muscle and tautened nerve, to squeeze sight into his blinded eyeball.

'That will do,' said the doctor.

Vision distorted with glare and atropine, Simpson watched the hazy figure go back to the desk and start writing again.

'What's the verdict, Doctor?' he asked.

Through the haze, Simpson saw the doctor's head lift.

'Pardon me, I did not catch what you said?'

'What are your . . . your findings?'

'I am writing a report – a highly technical report – for Dr. Westwood. He, of course, will assess the significance of each distinctive feature and, having an intimate knowledge of your case, will explain – in simple language, no doubt – the implications of this—' He tapped the paper.

'But I only met Dr. Westwood—'

'He is your medical adviser, Mr.—' He glanced down at his desk. '—Simpson. It is *he* who must exercise final judgement in your case.'

He bent again to his writing.

'What I meant to say is . . . Dr. Westwood hasn't . . . he isn't my . . . not exactly, that is . . .' The head stayed bent.

What was the use trying to explain? These gentry only talk to each other. They resent the patient cutting in with a few remarks of his own. Depressed and frustrated, Simpson sat listening to the scratch of the pen, the search for the envelope, the patting down of the moistened flap. At last the cheery confident voice:

229

'Therrrre we are now,' handing over the envelope. 'Just give this to Dr. Westwood.'

'What do I owe you, Doctor?' asked Simpson.

'Five guineas. My secretary will give you a receipt.'

'I can't see too well to write a cheque. Those damned drops.'

The doctor chuckled benevolently.

'Dooooon't worry, Mr. Stinson,' he said, soothing with gentle back pats. 'Miss Lynch will fill out the cheque for you. You need only sign. A regular happening here, you know.' He laughed again.

In an ante room, Simpson signed the completed cheque, pocketed his receipt and left, keeping his eyes averted from the sun as he walked the few paces back to Dr. Westwood's house.

There he was only kept a few minutes before being ushered once more into the consulting-room.

'You'll excuse me for a few moments,' the doctor said, waving Simpson towards a chair. He ripped open the evelope and scanned the contents rapidly.

'Humph,' he said. 'Retinal detachment affecting right eye only. Consequent loss of vision. Left eye. No sign of impairment. Danger of sympathetic ophthalmia. Neuralgic pains. Reduction of perception of light. Evidence of glitter points to. Possibility of. Must also be taken into account. Safe to say. Condition exists. Hmm. Central retinal vein. Just what I thought.'

He picked up a sheaf of papers. Clipped on the report. Put the lot into his desk drawer.

'That gives us a clear picture of the case,' he said, lifting a blank sheet of paper and commencing to write.

'Did he not mention the haemorrhages?' Simpson asked.

The doctor continued writing. At length he drew – slowly and firmly – a line across the page. Placed the pen carefully alongside the paper. Rested his elbows on the desk. Gazed at Simpson across his steepled hands.

'What we must do,' he announced, 'is to get at the cause of your complaint.' He paused, shifted the pen so that it lay along the top edge of the paper. Re-steepled his hands.

'Up to this, the concentration was laid on halting the progress of the disease. Very laudable and well-intentioned. But under the circumstances—' He spread his hands deprecatingly. '—hardly warranted. After all, it is now—' He stooped over the written page. '—over three months since the onset of this eye trouble. It is high time the disease, of which these haemorrhages are merely symptoms, was isolated and given treatment.'

Simpson moistened his lips.

'What disease?' he croaked.

Dr. Westwood sat back in his chair. Folded his hands across his waist-band. Stared at the lintel of the door.

'Haemorrhage of the retina is a feature of a number of diseases – from common rheumatism to haemophilia. It would be wiser if we start with the more commonplace.' He permitted himself a frosty smile. 'Don't you agree?'

'Whatever you . . . Oh, yes.'

'Well, then, Mr. Simpson, you might tell me if at any time you suffered from recurring pains in any particular part of your body? Legs? Arms? Back? More especially, in the joints, such as the elbows, knees or shoulders?'

'I never had a pain or ache in my life. Never a day off from work till now. No doctor ever got a shilling off me until this unfortunate—'

'Quite so. Quite so.' Dr. Westwood had the pen poised over the page. 'Did either of your parents suffer from rheumatism?'

'My father used to complain of backache. But there wasn't a thing the matter with him. It was only attention he wanted.'

'Your mother?'

'Healthy as a trout. A bit stiff with arthritis. But sure all old people get that.'

In dismay Simpson watched the pen race over the page.

'They both lived till over eighty,' he pleaded.

'Rheumatic pains are hereditary, Mr. Simpson. We can't overlook such an obvious indication.'

Simpson gulped.

'Do you indulge in alcohol?' Again the pen was poised.

'I do.'

'Much or little?'

'No more than the next fellow.'

'You never were attacked by gout?'

'Good God, no. I can't abide the taste of port.'

'Beer and stout are much more injurious to the system than

wine. Was there any tendency to gout in your family?'

Simpson's face reddened.

'Are you suggesting—?'

'I am not suggesting anything. Merely asking a question. Your family history is most important. Gout is another hereditary disease.'

'It was never known in our family.'

'Look here, Mr. Simpson. This is a very serious matter. We can't afford to ignore the smallest clue. I propose sending you to Dr. Hodge-Davis – the leading authority in these islands on diseases of the kidney. If there are any diabetic or albuminuric symptoms, he is the man to expose them.'

He picked up the telephone receiver and dialled. Cowed into silence, Simpson listened.

'Hullo ... Is that you, Miriam? ... Dr. Westwood speaking ... Put me through to the doctor, will you ... Oh, hullo, Cyril ... Busy? ... Good ... Could you see a patient of mine to-morrow? ... Fine ... three o'clock? ... Righto ... What's that? ... Oh, tonight ... I'd be charmed ... See you there, so ... Eight-thirty at the Buttery ... Good-bye for now.'

The doctor hung up. Scribbling a few lines on a scratch-pad, he ripped the leaf off and handed it to Simpson.

'Three o'clock tomorrow. Number 73. About five minutes' walk. Call back here with the report.'

He bowed his patient out of the room without offering his hand. Worried and bewildered, Simpson went back to the hotel, his mind whirling with possibilities – diabetes, albuminuria, gout, haemophilia.

And so began for him a week of coming and going. After Dr. Hodge-Davis, came a heart specialist, Dr. Stanfield ('a brilliant diagnostician'). His blood pressure was taken, a cardiograph test made. He ran up and down stairs so that the hammer beats of his heart might be noted. Back and chest he was stethoscoped. ('A diastolic heart beat, Mr. Simpson.') All for seven guineas.

Then came Dr. ('The finest chest man outside America') Irwin. Chest X-rayed and thorough examination. Three guineas and five guineas respectively.

Next a surgeon-dentist – Mr. Maynard Leith ('He has a European reputation') – discovered an infected tooth, pulled it and grew a culture from the suppurating pus. One injection of the vaccine was enough. Simpson woke that night violently ill. Puked his guts up. Watched, in horror, whilst lumps as big as billiard balls mushroomed on his arms and legs, disappearing without trace in an hour's time. This experience was relatively cheap. Examination and extraction two guineas. Preparation and injection of vaccine two more guineas.

One thing, at least, Simpson was thankful for. They all lived within a few minutes' walk of Dr. Westwood's house where, each day, the reports were handed in, digested and filed. The interrogation continued with continual emphasis laid on the importance of hereditary disease. On one occasion when Simpson had been protesting that his family boasted an absolutely clean bill of health, the doctor remarked drily:

'Two grandparents, one parent, two uncles and an aunt, three brothers: all suffering more of less from alcoholism, would we not be justified in postulating an hereditary tendency towards that disease in your family?' He waved Simpson to silence. 'It is all here, you know.' He pointed to his notes.

'You ... you ... you've got it all wrong. They took a tiddley right enough. But they weren't martyrs to the drink.'

'You mean they never drank to excess? Regularly? Even daily?'

'They might have taken a little drop too much now and again. That's all.'

'Ah, Mr. Simpson. The little more and how much it is.'

Baffled, Simpson watched the pen trace two more lines of bullshit across the page. This bloody man simply wasn't human. He couldn't understand that even the best of people get drunk now and again. A good man's fault, they say. And never was there a truer saying. If he were to get well scuttled himself once in a while, he'd be the better for it. Maybe he does. In one of those posh city bars. Wiring into wines or fancy liqueurs. Among a crowd of buck-teethed yapping lah-di-dahs.

The day after Simpson's visit to the dentist, Dr. Westwood announced:

'This is the day I send my blood samples—' He indicated a little rack containing labelled test-tubes of blood. '—to be tested.'

He picked up a large glass-barrelled syringe.

'Would you mind taking off your jacket and rolling up your shirt-sleeve. The left one will do.'

Strapping the upper arm, he slid the needle deftly into the swollen vein.

'Steady now,' he said. 'Don't move.'

He withdrew the plunger, sucking up the blood till the barrel was full. Squeezing a wisp of medicated gauze against the vein, he eased out the needle and pumped the contents of the syringe into a test-tube.

'These samples are numbered,' he said, affixing a label. 'No one but myself can tell to whom each sample belongs.'

He placed the test-tube in the rack along with the others.

'They go to the Pathology Department of a city hospital where, along with scores of others, the tests are carried out. You can be assured of absolute anonymity.'

Simpson nodded his head. There was no sense or meaning in this needless system of precaution. But by this time he had learnt to accept as normal the most outlandish practices. He rolled down his shirt sleeve and pulled on his jacket.

'Come back to me the day after tomorrow. Three o'clock. I will have the result of the test by then.'

There was a subtle change in Dr. Westwood's manner when Simpson presented himself two days later. It was impossible to pinpoint the difference but it was there all right. The urbanity was more urbane. The courteous manner even more correct. The air of civilized tolerance more pronounced. But with it all went an icy formality. A finicky withdrawal that in someone else would have been a sniff of disdain.

'We seem to be getting somewhere at last,' he said.

'God, that's great,' said Simpson, his face beaming with delight.

The doctor's lips curled slightly into an expression that could have been contempt. Or pity.

'Yes,' he said. 'The Wassermann reaction was positive. We can now say with something approaching certainty that we have discovered the causative factor in your retinal trouble.'

'What is this Wassermann yoke all about?' asked Simpson gaily.

Incredulously, the doctor stared at him.

'Do you mean to tell me you do not know what a Wassermann test is *for*?'

'No. Should I?'

'Tck! Tck!' The doctor clucked in distress. 'If I had

known that, I could have prepared you. Lessened the shock a little.'

'The – the – the shock? Lessen it. How do you mean?'

The doctor picked up the sheaf of papers. Head bent, as if reading from a medical text book, he announced in a low emotionless voice:

'The Wassermann Reaction is a biochemical method of diagnosing a venereal infection in the blood serum.'

'Venereal infection. Do you mean ... the ... the clap?'

Bewilderment, consternation, entreaty: all were mingled in Simpson's gaping stare.

'I fear, Mr. Simpson, it is a more serious complaint than that.'

Simpson swallowed noisily. Like cornered mice, his eyes scurried from side to side, seeking escape. At last he broke the lengthening silence.

'You mean,' he said, his voice thick and quavering. 'You mean ... it's ... it's that I've ... that I've clicked a dose of ...?'

'Precisely. The result of the Wassermann indicates that you are suffering from – suffering for a considerable time from – a syphilitic infection.'

'Dosed with syphilis! Good Jesus!' The note of outrage in Simpson's voice was high and shrill.

'Now! Now!' soothed Dr. Westwood. 'There is no need to panic. Venereal disease is as prevalent as ... as the common cold. Many famous men suffered from it. Gauguin. De Maupassant. Some authorities even suggest Shakespeare was a syphilitic.'

Simpson was glaring at the doctor with wild startled eyes.

'It's impossible,' he declared in a loud voice. 'It's bloody well impossible.'

'Why do you say that?'

'There was never a damned thing wrong with me. In that way, I mean. Wouldn't there be bound to be symptoms? Some evidence that you were dosed?'

'There should have been. The normal symptoms are unmistakable and could not go unnoticed. Chancres and swollen glands at the point of infection are almost invariable. Other symptoms follow, attacking the throat and mouth. Tumours and lesions set in.' He coughed apologetically. 'In some cases the hair falls out.'

'Well, I never had as much as a boil or an ulcer in my life. So the bloody Wassermann business is all wrong. Pure codology I call it.'

The doctor frowned.

'These tests are nearly 100 per cent accurate. Unfortunately syphilis is a law unto itself. It has been known for the disease to pass through the primary, secondary and tertiary stages without a single symptom showing up.'

'You want me to believe I've been nursing this disease for months without knowing it?'

'It is quite possible.'

'Isn't it far more likely that the test-tubes got mixed up and you've saddled me with one belonging to some poxy bastard from Ringsend or Goatstown?'

In agitation, the doctor jumped up and came round from behind his desk.

'This accusation is intolerable,' he said, 'and your language most offensive.'

'I'm sorry, doctor. But you can hardly blame me. You swept the feet from under me with that report of yours.'

'I know. I know. And if you wish me to get another test done I will do so. But I can assure you it is utterly unnecessary. The precautions taken in the laboratory are incredible. I really believe they render the test fool-proof.'

Simpson scowled up at the doctor, now leaning back, palms propped, against the front of the desk.

'Maybe you're right,' he said. 'But I still can't understand how I picked up a dose the like of that.'

There was irony in the doctor's voice when he drawled:

'Do you mean you have never actually known intimacy with a woman?'

'Ach, I don't mean that at all. It's just . . . that I never took up with . . . with . . . with the sort of bitches . . . that . . . that . . . that would be riddled with pox. Prostitutes and the like.'

'Syphilis is not always contracted from prostitutes, Mr Simpson. In fact it rarely is. To ply her trade a prostitute must remain healthy. If she contracts disease, the word gets round and in no time she is out of business. No. It is the young, ignorant, irresponsible girl who is often to blame for spreading the infection.'

Beads of sweat had begun to form on Simpson's forehead.

His lower lip jutted stubbornly. His two hands capped his knees as though to hold down his raging bulk.

'Be that as it may,' he growled. 'I never had truck with filthy young trollops of that sort.'

A sarcastic smile twisted Dr. Westwood's lips.

'Nobody nowadays believes that the germ can be picked up from a lavatory seat. Or from an infected towel. Or by the simple act of kissing. I'm afraid if we have to rule out sexual intercourse as the medium of infection, we can only conclude that you are the innocent victim of congenital syphilis.'

'Congenital?'

'Hereditary. There are numerous cases of eye disorder passed on by an infected parent.'

Simpson's face mottled with rage.

'Are you inferring ... Are ... are ... are you insinuating ... that ... if I thought for one moment that ... I'd ... I'd—'

Dr. Westwood interrupted, his voice cold with contempt.

'Don't you think we have had enough of these tantrums? What matter how you contracted the infection? The important thing is that we have discovered the cause of your retinal trouble. Rid yourself of the venereal infection and you will save the sight of one eye. Fail to do this and there is every possibility sympathetic ophthalmia will set in, with the inevitable result of complete blindness.'

Turning away, the doctor went over to a filing cabinet and commenced flicking through the pockets. Simpson sat, stunned and speechless. At length, in a high panic-stricken voice, he appealed:

'What am I to do, doctor?'

'I advise you to seek treatment.' He continued his search without looking round.

'Would – would you take on ... would you treat me yourself, doctor?'

Dr. Westwood's head swivelled round.

'I am a consulting physician, Mr. Simpson. Not a general practitioner.' He straightened up. 'Go to your own doctor for treatment. This is a situation that calls for someone you know intimately. A personal friend, if possible. Dr. Madden would appear to be the ideal person.'

He made a small gesture of dismissal.

Simpson got to his feet. Stumbled to the door. Wheeled about.

'What do I owe you, Doctor?'

'I will send you on my bill, Mr. Simpson.'

'I'd rather pay now, if you don't mind.'

'Very well,' said Dr. Westwood, his voice prickling with irritation. 'Twenty guineas.

'And three guineas for the Wassermann,' he added.

'You can give the cheque to my secretary,' he said, as he saw Simpson pull out his cheque-book. 'She will give you a receipt.'

He opened the door and stood, one hand on the handle, the other behind his back.

'You will find her in my office,' he said, as Simpson – dazed and sickened with shock – shambled past him. 'One word of advice.' Simpson halted. 'Strong emotions, such as fear and anger – the emotions you have exhibited here today – could very well provoke a retinal haemorrhage. So be sparing of them. Good day.'

Simpson started off early next morning for Glenard. He had slept little during the night. The ruin and havoc implicit in the doctor's verdict prowled his tormented thoughts and stalked his shallow fitful dreams. Grimmer and ever grimmer grew the possibilities of disaster. Like a leper, he was a source of destruction to his fellow man. Unable to warn by crying: 'Unclean! Unclean!' he still must avoid the society of his friends. Not because he might contaminate them with infection, but for fear they might read his secret in mottled skin or jaundiced eye, hands stricken with scaly flakes or nose cankered with scab and rash.

His flesh crept at the thought. Already he could feel corruption spread; eating into liver, heart, overtaxed kidneys: forcing its way to the surface of his skin to pullulate into stinking pus-ridden sores sending tentacles into the bony structure of his skull to spread destruction in throat and nose and brain: gnawing into the tender pulp of either eye to rob him of the last glimmer of sight.

Rolling and tossing in the bed, he felt his legs and arms burn with itch. As he rubbed his bare arms, the skin appeared coarse and rough-grained to the touch. Behind his eyeballs a dull grinding pain began. Even to blink his eyelids was painful. His heart thudded against his rib cage with the sinister double beat the doctor had described as diastolic. He was appalled at the sound of his own breathing, a harsh irregular rasp, that became worse when he tried to control his heaving, panic-stricken lungs.

At length, thoroughly terrified, he switched on the light and got out of bed.

His mirrored reflection told him nothing. Pink, healthy skin. Tongue a little furred, bur nothing out of the ordinary. Eyes? He bent over close to the mirror and, pulling back the lids of either eye, examined minutely. No sign of anything abnormal. Even the sightless eye had the appearance of normality. No one but himself could have told which one was blinded.

He forced himself to inspect the pale, hairless scalp, trying to keep at bay the memory of the doctor's remark: 'In some cases, the hair falls out.' He scrutinized its surface for sign of rash or pimple, scurf or scale. Nothing to be seen. Picking up the comb, he combed forward the rumpled top-knot so that once more the nakedness of his balded skull was mitigated. Even in the midst of his troubles, he was gratified to see how his shorn pigtail had grown back once more to maturity.

Next he threw off his pyjamas jacket. Arranged the wardrobe and dressing-table mirrors so that he was reflected back and front. Examined chest and back, shoulders and neck. Forearms. Upper arms. The armpits presented a problem. A thorough scrutiny was impossible without barbering them. He lifted the safety razor he now used since his incapacity. Put in a fresh blade. Tried to rake it down through the bristling hair. Wincing with pain, he desisted. The hair would have to be clipped first before he could shave it clean. As best he could, he examined each armpit, shifting the hair round so that he could see the surface of the skin. He found nothing.

Pulling off the pants of his pyjamas, he began to examine his legs, back and front. Four pimples he discovered. But by no stretch of the imagination could they be classified as infectious.

He rummaged around between his toes, holding them apart so that he could proddle their depths. He examined the soles of his feet.

With the aid of his pocket mirror, he scanned the backs of his thighs and calves. His loins and hips.

All this activity was only a ruse to postpone the scrutiny h
was at last forced to undertake. Gingerly, as though his hand
were those of a stranger anxious to avoid infection, he bega
to examine his genitals. Sick with anxiety, he probed and peered
groped and squeezed, his fingers shrinking from the horror
they might chance upon. Straddle-legged, he crouched down
mirror in hand, fumbling and cursing as he scrutinized groi
and crutch. To his delight, he could discover nothing. N
chancres or swollen glands. No lesions. No tumours. Of course
unless a barbering job was done, there could be no certainty
Still it looked as if the bloody doctor was talking out c
turn.

Pyjamas on, he was about to get back into bed, when he fe
an urge to relieve himself. He searched around. Blast them any
way, not a jerry to be found. It'll have to be the hand basin fo
it. Raising himself on tiptoe, he settled himself into position
And grunting, squeezed.

A lancinating pain shot back up into his stomach. In God'
name, what's this? The pain died away. He tried again. EUGH
Worse this time. Take it easy, you idiot, will you? If you carr
on like this, you'll do damage to yourself. By careful coaxing
he managed to start. Eyes closed, face scrooged up in pain, h
kept going. There's something wrong here all right. Kidney
must be affected in some way. What was it the fellows used t
say? If there was talk of one of them getting the clap?

> *Hell to yer sowl, ye'll have to pass*
> *Barbed wire and broken glass.*

So help me they weren't far wrong. I must have clicked a dos
all right. Internal. The bloody disease must be eating the pud
dings out of me at the present minute.

He dribbled to a close, shook off the droplets and stowe
away. But the spasms of pain continued as though he were sti
teetering with close shut eyes before the hand basin. Carefull
he climbed into bed. Coiled himself up to lessen the pain
Sought refuge from his troubles in prayer. An Act of Perfec
Contrition. And three Hail Marys to Our Lady of Dolours tha
she might pity him in the extremity of his need.

The pains died away. And, as if in answer to his prayer, i
came back to him that once before, many years ago, he ha
suffered a similar stricture. Some sort of bladder trouble. H

had got rid of it by taking somebody or other's backache kidney pills. First thing in the morning he must get some. He straightened out. Folded his hands across his chest. Before he dozed off, he reflected lovingly on the muddy blue colour he would be piddling tomorrow after taking the kidney pills.

He was hardly asleep when he awoke again, with Dr. Westwood's words ringing in his ears. *'Syphilis is a law unto itself. It has been known for the disease to pass through all its stages without a single symptom showing up.'*

Once more he rolled and tossed in distraction until able to convince himself of the absurdity of the doctor's diagnosis.

And so it went on through the night – fitful slumber alternating with desperate terrifying wakefulness – leaving him exhausted in the morning.

During the first spell of the journey from the city, the traffic was so heavy he was compelled to concentrate on his driving. But once out in the country, with nothing to hold his attention, there was ample opportunity for reflection.

The sense of outrage that had dominated his emotions the previous day, had now given way to a feeling of dismay. Events were happening too quickly. It was like one of the old silent comics, where the action was speeded up so that the jerky figures raced back and forth in an agony of uselessness. It seemed only a few days since he had suffered the first haemorrhage. Yet it was so long ago that it must surely have happened to a different person. Somebody strong. Healthy. Ruthless. Most important of all – uncaring.

With envy, he remembered this callous swaggering somebody, who barged his way through life, his very bulk insuring the respect of his fellows, contemptuous of the weak and ailing, harsh in his judgements, unrelenting in rancour. He had ridiculed love, scorned sobriety, despised respectability.

How welcome now would be the indiscriminate priapism, the ingrained mistrust, the ignorant uncaring dourness.

As the miles rolled by, he sought accommodation with his lot. After all, the doctor was right when he said: *'You will save your sight if you rid yourself of—'* (Even in his thoughts he shrank from using the ugly word.) All you have to do is get treatment. Yes, but where? This talk of going to a personal friend was pure bullshit. You'd look a nice idiot admitting to Madden that you'd picked up a dose, wouldn't you? When he'd

241

finished laughing his head off, he'd start reading you a lecture on the dangers of promiscuity. 'Keep it in your trousers, Jim,' he'd say. 'It's the safest place for it.' You'd never be fit to look him in the face again afterwards. No. It will have to be a stranger. Some doctor miles away that there'll be no chance of you ever meeting again. But then, if he's too far away, how could you attend for regular treatment? Didn't you read or hear somewhere that treatment of – (his hands tightened on the wheel) – syph entailed weekly injections for a period varying from six months to two years or more? If it got out that you were travelling thirty or forty miles each week to get medical attention, some of the local hard chaws would surely put two and two together. No use giving out that you were attending an eye specialist. That story could be checked upon too easily. Perhaps, in the long run, the local doctor would be the safest to attend. At least – if it was Madden – he'd keep his trap shut. But it would be a hell of a humiliating situation. Then, what if a better dispensary went vacant? Madden – dissatisfied with Greevan – could very well apply for a transfer. And get it. There would be a new doctor. What then?

Simpson's thoughts veered wildly away from this hazard. For the next ten minutes he booted up the speed, so that he was compelled to concentrate on his driving. In succession he passed out two cars, a bus and an empty cattle-lorry. The latter nearly proved his undoing. Its breadth and height obstructed his view. He kept edging out to the right, waiting for the straight stretch that would allow him to pass in safety. At last it came. Blowing for the road, he commenced to overtake. It was when the vehicles were nose to nose that he found he had underestimated the speed and width of the lorry. Ahead the road narrowed and swung into a right-hand corner. He was about to slow down and fall in behind the lorry when its horn sounded peremptorily. Out of the tail of his eye, he saw the driver shake his fist. This decided him. Pressing his foot down to the boards, he continued to overtake.

Again he had misjudged. Before he could take avoiding action, his off-side wheels were up on the grass verge. Clutching at the wheel, he held the bouncing, lurching car on its course until, reaching the corner, he was forced to swing across the bonnet of the lorry to reach his own side of the road. With the screech of locked tyres, the vicious hooting of a

orn and the pounding of his own heart in his ears, he fled
eadlong, never slowing down till he guessed the lorry to be
t least a couple of miles behind.

Once more he found himself reviewing his predicament.
What would he tell everyone when he got back? He would
ave to have some class of a story ready. Something fool-
proof. That would stand up to questioning. Mrs. Mahony
would be fussing around inquiring. So would McCann. He
would have to be careful with that little ferret. You could
e tripped up in that quarter handy enough. Surprising how
well read he is. Better not go into too much detail. Just hint
hat Westwood diagnosed some obscure disease. A disease of
he blood. Wait a moment. What was it he mentioned? It's
nocking at my ear-drums. Starts with an H. Haemo-some-
hing. Hold on, now. It's coming. Yes. Haemophilia. You can
ay it's something similar to that. Without being too specific.
A disease requiring long and patient treatment. That will stall
im off.

Then there's Hannah Murphy. She'll want to know what the
Dublin doctor had to say. And, of course – Delia. But what
was he going to tell *her*?

At one moment the urge to confide in someone – if only
o seek comfort from the cudgelling of fate – dictated that
e tell the truth to her: the next, he shied away from a course
of action that was bound to cripple, if not destroy, their re-
ationship. *'Open confession is good for the soul.'* How many
imes had he quoted that maxim to evasive customers? Well,
t was his turn now. It was only right that she should know.
Besides clearing his conscience, he was giving her a chance to
get ... if it was necessary ... that is, if she needed it ... to be
exact, if she had contracted – He slammed the gear lever into
hird and roared around a corner. Could you picture yourself
explaining the disease to her? Laying special emphasis on the
ugly and embarrassing nature of the probable symptoms? My
God, no! It couldn't be done, man. Nobody could be expected to face a job of that kind. It was everybody for himself
n this world. Wasn't there another precept: *'Man, mind thyself. Woman, do thou likewise.'* Anyway, if there was the least
hing the matter with her, wouldn't you have noticed it yourself? God knows, you had more than enough opportunities
for research.

Not recently, though. A lot could have happened in the la[st] few weeks.

Maybe. But that doesn't mean that you should be force[d] to act as a kind of sanitary inspector. No. '*Let sleeping do[gs] lie.*' Another very sensible saying.

A bloody lousy one – in this case, if you'll only look at it [in] the straight decent way. If anything's wrong with her, you'[re] to blame. So you had better find out before it is gone too fa[r]. Instead of skulking out of your responsibilities.

But if there's nothing wrong with her? What then? Th[e] cat'll be out of the bag then and no mistake. And what [a] bloody cat? You'll have made a right and proper balls-up [of] the whole affair. Nothing you could do or say would men[d] matters. Do you think she'd let you lay a hand on her wh[en] she learns the state you're in?

For the rest of the journey he tried to decide whether [or] not to tell Delia of Dr. Westwood's verdict. But he reache[d] Glenard without coming to any decision.

Mrs. Mahony was surprised to see him.

'I wasn't expecting you till next week,' she said. 'If y[ou] had only let me know in time, I could have had a ni[ce] bit of dinner ready for you. All I can give you now is [a] fry.'

'That will do very nicely. I'll garage the car and put aw[ay] my things. You can give me a shout when you're ready.'

As he unpacked his cases, he tried to prepare answers [to] the questions Mrs. Mahony was sure to ask.

The interrogation commenced when he sat down to ea[t]. Mrs. Mahony stood facing him at the far end of the tab[le]. Quizzing head tilted, folded arms nursing her massive elde[rs].

'What did the Dublin doctor say, Mr. Simpson?'

He popped a piece of liver into his mouth. Chewed indu[s]triously.

'Did he find out what's ailing you?'

Still chewing, he nodded.

'Was it good news or bad?'

He swallowed the last of the liver. Forked up a section [of] sausage. Plunged it into the egg-yolk. Paused to collect a tr[i]angular cutting of toast. Twirled the fork to stop the drip.

'A bit of both,' he said, conveying the fork-load to h[is] mouth.

'Aw, that's too bad,' she said.

He nodded his head lugubriously. Tongued out a piece of sausage meat jammed between denture and lip.

'One eye's gone for good,' he mumbled.

'Sweet Mother of God.'

'He thinks he can save the other one.' This time he sponged white of egg and sausage.

'How?'

'By undergoing a course of injections. Might take upwards of twelve months.' He continued eating rapidly while Mrs. Mahony lamented:

'Would you listen to him, for pity's sake? Injections! A course of injections lasting the guts of a year. Some people never learn sense. After being injected week in, week out, for months past! Wouldn't you think that would do him? But, no. He must start all over again. Gulping down tablets and having ould medicine composed of the dear knows what class of a gather-up squirted into you. If you could be sure it was only tap water you might be well enough off. For it's my firm belief they pump diseases into you instead of sucking them out. Don't you know right well, if there was no sickness or disease, the doctors and the chemists would die of starvation?'

Mouth bulging with food, he shook his head chidingly.

'No use trying to persuade me otherwise. There was nothing much the matter with you until you started going to those two specialists. They made a right job of you. If you had only done what you were told, this would never have happened. If you had eased off the drink. Stopped staying out late and slept your fill. Taken the herbs and the cordials that were ordained by the Creator for your benefit. But there was no prevailing on you . . .'

She broke off, sobbing.

Simpson jumped up. Went round the table. Patted her back, clumsily.

'Stop this nonsense, Annie. Didn't I tell you I'll have the sight of one eye. Isn't that good enough for anyone? No use in being greedy about these matters.'

'I know fine well what'll happen,' she moaned. 'You'll carry on the way you've been doing this while back. And you'll lose the sight of both your eyes.'

She gulped back a sob. Trembling, sought to regain her self-control. Sniffed convulsively.

'Your poor eyes,' she wailed. 'You'll lose the sight of both of them.'

She shook off his arm and made for the door. Turned back angry and red-eyed.

'There's ones to blame for this,' she burst out. 'Not a hundred miles from here. Idle young fly-by-nights with nothing better to do than make up to the men. Filthy trollops that would sooner be lying back with their clothes up than on their knees saying their prayers. If there's any justice to be had in this world, those are the hussies that'll get their deserts.'

Before he could speak, she had swung around and shuffled back to the kitchen.

Simpson decided to leave well alone. Annie was too disturbed by the news to be blamed for anything she said. The important thing was that she had asked no questions about the nature of the doctor's findings. If he got off as soft with McCann, there would be little to complain about. Perhaps the easiest way to handle him would be to bring the talk round as soon as possible to Bank business. He takes himself so seriously when he's doing relief work, there should be no trouble sidetracking him to a report on the state of the Branch.

And so it turned out. McCann had finished checking off the teller's cash and was helping him stow away the sacks and trays of bagged coin when Simpson interrupted them.

'How did it go, Manager?' McCann asked, when the relief cashier had gone. 'Was Westwood able to root up what was causing the trouble?'

For a few seconds Simpson was knocked groggy. Surely the little ferret couldn't have nosed out the truth. There was something odd about his attitude. He kept his eyes lowered. As if there was a smell of cat shit off your shoes. People who couldn't look you straight in the eye merited watching.

'He thinks he's on the right track,' said Simpson.

'He'll be able to save your sight?'

'I hope so. He doesn't seem to have any doubts himself.

'Of course,' he added, 'it was too late for him to do anything with the right eye. The vision is gone for good.'

'Pity you hadn't gone to him sooner, Manager. From what I hear he's a great doctor.'

What's this all about? Is he just making conversation? Or was he snooping around investigating?

'One of the best men in Dublin, they say. A most methodical, painstaking doctor. Leaves nothing to chance.' That puts the ball back in his court again.

'Yes, it's a great thing when you can have confidence in somebody. It's half the battle, I think,' said McCann.

You can say that again. There's no fear of anyone confiding in *you* at the moment. You'd be safer held at arm's length.

'I couldn't agree with you more, Mr. McCann.'

'Was he able to localize the cause of the haemorrhages?'

Would you listen to him? Talking like a fucking doctor himself. Better watch your step.

'It's the blood. Some obscure ailment of the blood. Dr. Westwood says it will yield to treatment.'

'Did he tell you the name of the disease? Head Office have asked me to report on your present state of health.'

On rubber legs, Simpson moved over to his desk, picked up the diary calendar and leafed over it slowly.

'It's . . . it's not a disease. It's more . . . a . . . more a condition of the blood. The blood—' He sought wildly for words. '—the blood won't—' Inspiration came to him. '—it won't scab.'

'Haemophilia! That's what it is. A hell of a rare disease.'

Simpson was staring blindly at an entry in the diary reading: *Emigrants' Remittances advised to Dublin.*

'The Spanish royal family suffered from it. Females transmit but do not suffer from it. Males contract it but do not pass it on.'

'It's only a mild form,' Simpson croaked.

'Still it would be better to mention it in the report.'

'No, we'd better stick to what Dr. Roche said in the first place. Retinitis. It'll only mix things up to change now. I'll get a certificate from Madden tomorrow.'

He turned over a page of the diary.

'I see you applied for £2,500 for Jim Lawson. What did the Directors say?'

'What do you think? Cut the overdraft down to £2,000 and set up a whine about the steep fall in the lodgements for the year. It's the same story all the time. "We do not warm to this advance." "Keep up the pressure for reductions." "Can applicant not get accommodation elsewhere?" You'd think by the tone of their letters that the arse was hanging out of their trousers.'

He's away for slates. It's only a matter of keeping him going now.

'Are they giving you trouble, Mac?'

'Trouble? They're never off my back. Every morning you open the Head Office letter, there's a couple of raspers in it. If it's not that, it's another batch of new forms. There must be a half-witted yahoo up in Head Office who does nothing else but think up an endless stream of forms setting out a new way of showing that two and two makes four. It would give you the green gawks filling them in.'

'Aye, it's bad all right. But I suppose they serve some purpose or other. If it's only to hang up in the lavatory.'

'The buffs must have great faith in human nature if they think the half of the forms are filled in correctly. Take that form for detailing farmers' livestock.'

'Is that Form 1B.12?'

'The very one. Well, you know the widow Heffernan? The gabby, ginger-haired one?'

'I do, of course. A decent woman. With a snug, well-stocked farm. A hard worker, I'd say. She's ploughing back her profits like any thrifty farmer would. In a few years' time that woman will have a nice fat credit balance. How does she stand now, tell me?'

'Over £1,800 debit.'

'A bit high. But we hold the deeds. And she's heavily stocked. Didn't she fill in one of those livestock forms for me a few months back?'

'Four months ago. Wait till you hear this. You'll bust a gut laughing.'

Simpson saw that McCann's eyes, now lifted to his own, were dancing with malice.

'The son came in to me last week. Looking for another thousand to stock up. I got him to detail the stock in 1B.12. And do you know what I found when I compared with the form the widow had filled in only four months before?'

'They hardly agreed anyway. These forms are not meant to be a hundred per cent accurate.'

'True enough. But ninety-eight cattle missing is a bit much.'

Ninety-eight beasts worth, at her own estimate, £5,000, dis-appearing, just like—' Two-handed, he fanned out curled magician's fingers. 'And not a shilling lodged to the account or a cheque cashed, to show evidence of a sale.'

'You wrote to her? Asking for an explanation?'

'I did. She was in today.'

'What did she say?'

'This is where the laugh comes in. She turned on me like a dog. Surely I wasn't suggesting she was trying to mislead the Bank. But where did the cattle go? Was I trying to make out that she was dishonest? No, but where did the cattle go? How, she asked, did I think she was to clothe, feed and educate nine children?' McCann gave a high caw of laughter.

'And what did you say?'

'I just said I hardly thought it was possible for the ten of them, herself included, to eat a bullock a day for four months. Unless, says I, you broke Canon Law and ate meat on the Fridays.'

Simpson joined in the laughter.

'What had she to say on that point?'

'It never shook a feather on her. She left the inner office without a stain on her character.'

'But,' he added, 'doesn't it go to show just how much reliance you can put on one of those completed 1B.12's?'

Simpson, satisfied with his diversionary tactics, agreed wholeheartedly and, excusing himself, made for the door. As he was opening it, McCann said:

'You'd never guess who's in town just now?'

Hand on the door knob, Simpson waited. Now, what's he getting at? There's a touch of spite in the way he asked that question.

'Who?'

'Brian Mullen.'

Simpson swung round, his two fists clenched.

'Are you serious?'

'Of course I am. I ran into him myself. In Snout's. He stood me a double brandy. And drinks for the rest of the house. Pulled out a fistful of notes. Fivers, tenners, singles. All jumbled up. A sight for sore eyes.'

He paused.

Is he trying to start something? Or did that last remark slip out accidentally?

'Did you tackle him about his overdraft?'

'You couldn't very well do that in the bar of a public house. Anyway he was in too much of a hurry. Gobbled up his drink and made for the next pub. He likes to keep on the move.'

'Did you not ask him to call in here?'

'He'll be here for a fortnight. He said he would look you up.'

'I'll believe that when I see him. He's a foxy gentleman, Mr. Mullen. If he's flying the notes, he has some good reason for it. Probably working up an alibi for himself.'

'How do you mean, Manager?' McCann was looking at him oddly.

'He's maybe got a dame tucked away some place. And laying a false trail to cover it up. You got a whiff of the aniseed yourself apparently.'

'The meed of us that trade in love.' McCann's voice oozed venom.

'What's that? What are you driving at?' Simpson said sharply. My God, surely he hasn't ferreted out . . .

'It's an old saying. Misquoted, no doubt. It doesn't do justice to poor Brian.'

'That's a funny way to put it.'

He opened the door again. Glanced back suspiciously.

'Humph!' he said, before he slammed it shut.

Shaken by this encounter, he decided it would be safer to keep his trap shut for a few days until things had returned to normal. So, during teatime, he concentrated on the paper propped against the milk jug, ignoring Mrs. Mahony's attempts to start a conversation. Eventually she said:

'You'll not be going out tonight?'

'No, Annie. I'll go to bed early. I'm tired.'

' 'Deed I'm sure you could do with a rest, Mr. Simpson. You're jaded looking.'

She finished clearing the table.

'I may go off, so?' she asked.

'You may.'

Ten minutes after she had gone he got the car out and started for Creevan. At Cleggan Cross he pulled in at Hannigan's. He surely deserved a drink after the day's skirmishings.

After the third glass of whiskey, everything began to slip into place. Annie, the poor angashore, was fretting over him like a broody hen. She meant well and it might be better to pass over her strictures. As for McCann, he was a foolish little fellow, crammed to the gullet with all sorts of nonsense he picks up in books. That silly saying of his. What was it? Something about trading in love. Absolute balderdash. The kind of tripe you'd find in a poetry book. Where he very likely found it. There was no double meaning in it whatsoever.

Another drink and he decided that it would be madness to tell Delia about the Dublin doctor's diagnosis. Time enough later on when he had got over the shock. It might be as well even to get a second opinion. In spite of what Westwood had insisted, those test tubes could very well have got ballsed up. Perhaps Madden might know of another – no, better leave John out of it altogether. 'Twould only complicate things further. Better let the hare sit for a little while. After this length of time, a few days more or less shouldn't make all that difference. All you have to do is to avoid getting angry or excited. Shouldn't be too hard.

'One for the road, Boss,' he called, throwing down a half-note. Better go – after this one. Must be in proper working order tonight. *There's no knowing what I'll give you* – isn't that what she said? When you were leaving for Dublin?

'There you are, Mr. Simpson. Out of the Parish Priest's bottle.'

'God bless.' Pocket the change. A drop of water in the whiskey. A trial sip to make sure he's not codding you. That's better. Now a small exchange of civilities.

'Nice weather we're having?'

'Aye. It'll shorten the winter.'

'The nights are beginning to close in, though.'

'Sure, it's only a few short weeks till Christmas.'

'It's hard to credit.'

'It won't be long flying.'

That's enough conversation! Drink up now! Good you boy, you. On your feet! That's the spirit.

'I'll be off now.'

'Good night, sir.'

'Good night.'

He drove slowly to Creevan. Gripped once again by guilt,

he felt raw and nervous. Delia was a shrewd customer. Would his story pass muster? What if she started probing and asking questions? Like McCann. He should have had another drink in Hannigan's. The best thing he could do was say nothing until he had another couple of jars under his belt. Any excuse would do. Tired after the journey. Fed up getting pushed around. Prefer not to say much about it tonight. Just mention permanent loss of vision in one eye. That should be sufficient to stall off any inquiries.

Before he realized it, he was at Hannah's. He drove past it and parked on the far side of the street. It would be less conspicuous than leaving it directly outside. If he happened to be a bit late getting home. Better lock it, too. Just to be on the safe side. He pocketed the keys. Then, straightening his shoulders and thrusting out his chest, he swaggered across to the bar door.

Hannah was behind the counter. Glasses down over her nose. Reading the paper. She looked up as he closed the door.

'My God,' she said, gazing at him in terrified apprehension. 'Is it yourself, Mr. Simpson?'

'I must look like a ghost, the way you're looking at me, Hannah.'

'It's not that. It's just ... we-we-we weren't expecting you.'

'I'm here now, anyway. And I might as well have a drink when I'm here. A ball of malt, when you're ready.'

She got up. Moved along the shelves, turning an uneasy bird-like head in every direction.

'Over there.' He pointed. 'Under the optic taps. The Jameson Ten. Surely you haven't forgotten?'

She settled the glasses back on the bridge of her nose. Gazed after his pointing finger.

'Tck! Tck! Tck!' she clucked. 'I must be wool-gathering.'

Holding the pewter measure over the glass, she poured carefully. From the drinking-room came a burst of laughter.

'There's a terrible shake in your hand the day, Hannah.' With relish he contemplated the overflowing measure.

She splashed the measured whiskey into his glass. Replaced the bottle. Looked round in agitation.

'I better get Delia. There's a crowd in the room. But she'll want to see you.'

'Don't budge. I want a quiet couple of drinks. Leave her be for a few minutes.'

'Would you not rather come down to the kitchen? You'll not be disturbed there.'

'I'm grand where I am.'

She stood at the counter while he drank, her fingers playing a distraught tune on the timber, her eyelids blinking rapidly.

Suddenly she clasped her hands together.

'God forgive me,' she said. 'I'm a terrible woman. What'll you think of me at all? I never asked you how you were. Or what the specialist in Dublin had to say—'

'Hussh!' He waved two soothing, two tolerant hands. 'Not now, Hannah. Please. I'll tell you about it later. In the meanwhile—'

He indicated, with stabbing forefinger, his empty glass.

'Please God, everything will turn out all right,' she said as she refilled the glass. The intense sincerity in her voice made it seem more like a prayer than a pious wish.

He sipped slowly. A rich glow of well-being pervaded him. Honey flowed through his veins. His limbs felt light and agile. From his stomach, the simmering guts rumbled pleasantly and sent up an occasional gentle burp, satisfying in its aftertaste. A godlike logic ruled the decreasing level of the whiskey in the glass: the changing features of the image in the mirror: the shaking off of the last restraint of worry and dread that had been nagging at him all day.

Miraculously the glass was empty again.

'Another potation, Hannah, if you'd be so kind.'

'A small one this time. Mr. Simpson?'

'The indications are that the ingestion of a gill of pot-still—' He winked at the smiling, witty face in the mirror.

'Would be grist to your mill,' said a voice at his elbow.

'Mind your own bloody business,' he said to the scowling, stand-no-fucking-nonsense reflection.

'Och, Mr. Simpson, it's not surely a naggin you want.'

'A gill, Hannah. A gill.'

'But it's one and the same thing. A naggin and a gill.'

'Are you trying to teach me the liquid measures?'

'No, but a naggin—'

'Never mind about your naggins. Aren't four gills one imperial pint?'

'Yes, but—'

'It's a glass of whiskey he wants, Hannah.'

'Would . . . You . . . Have . . . Manners. Didn't I tell you to shut up?' He turned round slowly, face buttoned up. 'Is it yourself, John?' he asked the dapper little man beside him. 'Two glasses of whiskey for myself and Mr. Vereker, Hannah.' He slapped his companion heartily on the back. 'Where have you been this long time, John? I haven't seen you in a month of Sundays.'

'Oh, just mucking arahnd. Trying to make an honest bob. How are you keeping, James? I heard you weren't so well.'

'You don't want to heed all you hear.' He frowned. This summoned up an unpleasant memory. What was it? 'Don't heed all you hear,' he repeated aggressively.

Vereker picked up his glass of whiskey from the counter. Raised it in salutation.

'Down the 'atch, chum,' he said.

He drained the glass. Wiped his mouth with the back of his hand.

'If you see Clancy, tell him I called, Hannah.'

He nodded brightly to the glowering figure.

'Ta-ta, mate,' he said and was gone.

'Bloody good riddance,' Simpson muttered into his glass.

Leaning over the counter, her face a mask of misery and dread, Hannah said:

'Will you excuse me, Mr. Simpson, till I fetch Delia.'

He placed the glass down carefully on the counter.

'You just do that, Hannah. Tell her I'm here.'

With Hannah gone, he tried to collect his thoughts. What would he say to Delia? What tell her of the doctor's discovery? He had had it all mapped out but somehow it had slipped his memory. The only solution was to play safe. Tell her nothing. Plead exhaustion. Say you've talked every day for a week to the doctors and you'd like to give it a rest. He yawned. God knows, it's a rest he could do with. The feeling of exaltation had passed. Already the drumming had started in his ears. His throat was dry and gritty. He was thirsty. He could do with a long cool bottle of stout.

The buzz of conversation had died out in the drinking-room. The house could have been deserted, so quiet was it. Yet when he door opened, the clink of glasses and the soft murmur of voices could be heard.

Delia and Hannah came out together. Stood whispering at the door. He thought he heard Hannah mutter: 'It's a sin and a shame, so it is.' Then she was gone and Delia was behind the counter, with a tray of empty glasses, her finger to her lips, saying: 'Hush! Wait till I come back.'

In silence she filled out two gins, two whiskeys and a stout. Opened a bottle of bitter lemon. Got change out of a pound. Started back with the tray, whispering: 'Don't move.'

Almost at once she returned, closing the door carefully after her. She crossed the room until she stood an arm's length from him. Let the pent-up breath whistle out through her lips.

'Blow me down,' she said. 'Would you look who's here?'

Hands on hips, she gazed at him, shaking her head sadly.

'No chance of a girl breaking out when she's in *your* stable.'

He had forgotten how lovely she looked. Fair hair, piled high. Smouldering grey eyes. Pouting lips, gleaming with mauve lipstick. Fresh unflawed skin. White jumper and plaid skirt moulded the saucy breasts and long elegant legs. She could have stepped straight from a chocolate-box cover.

She moved closer, kissed him gently on the lips and said:

'Well, Buster, how goes it?'

An aching hunger gripped him – obscure, passionless, frightening – as though this chocolate-box image was the pressed and packaged beauty of the day and night, soon to be pilfered from his sightless eyes.

Gathering her into his arms, he buried his face in the scented warmth of her neck, groaning at the boundless measure of his loss.

'Hey, there,' she said, pushing him away roughly. 'Behave yourself.'

Dodging his grasp, she slipped round behind the counter. Poured herself out a brandy. Sipped it slowly.

'What did the doctor say, Jim? Was he able to do anything for you?'

'He was and he wasn't.'

She reached out a casual forefinger and stroked gently the hand resting against the whiskey glass.

'Was it as bad as that, darling? Tell it all to Mummy.'

255

Like a flock of starlings, his thoughts wheeled and settled. The decision was made. Now was his chance to unburden himself. She would understand. Sympathize. Counsel.

'It came as a shock,' he said. 'You must believe me—' His appealing, outflung hand sent the glass of whiskey flying. Stooping to gather up the fragments, he swayed and staggered forward a pace.

'Leave it be, Jim. I'll sweep it up later.'

She filled another glass. Placed it before him.

'I don't know should I do this,' she said. 'You're well jarred you know.'

She wiped away the spilled whiskey from the counter.

'Aunt Hannah spotted it. She's worried about you. Thinks you should get no more drink.'

'Pay no attention to that old pooshey. It's scapulars and medals and rosary beads she should be selling instead of drink.'

He took a long slug. Left down the glass carefully. Belched deep in his throat – a moist, soggy, gurgle.

'Excuse me,' he said. 'Meaning no harm to your Aunt Hannah, I needn't tell you. A quiet decent woman.'

'You were going to tell me what the doctor said about your eye trouble?'

Suspiciously he squinted at her.

'You want to know it all, don't you? Like the rest of them. Questions. Questions. Nothing but questions.'

'You shouldn't say that, Jim. Damned well you know it's not curiosity makes me ask.'

'Sorry, Delia. I didn't mean that.' He drank again. 'It's just that I don't want to talk about it.' He filled his cheeks with air. Blew out through pursed lips. 'I've been every day for a week talking to one doctor after another. I could do with a rest. Talked out, that's what I am.'

'All right. Jim. You can tell me all about it later.'

She watched him drink, the whiskey swaying in the tilting glass, a look of ferocious concentration on his face.

'I think Aunt Han was right, darling. You're not in too good shape to drive a car, are you?'

He planked down the glass clumsily.

'Are you suggesting—' He picked his words carefully. '—that I am ... unfit ... to be in charge ... of a ... mechanically pro-pro-propelled vehicle?'

'Call it what you like, you shouldn't drive home tonight.'

Slowly the scowl cleared away, the creases reassembling in the form of a knowing leer.

'Do you mean . . . I should stay here tonight?'

'I can't see anything else for it.'

Tossing off the remains of his whiskey, he straightened up.

'Delighted to accept . . . your kind invitation. Lead the way, dear.'

'Stop the codding, Jim. Will you? This requires a bit of planning. There's a few snags to get over.'

'Snags! What snags?'

'We have a—' Delicately she chose the word. '—a visitor staying here at the moment . . . an old friend.

'Of Aunt Hannah's, of course,' she added.

'What has that got to do with it?'

'You can't sleep in the spare room, stupid. That's what it means. You'll have to sleep in my room.'

'But isn't that what we want?'

'Will . . . you . . . stop . . . interrupting?' Forefinger to her mouth, she deliberated. 'Aunt has gone to the chapel to do a Holy Hour. We have that much grace.'

Immersed in thought, she poured herself out another brandy. Sipped it slowly.

'Where have you the car parked?' she suddenly asked.

'Parked?' Frowning, he sought to recollect.

'Yes, fathead. Did you leave your car outside in the street?'

'Wait now. Don't rush me. It's up the road. A good piece away.'

'Which direction?' she asked impatiently.

'Down towards the bridge. On the opposite side of the street.'

'Good,' said Delia. 'She'll not pass it coming back from the chapel, so.' Thoughtfully she nibbled at her lower lip. 'Here's what we'll do. I'll sneak up to the room now. If we wait any longer, customers may start drifting in. When Aunt comes back, I'll tell her you were driven home. The crowd inside—' She nodded at the drinking room. '—are breaking up soon. They go through Glenard on their way home. What more likely than that one of them drove you home in your own car? Popped you into the house. And then went on with his own crowd.' She looked at him in triumph. 'How's that for a foolproof story?'

Eyebrows drawn down, he pondered.

'How do I get away in the morning?' he asked, at length.

'I'll set the alarm clock for five. You'll want to be out and away before Aunt wakes up at six.'

'But sure the clatter of the alarm'll wake up the house?'

'No such thing. It'll be under my pillow.'

He looked at her in admiration.

'Begod, you think of everything. You're a great bloody girl.'

'Stop prating and come on.' She started for the door.

'Hold on,' he said. 'You're not sending me away empty-handed?'

'You've a one-track mind,' she said, scooping up a bottle of Jameson. 'Here! Put this away.'

He took out his wallet and commenced fumbling in it.

'Come on,' she urged. 'You can pay me next time you're in.'

He followed her out to the hall and up the creaking stairs, moving with drunken caution. At the end of the corridor, she opened a door and switched on the light.

'Wait!' she said, rushing to the window and drawing the blind. 'That's better.' She looked around. Straightened the bed-clothes. Placed the two layered pillows side by side. 'Not much space, but 'twill do.'

'Aye,' he said. 'There's space to spare. The ceiling's not all that low.'

She grinned.

'Getting perky already.' She took the key out of the door lock. 'I'd better lock the door from the outside. Can't take any chances. Aunt Hannah might easily come in here for something.'

She took a final glance around.

'Put off the light before you get into bed. And make no noise.'

Blowing him a kiss, she went out the door. Peeped in again.

'For fear I forget in the morning. Aunt sleeps on the other side of the corridor, so go easy past her room when you're leaving.'

This time he heard the key turn in the lock.

Without opening the laces, he eased off his shoes. Padded

ver to the wash-stand, where he dumped the bottle of Jame-
on. Stretched himself out on the bed.

Sure enough, it was cramped all right. The width was in it
ut not the length. He would have to coil up like a hedgehog
 keep his feet under the bedclothes. What harm? It was all in a
ood cause.

He decided to have one drink before bedding down. Using
he tooth glass and a carafe of water, he knocked back a quick
ort. After some thought – a second one. Then feeling the
aves of sleep beginning to gather force, he peeled off his
lothes, scattering them on chair, bed and floor, switched off
he light and felt his way back to the bed. Curling himself
to a ball, right knuckle under chin, clothes happed into his
ack, he was soon sound asleep.

He seemed only to have closed his eyes when the light went
n again. Obstinately he refused to budge. Eyes tight shut.
reathing soft and shallow. He feigned sleep.

'Don't stir,' he heard her say softly. 'I just sneaked up to see
ow you were.' He felt her lips brush his cheek. Then:

'My God, what a mess. Were you never taught to hang
p your clothes? Tck! Tck! Tck! Would you look at the cut
f them! Jacket lying on the bed.' A creaking sound. (The
ardrobe door opening?) A flapping as something was shaken
igorously. Footsteps. 'Could you not put your shirt and socks
way properly? And your underpants?' Drawers opened and
losed. 'How do you expect to keep a crease in your pants
hen they are rolled into a ball like this?' More flapping,
ccompanied by jingling and the chink of silver. 'Aren't you
ery careless with your money, throwing your pants around
is way?' The creaking again, as the wardrobe door was
losed. 'I'm away now. There's a few still loitering in the bar.
hey'll be clearing off shortly. Be seeing you.' Again the warm
ressure of her lips. Darkness once more as she switched off
he light. The sound of the closing door. And the click of the
ock as it snapped home.

Gathering the clothes tighter round his shoulders, he
quirmed deep into the pillow. In the distance surf rumbled as
 broke on the empty beach. Or was it the gravel at the river
nouth, tossed to and fro as the incoming tide met the thrust
f the river? It could be the blood pounding in the ear pressed
o hard into the pillow. Thrusting fisted hand under cheek

bone, he lifted his head clear of the pillow. The throbbing continued. Like a car engine warming up. Being revved up mercilessly. Too tired to investigate he let the throbbing waves roll over him, engulfing him in sleep.

When he woke again, the car engine was still running. For an instant he was whisked back to that morning a lifetime ago when he had woken to the same throbbing noise. He listened for the sounds of Mrs. Mahony doing out the office. The silence worried him. Never had he known her to be late. He opened his eyes.

Holding his breath, he stared into the darkness. Surely it couldn't be? It was inconceivable that it would happen this way. During the night. Without warning. But isn't that how the other eye went? Lost its vision overnight? And as for warning, didn't you hear the engine running? Isn't that warning enough for you?

Panic-stricken, he glared around, trying to pierce the blanket of darkness that enshrouded him. A grey outline, faint but unmistakable, disclosed a window. Where it ought not to be. In a flash it all came back to him. The where. And the why.

What time was it at all? He was fumbling around over his head when he remembered there was no bed-light. Was it really worth all the trouble of getting out of bed, pawing around the walls seeking the switch, when all he had to do was cosy down and wait for Delia to come up? But what was keeping her? The way he felt he must have punched in a good few hours sleep. She should have been dossed down before this. He listened intently. Except for the throbbing in his ear (it must be that – what else could it be?) there was the silence of an empty house. Delia was probably tending bar. But Hannah and the visitor should surely to God be in bed by now. He strained his ears. No sound of cough or snore or creaking springs.

He swung his legs out of bed and sat, trying to get his bearings. Delia had warned him to make no noise. Carefully he groped his way along the wall, starting from the head of the bed, one hand steadying him against the wall while the other reached out as far as it would go. Then the feet, consolidating the ground won, shuffled noiselessly forward. Again the questing hand stretched out. Until at length the door jamb was

eached. Across the door to the far jamb. Then up and down
he wall till he felt the switch.

By this time he was sweating with tension. In the silence of
he house the click of the switch would sound like a gun shot.
Ie eased it down. Slowly. Slowly. Teeth clenched. Jaw muscles
ensed so that the noise might – in some miraculous fashion –
ɔe lessened.

In the sudden blaze of light, he heard no noise. He waited,
dazzled, staring at the wristwatch on his bare arm. At length
ais vision cleared. To his stupefaction, the time was ten past
hree. He held the watch to his ear. It was going, all right. Per-
aaps he had been regulating the watch and had forgotten to
ɔush back the winder? No. It was in the right position. It must
aave stopped during the night and started up again just now.
But what hell time would that leave it?

The best thing he could do was to slip out into the corridor.
Go as far as the head of the stairs. And find out what was
aappening down below in the bar. By the same token, there
was a clock in the hall. He could find the right time from it.

He turned the handle of the door. Very gingerly. Kept turning till it would go no further. Pulled it towards him gently.
Again. Tugged it viciously. Not a budge. The bloody door was
still locked.

To hell with this for a caper. Bad enough staying on in the
bar, serving drink to a shower of drunken gobshites. But keeping him a prisoner up here, at the same time, was a bit much.
The company falling asleep over their drinks. Taking an hour
to sink a pint. A proper pollution! Whatever they'd spend
wouldn't pay for the light. Too soft she is. She should turf
them out at closing time. Letting them stay on, night after
night, until all hours. It's asking for trouble. Some little skitter
of a Guard from the arse-end of nowhere that's looking for a
bit of notice from his superiors will take it into his head one
of these nights to put manners on her. 'And I suppose, Miss
Clifden,' he'll say, pulling out his notebook and looking
round at the assembled hallions, 'these gentlemen are your
guests? Well, there'll be no harm in taking their names anyway.' As if he didn't know the name, townland and political
pull of every man-jack that was in it. It'll be her own fault, all
right, if she's caught. She takes too many chances. You could
nearly offer odds that she's throwing back an odd brandy her-

self. Who could blame her? Or – remembering the Jameson bottle – blame him either if he took a wee sup of gander sauce?

Tiptoeing round to the wash-stand he picked up the bottle. Poured himself out a generous shot. Drank it standing up.

He shivered. Nippy enough to be lounging around in your pelt. You'd want trunks and vest for comfort. But where had Delia put away his clothes? She was as bad as Annie, hiding away anything she finds. Clearing up after you, it's called.

Where would he start? He could still remember her – half asleep though he'd been – moving about the room. Complaining about his untidiness. Opening and closing drawers. He would try the dressing-table first.

He drew a blank with the top right-hand drawer. It contained rolled-up stockings and undergarments neatly folded, sweaters, cardigans and jaunty woollen berets – all carefully put away. The next drawer – the top left – could have belonged to a different person. It was a hopeless jumble of scarves, odd gloves, ribbons, balls of wool, perfume boxes, bills, Christmas cards, ribbons, photographs, belts, lengths of material, ribbons. He was about to close the drawer when he noticed familiar handwriting on papers stuffed in at the back. Reaching in, he pulled them out.

They were letters. Two letters. One – there was no need to check the signature – from McCann. The other. He turned over the page. From George. Who would he be? Wait now! George. The sallow-faced waster from the 'Glass and Bottle'? What was his surname? Din-something. Yes, Dinsmore. That was it. Was that get still sniffing after her? He read:

My dear Delia, Got your note today. Many thanks for your kind and, I need hardly add, most welcome invitation. You can expect me any time after eight o'clock. I have thought of you many times since the Night of the High Wind. It is good to know you have not forgotten me. We have much leeway to make up!!! Until eight o'clock tomorrow. All my love. George.

P.S. Be sure and tie up that pet mastiff of yours. He's an ugly dangerous brute. You'd be better to have him put down before he savages someone. More love.

262

The second was longer.

My dear, I had to read your letter many times before I could credit that you were really serious. It is hard to understand how a shrewd sensible girl like yourself can suddenly go overboard the way you have done. Unmitigated bloody lunacy, that is what I call it. Still you have asked for my advice: the least I can do is give it. But remember – I am an interested party. And therefore suspect. Very definitely suspect. So here is my advice for what it is worth. Don't be a lug, darling. You have swallowed without question everything that outrageous blackguard has told you. But believe me, what he doesn't tell you is much more important. He is a randy ruffian whose boast is that he has seduced half the countryside. If you wish to avoid being the subject of one of his bar-room reminiscences, cut adrift from him before it is too late. I am giving this to Shaun the Post and will see you this evening. Perhaps I can persuade you to change your mind! At least I can try, can't I? Love. Frank.
Neither letter was dated.

Appalled, Simpson turned the letters over, re-reading the vicious slurs. *Pet mastiff. Ugly dangerous brute. Better have him put down.* Why hadn't he battered the bejasus out of Dinsmore? Instead of letting him off so lightly? The little whelp would bite the hand that stroked him. But, bad and all as Dinsmore was, McCann was worse. A treacherous cur. The village mongrel that waits till you pass, before rushing at you silently to sink his teeth in your leg. *Outrageous blackguard. Randy ruffian. Seduced half the countryside.* This from a member of your own staff. It was not to be tolerated.

Once more he read, grasping the hints and innuendoes. *Before I could credit that you were really serious. Unmitigated bloody lunacy. How can a shrewd sensible girl go suddenly overboard?* He must have thought that you and Delia weren't serious. When he found you were, he was driven frantic with jealousy. *I am an interested party.* It's there in black and white. But that's no excuse for his treachery. He was supposed to be a friend. Yet he stabs you in the back. *Cut adrift from him. Perhaps I can persuade you to change your mind.* He must have been working against you all along. Kept it to himself. A smarmy Judas, fawning on his boss. *You have swallowed without question everything he has told you. What he doesn't tell you is much more important*. He knows. Or he guesses what you're hiding. He's hinting at it. Just as he was today. What was it the little scorpion said? The something of. Them. That trade in love. The gift? The token? No. It's more a kind of compensation. Reward? Prize? I've got it. The meed. *The meed of those that trade in love*. Could any innuendo be more pointed? Has he told her, I wonder? *I will see you this evening. I can try, can't I? To make you change your mind*. Wait a moment! What does that bastard Dinsmore say? *Until eight o'clock tomorrow*. And neither of the bloody letters dated. They were received the same day or they wouldn't have been stuffed into the drawer together. Could it possibly be ... that his ... watch was—

He looked at it. Three thirty-five. What was she doing till now? Dry-mouthed, on shaky props, he made his way round to the wash-stand. Poured himself out a drink. Sat down on the bed.

His head ached abominably. The drumming had recommenced in his ears. Lassitude weighed him down, hunching his shoulders, curving his spine. He drank slowly. Three deep slugs. Picked up the letters again.

It is good to know you have not forgotten me. We have much leeway to make up!!! There wasn't much doubt what *he* had in mind. The three exclamation marks aren't inserted there for nothing ... He must have been tricking at her the last time. And going to start where he left off, when he meets her at *eight o'clock tomorrow*. Maybe that's what's keeping her. Tomorrow is now today. And she's away off with him as she did before. But you couldn't be sure. That's only guesswork. After all, wouldn't the same argument apply to the other letter?

He turned to it. *I am giving this to Shaun the Post and will see you this evening*. That could be now. This very night. What else does he say? *Perhaps I can persuade you to change your mind!* The bloody exclamation mark again. Take care but he's trying to get on the inside of you. The letter was written before you got back to Glenard today. He probably thinks you'd be too tired to stir out after the long run. And he's with her now. Somewhere. How does he finish the letter? *At least I can try, can't I?*

He shook his head violently, seeking to rid himself of his

264

memories, his suspicions, his forebodings. At once the pain gnawing at his forehead, raked the back of his eyes with slashing claws, a searing stabbing pain, lasting hardly more than a second but leaving him agitated and breathless.

Cautiously he conveyed the glass to his mouth. Took a steadying drink.

It must have been the sudden movement brought on the pain, he decided. But that could not have anything to do with the eye trouble. Whatever other daft things he had been told to avoid – stooping, coughing, sneezing, even paddling – shaking his head was not one of them. It would be a poor day when he'd have to go round with head held rigid as though he'd a crick in the neck.

The headache and the throbbing in his ears still continued. But in a subdued form. More than likely Westwood was right. A strong emotional upset was harmful. That made more sense than all the other footling prohibitions. Rage or vexation might possibly send the blood shooting up to the head. Make you more liable to suffer a haemorrhage. All well and good. But have these medicine men any pill or injection to keep you cool and collected under every eventuality? Wouldn't tonight's carry-on break anyone's temper? Locked up in a bloody bedroom till . . . what time is it? . . . after four o'clock in the morning. Compromising letters left under your nose. Discovering that a so-called friend – a member of your own staff – was knifing . . . That noise? What was it?

He sat up. Head cocked to one side. Waiting. Again it came. A faint scraping sound. A door – the hall door, warped and tight-fitting, was being thrust in gently. Quickly he was on his feet. Downed the drink. Crossed to the dressing-table. Stuffed away the letters and pushed in the drawer. Took a last look round before he switched off the light. Slid back into bed.

Downstairs the scraping had ceased. Instead there was an intermittent grating noise. The door being forced shut. Carefully. Too carefully, it was pushed back till at last with a loud click, the lock snapped shut. In his mind's eye, Simpson could see her standing motionless, both hands still gripping the knob of the door lock. Listening. Waiting for the challenging cry. Certain the noise must have awakened someone. At length, starting off along the hall. No-no! Shoes off first. Then padding along, holding them in one hand, the other feeling along the wall. Step by swaying step, she was creeping along, eyes trying to pierce the darkness ahead, ears strained to catch the smallest sound, teeth clenched in concentration on her lower lip. Soon she would be at the stair-foot, starting the slow, cautious—

A loud bump. A muttered curse. Creaking – loud and continuous. What the hell did Delia think she was doing at four in the morning clumping up the stairs in this fashion? Her progress could be followed stair by stair till she reached the top. Then silence once more. Now she must be creeping up the corridor, key in one hand, shoes in the other. She should reach the door at any moment. Ah, here we are. The key was inserted in the lock. Eased round carefully. Now the handle was being turned. Very, very slowly. He could hear her breathing as the door was opened. She was fumbling with the key now. Shifting it from the outside to the inside. The door was being closed. And ... (there was a click) ... locked. More fumbling. She must be feeling for the switch. No, she was standing quite still. Uncertain what to do. Don't pretend you are awake. Breathe softly. Deep. Gentle. Through your open mouth. That's it.

The light was switched on. Don't move. Keep up the pretence of sleep. See what happens.

'Cum'on, Brer Fox. Who dj'you think you're coddin'?' Her voice husky. The words slurred. 'I heardj'you. Holding yer breath. Listenin'.'

He lay doggo. A shadow darkened the closed eyelid of his left eye. She was standing over the bed.

'I spy, with my li'le eye, something beginning with "K".' There was a jingling sound. 'Snap out of it, buster. You hear ev'ry word I say.'

Opening his eyes, he looked up at her. Her hair was tossed and matted: her face caked with dried blood and dirt. The white jumper was mud-stained and fouled with patches of green scum. One of her stockings was ripped at the knee, exposing an ugly gash from which blood still welled. Her mouth was twisted into a pugnacious sneer and she teetered backwards and forwards on her heels. She was very drunk.

'In God's name, what happened to you? Or where have you been?' he asked.

'D'you want these back or d'you not?' Again the jingling.

266

She was holding aloft his car keys. 'There,' she said, walking to the dressing-table and flinging them down. 'You can't say I lost them on you.'

'Hush! You'll waken the house.' He listened. Not a sound. 'What did you want with the keys of the car? Did you think I would follow after you? And catch you out? And how did you get the keys anyway?' He was sitting up in bed, his face gathered up into a frown of concentration.

She paused in the act of rolling down the torn stocking.

'How d'you think?' she said contemptuously.

Take it easy, he warned himself. Don't lose your temper.

'Who were you out with?' he asked.

Ignoring him, she finished peeling off the other stocking.

'Don't think you can bamboozle me! Bloody well I know who it was.'

Getting to her feet, she started pulling the jumper over her head.

'Who was it?' he demanded.

She tugged the neck of the jumper free of her head. Shook out her hair. Dumped the jumper on a chair and unzipped her skirt.

'Why don't you tell *me* if you know all about it?' she said.

He leapt out of bed. Padded across. Stood over her.

'Listen, you bitch.' He spat the words, trying to keep his voice low. 'Was it that little upstart, Dinsmore?'

She unhooked her brassiere and tossed it across the room. 'You'd like to know, wouldn't you?'

The familiar ache gripped him – a massive hand squeezing his heart as he looked at the slim lovely body marred by the grimy sneering face and mangled knee.

'Was it McCann?' he asked hoarsely. 'Were you out with that mean treacherous get?'

She stepped out of her panties. Crossed to the wardrobe mirror. Stroked with sensuous hands her breasts, belly and flanks. He could see her reflected face break into a furtive smile, whilst the tip of her tongue moved slowly across her lips, savouring a secret memory.

She wheeled around.

'What's it matter to you who I was out with? I'm here now, amn't I?'

She swaggered past him, reeking of stirred-up, still unsatisfied lust. Stretched herself out on the bed, knees raised, arms outflung.

'Come on, lover-boy,' she jeered. 'What's keeping you?'

Hating every humiliating step he took, loathing the rising tide of passion that disgust could not even quench, fearing the throb and pound of his riotous blood, he flung himself on her, gathering her fiercely into his arms, mindless of anger, suspicion, jealousy, conscious only of the fierce devouring urge for fulfilment, that put him threshing around savagely with clenched teeth and tight-shut eyes until, slaked of his hunger, he rolled over on his back – spent ... unhappy ... alone.

Gasping for breath, he lay inertly, clamped across his forehead a crushing band of pain screwed tighter with every beat of his thundering blood. His lungs were emptied of air and he sucked in noisy gulping breaths that were squeezed out again immediately. He struggled to a sitting posture, gripped his head with both hands and groaned.

'Huh!' she said. 'Listen to him. You'd think he was dying. And not a minute ago, carrying on like a jack donkey.'

'I don't feel so good,' he panted. 'The breath's ... caught up in me somehow and I've ... I've a splitting headache.'

'What d'you expect? Nothing would do you but a naughty. And now, look at the cut of you.' She sat up. And, pointing, giggled. 'If you only saw yourself. Slouching there with your head in your hands and this ridiculous fringe of hair, that I had shorn off, grown in the new and streeling down over your shoulders. You – you're like something that climbed up out of—'

'Would you, for Jesus' sake, lay off. I feel bad enough without you weighing into me.'

'There you go again. Losing your temper over nothing. The way you talk to me you'd think you owned me. Where were you? Who were you with? Questions, questions, all the time. You haven't got *me* in your pocket, remember.'

He got to his feet.

'Where are you off to now? Like all the men. When you've got what you want, you're ready for home.'

'My clothes. Where are they? And why did you take the car keys?'

A cunning expression crossed her face. She looked at him, slit-eyed.

'Clothes? Keys? What on earth are you talking about?'

'The keys of the car, you idiot. What did you want with them?'

'The car keys!' She broke into another fit of giggling. 'Oh, dear, it was so funny. Every time he went to start the car, it went ... Ugh! ... Ugh!' She jerked her body violently in demonstration. Flung her head back and laughed.

Quickly he put a hand over her mouth.

'Quiet!' he hissed. 'You'll have Hannah in on top of us if you don't pipe down.' He took his hand away. 'What was that you were saying about the car?'

'There's something wrong with it, Jim. It jumps all the time. Every time that gadget in the floor is pressed – the car jumps.'

'It jumps ... does it? Each time ... the accelerator ... is pressed?' He strove to keep his voice under control.

'Don't I know it? Every time it jumped I fell on my mouth and nose. See!' She indicated knee, palm of hand, cheek. 'Of course, it was grass. So it wasn't so bad.'

'Grass? How do you mean – grass?'

'We went off the road. Into the grass verge. I had to help push it out. And when it was clear, it jumped again. Shot across the road and nearly went in again at the far side. 'She giggled softly. 'I'm afraid he's not a very good driver.'

Hands on the bed, he leant forward till his face was close to hers.

'Are you trying to tell me ... that you took my car ... you and some other drunken fool ... and that you-you-you ditched it?'

'What do you think I took the keys for? And I wasn't driving it!' Her voice rose belligerently.

'Hush!' he hissed. 'Keep your bloody voice down.' Instinctively, he straightened up. Let the angry gathered-up breath wheeze out from flared nostrils. 'Who was driving the car?' he asked, at length. Very softly.

'That would be telling,' she said pertly.

'Was it Dinsmore?'

'No.'

'McCann?'

269

'Why are you all the time harping on about Frank McCann? Isn't he supposed to be a friend of yours?'

'Friend, my arse. He'd knife me in the back, if it paid him to. Was he the treacherous cur that stole my car?'

'It was not. And it wasn't stolen.' She hesitated. The cunning look crept into her face again. 'But I'll tell you something, Jim. It was another friend of yours.'

For a moment, the shock of this statement kept at bay the rage that was consuming him.

'An old friend of mine, too,' she gibed.

Cold sweat broke out on his forehead. He leant towards her again.

'Who?' he demanded. 'Who was it?'

'He's never done talking about you. Always singing your praises. Or nearly always.'

'Who?' he pleaded hoarsely.

'Ach, for God's sake, who do you think, stupid? Brian Mullen, of course.'

Knees buckling under him, he flopped down on the bed. From afar off he heard, unheeding, her voice toll on.

'He has a marvellous job in London ... making stacks of money ... getting me a post ... manageress, if you don't mind ... swanky lounge bar ... in the West End ...'

He tried to gather his scattered wits. This bastard, Mullen, has pulled a fast one. Often you heard him boast that no one ever got the better of him. Cutting in on Delia is his way of getting his own back for the dishonoured cheques. A dirty, rotten trick. After all, you were only doing your duty as a Bank Manager. He lied to you, obtained money under false pretences and then absconded to England. He had to be disciplined. Or he'd have stuck the Bank for the full hundred pounds. Maybe more. As it was, didn't he sting them for over seventy pounds? And now this business of the car. It's too much. He's getting away with—

Hold on a minute. You can charge him with the theft of the car. It's probably damaged and the District Justice always takes a serious view of things when that happens. Could very well mean a stretch in jail. That would put manners on the hoor.

What about Delia, though? She'll have to give evidence as a witness. It'll all come out. How she locked you into her bedroom whilst she and her young man went off in your car. Parking it in some quiet side-road or the grass-grown driveway leading to a ruined mansion. Switching off the lights and creeping into the back seat, to pollute and befoul it with their scrabbling, shameless contortions. Then, on the way back, gorged and drowsy with coupling, ditching the car through careless driving.

Frustrated rage gripped him. Surely to Christ you hadn't to swallow a humiliation like this. An indignity that no decent Christian should be asked to bear. Delia's voice merged into the ferment of his thoughts:

'He's going back next week. And I'm going back with him. After all, I knew him long before I got friendly with you.'

His memory swung back to the last time he had heard Brian's voice. On the phone.

Hey! Someone's just after passing. An old playmate of mine. A good sort. Must be on her holidays.

It was Delia he had seen, of course. Spotted her out of the telephone booth. No chance to contact her at the time. But later—

He must have written to her. Kept in touch with her. Then, when she found you were going to Dublin, she passed the word on. He took the opportunity to move in. And take over. They must have met in London, where Mullen worked for a while. 'Got friendly,' as she put it. My God, that young blackguard wouldn't waste his time getting friendly with a woman. It's tail he's after. And tail he gets. He must have been shagging away at her in a flat in London. Like the other bitch. What's her name Wingate. Then he has the bloody neck to tip you off over the phone. In return for a sanctioned overdraft. *An old playmate. A good sort.* Why in hell didn't you catch on at the time what he was hinting at? It could hardly have been plainer. The dirty bowsie. Giving you the low down about a decent girl. That she was a good thing. An easy jaunt.

The rage and hatred mounted in Simpson as he realized that Mullen was quite right. She *was* a good thing. A proper nympho. Didn't you find that out the night of the weight lifting? When you took her down to the Hermit's Cove. No coaxing or wrestling or preliminaries of any kind needed. Hardly out of sight of Hannah's than she had your fly unbuttoned. From then on, till she flung herself down (like

271

tonight) on the broad of her arse in the Cove, she kept a tight hold of Fagan. As if she feared you would take off for the hills, if she let go. God's curse on her, she's every bit as bad as Mullen.

She was still chattering away to herself:

'He works for a big firm of importers. Bringing in luxury goods from the Far East. Silks and satins and jewellery and carpets and furs. Priceless materials of every kind. The only snag is that you're exposed to a variety of foreign diseases if you handle them. Of course they take all precautions . . .'

Disease! What was this she was coming out with? Giving you a hint, eh? As the idea took root, he shivered with fury, digging his fingers into his bare thighs. Here – there was no doubt about it – in this very room was the source of his ills and afflictions. An indiscriminate slut that would let the whole countryside line up and tread her: a wanton ravening trollop scalded to the welt with the itch for crowbar: a treacherous bitch, ready, when it suited her, to cast him contemptuously aside; Delia it was who had dosed and destroyed him. What matter who she got it from? Mullen or a hundred others? It was he who had been made to suffer. And to think he had been bent upon confessing everything to her. Warning her, so that she might avoid infection.

He let his anger have its way. Swung round and faced her.

'There's nothing for a girl in this country, anyway,' she was assuring herself in a mindless whisper, when he gripped her shoulders.

'Shut up!' he hissed.

Squirming, she strove to break his grip.

'Let go! You're hurting me.'

He leaned close. Mouthing the words into her face.

'Did that fucker Mullen give you a dose?'

Wide-eyed, she stared back at him.

'What are you talking about, Jim?'

He shook her. Two swift jerks.

'Did he dose you?'

'Don't do that. It's sore.'

'Answer me, then.'

'How can I answer you when I don't know what you're talking about? What do you mean by "dosing"?'

'Don't be acting the innocent. Did you click a dose?'

'A dose of what?'

'Clap. V.D. Syph. Pox. Whatever you like to call it.'

Understanding, astonishment, anger, chased across her features.

'Are you suggesting I'm infected?' she demanded. 'What right have you ... why do you accuse ... say such things to me?'

He shook her again. Roughly.

'Because you've passed it on to me, you bitch. The dose you got from Mullen. Or any one of those bastards who were riding you.'

Breathless, trembling, she pointed a finger at his glowering face.

'You-you mean ... you're ... you're infected?'

'The Dublin doctor did a blood test. He says I'm dosed. With ... with ... with ... syphilis.' He spat out the hated word.

Her face broke into a delighted grin.

'A Bank manager ... a respectable Bank manager ... infected with ... Oh, I can't believe it! It's too priceless!' She threw back her head and laughed.

The damned-up fury burst out, raging through his body. Violently he shook her, jarring the gay laugh into a choking cry.

'You dosed me,' he kept repeating in a hoarse whisper. 'You jeering hoor, you dosed me.'

Unheeding the tugging and tearing hands, he persisted. Strength, the almost-forgotten strength, soured and buttressed by wrath, came coursing back. His fingers, heedless of those others clutching and pulling at his own, secured their purchase. Shoulders, biceps, forearms, worked smoothly together – jarring, jolting, jerking. Back in a world where physical force was the measure, he shook the struggling body back and forth, just as in the old days, maybe not so long ago, he had dealt in the same way with the half-hundreds. Treating them like dumb-bells and counting aloud, a double jerk to each command. 'One! Two! One! Two!' As if he were in a drill hall. Barking out the tally and urging himself on. 'One! Two! One! Two!' Heaving chest keeping pace with the piston motion of the arms. 'One! Two! One! Two!' Ignoring the limp arms, the slack wildly-flopping head, the thud of bone on iron. 'One! Two! One! Two!' Until it happened. As he had feared it would happen. As he had seen it happen so many times before.

Against the white wallpaper, it showed up as on a cinema screen. The scarlet column rising to a plume at the top, like a volcanic eruption. The plume thickening to a mushroom cloud as the blood flowed from the ruptured blood vessel.

He tried to collect his thoughts. Caution was the most important thing now. On no account must he either jerk or lower his head. He must stare straight in front of him, never shifting his gaze, for the slightest motion of an eyeball would spread the haemorrhage, leaving him sightless. And speed was essential if he was to get out of here before it was too late. Had Delia been at herself, she could have helped. As it was—

Carefully, very carefully he eased her back on to the pillow, staring straight before him, his head stiff and erect as if clamped in a vice. She lay limp, arms outstretched, head lying across her shoulder at a grotesque angle. Like a stricken bird. An impossible position really. But . . . no time to investigate. Get to hell out of here, as quickly and quietly as you can.

Warily he got to his feet, mindful lest a lurch or a stagger would smear the blood across his vision. Sweat rolled down his face, salting his mouth, smarting the glaring eye. He dared not wipe it away. Flat-footed, he worked his way across the room, fixing his gaze on the lintel of the door.

At last he reached it. His extended hand travelled down the wood to the brass knob. Turned it stealthily. Locked – as he had expected. His fingers fumbled across the lock till they found the keyhole. Groped around for three valuable seconds before the sickening truth was borne in on him. The key was gone. Again he turned the door knob. Just to make certain. No use. It was locked all right.

For a moment, he panicked. Jesus Christ, there'll be a bloody awful scandal when you are found here. When it comes to the ears of the buffs in Head Office, there'll be hell to pay. If you're not sacked out of your job, you'll be lucky. Then he remembered. Delia had turned the key from the inside. It must be in the room. Somewhere.

But where? Better try the floor first. It may have fallen.

He backed away until his levelled gaze included in his vision the varnished boards around the door. Nothing was to be seen. He moved further back to scan the carpet. Still nothing.

Hold on now! Don't lose your rattley. Try to think back. Go over what she did when she came into the room a while back. What you heard. The handle turning. Yes. The door opening. Breathing. Yes. The key being taken out. The door closing. And – That's it! A fumbling noise. She put the key by mistake into her handbag.

From where he stood he could see that the handbag was not on the dressing-table. Where could it be then? Underclothes were strewn over the floor. Flung on a chair were skirt and jumper. Worth trying.

As he shuffled across the room, his gaze now fixed on a picture of the Sacred Heart, he discovered, to his horror, that the mushroom cloud was spreading and thickening. There was no time to lose. He quickened his pace, lowering his gaze fractionally, like a marksman sighting on a target.

Reaching the chair, he hunkered down cautiously. Lifted the two garments. Nothing underneath. Shook them out. Nothing.

His breathing was now rapid and shallow. The strain of keeping his eyes fixed had become further aggravated by the need to curb the overwhelming urge to knuckle and rub, scratch and poke at the eye sockets where a violent itching had broken out.

Where next? he asked himself. Still crouching, he hobbled round the floor, searching amongst the discarded underclothes. In vain.

He straightened up. Swung his head slowly round. Pointed like a gun dog. A drawer in the dressing-table was not quite closed. The drawer in which he had discovered the letters. He must not have pushed it fully home when he had heard her at the hall door. This was where she had put the handbag containing the key. It had to be.

Quickly – the risk must be taken – he crossed the room. Squatted down on one knee in the posture of latecomers at the back of the chapel. Eased the drawer further open. Further still. Right out till he could see the two letters stuffed in at the back. Poked wildly around among the jumbled contents. No bag. His agitation rose as he opened drawer after drawer,

275

tossing everything around in mad confusion. At length he desisted. Wherever the bag was, it was not here.

He rested a moment, panting and sweating, his gaze fixed on a satin slip hanging out of the top right hand drawer. Against its whiteness, he watched in horrified fascination the gathering blood, now a red plush curtain descending slowly, inexorably, on the brightly lit stage – for the positively last performance. Already it was almost half-way down.

Hurry up, you fool, he urged. Do something. Or it will be too late to get out of here.

He straightened up at the same time as the burly, bald-headed, middle-aged gentleman who was staring back at him aghast. He saw his lips move.

'You fucking idiot! You are ballocks naked!'

Forget about the bloody handbag and get your clothes. You can go nowhere without them. Where hell did you put them, you bitch, he asked the reflected figure sprawled out on the bed. Nice state of affairs. Stretched out drunk on the bed and not giving one damn what happens to a fellow.

Steady on now. There's only one place they can be. The wardrobe. Didn't you hear it creaking last night when she was complaining about you leaving your clothes lying around. The time she came back to pinch the car keys.

Anger rose in him at the recollection. And boiled over when he found the wardrobe door would not open. God blast your maggoty soul, did you lock this door too?

Rolling his arms to flex the shoulder muscles, he spat on his hands, rubbed them together and gripped the small brass handle. Feet spread apart, knees bent, shoulders hunched, he tightened his grip on the handle.

'Now!' he urged, flinging himself back with a mighty jerk.

The wardrobe was already falling when its door burst open, flinging him completely off balance. Down he crashed with the heavy mahogany wardrobe on top of him, the sound of its fall being smothered by his own body and the huge mass of flapping clothes. Stunned by the fall, he lay, for God knows how long, under the pile of clothing, a deep gash across his forehead where some projection, metal or wood, had scored a furrow.

It was the smell of camphor that wakened him. Threshing

276

and struggling among coats, frocks, costumes, hats cursing and praying with indiscriminate fervour: too dazed to know where he was or what had happened to him: he at length crawled out from under the heavy, stifling, unaccountable weight. To utter and absolute darkness.

He crouched on the floor, trying to marshal his whirling memories. Something had fallen – that was certain. And falling, had most likely banjaxed the light. But what the hell had fallen on him? Feeling over its surface conveyed nothing to him except that it was large and made of wood.

The drenching sweat from his stuffy confinement had dried on. Shivering, he rubbed the goose flesh on his thighs. It was bloody cold in here, wherever it was. But, good God, what are you doing anyway in your naked pelt?

Remembrance rushed back to him. And with it, panic fright. Had the light bulb really been broken or had he at last – and finally – lost his sight? From side to side, like a questing dog, he turned his head, seeking a glimmer of light. Surely the grey of dawn should be beginning to show in the window? Hold on now! Don't get excited. Delia drew the blind last night. Remember?

He flung his head back and glared up at where he thought the hanging light should be. He'd know by the heat if it was on or off. Pull yourself together, man. Why waste time trying to place the whereabouts of a fused bulb?

Worried and confused, he scrambled to his feet. Better find out if the light is switched on.

He faced in the direction where he thought the door should be, stretched his arms out in front of him like a strip cartoon sleepwalker, crept forward, step by cagey step, in an uncertain teetering shuffle. Before he had gone more than a few paces, it was manifest that he was holding his hands too high. A chair, or some other small obstacle, could pass under his outstretched arms and trip him up. Lowering his arms, he started forward again, crouching on bent knees.

At length, the finger-tips of his right hand brushed against a cold rough surface, producing a faint ringing sound.

He halted. Felt around with his other hand until it, too, rested on the unknown object. Like antennae his fingers crawled around trying to make out shape and substance, creating as they did so a continuous resonance – familiar,

277

hollow. They rested, as far as he could make out, on the curving lip of some large object, the underpart of which was smooth, the upper corrugated. The inside, too, was smooth, dropping away steeply to meet— Why hadn't he guessed it at once? The delft wash bowl. And beside it. To the right. Was ... Careful now ... Move your fingers very slowly ... Once more a faint ping, as his finger-nails tapped something. It was a higher note. Not the hollow emptiness that sounded from the wash bowl. Yes ... Here it was. His fingers circled it, savouring the grainy feel of the label. It was the whiskey bottle.

Sliding his hand up till it clutched the neck, he lifted it gingerly, so that it would not clang off some toilet vessel. Only when it was clutched to his chest by both hands did he relax.

Now all that was required was to negotiate the couple of paces to the bed. Take no chances, though. If you turn around, you may start off in the wrong direction.

Releasing his left hand from the bottle, he placed his fingers on the curved lip of the wash bowl. Then he backed away slowly, leaning further and further forward, until his balance was threatened. Straightening up, he reached out behind him. Further. Further. He sighed with relief as his hand touched the bedclothes.

His teeth were chattering as he eased himself down on the bed. If ever in your life you needed a drink, he affirmed, this is the occasion.

Suddenly he thought of Delia. Poor thing, she must be like an icicle, lying there in her pelt. He reached across. My God, she was frozen stiff. One handed, he fumbled the two ends of the eiderdown over her so that she was encased in a cocoon of warmth. A good bumper of whiskey would thaw her out. But she was too drunk. There would only be more trouble. And eventual disaster.

He uncorked the bottle. Put it to his mouth. Drank deeply. Gulping back the raw whiskey in avid mouthfuls.

Placing the bottle on the floor between his clamped feet, he sat waiting. Soon the expected glow started. In the pit of the stomach, a tiny spark. A flush of heat creeping over his face and scalp, stretching the dry crackling skin across the bones till it felt taut as a drum head. An incandescence that swept his body – chest to limb tips. An enormous feeling of general well-being.

He picked up the bottle. Drank a long steady gurgling draught. Left the bottle down beside his right foot. Lay back on his elbows, shoulders resting comfortably on the quiet eiderdowned figure.

It was time to take stock. Comforted by the clarity, the logic, the fearless judgement that whiskey always imparted to him, he reviewed his plight. The door locked. The key not to be found. His clothes somewhere in a heap in the – he yawned – in the—

Oh, Lord, but he was sleepy. It would be grand to stretch out. Just for a few minutes. His eyes were burning. The half hundreds hanging from the lids. A catnap – five minutes itself – would be the making of him. Can't have that though.

He straightened up. Better take another drink. The only thing to keep you awake. He reached down between his legs. Groped around on the floor. Where was it gone? Did it topple over and roll away? He was about to heave himself off the bed and get down on hands and knees to search when he remembered. Tck! Tck! Tck! What were you thinking of? Sitting right here beside you all the time.

He picked it up. Hefted it. Not a lot left, eh? No use in making two bites of a cherry, what? He drank. And drank again. Single gulps, swallowed back noisily. He yawned again. Getting damned stuffy in here. Bloody window should be open. I'm tired telling her that. But she pays no attention. Might as well be talking to the bloody wall. He burped. Shook the bottle. Put it to his head and tipped it back. That's better. No use in leaving things for the sweeper. Clumsily he put down the bottle. And, uncaring, heard it fall and roll. Something would have to be done. There'd be no sleep in this sweltering heat if he didn't get the window open.

He pushed himself to his feet. Stood swaying. Glaring into the darkness. Where in the name of God is the window? Silly slob. She must have pulled down the blind. Bloody awful dark. Have to switch on the light.

Feeling his way to the bottom of the bed, he clung to the bed-end for a second to steady himself. Then launched himself into the darkness. He staggered three steps forward. Stopped. Pawed around. The damned door should be here.

279

Another step. Still no door. The whole geography of the place was altered. She must have been shifting the furniture around.

Bewildered he stood, his extended hands groping about in the blackness ahead. Another hesitant step. And – CRASH. He had tripped over something on the floor, shot forward to the wall and clutching for support had pulled down a mirror. Where none should be.

He was getting desperate now. The bloody woman had turned the place upside-down. There was no sense or reason in this constant spring-cleaning. Now he didn't know in the name of Christ where he was.

From side to side he turned, but ahead of him everywhere was inky blackness. At random he took a step forward and found his path blocked by ... What in fuck's name is this? More of her handiwork? A bloody great wooden barricade. Does she think that will stop me getting out?

Muttering curses, he scrambled clumsily up on it. Clambered to his feet and was about to move forward – when it gave a lurch. Swaying, tottering, striving to regain his balance, one of his wildly clutching hands grabbed a round, dangling, almost red-hot object, which burst in his grasp with a loud report.

'JEEEEESUS!' he roared in agony, as he staggered backwards, struck the wall and, spinning sideways, crashed against a frail piece of furniture, fetching up sprawled on the bed with the ruinous din of shattering china in his ears. In the silence that followed, he seemed to hear the house itself holding its breath.

God knows, it was good to get back to bed. Better get cosied down before you get your death of cold. As he hoisted his feet on to the bed, he heard a bottle roll across the floor. He made to rise but settled himself back on the pillow. Pure idiocy groping around in the darkness looking for anything. Hadn't he lost himself once before in his own bedroom? A clothes closet – that's where he had found himself. Took him hours to get out. Pure madness. Wasn't the bulb fused anyway? He licked the still smarting palm of his hand. Shivered. Pulled the clothes around him, folded his arms across his chest and burrowed for warmth under the weight resting against his back.

He settled his breathing into a slow steady rhythm, began a

Hail Mary, knowing sleep would come before the prayer would be finished. In the distance – far away – he could hear voices murmuring. Irrelevantly. Then—

Tap-tap-tap.

He groaned. What's the matter now? Go away, will you? Can't you let a fellow sleep?

Tap-tap-tap.

'Delia, are you all right?'

He pulled the clothes over his head. Hunched down deeper under the comforting weight.

Tap-tap-tap.

Loud. Urgent. Imperative.

'Delia, are you all right? Is there anything the matter?'

The door handle rattled.

Eyes tight shut, he pushed back the clothes and levered himself round till he was sitting on the side of the bed. He yawned widely. God, he was bloody tired. It was a shame having to get up. He scratched his chest abstractedly. Shifted his weight from one hip to the other. What the hell was he sitting on? Slid his hand under his buttocks. Drew out something ... oyster shaped ... made of ... leather ... with a steel ... clasp! Without opening his eyes he knew what it was. A bloody handbag! Tck! Tck! Tck! Don't they have heads like sieves, these silly creatures? he mused, with affectionate tolerance. First black satin panties. Now a handbag. What on earth will it be next?

Outside the bedroom door, the voices were louder.

A frantic rapping broke out. The door was shaken savagely. He yawned again. Stretched himself amply.

'All right. Annie. All right,' he growled irritably. 'I'll be down in a moment.'

Other Panthers For Your Enjoyment

Man and Woman

☐ Gore Vidal   **MYRA BRECKINRIDGE**
                                                 40p

The elegantly outrageous novel that demolishes lots of American sexual myths. Vidal's piercing invention is at its most dazzling in this story of Hollywood sex-changes.

☐ Martin Seymour-Smith   **FALLEN WOMEN**   40p
The strumpet in literature – from the Old Testament right up to today's highly professional porn. The author does it with insight, sympathy and wit, and his conclusions are controversial – or, as the *New Statesman* puts it, 'Provocative'.

☐ Trans. Charles Plumb   **THE SATIRES OF**
                                        JUVENAL   42p
The vices – and what vices! – of Imperial Rome by one who was there. A translation for the 1970's – direct, witty, lewd.

☐ Jean Genet   **QUERELLE OF BREST** 60p
The criminal-homosexual world so sensuously evoked by Genet is a taboo subject in suburbia. Elsewhere, Genet is 'Matchless . . . any comment at once becomes presumptuous' – Terry Southern

☐ Jean Genet   **OUR LADY OF THE**
                                        FLOWERS   40p
The great sensual novel about the criminal-homosexual world with which Genet overturned middle class values.

☐ John Rechy   **CITY OF NIGHT**   40p
Rechy's city of dreadful night is any downtown American city after dark, when lonely homosexuals begin their frantic prowl in search of companionship.

Outsize Heroes

☐ **Henri Charrière**   **PAPILLON**   60p
Charrière, known as Papillon (Butterfly), is probably the greatest
escaper of modern times not only because of his numerous
indefatigable and finally successful attempts but also because of the
prison he escaped from — Devil's Island. Reads like a Hammond
Innes novel, yet it's stark fact, every incident verifiable.

☐ **Phillip Knightley and**   **THE SECRET LIVES OF**
   Colin Simpson   **LAWRENCE OF**
                                                ARABIA   40p
Boy Scout hero or masochist. The authors examine the myth in the
light of the latest information. T. E. Lawrence may well be
diminished in this cool study, but he does emerge, for the first time
in the numerous accounts of his ambiguous life, as a human being.
'Explosive — biographical dynamite' — *Evening Standard*

☐ **Jan Cremer**   **I, JAN CREMER**   50p
This roaring, raucous, autobiographical novel of its young author's
sexual conquests in Europe and the US is scandalous, sadistic and
funny.

☐ **Jan Cremer**   **JAN CREMER 2**   50p
Continues the roaring, raucous account of Cremer's one-man
assault on our sacred cows — the opening moves in which were
revealed to a disbelieving world in his international bestseller
I, JAN CREMER. 'I'm nervous, schizophrenic, sadistic, perverted,
and an inspirer of riots', Mr. Cremer admits — and lives up to every
word of it.

☐ **Heinz Werner Schmidt**   **WITH ROMMEL IN**
                                                THE DESERT   25p
By a high-ranking officer of the Afrika Korps — the inside story of
Rommel's vicious fight to destroy the Allies in North Africa.

☐ **William Rodgers**   **THINK: a biography of**
                                                the Watsons and IBM   50p
International Business Machines is the largest single corporation in
the western world, and its policy decisions may well shape your
future. Consider this: £1,000 invested in IBM when Watson started
it in 1914 would be worth £6,000,000 today. This ominous account
has delved into every source — except one. IBM flatly refused to give
the author any information whatsoever. The reader will understand
why.

Bestsellers

□ **Patrick Skene Catling** THE EXPERIMENT **40p**
Laboratory sex as a scientific experiment. The cameras grind.
So do the performers.

□ **Patrick Skene Catling** FREDDY HILL **35p**
(The story of a modern man of pleasure). Freddy is a spiritual
descendent of Fanny Hill. His engagingly innocent progress down
the primrose path to the everlasting bonfire leads him to an
ambiguous job in a male bordello. In the end Freddy manages, but
only just manages, to get out from under. . . . Even so, somewhere
there, over the horizon, flames the everlasting bonfire. 'Patrick Skene
Catling makes you laugh . . . and also makes you think' –
P. G. Wodehouse

□ **Bill Naughton** ALFIE **30p**
'Alfie is a cockney Pan, always willing to oblige a lady, and you
can't say fairer than that, can you?' – *Sunday Times*

□ **Bill Naughton** ALFIE DARLING **35p**
Anything that Our Alfie did in the bestseller ALFIE (and what
didn't he do!) he does even better in this sequel. Pushing a truck
down the M1 the lad stops over from time to time for a rest – and
to console various lonely ladies . . . all out of the goodness of his
heart of course. ALFIE DARLING is swinging 1970's stuff.

□ **Margaret Forster** GEORGY GIRL **25p**
The bestselling saga of a rather plain, very ordinary girl's
successful quest for sexual fulfilment and social success. It made a
great film.

□ **James Leo Herlihy** MIDNIGHT COWBOY **35p**
No one had raised Joe Buck, loved him, led or misled him, taught
him anything. Joe understands only one thing: his body. Adorning
it in a dazzling cowboy outfit he takes off hopefully to New
York where there are no great-looking cowhands, and beautiful
rich women will surely pay to sleep with him. Joe's descent into
the jungle of night-time New York is swift and brutal.

Today's Fiction

☐ **Alexis Lykiard**   **ZONES**   **30p**
A young man's mental and erotic awakening, and his free-wheeling swing from London to Paris to Spain. 'Bursting at the seams with vitality' – *Sunday Telegraph*

☐ **Donald Barthelme**   **SNOW WHITE**   **30p**
The novel with the big underground reputation. 'A wised-up story of our time' – *Newsweek*. The lady is a tall dark beauty. She lives with seven men who, to earn their daily bread, do various odd jobs, and in between make love to the tall dark beauty in the shower – more or less one at a time. 'No matter what you look for in a book you can find it here' – *Boston Herald*

☐ **Colin Spencer**   **ANARCHISTS IN**
                             LOVE   **30p**
They were young, and unattached – and *very much* uncommitted; and passionate love-making on the night beaches of summertime Brighton was their be-all.

☐ **Julian Gloag**   **MAUNDY**   **40p**
Maundy is a young man starting on a banking career . . . but his fate is hallucination, rape and final destruction. 'Fantastically clever; it illustrates a case of obsessive sanity falling to bits in slow motion: coldly erotic' – Kay Dick, *Queen*

☐ **James Leigh**   **THE RASMUSSEN**
                           DISASTERS   **35p**
Rasmussen is a second – maybe third – generation American in southern California where he runs a liquor store. Rasmussen is by no means an eccentric, but the mob that suddenly home in on his rather staid life by god are. Order is finally restored by a local fascist and his thugs and – hold it – a bowling team. Only California could be like this.

☐ **Ivan Gold**   **SICK FRIENDS**   **40p**
Not since Henry Miller has any writer explored so frankly the limits of love and sex. Its outspokenness may startle, but it is not a 'shocking' book – simply an honest one.

Highly-Praised Modern Novels

☐ **John Fowles** **THE FRENCH LIEUTENANT'S WOMAN** 50p

Although Fowles is an English – and *how* – writer his novel has been on the American bestseller lists for months. To read it is an experience. 'When the book's one sexual encounter takes place it's so explosive it nearly blows the top of your head off' – *New York Saturday Review*

☐ **David Caute** **THE DECLINE OF THE WEST** 60p

A newly independent African state in bloody turmoil, and the world's adventurers – male and female – home in like vultures. Strong reading.

☐ **John Barth** **THE SOT-WEED FACTOR** 75p

The story of a mid-eighteenth century man of fortune, told in a modern spirit by one of America's great writers. 'Most magnificent, totally scandalous' – Patrick Campbell, *The Sunday Times*

☐ **Elizabeth Bowen** **EVA TROUT** 35p

'Elizabeth Bowen is a splendid artist, intelligent, generous and acutely aware, who has been telling her readers for years that love is a necessity, and that its loss or absence is the greatest tragedy man knows' – *Financial Times*

☐ **Norman Mailer** **THE NAKED AND THE DEAD** 60p

The greatest novel from world war two.

☐ **Mordecai Richler** **COCKSURE** 40p

Constantly reprinted by public demand. The brilliant satiric picture of a tycoon whose business and sexual appetites know no limits.

Fictional Diversions

☐ **Violette Leduc**   **LA BATARDE**   60p
In this famous autobiographical novel a great writer lays bare the secrets of her checkered life and her loves — largely for other women.

☐ **Violette Leduc**   **RAVAGES**   50p
'Violette Leduc has a wonderful feeling for all kinds of sensual happiness' — *Daily Mail*. A novel with all the candour and poignancy of LA BATARDE.

☐ **Angus Stewart**   **SANDEL**   30p
The well-reviewed novel of a young man's relationship with a boy. 'A controlled and beautifully written love story, at once passionate and pure' — *New Statesman*

☐ **Henri Barbusse**   **HELL**   30p
Life in a Parisian girl's bedsitter viewed through a hole in the wall by her next door neighbour, an impoverished and struggling young student. Cold, French realism working at its coldest. By the famous author of *Under Fire*.

☐ **Maureen Duffy**   **WOUNDS**   30p
A man and a woman making love: tenderly they explore each other's body and mind. No taboos, no shame. Flesh is there to be caressed, thoughts to be exchanged. But — outside this sensual, very private world the world is harsh. This story of pain and pleasure has an honesty rare in contemporary fiction. *Here*, says the author, is, where life inflicts its wounds.

☐ **Kingsley Amis**   **I WANT IT NOW**   35p
A poor little rich girl, Simona, and a TV interviewer, Ronnie, meet, merge, and strive for the things that *they* want tout de suite. In a word, that knowing, sardonic Amis is at it again in another bestselling high comedy. 'Wickedly entertaining' — *Sunday Times*

Obtainable from all booksellers and newsagents. If you have any difficulty please send purchase price plus 7p postage per book to Panther Cash Sales, P.O. Box 11, Falmouth, Cornwall.

I enclose a cheque/postal order for titles ticked above plus 7p a book to cover postage and packing.

Name ——————————————————————————

Address ——————————————————————————

——————————————————————————————